CW00540383

Sweat

Also by Emma Healey

Elizabeth Is Missing
Whistle in the Dark

Sweat

EMMA HEALEY

HUTCHINSON
HEINEMANN

1 3 5 7 9 10 8 6 4 2

Hutchinson Heinemann
Penguin Random House UK
One Embassy Gardens
8 Viaduct Gardens
London SW11 7BW

Hutchinson Heinemann is part of the Penguin Random House group of companies
whose addresses can be found at global.penguinrandomhouse.com.

www.penguin.co.uk

A CIP catalogue record for this book is available from the British Library.

ISBN (Hardback): 9781529154122
ISBN (Trade paperback): 9781529154139

Typeset in 13.5/16pt Garamond MT Std by Jouve (UK), Milton Keynes
Printed and bound in Great Britain by Clays Ltd, Elcograf S.p.A.

The authorised representative in the EEA is Penguin Random House Ireland,
Morrison Chambers, 32 Nassau Street, Dublin D02 YH68

Penguin Random House is committed to a sustainable future
for our business, our readers and our planet. This book is made
from Forest Stewardship Council® certified paper.

To my husband, Andrew McKechnie

Week One

After seventeen hours of social-media humiliation, our CEO's public apology finally appeared; his profile picture changed from a tongue-out, abs-out pout to a sombre workout, workday portrait.

You're a piece of work. That was the nicest response I could find. And I searched – spent a long time scrolling through comment threads while rain ran down the gym's tinted windows.

As a new employee I was invested in the controversy, had skin in the game. Smooth, drill-toned, clean-taut skin, skin to advertise, to sell, to make you think training with me would get you fit, keep you young.

Not that I'd done much advertising. It could be dangerous, and I knew what it was like to have your accounts scoured and sieved. So I was relieved when the morally outraged mobs scattered and became scarce after the CEO's damage-control post:

Absolute abject apols. What can I say? I'm an idiot sometimes. I didn't intend to cause harm, but accept now that what I said and did was insensitive. To the max. I promise to try harder to make

our gyms more inclusive for people marginalised by disability.
Starting with this new offer.

The offering? Twelve weeks of half-priced personal training sessions for clients who were blind, deaf, in wheelchairs, had prosthetic limbs, or lived with learning difficulties. Twelve weeks to make it up to everyone the ex-international-rugby-playing entrepreneur had mocked in a now-deleted twelve-minute YouTube video.

I'd only been working for the company twelve weeks, and the symmetry was satisfying. I love a bit of numerical synchronicity. But I knew about men like our CEO, full of abject apols. Men like my colleague, Tommy, with his furtive little face as he ducked into the office.

'Really sorry, Cassie, but I can't make my one o'clock.'

A creak as I moved. From me or the old wheelie office chair? I was stiff from barbell squats, and had a pain like a splash of cold water along my lower spine. I'd skimped my post-workout stretches that morning, taught a spin class under the spotlights, then sat in the frigid artificial breeze to reissue a dozen access codes and update machine maintenance records. Sweat cooling, joints rusting. There was another creak; it felt like it came from me.

Tommy stood, oblique, in the reception doorway, letting a song's crisp percussion skate into the quiet of the office. Of course it was the female PTs who got most of the half-price clients.

'Can you take him, Cass?' Tommy asked. 'I said I'd get Steph to fill in, but I can't find her.'

I glanced past Tommy, looking for Steph's fake-formalwear figure. To prove her managerial status, she always wore those black yoga pants they advertise in the flashing sidebars of celebrity-gossip websites, the ones that stretch like leggings but look like proper work trousers. I could scoff, but who was I to judge? I'd started wearing stacked trainers to meet clients, hoping the extra couple of inches would lend me authority.

'He's here already,' Tommy said. 'He's blind. You've just got to help him to the machines, set the timers. You'll be good. Right?'

'Yeah. Sure. I'm caring, *right*?'

'Eh?'

'I'm the caring one.' I cupped myself between my legs, to prove I was the nurturing sex.

'You make me laugh.'

I didn't; he never even cracked a smile. Not a sour person, Tommy, just smooth-faced, glassy, always a few seconds behind. No stacked trainers for him, he's already tall: six five, six six? Maybe it takes longer for meaning to reach him up there.

His client was waiting behind the reception's obscure glass, a blur of peach and brown that had arranged itself in the pattern of a human. A very still human. Extremely still. Well, he couldn't see, didn't know where the edges were, or what he might come up against if he moved. He was about to come up against me. But I was the one who got the shock.

'Sorry, buddy. I have to get off,' Tommy told the client

while staring at my Lycra'd crotch. My fault for drawing attention to it. 'I'll leave you in my colleague's capable hands.'

I sighed and stepped through the door.

And there he was. Liam.

Fear isn't what it was like. Imagine someone pulls a gun on you, imagine what you feel in that moment. That wasn't it. Nothing so pure and clean. What it was really like was, well, imagine you've been dropped into an underground maze and you get to look at a map for thirty seconds. Thirty seconds to plan your route so you can make it out alive. That's closer.

And suddenly everything was sharp and clear. The colour-changing column lights, the magic-eye carpet tiles, the unspooled blue paper rolls, the mess of gun-metal pipes on the ceiling. A weightlifter's neon-yellow stringer vest piercing my periphery. I could smell sweat and body spray, watered-down lemon cleaning fluid and the milky, foetid stink of protein shakes. I was trembling, but it was the music, the sludgy bass rising up through the soles of my trainers, through padded ankle socks.

Two years ago, I'd changed *my* profile picture and walked out of my flat, away from my boyfriend, from our life, from our regime. Liam hadn't been pleased. He hadn't been pleased for a while. But recently his interest had dwindled to apathetic phone harassment and I hadn't had a glimpse of his brooding profile for over five months. I'd seen nothing. Not the curl of his eyelashes, not that familiar scar across one eyebrow, not the flat mole behind his ear. For five months he'd made himself an absence instead of a presence, a gummy gap rather than an abscessed tooth.

And now here he was, man of my dreams, fire of my loins, star of my nightmares, my mentor, my shadow, my ex-boyfriend, looking at me.

Or was he?

Blind, Tommy had said. I shifted, bouncing on air-cushioned toes, a fighter's footwork. Liam's green gaze was steady, resting somewhere near the reception door's combination lock. I slid right again. He caught the movement but his eyes didn't catch me. By rocking side to side, I could let him lay that gaze over my cheek-bones, the bridge of my nose, or I could leave it hanging in the air.

I had an idea, several ideas, and I let them tumble over each other.

The first was to call Tommy back, go begging to Steph, retreat into the office until the threat was gone and the place had been swept for emotional landmines, but, well, I didn't want to. I didn't want to explain my personal life to my new colleagues, I didn't want to ask for help, for sympathy, for special favours. I wasn't full of abject apols, I was full of . . . something else. Curios-ity, wonder, mischief?

For months – years – I'd moved, hidden, ducked, grateful to avoid Liam's scrutiny. That was over. I didn't have to hide any more. I could look at him. It was my turn.

Five minutes. That's all I wanted, that's all it'd take. What's five minutes? Only the length of one and a bit songs, barely time enough for a warm-up run, a little cycle, a quick row or three sets of lateral raises (if you're resting properly in between). That's all I'd do: five minutes with a different name, voice, manner. I could keep up anything for five minutes, surely.

'All right?' My voice was low, my *l*'s more like a *w*.

He gave a sharp little animal movement, like he was scenting something, and I stepped back, out of range, a freezing stream from the air conditioner like a screen between us. That morning someone had left a nearly new bottle of Armani Code in the locker I usually used and I'd sprayed a little cloud for myself before dropping it into the lost-property box. Perhaps he was sniffing that.

'Hi?' he said.

'Sorry. Liam, is it?' I cleared my throat. 'First time, mate?'

I was doing a parody of my brother's voice. An impression of his bouncy South London salesman's affability, forcing my tone deeper, staying a shade too quiet in this noisy room. We kept the music loud in the gym. To boost the mood, to motivate people, as if the beat itself could lift a weight, as if it didn't press you down, down, eardrum to the mat, hairs flattening inside your cochlea. Was it covering my real voice? I searched

6

Liam's face for clues; he was frowning, head cocked, as if trying to catch my words.

I needed more words, but what was I supposed to say?

Nice to meet you. Let's get started. What d'you want to focus on? Give me the rundown. What are your goals? DO YOU KNOW WHO I AM?

'You're Steph?'

I choked on a breath.

'Yeah,' I said, coughing. 'Yep, that's me. That's me, mate, one hundred per cent.'

'Great. Wanted to make sure I'd heard right. They say your other senses take over, but . . .' He shrugged, bared his teeth in what anyone else might have mistaken for a smile. I shrugged too, but he didn't know it.

Because he was blind.

'You're all good, mate,' I said. I needed to stop saying 'mate'. 'Got your gear on, I see. Want me to chuck your stuff in a locker?'

He did. I took his bag and carried it away while I got my breathing sorted, forced the air from my throat to my lungs. And I unzipped the bag as I stashed it, rooting through. He'd changed his aluminium-free deodorant from fresh mint to fresh citrus, and his protein bars were peanut butter not caramel. But otherwise it was familiar in its meticulous organisation. He'd have been able to pack with his eyes shut. Which was lucky, wasn't it?

I packed for workouts the same way, the way he taught me, trainers in their own compartment, headphone wires wrapped around a ball of socks, water bottle swaddled in a microfibre towel, wrist braces, knee braces, spare shoelaces coiled into a side pocket.

I imagined stealing the shoelaces, sliding them into the pocket of my leggings and feeling the folded length writhe against my thigh. In the labyrinth, you get to make a new map, redraw it, mark the turns that end dead, and the ones that never end. Theseus had thread (I've been to Crete); shoelaces might come in handy. But I left them where they were, zipped the bag closed, shut the locker.

Liam stood where I'd left him, waiting. If he *could* see, if he saw me rooting through his things, he didn't object. It was all the proof I was going to get and there wasn't much time to wonder, because I had a sacrifice to make: my arm, bare, the downy hairs raised in protest. Could he feel them as his fingers ran past my elbow to my bicep and curled over the flexors and extensors? Could he feel the tremor, and could he guess what it meant? He was good at guessing, good at knowing how I felt, even when I didn't know myself.

I met Liam at a park bootcamp session. My friend Tanya was trying to shift the baby weight. We'd already tried a load of different classes, spin, Zumba, Pilates, and found them too intimidating – all those people who were just *better* than us at moving their bodies – so we'd dropped out. I didn't have a baby, just the weight, and my optimism was low, but I'd thought an outdoor class might be different, that being near nature might give us confidence. Tanya came reluctantly – scowling at the rain clouds, at the skipping ropes, at the sweatbanded crew already warming up with star jumps – pessimistic about her pelvic floor.

'Dammit, why did I have a kid?'

'What's a bit of misplaced wee,' I said, 'in return for gorgeous little Ashlie?'

'I feel like my whole life is a battle against liquid. All dribble bibs and extra-thick sanitary towels and praying it doesn't rain so we can get out of the house.'

I handed her a pocket pack of tissues. 'Stuff this in your knickers if you're worried. And shut up. The instructor's coming over.'

The instructor was Liam.

He was fresh-scented and friendly, bouncing through the participants, pleased, proud, a cockerel amongst his rare-breed hens. His shouted commands were a punishment and a thrill. The regulars all worked hard to get his attention, to get a nod, a 'Great work!', a pat on the shoulder. I didn't work hard, I resisted, rolled my eyes at the motivational messages, the spontaneous cheers, the breathless enthusiasm.

I thought I'd avoided his notice. Then his deep voice behind me as I lifted a tyre over my head: 'Excellent control, Cassie.'

'Er. Thanks.'

'But you're holding back.'

'Am I?'

'You think you'll be bad at it. You think you'll look stupid if you try.'

'Everyone here looks stupid. Sorry to inform you. No one looks good dragging a weight on chains.' Or slipping on wet grass, or doing push-ups wearing punch pads.

'*You* look good.'

'What?'

A slow smile, skewed a little to the left. 'Stop fighting it.'

I wasn't totally clear what I was supposed to stop fighting, but I refrained from eye-rolling and sprinted rather than jogged between plastic cones, and even gave a little cheer when my team won a tug of war. And I found I was enjoying myself. He was right. I'd been afraid of humiliation, of trying and failing.

I had to hide my delight when he called across the field, 'Looking great, Cassie!'

'Fuck, he's hot,' Tanya said, recovering after a set of mountain climbers, flattening the damp grass with her back, legs bent, knees spread.

'Want me to call him over, tell him you're ready, right here, right now?'

'Wouldn't say no.'

'What was it you were saying about everything being wet all the time?'

'Ugh. Too far, Cass.' She threw my (mercifully unused) pack of tissues at me, did a couple of suggestive bridges. 'If I wasn't happily married, though, I'd let him increase my reps, if you know what I mean.'

We laughed. She'd always been the sexy one. But it was me Liam backed against the children's climbing frame at the end of the session.

'This feels inappropriate.' I was performatively breathy, frog-shaped handholds digging into my spine. The sun had gone down and there was a misting sort of rain, the air condensing where it avoided contact with Liam.

'No kids here this time of day. They won't know.'

It was true, the park was empty, and when he leaned into me I felt him, hard against my belly (which was a gentle curve then, still soft). We kissed. I got a noseful of that mint deodorant. He got my number. He'd already *got my number*. Because what I'd done, after his little pep talk, was follow his every instruction. What I'd *done* was bow to each suggestion. What I'd done was give him a taste of my unqualified obedience.

I went back to bootcamp even after Tanya dropped out. All through the winter, I did my star jumps and hula hoops, I hefted ropes and crawled through muddy tubes and gave other women piggybacks. And afterwards I waited for Liam to rub a towel through his hair, his biceps gently flexing, waited for him to take me home and cook me salmon with butter beans and harissa and run me through stretches.

I waited, and while I waited, I marvelled. I couldn't believe it was me he was cooking for, me he was taking time to explain muscle groups to, me getting those end-of-session massages. I'd never been picked out of a crowd before, and though I'd always liked being part of a crowd, I suddenly realised what I'd been missing. It was like I'd gone around wearing a disguise my whole life, not knowing it, and he'd slipped it off and discovered something special.

He was the one wearing a disguise now: long hair, pulled into a bun, a blond-brown beard, tufted, scruffy, and a new covering. Not fat exactly. Flesh. Padding. A rounding of the slopes and ridges he'd had. The dip under his deltoid was no longer there, nor the hollow between his shoulder blades; instead his T-shirt stretched, ever so slightly, across his lower back.

In the past there'd have been a trench-coat sheen to his skin, but he was pale and dry-looking, like an old pillowcase found at the back of the airing cupboard. He smelled unfamiliar, too, the citrus deodorant perhaps, or maybe my memory of him had faded. He looked knotted, creased, packed away behind those unseeing eyes.

My eyes rushed to cover every inch of him, and my fingers itched to touch, to poke, to feel for themselves if that extra layer was real.

Tommy had shouldered his bag, a signal he was on his way out. To me he was just a whisper of polyester tracksuit, but of course he noticed I hadn't moved. 'Everything all right—'

I saw the muscle in his throat as he began to make the *C* of 'Cassie'.

'Yep!' I interrupted before he could say my name. 'Yep, all good.' But I saw now there was a gauntlet to run, an obstacle course of verbal greetings. Dani, Roland, our manager Steph. Any of them could casually say my name on the way to the blood pressure monitor, the scales, the new-client forms.

'You've been assessed already?' I asked Liam, crossing my fingers.

'No. But. If you don't mind . . . I was hoping to try a couple of machines first. See whether it's worth signing up.' A catch in his breath, the ghost of a consonant. 'I'm not sure how I'll manage. Like this. It's . . . new.'

'Ah. Gotcha. *Gotcha.*' I glanced at Steph, the real Steph, as she directed Roland in replacing a water filter, watched Dani fill her business-card slot with more tiny hot-pink oblongs. 'Okay. Let's . . . let's get moving.' I tried a pat, too light, then harder, expecting my fingers to tingle, expecting a flash, a roar, a blistering. Nothing happened. 'Come on, then,' I said. 'We're gonna give this thing a shot.'

He let me guide him, but he skated a white stick over the smooth floor, following its clues – the muffling purr of carpet, the clack against a step trainer.

We started on an upright bike, for a warm-up, for a test, and I made a show of adjusting the seat too low, as if I didn't know how long his legs were. He wasn't so tall as Tommy – a more conservative six one – but he looked like a grasshopper with his knees raised above his hips.

No complaints, though. Not a word. He laboured on. And it was labour, it was hard work.

'I'll let you decide how hard you want to push yourself,' I told him. 'Here, I'll put your fingers on the resistance button.' I said it *bu'on*.

Once upon a time, I'd spent hours in front of a mirror, repeating my *t*'s. Bo*tt*le, be*tt*er, bu*tt*er. Chasing away the glottal stops, annunciating till my tongue ached. Now I relaxed, let them slip back in.

'Want some more wa'er?'

What he wanted was the lowest setting, a longer warm-up, an easier programme. What he wanted was a rest while he got his breath back. I watched from a few paces away, hardly believing he was Liam. The Liam who'd forced his body through imagined battles, who'd always chiselled his way through life. Now he hung his wrists over the handlebars, fingers dangling lazily, and lifted his face towards the nearest TV screen. Was this just the ingrained reaction of a modern human, did our exposed skin seek screens the way sunflowers follow the sun, or could he really see it? Was this an act? Was he deceiving me? I had to know.

'What are you doing?'

I dropped my arm.

'I can see shadows,' he said, 'if that's what you're wondering. I can see you waving something in front of my face.'

'Sorry.' I froze at his tone, an automatic response, a muscle memory.

'D'you do that to every visually impaired person you train?'

'Of course not.' Indignant, I nearly forgot to drop my *t*. 'It's just we've had clients try and get cheap sessions.' This was true; other branches had reported issues. People will do anything for money off. 'And you seem very . . .'

'What?'

'Sure of yourself.'

The line between his brows deepened, the corner of his mouth twitched up; he seemed to be trying to decide whether or not I'd insulted him. Finally he gave it up.

'I'm not faking it.'

'Okay. I believe you.'

I looked around the gym. At the unmoving navy and purple surfaces, at the shimmering TV screens, at the people, their swan-neck limbs delicately extending. If he was really blind, that meant he couldn't see any of it: how big the space was, or which machine was which. He couldn't see the orderly row of weights or the unrestrained balance balls drifting to a soft bounce against the mirror. He couldn't see my face, my expression, my height, my colouring. My identity.

None of it. He could see none of it. I was a blur, a shape, like he had been behind the reception glass. Less than that: I was a smudge of dark against light. My muscles relaxed. I couldn't stop my grin. I didn't stop it. He wouldn't know. He wouldn't *know*! I could have laughed, but I felt my face instead, checking it was still there, that it existed even though Liam couldn't see it, couldn't add my stretched mouth, my raised eyebrows, to some list he kept of my expressions and transgressions.

For two and a half years I'd barely smiled without it being logged. Calories, workouts, menstrual cycle. There was an app for each one. But it wasn't me who tapped on the boxes, recording the second slice of turkey I'd eaten at lunch, the extra six minutes I'd needed to finish my 5K, or the raw-egg-white consistency of my cervical fluid. And how could I be sure I was alive without a constantly updating list of each coffee I drank, every fluctuation in my heart rate, the strength of my mittel-schmerz cramps?

Old Cassie had managed without knowing. But I was busy shedding her. The Cassie who wheezed after two minutes of running, the Cassie who always ordered a large deep-pan pepperoni and always ate the entire thing, the Cassie who never looked at her body in the mirror, and didn't expect anyone else to look either.

Old Cassie hadn't been worth documenting. But *Liam's* Cassie. She was coddled and studied, she was energetic and focused, she was controlled. She was looked at. She was worth looking at.

And Liam did more than look.

Like that Sunday afternoon, curtains shut against the

light. A breeze repeatedly sucking the chevroned fabric into the open window cavity. I'd spent the morning with friends and my brunch wear was lying on the bedroom floor. Liam braced above me in the grey dark.

'You stuck to coffee?' His breath hot against my ear, one hand smoothing my waist, as if it already showed signs of inflating. 'You didn't get a muffin?'

'No.'

A kiss on my neck. 'Did you?'

'No.' I was laughing. The bakery I'd gone to was famous for these fresh cranberry muffins, sharp with orange zest and almost too tangy. I loved them. He knew I loved them.

The softest touch of teeth to my jugular. 'You resisted? Completely?'

'Maybe.'

He bit my jaw. Not rough, only hard enough to cause a shiver.

'Half – I had half.'

'You're such a bad girl.'

'Uh-huh.'

The unwelcome glare of a phone screen waking up. I opened my eyes. He'd rolled onto his back.

'What are you doing?'

'Cranberry muffin? You swear it was half?'

I nodded, watched his thumbs tapping.

'I'm going to guess . . . two hundred and sixty calories.'

'Okay.'

'Okay.' The room went dark again as the screen locked. 'Suppose I'd better help you work that off, then.'

There was always something to work off or work on. Progress to make, or time to make up for. True now more than ever, for him anyway – he obviously hadn't been in a gym for months. I had to cut short his second cardio session, drop the weight pin to a hundred and forty pounds, fetch him lighter dumbbells. His lateral raises were wobbly.

'I'm done,' he said after his tenth rep. 'I'm at my limit.'

'Nah. You can do more than that.'

He leaned forward, his T-shirt clinging to a fascinating new facet of his physique: a fine line of flab. 'I can't.'

'One more set.' I never did this, I never argued with clients. I blamed my brother's voice, his sale-closing attitude; I blamed my need to needle Liam. I really wanted to needle him. 'Don't you know the age of the man bun is over?' I said.

He turned his face, half a scowl, not sure if he was ready for banter.

'And beards are on their way out.'

Two full seconds before he allowed himself a grimace. 'Haven't mastered shaving without a mirror,' he said. 'And I don't trust anyone else.'

Fair enough. If he let me do it, I'd have been tempted to slit his throat.

'You normally cut your own hair, too?'

'I'm growing my hair.'

'Deliberately?'

'I'm hoping it'll give me my strength back.' His smile was self-conscious, a flash of dimple in his cheek. That defenceless little dimple, shy to show itself. 'Actually, I'm hoping *this* will give me my strength back. Coming here.'

'Yeah? You committing, then?'

'I think so. Should I let them know at reception?'

'No, no. I can do that. I can sort out the schedule. There's always a mix-up. With names and stuff. There's always a fuss.' I was talking too much, overexplaining, but I couldn't let him speak to anyone else, say my name, say what he thought was my name. I couldn't let him be corrected, informed, empowered. So I kept going like I always did when I was on my last leg, the final kilometre, the closing minutes of a run. 'We're good at fitness here, I promise, just not so much at admin. But I can sort it, and we'll worry about details, your bank and that, next week. Okay? Next week.'

'Okay.'

'Great.' It came out strangled. 'So. One more set, huh? Let's go.'

A nod, persuaded, purposeful. He took a deep breath before he started, and I took a deep breath too, putting my hands out, ready to catch a dumbbell. Ready to catch him. Ready to catch myself, to crush the overwhelming desire to pinch that tiny, tiny fold of flesh sitting above his waistband.

I could imagine how it would feel, the swell of it, soft, pliable, with a bite of muscle underneath. I could imagine rolling it between my fingers. I could imagine the lateral raises too. They're one of the exercises I love to skip. It feels unnatural to me, uncomfortable. The drag down the side of my neck, the hot flare at the shoulder, the reminder that arms are only connected to bodies by one complicated and breakable joint. I hate the fragility of the phrase 'rotator cuff'.

I didn't blame Liam for wanting to give up.

He tried, trembled, sagged, slumped. 'Sorry,' he said, but it was hardly a word, hardly a breath.

His hands fisted, jaw clenched. He was upset. He was raging. But not at me. I was a shadow, I was a ghost, I was the fucking Scarlet Pimpernel. I could slide behind him and gloat over the loss of muscle definition, the way his hand shook on the barbell, how close he came to hitting his head on the pull-up bar. He was frustrated, he was scared, he was vulnerable. I was fascinated, vindicated, delighted. I'd had my five minutes, but I wanted more.

I steered him, stumblingly, through the narrow path in the strength-training section and watched as his shoulder clipped the rubber handle of an assisted dip machine. He flinched at the contact, but he hadn't swerved, hadn't shrunk back, hadn't saved himself. He hadn't known it was there.

I smirked, full-on smirked, and caught sight of myself in the mirror. I was happy. It had been a while since I'd felt that way, but I recognised it, and recognised the danger. I always did do crazy things when I was happy.

Like getting fired for misconduct. Like transferring funds between my own account and a customer's. Like breaking both procedure and trust.

I had worked at the bank eight years, part-time, full-time, as an assistant, an administrator, an advisor. Hopping from one creaking, closing branch to the next, accepting the changes: the coffee machines, the arm-chairs, the colour of the piping on our blazers. I'd memorised the terms of all our accounts, I could explain mortgage repayments, I'd learned to tie a silk scarf in a bow at the side of my neck, and I knew the regular customers.

Once a month, an old couple came in to withdraw cash. Mr and Mrs Dacosta, both kind of bundled up and frail. I liked how the husband was so attentive to his wife, getting her a seat while he queued and helping her up when it was their turn at the counter, and how she patted his hand when he put the banknotes in the inside pocket of his suit jacket.

They had a joint current account that received a tiny pension payment each month. Spending money, they told me. And they only ever spent it on one thing: taking their grandson out for the day.

There was some estrangement in the family that I never totally understood, but this day with their grandson was a big deal. A chance of some kind, maybe a second chance.

I liked it when they came in, quietly excited, looking forward to something. A trip to the Science Museum or the Rainforest Café or some place with a zipwire. The grandson loved sloths, they told me. 'Not because he's lazy, you understand. He's a very hard-working boy.'

He was going to be a vet and move to Costa Rica when he grew up. They seemed thrilled by his ambition, and they were planning on visiting a zoo in Sussex where a kid could meet an actual sloth.

So it was less than thrilling to find there wasn't enough in the account for a withdrawal. No extravagances on their part; the pension payment just hadn't materialised that month. A blank in the credit column.

Mr and Mrs Dacosta didn't argue; they merely, meekly, looked at the statement I'd printed, looked for several minutes, as if they couldn't bear to look away, couldn't bear for the moment to be over because then they'd have to deal with the consequences of the moment instead: their disappointment, their grandson's disappointment.

I offered to get an advisor, though I was reluctant because of the danger they'd be talked into a credit card or offered a loan. But there was no need to worry – they refused help, refused pity, refused eye contact.

The next month was the same. They came in, there was nothing for them, they went away. Only this time the wife cried. She often wore these quilted jackets, soft like bedding, with batik designs on them, and she used a cloudy sleeve to soak up the tears. Her walking stick had a jungle plants design, and a tiny sloth had been marker-penned on, between the leaves.

At any other time I'd probably have tutted and sympathised and then shrugged it off, but just then I was so happy – I'd replaced hangovers with workout highs, lost four kilos, mastered proper push-ups, and Liam had bought me a bunch of workout gear to leave at his place so I could stay overnight and train in the morning. It was unnaturally painful to think of anyone else being sad.

So I brooded over the account and kept an eye on it for the next few weeks. No funds received. The numbers stayed the same, and by the end of that month I couldn't stand it. When I saw Mr and Mrs Dacosta come in, I opened my own account and transferred them the hundred and eighty quid.

I didn't say anything. I didn't think they'd ever know. Or that anyone would know. It wasn't a huge amount of money, it wasn't a life-changing amount. I just needed to do something. To spread a little joy. To stop anything interfering with my high.

But then the pension payment came through, back-dated, itemised, and Mrs Dacosta was puzzled by the discrepancy and Mr Dacosta asked one of my colleagues to look into the mystery.

Company policy states that no employee should ever interact with their own account while at work, either on the premises or when working from home. It was a dismissible offence.

I argued, of course I argued, but my manager took my piped blazer and my silk scarf and told me I'd probably be banned from working anywhere in the financial industry. She said I'd thrown away my career. She said I needed to 'rein it in'.

Then she cleared my locker while I sat on a chair inside the main door, watched by the Sudanese security guard, who helped me pass the time by teaching me numbers one to ten in Arabic.

'For your reps,' he said, mimicking a bicep curl. Exercise had dominated most of my recent conversation at work.

I'd perfected the *kh* sound at the beginning of five by the time my stuff had been gathered.

There was a lot of shit in my locker: tote bags and tampons and desiccated tangerines between a subsoil of crumbling eyeshadow and powdered paracetamol and a topsoil of discarded tissues and laddered tights. The sad strata came out to me stuffed into a big plastic carrier bag.

So that's what I was holding as I walked up the hill, an archaeological dig's worth of crap, my ballet pumps slapping on grey cement slabs, my knuckles knocking against walls and railings, against trimmed privet and gaping passionflower. I was a gaping passionflower.

Garish and disturbing and too much, always too much. I let out a little sob.

Some toddlers in collared grey smocks were sticking tissue-paper butterflies on the windows of a Montessori nursery. They'd started waving before they clocked my forlorn expression and a series of hands dropped, like they were counting the seconds at the beginning of a race.

The pavement, narrowed by rows of parked four-by-fours, had given a false sense of privacy, but anyone could see me, mascara running down my cheeks, and as I stood at the edge of the common, a ray of light shone right in my face, underlining the point.

Beyond a band of London plane trees, though, I could see Liam's silhouette: he was setting up for his first evening session, measuring his territory with long strides. The low sun brought out the blond and red in his hair, made his broad shoulders look even more solid. I watched him concentrate on spreading the equipment out, everything at set intervals. So diligent, so competent. The hot dry breeze flattening his T-shirt to his abs. The grass behind him was tall and golden with fluffy, airy seed heads. I'd run through that grass last week and come home with a tick on my belly. Liam had deftly tweezered it out, and been kind while I panicked about Lyme disease, letting me obsess over the Mayo Clinic symptom list until dinner was ready.

He'd added the tweezers to the first-aid kit he always carried. That he was required to carry. That he never forgot to carry. Because he was good at following rules and having a job and not making mistakes, and not suddenly ending up unemployed.

I was crying again.

'Cassie?'

I made a silly sort of wail, my shoes flapping off as I shuffled towards him. I let them stay where they were, dropped my plastic bag and covered the last ten metres in stockinged feet, the short dry grass poking between my toes, making holes in my tights, probably, cutting my skin, probably. Who cared? I wouldn't be wearing tights tomorrow. I wouldn't be leaving my flat tomorrow. Probably.

'What's happened?'

'Been sacked.'

He dropped the cone he'd been holding – a hollow clop on the hard ground – and jogged to my side.

'How? Why? What—'

I was really crying now, and he held my face, hands smelling like grass and dry soil, wiping the tears with his thumbs. 'Hey, hey,' he said, soft and warm. 'Stop. You have to stop crying. Now, Cassie. Stop.'

But I couldn't stop. The tears ran faster, my throat aching, sobs wracking my body. I felt drunk with it.

Liam gave me a gentle shake. 'Okay. Focus, sweetheart. Focus on me. I'm here. I'm here and I'm going to make you happy.'

Kisses, that was the first thing. On my mouth, my wet cheeks, my jaw, my neck. Then he stood back and started unzipping my newly obsolete work skirt.

'You need to get the feelings out.'

For a second I thought he meant we were going to fuck right there, in the middle of the park. But no.

'Run to the path and back.'

I sniffed, wiped my nose on my sleeve. 'You what?'

'Trust me. You'll feel better.'

I sniffed again. The path was about two hundred metres away. My skirt slid to the floor while I calculated and Liam tugged it from one, then the other foot. I was left in thick tights and a buttoned shirt.

'Go on, Cass.' A hand in the small of my back, a tiny shove.

I started walking, then jogged a few steps. Breath just dry dust. I felt like a clown. Two teenagers, tessellated on a nearby bench, snorted. I could imagine what I looked like – an escaped hostage from a bank robbery gone wrong. But in a sitcom, where no one is supposed to spoil the fun by sympathising. I nearly stopped.

Except. I could blank out those feelings: embarrassment, shyness. I could control that. I'd practised that: not caring that I made a foolish face when I was doing overhead lifts; shrugging at the lurid pink of my forehead after a hard row.

I jogged a few more steps. Relaxed, jumped, ran, sprinted. The ground was prickly and rough and I stumbled whenever anything poked my arches. Wispy bits of seeds hung in the air and got in my nostrils, sticking to my still-damp face. But I didn't object when Liam told me to do it again. And again.

Then push-ups, then kettle-bell lunges, then Russian twists.

'Another set of ten,' he called, not looking at me while he counted boxing gloves. 'Keep going.'

By the time the first bootcamp members arrived, my tights were shredded and my work shirt was drenched in sweat, and I was grinning like an idiot.

Liam was grinning too. 'My girlfriend forgot her kit,' he told the three women and one man. 'Let this be a lesson to you all.'

I got another kiss, in front of everyone, and he made a soft little grunt in his throat, then he pushed a bottle of water on me and told me to go and wait in his car. I fell asleep on the back seat, too tired to worry about my job, too tired for *any* worries, and when I woke we were driving back to his place.

'Feel better?' He studied me in the rear-view mirror.

'Yeah.'

'Told you.'

I stuck out my tongue to make him laugh.

Would he laugh now, if I stuck out my tongue? Would he see it? Could I catch him out that easily? The gym had a long mirrored wall behind the weight racks and Liam was sitting facing it, spine braced against a tilted bench as he attempted a final set of seated single-arm lateral raises. In his reflected expression the line of concentration between his straight brows was clear, the clench of his jaw distinct. I usually try to ignore the mirrors – it can be awkward, catching a client's eye over and over, giving that toothless smile to say without words: I'm not studying you, I'm not spying, I'm not checking you out or giving you evils. I'm just looking, looking, looking.

Which was all Liam was ever doing in the months after we broke up – leaving comments on my Instagram photos, or parking outside my flat at night, or carrying an empty basket round my local supermarket, or nursing a kale smoothie in the garden of my favourite vegan café. He was only looking, staring me into a tighter and tighter space.

Maybe that was it, I thought, watching each smooth move, his perfect hand-to-shoulder alignment as he forced the dumbbells up and paused for a second before slowly lowering them. Maybe he'd hurt his eyes with all that watching. Maybe if I'd stayed by his side, like a good girl, his retinas or corneas, or whatever, wouldn't have worn out.

I'd thought a lot about vision when I was with Liam, under his eternal assessment, in his circling gaze. About how it worked. The light flipping through the lens and hitting the retina. I saw myself as a tiny upside-down picture projected onto Liam's brain, running, running, but never getting anywhere, one of those horses in an old zoetrope, galloping for eternity, or until the drum ran out of momentum.

Was that image still there? A miniature Cassie, trapped in his head, forever trying to get away? Even if he couldn't see me, he could remember, surely. Conjure me. He'd spent enough time revising, it wouldn't test his imagination too hard.

Visualisation is big in fitness. Imagining the movement you're going to do, the goal you're trying to achieve. 'Seeing' yourself crossing the finish line, or hefting that weight over your head. They talked about it on my PT course: what to do if your client *can't* visualise. There was nothing on what to do if your client can't see at all.

I got out my phone and googled 'blindness'. Probability of, types of, causes of. Liam wasn't diabetic. I didn't think he had cataracts or glaucoma or macular degeneration. He was only in his thirties. Was it an injury, then? An accident?

One time, at a party, a girl in my GCSE biology class was hit by a scaffolding pole. No, that's not right. What happened was a boy hit her with a pole. He was active, she was passive. He got her in the forehead, but it was her eyes that swelled shut. Had something like that happened to Liam? Had *anything* happened, or was this all a trick?

I squatted down, shifted into his eyeline, waited for him to settle the dumbbells on his thighs for a rest, and stuck out my tongue. There was no reaction, not the tiniest twitch of a muscle in snout or brow. The Minotaur hadn't found me yet.

Week Two

There was no competition when I said I'd carry on training Liam; Tommy nearly fell off a treadmill in his hurry to sign the paperwork.

'Only, can you put a note on the file?' I asked. 'He thinks my name is Steph. Too awkward to correct him now.'

'Sure, no probs. No probs at all.'

So that was it. I was sorted, I was ready. But the minute I stuck the form in the filing cabinet, a cold, brittle sensation rattled up my limbs.

I started expecting Liam to jump out from behind every bus stop or tree, I listened for his voice in the night, I watched for him from my window. I was living in the past, living like I had last autumn, catching shadows in the light, hearing footsteps when there was silence. My resting heart rate was up, which was annoying when I'd worked so hard to bring it down.

Fear and exercise produce the same results: faster breathing; increased heart rate; sweating; muscle discomfort; needing to wee, even. This is why you shouldn't be too hard on a client who seems to be afraid of exercise. It's not laziness, it's self-protection. And it's more pronounced in someone who's suffered trauma. Of course they don't want to get in a situation where they experience the exact same feelings they had during a terrible event. It's natural, it's sensible.

For me the exercise and the trauma were chain-linked. Getting fit was what I did with Liam, it was how I lived with Liam. It was the legacy, one of the legacies, he left me.

I wasn't fat when we met, I wasn't even overweight, but I was soft, nondescript. I walked to work, I swam on holiday. Tanya and I occasionally went to the gym, where we'd do a ten-minute warm-up on recumbent bikes, then move to the mats to gossip for twenty minutes, our bodies cooling and stiffening while our minds lithely wormed through every problem, analysing each personality in our friendship group.

Lauren revenge-cheating on Craig, Reece emotionally blackmailing Michelle, Daria miserably ignoring Jamie's philandering Facebook posts. Everyone had something going on. Except Tanya – who'd been with steady Steve since sixth form – and me. I was often single because I famously 'didn't put up with any shit'. And your relationship had to last more than a few months to turn into anything gossip-worthy.

Sometimes our gym chats gained momentum and action needed to be taken. Like blocking Craig's number from Lauren's phone, or packing Reece's belongings into Tanya's Ford Focus and taking them back to his mum's.

What we liked best, though, was an intervention.

Wine, earnest advice, righteous arguments, imaginative insults, laughter, sweaty hugs, more wine, declarations of love, declarations of undying friendship, more wine. They were great nights.

Daria's intervention was in a pub on Clapham High Street. Big new wooden tables, warm white fairy lights, sturdy, shiny glasses, everything matching. It smelled of lemon and lager, was airy and had ceiling fans, and the windows could all slide fully open in the summer – we were into good ventilation long before it was fashionable.

Daria sat on a well-polished leather sofa, next to Tanya, who'd be leading the charge. Lauren, Michelle and me on pouffes – backup, the chorus, our words just punctuation to Tanya's presentation.

She'd started with the usual opener. *We're just worried about you, love.* Then got more specific.

'You said Jamie has fake Instagram accounts.'

'Not fake, just different names.' Daria hooked her forearm through the straps of her bag, as if it was a shield.

'Fake names,' we insisted.

'Jakey.'

'Also Jonny.'

'He's got one under José. Think he knows how it's pronounced?'

'He uses his own pictures, though,' Daria said.

Tanya and I exchanged glances.

'But what's he got extra accounts for?' Tanya asked.

'He finds it hard to make friends.'

Lauren snorted.

'Why's that funny?' Daria was squirming on her seat, looking out the window.

'Who's he making friends with, Dar? Fourteen- and fifteen-year-olds. He's a creep.'

'A fucking paedo.'

'He's not that! He's not a creep. He can't help who likes his posts.'

'He can help listing his age as eighteen when he's actually twenty-nine.'

'He probably just forgot to update the default setting or something.'

'Default. Right.'

We all reached for our wine glasses, took big gulps. Outside, the day was fading; inside, the fairy lights were gaining power.

'How can you not see it, Dar? You're amazing.'

'Yeah,' we stressed, 'you're gorgeous, Dar.'

'You're incredible.'

'Yeah, and he's a loser.'

'Gold-plated pond scum.'

'Fucking glittering nonce.'

'You thought he was cheating before.' Tanya again. So gentle.

'I was wrong about that.'

'And he lied about having a conviction.'

'That was a misunderstanding. I told you.'

'But . . . Daria. You can do so much better.'

Daria sighed, slouching on the couch, shoulders rounding under fussy polka-dot sleeves. 'You don't know him like I do. I know he sometimes comes across wrong, but it's anxiety. He gets shy. He's different with me. And he has lots of really lovely qualities.'

'Like what?'

'Yeah, list them.'

A quick dry swallow; her wine sat untouched. 'He listens. And he's interested when I'm having trouble at work or with my dad or whatever. And he always takes my side.'

Unlike us, her tone said. We'd crossed some territorial boundary, we were a foreign power, colonisers, enemies. Tanya shifted closer, sliding easily along the leather sofa cushions.

'And he lets me decide what we watch on telly, and he always comes to pick me up from the station or the bus to walk me home. And he adopted a panda for me. She's called Jenny.'

Her voice was getting whinier, greasier somehow, like it might help her slip out of the conversation. She was restless, scrabbling in her bag, turning to look at the door.

'Is that enough for you?' Tanya asked.

'And where the fuck's Jenny? That's the real question. I've never seen you with a panda.'

'Shut up, Lauren.'

'It's not funny.'

'It's kind of funny.'

'You might not like him, but he's not *your* boyfriend.'

'You really trust him, Dar?'

'Like, with your life.'

'With your heart?'

'I trust him.'

That's when Jamie walked in. Five foot six, acne all round his mouth, hair shaved to the skin except for a feathery mop on top, T-shirt that read *Keep Calm and Bite the Pillow*.

'God, he's a prick.'

Lauren nudged me. 'Hey, Terrier, get him, will you?'

The girls cheered, and I bared my teeth in a mock growl.

Jamie took a step back. 'Fuck's your problem?'

'You are,' Tanya answered, and then looked like she wanted to slap a hand over her mouth.

'Where d'you get the shirt?' I asked, tugging his furious gaze to me. 'Rapists R Us?'

'Where d'you get your face? Cunts R Us?'

There were some sucked-in breaths, but I had to laugh. 'Nah, that's where your dad picked up your mum.'

'Cassie!'

'Jesus Christ. You're a fucking bitch. You coming, Daria?'

'No,' Tanya said. 'She's having a night out with her friends. What are you even doing here?'

'She fucking asked me to come and get her.'

We all turned to stare at Daria in betrayal. She'd been texting him while she had her hands in her bag, secretly asking him to come to her rescue. This wasn't how it was supposed to go. Where were the group hugs?

She was unashamed. 'Told you he always walks me home.'

I was livid. 'I'd rather walk home alone than go anywhere with that shit advert for Clearasil.'

'Yeah?' Jamie said. 'Well, I'd feel sorry for any guy stuck delivering you back to the dog shelter. I'll wait for you at the bar, Dars. I need a fucking drink.'

'I cannot believe this,' Tanya said when he was out of earshot. 'You must be able to see it, Dar. The way he is. You're being deliberately blind.'

'Cassie's the one insulted him first.'

'But he's a classic predator. Turning you against your friends. We're not blaming *you*. You were vulnerable after your mum died. He took advantage.'

'He supported me. He makes me happy.'

'Okay,' Michelle said. 'I mean, I guess if she says she's happy.'

The rest of us were *not* there for that kind of sentiment. We already had a verdict, and there was no chance of appeal.

'She's not happy!'

'Definitely not happy.'

'Just look at her.'

Daria went very red. 'D'you know what, Cass, you've got a fucking cheek coming here for this. You've never had a lad last more than a couple of fucks. Maybe you should think about that. You think when they call you Terrier it's a good thing? You'll never find anyone.'

She got up and let Jamie walk her out. As they reached the doors, I stood up and barked loudly. I might also have made an obscene gesture. The girls cheered again, but when I sat down, I found I was very ready to get drunk.

Was I still a terrier? I didn't feel like one. Liam had stripped me of aggression, that lack of control. I rarely went *too far* now. Which was good, a relief, proof of maturity. But had I lost something valuable too? A particular kind of courage?

On the morning of Liam's second session, I woke with a weight on my chest, a sinister tingling in my limbs, and I reached my cardio limit early. My usual mid-workout energy surge never came. My body was heavy and there was a heavy atmosphere. The trees outside, weighed down by the July heat, flexed their branches, leaves quivering, doing their best to keep the sun off the ground. I wondered how long they could hold it, how many reps those old trunks had left in them.

I forced down a few glasses of water, but liquid was the last thing I wanted. The day before, I'd tried out a

juice fast and I was still crunching on antacids to coun-
teract the sloshy burn, a thick white paste forming in the
corners of my mouth.

I licked at the chalky peppermint as I watched Liam
arrive, struggling with the cab door, hesitating on the
pavement. He had his stick again. A white one with a little
ball at the end, like a real blind person would carry. If this
was a performance, he'd really committed to the role.

He stood, feet planted, head tucked into his spine.
Unmoving. In the past, his ability to stay absolutely still
had frightened me. He was like an ambush predator, a
trapdoor spider, waiting for the moment to strike. Now
there was a tiny sway, as if he was subject to a very, very
slight breeze. If I'd been a beetle, I'd have spotted him
waiting in his web.

But when he took my arm I was just as caught.

'I wasn't sure I'd get you again,' he said.

'Why not?'

He paused, stretching his neck. Was he thinking, or
was this some new habit that blindness had fostered?

'After the change last week,' he said finally. 'I was
meant to be with a bloke originally. Tommy? But then I
got you. So I thought I might get passed around. And
you said admin wasn't your forte.'

'We try and stick with clients . . .' I stopped. That was
too earnest, too middle class. 'Can't get out of assessments that easy,' I said instead, my cheeky-salesman
voice all rusty and false. 'I want to make sure you're
giving me a hundred and ten per cent.'

I'd looked up ways to disguise your voice when I'd decided to train him again. Mostly I was doing the right things: lowering my pitch, pronouncing words differently, attempting an impression of someone else. I'd tried calling my brother, to practise following his catchy kind of cadence and replenish my well of chirpy business clichés, but I'd only got his voicemail. *Congrats! You've reached Gavin from the Croydon office. I'm mid-hustle and can't take your call right now, but if you leave a message I absolutely solemnly promise I will call you back.*

I left a message, but I'd grown up with Gav and his solemn promises, and I didn't expect to hear from him soon.

In the meantime, I needed to widen or purse my mouth, and I needed to watch out for favourite phrases and inflections. I'd listened to an AI impersonation of someone famous and realised that it was the highs and lows that confirmed the speaker's identity. If I stuck to mid tones I would be less likely to give myself away.

'Okay, let's crack on. Get you back on track. No slacking.' Not my phrases, not my voice. But I had to be careful not to become a caricature of my brother or make 'Steph's' parodic expressions more suspicious than Cassie's normal speech.

The gym receded as I guided Liam inside, but I was used to that. There'd always been two settings in his presence: visual overload, when I saw *everything*, like an acid-hopped Sherlock Holmes, nothing escaping my notice – shoes, cars, brickwork, foliage, litter – or tunnel vision, when I could barely look up from my own feet, missed it all and saw nothing. Except him.

'We really *should* do an assessment this week,' I said, flat, determined, wanting to take charge, to take shelter behind my own professionalism.

'Why do I get the impression you've already got the calipers out?'

The laugh caught me by surprise. 'Yeah, I've been waiting for an excuse to give you a pinch.'

'Have you? Well, I'm right here.'

'Yes, you are.' And close, too, his body tucked behind mine.

I went cold, like when I've worked out hard after a fast and my blood sugar's dropped too low. I couldn't do it. I couldn't do this. Not even for five more minutes. I *was* going to pass him on to another trainer. I stopped and looked for Tommy, but there was just a bench-presser in a bright violet T-shirt, and a runner with navy neck tattoos. Both normal human height.

'Steph?' Liam said, and it took a moment to realise he wasn't suggesting I find my manager, that he was addressing me.

'Gimme a sec.' I hoped the panic wasn't clear in my voice. Dani was setting up for a spin class, sliding on three sets of terry-cloth wristbands, ready for the sweat she said always ran down her arms. There was a PT at the pull-up bars, coaching a woman with obvious butt implants, but she wasn't staff. There was a cleaner in the gym uniform, but she'd get a shock if I asked her to train someone.

'Can't find the calipers after all?' Liam asked. His voice was gentle, soft, forgiving, his smile tentative, his hand on my arm steady. Is this what he was like with other people? Reassuring, patient? Is this what he'd been like with me, once?

'To be honest, we usually use the body composition scales,' I said, feeling my blood grow calmer in my veins. 'I know it's not as accurate, but most clients don't want to be pinched.'

'Is that the plan, then?'

'Sure.' As good as any.

I took him into the office, pulled out a chair and let him feel for the seat. He'd used a body fat monitor before and knew to take off his socks and shoes, but he fumbled with his trainers for long enough that not offering to help would seem weird.

'Need a hand?'

'It's this knot. I seem to be making it worse somehow,' he said.

Hesitation, irritation, then I knelt in front of him and dug my nails into the tangled laces. There was a slight sports-shoe smell, but it was more rubber and plastic than anything. 'Jeez, yeah, this is a tight one. Let me just . . .' I shifted – my cheek near his shin, one knee between his feet – and worked the knot free. His leg hair tickled my collarbone, and was that his breath on the back of my neck?

'Done,' I said, and just as I was about to stand, he

snapped his legs shut, catching my shoulder between his thighs.

I yelped, and swore – half swore, my tongue not quite able to tackle a full word.

'Sorry.' He spread his legs again instantly, letting me go, letting me sprawl out across the room, letting me curl away and stare.

'Sorry,' he said again. 'I didn't realise . . . I thought you'd moved already.'

'You're okay,' I told him, but I kept back behind the desk while he pulled off his socks and I was reluctant when helping him onto the scales.

He gave a grunt at the reading, said he was probably a bit dehydrated.

'No worries,' I told him. 'It's just a guide.' Which was lucky because I hadn't been able to hold the numbers in my head long enough to write them down. All I could think about was the strength of his legs, pinning me, one knee digging into my chest, the other into my back. A split second, that was all it was, but the sensation wouldn't fade.

'Get your things back on.' Voice too high. Was I managing *cheerful*, or did I sound as wound up as I felt?

He rolled on his socks. One was inside out and I watched his face to see if he'd notice, but his expression didn't change. He tightened his laces with a sharp tug, the sound like a hissed word in another language, one Liam was fluent in, a language that said it was time for a run, it was time for him to leave, it was time to do what he wanted. I hadn't expected to hear it again.

'That it?' he asked. 'You have my height and everything, right?'

'Right.'

'Blood pressure?'

'Right.'

'D'you want to take it?'

'Oh. I see. Yeah. Yes, we should do that.' I found the machine, set it up, laid his arm on the desk and wrapped the cuff around his bicep. He flexed once before relaxing and it felt like a warning.

'It might be a bit elevated,' he said.

'You nervous?'

'Not now you've dropped the caliper idea, but I'm taking quite heavy-duty steroids at the moment. They aren't the fun kind either.'

'Oh, for . . . for your eyes, you mean.'

The machine whirred, the cuff swelled, Velcro crackling, and Liam blew out steadily, tipping his head back.

'So, your . . . diagnosis, or whatever. I mean, d'you mind me asking . . . ?'

'I have a brain tumour.' He turned his face to me and for a second I thought he was studying my reaction.

What was my reaction? I didn't say I was sorry, I didn't tell him it was awful. You have to be able to breathe for that. And I wasn't breathing. Or moving or thinking. I was trying to disappear, like a mouse cornered against a skirting board, hoping to go unnoticed. It was a ruse I'd tried in the past – he couldn't get me if he didn't know where I was.

The cuff began to deflate, the machine's whir a little more disappointed on the way down.

'Steph? You still there?'

I *had* disappeared. It had never worked before.

'I'm here,' I said. 'Wow. Brain tumour. That's a biggie.'

'Yeah.' He smiled at the ceiling. He really was beautiful. That flash of teeth like a cat, like a threat, the muscles in his neck moving beneath the beard. 'A biggie. The official medical term.'

'How did you find out?'

'It's been growing a while. I had symptoms, but I didn't know what they meant. Didn't want to know. Finally went to the doctor a few months ago.'

A few months ago, he'd been outside my old flat, clean-shaven, poised, following me down the street when I'd been forced out by an empty fridge. *I just want to talk, Cass. Give me a chance, will you?* The phrases unimaginative, the follow-up phone calls routine. I'd joked he was growing lazy, but no, he was growing blind.

'What kind of symptoms?' I asked, finally unwrapping the blood pressure cuff.

'Headaches, mainly, and I was tired all the time, getting blurred vision. I had to stop driving. Even then, I thought it was migraines or something.'

'But it was cancer.'

'No. Not cancer. The tumour's benign.'

*

So, he wasn't dying, then. Which would have been the ultimate win for me. Especially as he'd planned to live for ever, or past one hundred at least. He'd been obsessed with those places in the world where everyone makes it to their centenary. The blue zones: Sardinia, Okinawa, California, Costa Rica and somewhere in Greece. Places where they eat local, unprocessed food, exercise every day and work till they're ninety. He was going to be like them. We both were.

Part of that plan meant living together.

'It makes sense, doesn't it?' he'd said, a few months after we'd got together, the menthol sweat of his post-run T-shirt confusing the atmosphere of his kitchen, his hand leaving a print on the gleaming stainless-steel fridge. He'd asked me to move in with him towards the end of a really long run and I'd thought I was hallucinating.

'This way we can train together. Push each other. You can keep me on course and I can do the same for you.' He scooped low-carb strawberry protein powder into a glass, added water, handed it to me. 'I want to look after you.'

And I wanted to stay on course. I wanted to be pushed. I wanted to be looked after.

'If you need to break your lease, I can help with that,' he was saying, his voice running now his body was stationary. 'And you don't have to worry about rent until you find another job. In fact, I've been thinking – why don't you train as a PT? I can mentor you. Then later you could even work for me.'

I stirred my protein shake, sucked some off the spoon. 'I'm not sure I want to spend my life barking at a bunch of brightly dressed marketing managers.'

'Do in-gym stuff, then. That part doesn't matter.'

What did matter? Eating right, training right, doing the plosive movements while you had the most energy, getting the cardio in before paying attention to the minor muscle groups. Getting focused, staying focused. Setting goals and keeping lists and creating visual aids.

Liam's visual aids were pictures of people who were super fit at seventy or eighty or ninety. He put them up in the flat, on the mirror, on the fridge. There was one particular couple on a beach, the grey-haired woman in a sarong, dancing with her leathery husband in front of a sunset. I couldn't help giving her a sarcastic smile every time I reached for the milk.

'Do we have to have all these old people staring at us all the time?' I asked a few weeks after I moved in, when I thought I couldn't stand sarong woman any longer. 'My mate Lauren thinks you're into granny porn. It's kind of embarrassing.'

'Why d'you care what *your mate Lauren* thinks?'

'She's . . . part of the group. I don't want her spreading rumours, or whatever.' Lauren had managed to stay friends with Daria. She and Tanya had met her for dinner a few days ago, after popping in on me. I would have bet my favourite trainers on them discussing sarong woman and Liam's photos of ninety-year-old Japanese cheerleaders. I bet they'd had a good laugh too.

'If you're embarrassed, don't invite her again,' Liam said. '*I'm* your future, Cass. In a hundred years Lauren won't matter – you won't even remember her, or any of those people, or what they said about the pictures in our flat.'

'In a hundred years we'll be dead.'

His cup slammed down. The handle cracked off. Camomile tea everywhere.

He didn't like to be reminded of his mortality, he wasn't calm in the face of death. There were words I avoided because they made him moody. Cancer was one of them. Growth, death, dying, ageing, shrivelling, atrophy, arthritis, wrinkles, obesity. I started collecting them in the back of my mind, cutting them out of my speech. It was easily done. Who wants to talk about depressing things with their sexy new boyfriend anyway?

'So, is it like a mutation?' I asked, using another word I knew he didn't like. To compensate, I shifted the exercise bike's saddle to the correct height. 'Your tumour, I mean. Or is that just the *cancerous* types?'

A pause as he laid his stick on the ground. 'It's, no, it's just . . . abnormal cells. Just a . . .'

'Growth?' I pronounced the *th* as an *f*, but the word still packed a punch.

'Anomaly.' He gripped the bike's handles hard, starting on his mid-session cardio, reheating his congealed muscles.

I was silent but curious, trying to picture the moment of his diagnosis. How had he taken the news? What had it been like for him in that moment, hearing the words? Had he cried? Had he raged at the doctor? I imagined him red-faced, burning. It was easy to imagine.

The heat that came off him now – feverish – I'd forgotten that. How hard it was to keep cool, in every sense, like trying to take a maths exam during an Ibizan heatwave. I held a palm close to one thigh, warming it as if he were a blazing wood burner. His skin brushed mine as he pedalled, and he reached for me. There were plasters on three of his fingers.

'You hurt yourself?'

'Tried to chop a pepper.'

'That wise?' There were half-healed cuts on his thumbs, I noticed, and a burn on the back of his hand.

'I'm sick of stuff from the microwave,' he said. 'I've been living off absolute crap for months. I thought maybe I could manage something else, something better. But it's hard to avoid hot things and sharp things when you're going by feel. So, no, not wise.'

'Isn't there anyone to help you?'

He shook his head with a single sharp turn and tucked his wounded fingers into his palm, hiding the plasters for a moment. 'I have a care worker once a day, to make sure I'm not dead. But the people I thought might be there for me aren't. The people I thought I could count on.' He palmed the handlebar, massaging his thumb muscle. 'Though I have to admit it's partly my fault. My pride. Lots of my friends don't know. I didn't exactly want to make a Facebook announcement. Ollie – my mate Ollie – drops by sometimes, but he's busy keeping our business afloat. We run a park bootcamp. Franchise it. Programmes, equipment, permits, advertising. I put everything into it. Thought I'd worry about relationships later. So. No. I don't really have anyone else now.'

'Not even family? What about your mum? Er. Or dad?' I knew his dad wasn't in the picture, but *Steph* didn't.

'No chance.' He said it on a laugh, a humourless one. 'My mother's not exactly a great cook, anyway.'

'What would you ask her to make, though, if you could?' But that was too like me, so I rephrased, said it how my brother would: 'What's your top dish?'

He lifted his head. 'Tuna steak. With bean and courgette salad. Mint and caper dressing. Bit of lemon and chilli.'

'Sounds . . .' I cleared my throat. 'Sounds delicious.' It was. I knew that recipe, I could practically taste it. He'd made it for me often. I could remember it served with

SWEAT

water icy from the fridge, Liam setting my plate down, a kiss on my head. He'd wanted me to love that meal – the taste, yes, but the benefits too. The protein and the fibre and the antioxidants. He'd really cared I got enough anti-oxidants. He'd cared about my vitamin A intake and my need for iron and selenium; he'd wanted me to get more fatty acids. He'd designed the meal for me, and he'd made it tasty too.

'I'd offer to make it for you sometime,' he said, 'but I can't even handle a pepper.'

He cupped his hand as if he held the pepper now, and the tips of his fingers grazed my ribs. They grazed the material of my breathable T-shirt, my collagen-fed skin, the thin (very thin) layer of subcutaneous fat before they reached bone, but I may as well have been a skeleton. I felt exposed. I was standing too close.

'Maybe I could persuade someone else to make it sometime.' A lilt to his words, like he was asking, like he was hopeful.

'Maybe . . . we should wrap up the cardio.' The offer had nearly been out – I was already watching myself drizzle oil over courgette circles. I must be sick in the head. It was pure manipulation and I was still ripe for it. Too ripe. I was the ingredient for a fucking smoothie.

He had recipes for those, too, full of hemp seeds and Greek yogurt, full of anti-inflammatories and amino acids.

'I love food,' he said, settling into the cooldown phase as I tried to settle into my own. 'People used to think I

51

didn't, because I was careful about what I ate, because I understand restraint, balance. But I've been stuffing my face for the past few months, munching on double bacon cheeseburgers and double-cream lasagnes, and I can tell you it's the people who choose that shit willingly – they're the ones who don't love food. The people who gobble their way through whole boxes of chocolates.'

That made me start, made me clutch the cupholder, made me add three unnecessary minutes to his timer. Because *I* was the chocolate gobbler. I was one of those people. 'They just care about taste, you mean?'

'If you can say those things have a taste, beyond the salt and corn syrup. I miss *flavour*, the combination of sharp and earthy, of bitter and creamy, of rich and fresh. I know what I'm *supposed* to be eating. It's not fair.'

'Yeah,' I said, feeling his hot, angry breath even as I moved away. 'Pity you're stuck with microwave crap, then, isn't it?'

Because, yes, Liam knew about food, how to use it to build muscle or boost energy, how to pack nutrients into every meal. He knew which vegetables we were supposed to eat and what season they grew, what family they belonged to and whether they contained flavanols or anthocyanins.

We went shopping on Friday mornings. Under the

grey arches of a railway, then under the green arches of the market, where it was crowded and smelly and there were always tourists taking photos.

'D'you fucking mind?' I said one morning as I squeezed a grapefruit.

Two curly-haired Spanish girls pulled their phones against their chests.

'What d'you think I'm going to do? Make it disappear? I'm not Debbie fucking McGee.'

'Nice reference,' Liam said, shifting a bunch of kale into the crook of his arm. 'I'm sure that will make a lot of sense to them.'

The tourists raised their hands to apologise and slipped away with a large group of other bland, tanned teenagers. I was pissed off. The coffee stand had a big stack of cinnamon buns the size of a balance ball, and I knew I wouldn't be allowed one. Instead, Liam bought a fat pumpkin and dropped it into my backpack.

'Weight training,' he said, with a wink for my scowl. 'Keep your core tight, Cassie.'

'There are these places with trolleys,' I told him, heavily, as we left the vegetable stall behind. 'Sainsbury's, Tesco. Have you heard of them? And you know they're called *super*markets . . .'

'You think the food in Tesco is better than here?'

'I think the food in Tesco doesn't require me to *keep my core tight.*'

'But the experience is important, my darling Cassie. The sight and smells, the connection with each vendor, being deliberate about what we buy, paying attention to the season. And working up an appetite.'

I grimaced. No chance of that at the fish stall, where I concentrated on not looking at the pink octopuses draped over the front of a table like party streamers. Liam bought several kilograms of wolf fish to take home and bake with ginger and green beans. He said it was high in protein, but I was sure he'd been seduced by the name. And they looked absolutely horrific. Honestly, I could have done without seeing their great big tusky faces. I like my fish in neat plastic-wrapped fillets.

The bread stall was consoling after that. Nothing dangly or gelatinous to avoid. All sweet, doughy warmth.

'No, come on, Cass, away from there.' He had his arm on my shoulders, guiding.

'I'm not a kid, you know.'

'You look like one. Staring at the sourdough like that.'

'I thought sourdough was good for you.'

His arm tightened, he lowered his voice. 'Cassie, I don't want to have an argument here. You know you can't have bread. We don't eat bread.'

I blinked. That was new. I could have sworn we'd bought a rye loaf a fortnight ago. But the rules changed every week. Carbs were good, carbs were bad, cheese was healthy, cheese was poison, coffee made you live longer, coffee shrank your brain. It wasn't Liam's fault. That's just science. No one can keep up with it.

I helped Liam to his taxi at the end of the session, feeling the span of his hand, the blunt ends of his fingers, and then I turned my head away and wondered if I could guess his height from the angle of his hold on my arm, if I could find any familiarity in his form. The experiment was inconclusive, but then this wasn't a blind test.

Week Three

I experimented a lot over the next few days, in shops and cafés, at home and in the gym, asking myself: what was life like for Liam now? I wanted to know, I wanted to *feel* it. I let my eyes shut while I queued at a checkout, while I counted reps for a client, while I waited for my coffee.

'Black Americano for Cassie?'

The voice was veined with conflicting noise, with crossed chords of sound: a soft-voiced song over speakers, the clink of metal spoons on china, the harsh, hollow hiss of the milk frother.

I stretched towards the barista, eyes closed: 'Can you put the cup directly in my hand?'

'It's very hot, ma'am.'

'I'll be okay.'

Fuck, it was fucking hot. That was a mistake. I nearly dropped it.

And I remembered a habit of Liam's when we were together: his way of making me take something from his hand. Because if you leave an object for someone — a milk carton on a counter, for instance — they can get it in their own time. But if you hand it to them, they're on *your* time, they have to take the carton *now*, the way you want. He'd done it in the gym the last two weeks — handing me his bag, handing me the weights, handing over his water bottle for a refill. I'd hardly noticed, because it was what he'd always done, and because it seemed natural when a person couldn't see a surface, let alone the proffered thing.

But either way, it felt like I'd been played. I'd thought I was lording it over him, but the blindness had made me serve him better, with even less resistance.

On the way home, I went and bought courgettes. I bought tuna steak and flageolet beans too. Mint, lemon, chilli. I'd been craving this meal since he'd mentioned it, but when I got to the till, I wondered: was cooking his favourite dish revenge or reverence?

The shopping bag was heavy, so I lifted it as I walked. Sneaking in a little extra weight training. I'd repped about twenty on my left side, thirty on my right, when I got to the ornamental gates of an old cemetery.

I'd been in there once before, after a fight with Liam. A fight about food. I hadn't properly followed his recipe for hake and Puy lentils: I'd added too much olive oil, I'd messed up the fat–protein ratio, and that proved I didn't care about him, about us, about what he'd been trying to do for us. I think that was the first time he'd really frightened me, though I couldn't have explained what was so scary; there hadn't been any shouting, and he'd never touched me. But I'd been panicked enough to leave, flee-ing out the door, the laces of my trainers trailing on the pavement.

Unthinking, I'd headed towards my parents', then realised their house wasn't the sanctuary I needed. The cemetery had seemed like a good place to hide. Liam hated a cemetery, the way he hated any reminder of death. And the place looked like it had been designed to hide in. The long Gothic chapel, the dense evergreens, the big stone statues and plinths. The ground had been dark from a week of rain, the trees stacked with tattered pink cherry blossom.

I'd walked round and round, methodically wiping Liam's texts and emails. Every note he'd sent me, senti-mental and practical, every tentative offer of romance, every demand for domesticity. I sent them into the eter-nal ether.

Later, I felt I'd burned important evidence, all the clues to how I'd got here, the subtleties I couldn't remem-ber. The accidental documentation of a slow decline, or a fast tumble. I'd never know.

Finally, I had been calm, regretful, sure I'd over-reacted and ready to go home. Home, where Liam asked what had got into me, where lunch had been remade and kept warm, where my nan's pretty stoneware measuring spoons had been accidentally dropped and smashed, where Liam's trainers were wet and muddy. Something had happened while I was out, there had been a series of events, but piecing them together was disloyal, ungrateful and completely pointless when my boyfriend was lovely again.

The cemetery looked different now, full of fallen leaves. Autumn had come early, the trees giving up in the heat. Purple wild flowers waved above the oldest graves, and a couple of guys in monogrammed green polo shirts were raking the paths.

I sat on a bench, let the shopping bag flop onto my trainers, and closed my eyes, a sliver of sun on my face. The smell of hot dust, of grass cuttings, a weak waft of exhaust fumes. Liam couldn't break my stuff now, he couldn't chase after me or come looking, kicking through the paths on my usual running route. So why was I here? Why did I still feel the need to hide?

'Mind if I . . . ?' A woman with a stick. She was pointing it at the seat next to me, hunched, gasping. 'The other bench is too far.'

I scooted along. She gave me a side-on inspection and pulled up a blue surgical mask as she collapsed back against the wooden slats.

I turned my face away, breathing over the victims of consumption and typhoid and smallpox, and whatever else Victorian people died of.

'Peaceful, isn't it?' the woman said. 'I worry they'll develop it one day, build flats, but hopefully they won't want to deal with all the old bones. No one likes dealing with old bones. Just ask my GP.'

I gave the little laugh she'd been angling for, and

wondered how old she was. Seventies? Eighties? She
wouldn't have made it onto Liam's wall, wouldn't be
modelling a sarong or competing in a cheerleading team,
or herding sheep up a Sardinian hill at a hundred. I liked
her just for that. My phone was buzzing in my pocket
and I silenced it without looking.

'What brings you here?' she asked.

'Er . . .'

'Go on, you're all right.' She tugged down her mask.
'I'll risk it.'

'My ex is scared of death,' I said. 'This is a place I
know I'll never run into him.'

She gave me an impressed look. Not the bland answer
she was expecting. 'He got a lowered immune system,
then?'

'Maybe. He's got a brain tumour.'

'Well, Christ. That blows my COPD out of the water.'

'It's not a competition.'

'It bloody well is. It is in this market.' She was digging
in her bag, and I hoped she wasn't looking for test results
or something. My phone buzzed again.

A nasty little treacherous excitement built in my stomach. That was me thinking it was Liam. Hoping it was
Liam. Not a true hope, more like a muscle memory, an
atavistic animal instinct, a disgusting evolutionary trait I
hadn't managed to overcome, no matter how civilised I
thought I was. Sickening.

I checked the screen. *No Caller ID.* The excitement
didn't dim. I hit decline.

'Brain tumour.' The woman was shaking her head. There were no test results; she was holding a small sketchbook and a thin-nibbed pen, and she was drawing a tree. Within a few strokes, I could see it was a cherry tree in the middle distance, the lowest branch arched sharp and awkward, a rough ball of fungus growing on the trunk.

'That's good,' I said.

'Not really.' She made an artless little scribble where a leaf might be, deliberately spoiling the picture. 'I used to be better.' She shut the book. 'What d'you think of that monument over there?'

She was pointing at a grave a few rows back. A column that looked like it was supporting a big stone bowl full of jelly.

'It's a goblet of fire,' she told me before I could say anything. 'For a Zoroastrian. A Parsee. An Indian. You're not supposed to bury Zoroastrians, but I don't suppose there were any Towers of Silence in London in eighteen hundred and whatever-it-was. Or any vultures.'

I had literally nothing to say to that, and my phone was at it again, throbbing against my thigh.

'I'd love to be left to the elements,' she carried on. 'Especially somewhere hot. So, I'm going to leave my body to medical science and hope I pop off in the summer.' A crow darted down onto the path, eyeing us. The woman eyed it back and wagged her finger at it. 'There'll be nothing left for you.'

There'd be *some*thing; she wasn't skinny. But would I

be worried about my body mass index at her age? I hoped not. I hoped I'd be over it. Surely at some point flesh could be set aside and food could just be enjoyed, and the sweaty straining of youth would be looked at as something slightly embarrassing. The way remembering games of kiss chase made me blush for six-year-old Cassie.

The woman's phone started ringing then, a sound like a robotic woodpecker, which suited her jabbing movements as she made a mad scrabble in her bag, found the mobile and put it on speaker.

'I'm in the middle of talking to someone, can I call you back?'

'Oh, right, sorry,' the voice said, shrinking and sheepish, as if they should have known she'd be having a conversation with a stranger in a cemetery at this time.

'No bother. What's the weather like there?'

'Er . . . yes, nice, but if you're busy, I won't keep you.'

'I need to tell you about the hedgehog I saw in the garden.'

'Now?'

'No, not now. Later. I'll speak to you later. Okay?' She hung up. 'People just love interrupting.'

My phone rang again as if to prove her point.

She chuckled. 'Go on, you can answer it.'

I did. The buzzing stopped, but there was silence on the line, or perhaps a little static. No Liam. 'Hello?' I said. 'Hello?' I hung up, shrugged. 'No one there.'

'Scam, then. Or one of these marketing calls. Same

thing half the time. *Every* call is a nuisance, actually, if you ask me.'

'Yeah.'

She was rooting through her bag again. 'People do survive brain tumours nowadays.' There was an inhaler in her hand. 'There's no cure for COPD, though.'

'He's gone blind.'

'I've got cataracts.'

'You can get them fixed.'

'He might be able to get *his* thing fixed.'

I snorted, gave in. 'True.'

She sucked on her inhaler and then gave a deep cough. 'How's this your only sanctuary, if he's blind?'

'I didn't say it was my only sanctuary. Anyway, he might be faking.'

'A fake tumour?'

'Fake everything.'

'Fake fear of cemeteries?'

'No, he was scared of them before the tumour.'

She put her inhaler away. 'An interesting psychological study.'

'If you say so.'

'Hard to live with, was he?'

'That's one way of putting it.'

She nodded. 'You shouldn't trust anyone who refuses to face death. But, on the other hand, you shouldn't trust anyone who takes too much of a comfort in the idea.'

I rolled my eyes. 'I'll try and remember that.'

We sat quietly for a while. Looked at the Zoroastrian

grave, leaves blowing around our ankles. I watched the crow peck at a snail, stabbing the insides until – seeming to lose patience – it picked up the shell and smashed it against the stone path.

'I probably won't leave my body to medical science,' the woman said, her eyes following the crow as it flew off. 'What would they want with it anyway? Doubt my organs are much good to anyone. I've got a fatty liver. Forgot to tell you about *that*, didn't I?'

I took a long walk after I said goodbye, absorbing the evening sun through my shirt, absorbing the beer and cigarettes and laughter from the crowds of drinkers outside different pubs. I hadn't stood outside with a pint for years. I hadn't smoked or laughed like that for years.

I probably didn't have a fatty liver and maybe I should leave my body to medical science, or at least get a donor card. I wondered if Liam had a donor card. Surely he wouldn't want his omega-3-fed, forty-beats-a-minute, cholesterol-free heart to go to waste. It might be black in the psychological sense, but it had always been golden in the medical one.

I'd ask when I saw him; that would wind him up.

I was nearly home. As I turned into my street, I saw my bin lying on its side, contents strewn over tarmac: cartons and cans, crumpled cling film, clumps of kitchen towel. Foxes, I told myself. But there was a nasty shimmer of familiarity around the scene. Liam had gone through my bins after we'd broken up.

Closer, I realised it wasn't only the waste bin that had spilled. The council-issued paper-recycling bag had a tear, the clear plastic stretched and cloudy. Ripped strips of old insurance policies and mobile-phone bills littered the pavement, glowing against the dark ground.

My paper waste hadn't interested Liam in the month after our break-up. It was the proper rubbish he'd groped through, that he'd documented, sending me dozens – hundreds – of messages. Pictures, too, photos of my own refuse.

Crisps, Cass? Really?

Ready meals?

Fruit juice is very high in sugar.

Diet drinks are linked to liver failure and dementia.

You've started getting your periods again, I see.

You're not taking your supplements regularly. I know because you should have used up that bottle of glucosamine by now. And yet . . . I can't find it.

What did I tell you about cheap meat substitutes? Starch is not a nutrient.

What are the plasters for? Have you got blisters again? You need to take better care of yourself.

Why won't you let me take care of you?

I just want you to stay healthy, Cassie.

You need me.

On and on and on, for hours. Knowing I couldn't look away, that I felt every scold as a scald.

Was it about to start again?

That evening I watched my phone like it was a

comedian threatening audience participation, and felt that fist of fear when the screen lit up. But it was just my mum: *Can you give me a call at some point, assuming you're still alive?*

I went to bed with a self-conscious smile. Of course that was the only message; a blind man can't look through your bin.

A blind man can't follow you either, but I found myself acting like a secret agent the next morning: changing my route to work, stepping onto a waiting bus at the very last minute. Suspicious. Of Liam, of life, of myself.

The heat had dampened and the windows were steamy. I climbed to the top deck and swiped at the condensation so I could scan the street below. No Liam. No soft felt hats or dark glasses or newspapers with eyeholes. I relaxed, settled, sat back, and then flinched when a tree branch scraped the roof of the bus. I needed distraction. I called my mum.

'You on your way somewhere, then?' she asked when she picked up.

'Why d'you say that?'

'You only call me when you're on the move.'

'That's not true.'

'Yes, it is, but I'm not going to argue with you. What's happening? What's the news?'

'I thought *you* had news.'

'Did I say that?'

'You said . . . No. Never mind.' I closed my eyes for a

second, felt the sway of the bus, breathed in the dusty scent of the warm, carpety seats. 'I've got a blind client.' I was *this* close to telling her it was Liam. I wanted to do it, the way I wanted to throw myself off the cliffs at Seaford Head. A sudden irrational desire for absolute, meaningless destruction.

Because Mum *loved* Liam. Thought he was the best thing that ever happened to me and took his side in everything. She'd been livid when we broke up, and refused to accept he wasn't just 'madly in love' when I found him waiting outside my flat or following me around a shopping mall.

'A blind client?' she said. 'That must be hard.'

'It's been fine so far. I only have to get him to the machines, press the buttons.'

'So does he . . . you know . . . feel your face?'

'What? No, of course not. Don't be daft.'

'Why you getting narky? It's a reasonable question.'

The bus lurched to a stop. 'Mum, no blind people actually do that.'

'They do in films.'

'What d'you think they'd get out of touching your face?'

'That's how they build a picture of you, in their *mind's* eye.'

'You can't really believe that.' I pressed my knee into the seat in front as the bus set off again.

'All right. Whatever. He doesn't do it. Let's talk about something else.'

There was a thunder of feet up the stairs and a teenager with a fluffy pom-pom headband landed next to me. I shifted and switched the phone to my other ear.

'And young Gemma got ten thousand likes – or views, is it? – for that TikTok challenge with a skipping rope,' Mum was saying. 'Sal's been bragging. *You* should do one of those.'

'Should I?'

'Be easy for you, jumping about and that. Hanging from bars, lifting things. You do it anyway.'

'Yeah, I'm always hanging from bars, me.'

'Good for business too, I'd imagine.'

'You're probably right.' I didn't want to argue, and perhaps I *was* missing my chance, but I didn't want to be watched and analysed – I'd had enough of that.

'Course I'm right. By the way, when are you coming round? Gemma lives in Birmingham and she visits Sal more than you visit me. You'd think you were in a different country rather than the same bloody borough, the amount we see you.'

The sound of the kettle being switched on in the background made me think of the hot little kitchen. All white. Spotless. Toast under the grill. My parents bought their council house in the eighties and then sold it in the nineties to buy something that looked almost exactly like a council house. It was the most comfortable place in the world, physically. Always warm, stuffed with recliners and thickly underlaid carpets, the TV volume never above twelve. Lots of uplighters with dimmer switches, and fake fur blankets to pull over your lap. It was like going back into the womb.

Not something Liam appreciated. Liam, who only saw the ugly textured wallpaper and the too-big telly. He was from a more draughty habitat. A place where televisions were kept in cupboards, like skeletons, and the sofas were filled with actual horsehair.

So it was doubly uncomfortable to find him, couched and cosy, at my parents' place a couple of weeks after we broke up.

Mum had answered the door to me with a suppressed smile. 'Liam's in the lounge.'

I stopped with my foot on the step. 'What's he doing here?'

She flicked a look back inside. 'He just wants to talk to you, Cassie. He loves you. The least you can do is listen to him.'

'I have listened to him. He's left me fifty voicemails in the past three days.'

'You know how keen he is to talk to you, then.'

'Too keen. Desperate.'

'You're making him desperate by not answering.'

'Oh, it's my fault?'

'Cassie, you're lucky to have someone worry about you like that. Your dad never worries about me. I could be absent forty-eight hours and he'd just say, "Best crack on." '

She wasn't wrong. My dad was excellent at ignoring a crisis. But this was a conversation we'd had before. My mother's idea of love was intrinsically linked with worry. If you wanted to prove you loved her, you only had to tell her to go to the doctor. 'Oh, Mum, I really think you should book an appointment, get that checked out.' She'd pat you then, pleased. So it was hard to argue that a man who'd personally take you to the GP and sit in the waiting room, and even come into the consulting room with you, wasn't the best catch in the world.

'There's worry and there's worry, though, Mum. He's worried he's lost a possession. That's not actually very romantic.'

'Oh, I don't know about *romantic*. I just know he's a good boy.'

She tugged me over the threshold and shut the door, flapping her hands to get me to walk down the hallway. The wall was covered with photos of me and my brother at five, ten, fifteen years old, in school sweatshirts or school ties, gap-toothed or slick-haired, but always grinning grinning grinning. What smug little fucks we'd been. How easy life was then.

The door closed behind me, trapping the heat, trapping me. This house was where I'd grown up, the place I still thought of when people said the word 'safe'. And Liam was here. An invader.

In the living room, the TV was on and my dad was

watching it, despite the muted volume, irritated to be
kept from the local news. Liam was on the sofa under
the window, sad eyes, repentant pose. He was wearing a
fisherman's jumper. I knew the pleasure of forcing my
face against its collar, feeling the contrast of coarse wool
and smooth skin.

'Hello, Cassie. How are you? You *look* great.'

'Liam.' There was no good way to play this. If I was
impolite it'd be my fault, if I was placating it would
prove he wasn't that bad. 'Mum said you wanted to talk
to me.'

'You haven't answered my messages.'

'I think we need some space. From each other.'

'I'm worried about you.'

I sighed and sat down opposite him, resting my elbows
on my knees. 'I'm fine.'

'Watch your posture.'

We both heard the tone change as the words left his
mouth. I watched him curl a fist, getting himself in
check. 'Women have to be careful of their spines, Cassie.
You're more prone to curvature.'

My dad made a sort of grunt, to let us know he was
now part of the conversation. 'You'll get a widow's
hump, he means, Cass. Like your mother.'

'Ooh. You. I've no such thing.' Mum was coming in
with a tray of mugs and she sloshed tea over the sides as
she tried to stand up straight. 'Quality Street?' she offered
as she sat down. The tin was new and she was peeling
the plastic sealing strip from the lid.

Suddenly Liam's eyes were on me, that pleading look gone. He was waiting to see what I'd do.

'Here you are, love. Strawberry Delight,' Mum said, chucking me the chocolate.

I picked it up, fingering its stiff twist of red paper, still looking at Liam.

'Go on, then,' she said, around a toffee. 'Don't tell me they're not your favourite any more?'

The chocolate under the wrapper had a pale bloom, the shell a little too soft. And when I bit into it, the white cream inside was just as headache-inducingly sweet as I remembered. I swallowed it down quick, trying to lick my teeth clean, but the flavour clung on, turning my stomach. Liam looked away, his lip perhaps just a little curled at my family's display of sugar feasting. A series of overflowing wheelie bins was being shown on the TV.

'And the Roses version,' Mum said, approving, re-assured. 'She always liked them too. Milk chocolate, aren't they, though? Rather than dark.'

We were connoisseurs of confectionery in my house. Mum shook the tin at Liam and he practically recoiled. I'd acted as a buffer before, when we were together, my own cravings coming between him and any temptation, any offending food or drink. He'd had to be strong for us both. Now he was fending for himself.

'I've never . . .' he said. 'I wouldn't know the difference between these and Roses. I don't eat anything like that.'

Mum made a face – *lah-di-dah* – but she was pleased too. *Look at this quality man*, her face said, *his body is a temple.* Turning up his nose at our snacks only proved his worth. 'Oh, fitness,' she'd said when I started my PT course. 'We did that in the eighties. That or heroin. You're not so fancy.' But Liam was fancy.

'You haven't drunk your tea,' she said.

'I don't take it with milk.'

Mum nearly bounced with excitement next to me.

He shifted a little, pulling at the thick wool of his jumper. It was too hot in my parents' place for proper winter clothing. 'Could we go somewhere, Cassie? To talk?'

'You can talk to me here.'

Mum tutted. 'Don't be silly, Cass. A man's entitled to privacy. Use your old room.'

I made Liam go up ahead and hastily ducked into the bathroom to rinse away the taste of the chocolate. Liam had put me off strawberry creams for ever.

It was cold in the box room, with the chill that an unused space breeds, even in an overheated house. This had been mine once, now it was just storage for interior design mistakes – shelves of unused cat-print curtains, gold-spackled shabby-chic lampstands and nautical-themed artwork (sloppily painted lifebuoys glued to squares of MDF).

Nothing was left of my teenage preferences, no posters or black paint or filmy curtains. My parents were conscientious, regular redecorators and my dad was often stirring a tub of wallpaper paste when I visited.

'Will you shut the door?' Liam asked as I edged in.

'No.'

'Okay, fine.' He shifted, put one foot on the lowest rung of a stepladder. 'Cass . . . I've already told you I'm sorry.'

'And I told you we're done.'

'But I came here because you need me. Look at you, Cassie. Letting yourself go. Eating sugar. I bet you're drinking. Are you? It's not good for you.'

'*You're* not good for me.'

'Why? Is there someone else?'

I gave a bitter little laugh, a humiliating glimpse into my uncontrolled, uncontrollable emotions. 'As if I could even *think* about dating someone after you.'

A smile. He was pleased.

'That's not a compliment.'

The smile stayed put. 'Sweetheart, if you were unhappy you should have said. I pushed you, yes, I'm a perfectionist. But I'd never do anything to hurt you.'

'You *did* hurt me.'

'Well, you hurt *me*.' The ladder rattled as he pushed away from it. 'You know that? You hurt me too. Walking out like that. Leaving like that. You're not innocent. I did everything I could for you. I helped you – *made* you. Are you listening, Cass? Listen to me.'

He reached past to shut the door and fear sucked me dry, my insides shrivelling from tongue to colon.

'I'm just asking for an honest answer. How can you do this? To us? You know I love you. How can you throw everything away like this?'

The desiccating ache intensified while he spoke, while he berated and coaxed and rewrote our history, while he described our last moments in the flat. I said nothing. I stared at the shiny brass handle, counting the steps from here to the living room.

Finally, leaning on the door, he dropped his voice. 'Come back with me now. It's what we both want. Cass? You're safe with me. And I'm nothing without you.'

That splashed my brain, woke me up, stopped the counting and the staring. I looked him in the eyes. 'Then you're nothing,' I said, mouth suddenly full of saliva. And saying those words was like stepping off a cliff. I glanced at the painted lifebuoys, reached past him to grasp the doorknob.

'Your mum says you've moved out of Tanya's place,' he told me, his tone turning, deepening: silky, sulky. 'Is that to avoid me?'

There was no sense in answering, so I studied his face. The bland expression struggling against the narrowing of his eyes and jutting of his jaw.

'If you think I'll give up, if you think I won't find you, you're kidding yourself.'

Dread. That's what I used to feel when I thought about Liam after our break-up, when I felt his spitting, lurking fury. But I knew I could get over it; I just had to wait it out. Things change. I used to dread going to the gym too. Squinting against the lights, shuffling past the complicated machines, dithering at the edge of the free-weights section. Then there was always a guy ambling across the floor to chat about foot position midway through a run, or give an opinion on the dangers of dynamic stretching.

The gym can seem like a harsh place. Hard surfaces, heavy equipment, flashing TV screens. Men wearing T-shirts that read DOMINATE or EXECUTE; the thump of some bellend dropping his barbell every couple of minutes. Constant pop music, not interesting enough to take a person's mind off the slow seconds of a bike ride, but insistent all the same, with a little trumpet or whistle that will pinch out thoughts over and over.

So when someone walks in and looks around with wide eyes, like it's their first time, I want to go and tell them it's okay, that the gym is just like a big old cushion. The crazy carpet tiles, the squidgy balance balls, the thick workout mats, the bubbling water cooler, and the bouncy treadmills. The pleasure of watching runners begin to match their pace, all bobbing in time with each other. That's what I want them to see.

Newbies had been arriving a lot since our CEO's video-atonement offer and I was suddenly training half a dozen new clients. Including Sophie.

Blonde, soft-limbed and the grumpiest client I'd ever had, Sophie had Down's syndrome and was five stone overweight. She wasn't keen on counting reps, which was weird for me, and she often stopped halfway through a set, which I found disorientating, but I quickly learned to keep moving. As long as I had another activity ready, another piece of equipment, another way to raise her heart rate, we were fine.

Oh, you're done with crunches? No worries, let's do bridges. You're done with bridges? Cool, let's hop on the chest press. You don't like the chest press? What about a balance ball?

She could see me running out of ideas some weeks and got a sneaky look that made me laugh. I liked training her. She wouldn't do any exercise alone, so I got a workout too while she mirrored my movements.

'You're not going to beat me,' I told her.

She smiled at that. 'Maybe . . . we'll see.'

I was determined to make her enjoy our sessions. Even if I had to look like an idiot to do it. We invented a light dumbbell routine based on 'Heads, Shoulders, Knees and Toes' and she made me sing it in front of the meatheads at the free weights. She was threatening to make me do 'Incy Wincy Spider' next time.

It was harder to get her to focus on cardio. Two minutes on a cross-trainer, one minute on a bike and one minute on a step trainer wasn't doing much for her aerobic capacity. But I had an idea.

I got permission from Steph, the real Steph, to turn down the music, chose the loneliest corner of the gym, the treadmill furthest away from anyone else, and switched off the TV. Sophie was suspicious, but in the relative quiet she seemed to relax.

'We're going to start on the treadmill, but . . .' I was already chuckling at her exaggerated expression of annoyance '. . . it'll be fun, I promise. I'm not going to make you run. We're going to do inclines.'

'What's that?'

'Every one and a half minutes, the treadmill is going to lift or lower. It'll be just like a roller coaster.'

'You been on a roller coaster?'

'Give me a chance. It's better than going for a walk outside.' I knew she hated that, the sun and the noise. It was much better in here. I could prove it.

I like training people. I like figuring out mindsets and motivations. I don't like teaching classes nearly as much. It's often a good workout, but I'm not keen on everyone looking at me, expecting, copying, struggling. I hate having to smile all the time and say blandly encouraging shit. *Great work, squad. Let's smash those goals.* I got an average mark for my class instruction on the final personal training assessment. I still passed, but it was the one-to-one training that got me the qualification.

The tests were in a fancy suburban leisure centre, thirty of us drawing arrows to muscle groups, calculating metabolic rates and role-playing client sessions. I'd been paired with a guy called Jamal most of the day. He was nice. Big wet eyes. Non-threatening despite all the wiry strength in his upper body. A climber.

'Enthusiast turned professional,' he said, pinching the skin on the backs of my arms, my abdomen, my thigh. 'Hope I haven't just ruined my hobby.'

He was measuring my body fat percentage (twenty-three), and I'd done the same for him (eleven per cent). I'd been excellent at tailoring my workout to his passion, apparently, and I was an encouraging and enthusiastic motivator. I'd also shown a good knowledge of, and interest in, nutrition.

Hard not to show interest: Jamal had brought an insane amount of falafels with him – two big Tupperwares. And he just threw them into his mouth all day, like they were popcorn.

'How are you so lean when you eat chickpeas by the bucket?' I asked him as we thanked the assessors and left the fancy glass foyer.

'Veganism's the future, baby.' He blinked as he said 'baby', like he'd shocked himself. 'They're high in protein and fibre,' he told me in a more sober tone. 'And it's better than the raw chocolate almonds I used to be addicted to. Talk about high fat content. Ha ha ha.'

'Yeah, sucking on nuts is never a healthy habit.'

The puff of surprised laughter told me he'd caught my tone. 'Anyway,' he said. 'Good luck with training. If you ever want to try climbing, let me know.'

There was an awkward dance as we negotiated a half

hug, half pat and said goodbye. Then I turned and walked straight into Liam.

'Who was that?'

'Oh, hi. What are you doing here?'

'I told you I'd come and pick you up. Who. Was. That?'

I looked back at the neat figure heading to an idling bus. 'That's Jamal. He was my assessment partner. I don't remember you saying you'd pick me up.'

'You were flirting with him.'

'I wasn't.'

His eyes snapped to mine. 'I'm not simple, Cassie. I was waiting. I watched you.'

'If you were watching, then you know. I *wasn't* flirting.'

'Touching his arm, flicking your hair.'

'That's ridiculous. That's not me. That's not like me.'

'Yeah, I know, why d'you think I'm so surprised? You must really fancy him.'

The bus had pulled out, brakes hissing, and as it drove past us there was a movement, a hand waving behind the window. I ignored it. 'Seriously, Liam. I don't fancy Jamal. I was not flirting with him. I swear to God.'

'Do you?' He studied my face and I wondered what my expression showed. 'Go on, then.'

'Go on, what?'

'Swear to God.' He lifted his chin, pointing.

I turned to see a church on the corner. A big brick church, with a pointy tower and all the narrow windows and everything.

'What? In there?'

'God's house, isn't it? That's what they call it. Swear. In there.'

I rolled my shoulders, looking about. 'Are we allowed?'

'Of course we're allowed.' He gestured at a blue sign screwed to the railings: *Church Open. Jesus Welcomes All.*

Pretty definitive.

'Okay.' I brushed my clothes down, pulled the zip on my fleece to my chin.

The door was wooden, heavy, arched, and I struggled with it for a second before realising there was a smaller panel cut into one side. The clang of the latch echoed. I really hoped there wasn't a funeral or something going on. A prayer meeting. A solemn service.

It smelled of candles and polish and old coins, and it was gloomy: ugly energy-saving bulbs in the candelabra, and not much light coming in through the stained-glass windows. I studied the images of birds and lambs, and of people holding dishes like they were waiters and waitresses, the lowering sun only just picking out their colours.

'My nan used to go to church,' I said, hushed. 'She made a big fuss about my brother getting baptised, then took him to a priest without my parents knowing. But I think she was over it by the time I was born.'

'Sure, you're every kind of cliché.'

I looked at him. I'd wanted to tell him something. Make him know me. But he was too angry to hear me now.

He touched my back, urging me into one of the pews.

I glanced at the altar, at the candlesticks, at the painting of a skinny Jesus nailed to a gnarly-looking cross. We weren't supposed to be in here; I needed to get this over with. 'I swear—'

'No. Pray first.'

'Huh?'

'On your knees. Pray.'

I glanced at Jesus again. 'You kidding me?'

Liam smiled, a little twitch at the corner of his mouth, but that didn't mean he wasn't serious.

'Fine.' I found a cross-stitch cushion – white dove on a blue background – and dropped it in front of me, then waited for a second, almost expecting Liam to forbid the cushion, but he said nothing. So, I got on my knees, head down, hands clasped, eyes closed. Now what?

Hi, God. Sorry to bother you . . . I blew out a breath. *Er, I'm just here to say . . . hallowed be thy name? Um. Please can we have world peace and all that? Also, I'd love to get my body fat percentage down to twenty. Nineteen, if it's not too much trouble.*

I could feel a gaze on me, someone watching. God or Liam? I kept my eyes shut.

I know some people say nineteen per cent is too low for a woman, but if you look at the research . . . Well, you probably know all about that. You apparently designed us in your image. That made me wonder. What image? Was God in good shape? Was He ripped? Or had He let Himself go after all these years?

Liam coughed and I clasped my hands tighter.

So, nineteen or twenty. That would be great. And the world peace thing. Thanks very much.

'Amen,' I said. I looked up at Liam, at the indentations under his jawbone. 'I swear to God,' another glance at the altar, 'that I was not flirting with Jamal, who I do not fancy in any way.'

Liam waited a moment, then nodded, started laughing. 'You should see your face,' he said. 'You look like you expect to be struck by lightning.'

I stood and hung my cushion on its little hook. I was a bit stiff, a bit offended. 'I can't be struck by lightning if I'm telling the truth.'

'Okay.'

'Do you believe me now?'

'Of course I believe you.' He caught me up. 'Did you really think I was angry?' He laughed again, kissing my temple, the corner of my eye, the bridge of my nose. I slowly relaxed into him, one muscle at a time, the way I relaxed in guided meditations. Letting go of my irritation.

'I love you, you know, Cassie? I *love* you.' He squeezed me to him, rubbed his cheek against my hair, sighed as he tilted his head back to look around. 'We should get married here.'

'That a proposal?' I asked his collarbone.

'No. It'll be a lot more elaborate when I officially ask you.'

'Wow. Something to look forward to.'

'We've got lots to look forward to, you and me.'

Liam took my arm and I walked down the aisle with him, imagining my mum in an organza hat, my dad in a suit, my aunties, my cousins, Tanya. *Daria*. That would show her. He stopped by the door to drop a fiver in the donation box.

'Call it a deposit,' he said, winking.

And everything was great again, everything was fine. But it was like . . . like the corner of a floor tile had lifted, just slightly. It was barely noticeable, but I'd know if I saw it again; if I came this way in the labyrinth again, I'd know it.

The tiles in our gym hadn't lifted. The place was relatively new and the smooth grey porcelain in the changing rooms, the narrow rectangles of fake wood by the cardio area, those short-napped squares of durable carpet in the foyer were all undamaged. Nothing out of place, nothing to trip on. Liam was cautious as he walked in, though, pausing in the doorway.

I couldn't imagine him going through my recycling.

'Hello,' he said. 'Is anyone around?' More expectant than anxious, but an appeal all the same.

I could have left him hanging, pretended I wasn't there, stared at his face till it creased with worry. I could have asked someone else to take over, left my resignation letter on the desk, walked out and never come back.

But Sophie had stayed on that damned treadmill for twenty-three long minutes. I liked it here.

So, closing the office door, I called: 'Hi, Liam. It's me. Ready to rumble?' I was still trying to use my brother's phrases, to step outside myself.

Liam turned, relieved, relaxed, and took my arm as if it was the most natural action in the world, as if I existed just to guide him, as if my arm was made to be clutched by his hand. A soft touch.

I was a soft fucking touch, I thought, as I took him towards the cross-trainers and let him warm up. I was a cross trainer. Cross with myself. Cross with him.

The air-con currents scrubbed my skin and forced the smell of Armani Code into my nose. No one had come to claim the bottle and the scent was now the scent of Steph, of glottal stops and hard fingers on my brachial artery, my blood pumping against his grip.

I was getting too used to it. So was Liam.

When I'd gone to stow his bag, he'd already been facing the cardio suite, left hand against the glass of a vending machine; knowing that set him on the right course. He was getting used to the layout in here, getting cosy, getting confident.

Meanwhile, the gym seemed less familiar to me, the space an alien landscape when he was in it. I wished I could move things around, trip him up. But perhaps I didn't have to go that far. Perhaps I could redraw it for him.

After his warm-up, I guided him to the end of the

cardio machines, ignored a central cut-through and then walked all the way to the foyer before turning back.

'Up this step. And then down again,' I narrated, navigating over a low bench. 'Narrower gap here.' We were in an open space.

I walked him right round, past the office and the toilets, past bulky men propped against mirrors, past a woman in mesh leggings rubbing her calf as if it were a pet, a little animal that needed reassurance. I was recreating the gym in Liam's head, making it bigger, stranger, differently shaped. We took a tangled route across the main floor. If anyone noticed, they didn't say anything; perhaps they thought I was helping him acclimatise.

And why not redraw the route? The other people in the gym were all busy constructing paths of their own, digging, sifting, shifting stones, packing down sand, treading it flat. What were the battle ropes if not a guiding line? I didn't know where these workout wanderers' paths were going, and they didn't have maps for mine.

'I like this song,' Liam said as we weaved through rows of riderless spin bikes in the studio.

I hadn't been listening to the music: a breathy female singer introing a nasal male voice, lots of synthed echoing. I made a noise, not quite agreement.

Our gym, like most gyms, played a narrow form of pop on repeat, vaguely upbeat but not rousing, euphemistic lyrics about being crazy, or getting over ex-boyfriends, or doing things *all night*. Mostly the melodies

washed clean through my ears and I hardly noticed one
track merging with the next.

I have two playlists, both for working out. Upbeat
stuff – rousing choruses, rhythmic singing, rising keys,
time kept by snaps and hand claps. Songs that swell with
the swelling of muscles and form a symbiotic relationship with my endorphin high. Hoedown music, Liam
called it, accusing me of being a closet redneck. The
other playlist is darker – metal-core, battle rock, the
lyrics full of self-loathing and regret, or violent promises
and abstract threats. For when working out feels like
war. 'Zombie video-game trailer music,' Liam used to
say. 'What are you? A fourteen-year-old boy?'

At least there was a funky guitar melody in the song
Liam was bopping his head to now.

'Not your thing?' he asked.

'It's okay.' We were back at the cross-trainers and I
watched him in the mirror to see if he knew we were
walking in circles.

He sighed. 'It used to be a background thing. Before.
I knew what I was supposed to like, I could give the right
opinions, disapprove with the best of them. But these
days I really *listen* to music, you know?'

'Your tastes have changed?'

'Widened, maybe, yeah. I've found lots of new inter-
ests. Podcasts help, and audiobooks. Technology is
beautiful. Even texts can be audio now.' He slowed
slightly. 'Where are we going?'

'Nearly there.' We needed to stop. I couldn't keep the

walking up much longer, but I was thinking about the phone calls in the graveyard. Probably marketing, possibly scammers, but perhaps . . . Liam? I imagined him at home, lying back on the sofa cushions. *Siri, harass my ex-girlfriend.*

'Seriously.' He squeezed my arm. 'Feels like we've been walking ages. How big *is* this gym?'

'It's big,' I told him. 'Massive.'

He frowned, moved his head as if he could judge, but he couldn't judge, he had to trust me. How many times had he asked me to trust him, or accused me of not trusting him, or lost his temper because I'd proved I didn't trust him? Now I was in charge, the custodian of our athletic adventures.

'Okay, well, are we near any water?' he asked, a little sulky. 'I'm thirsty.'

I filled his bottle, and then I did another circuit as punishment, but it felt uncomfortably restrained. I wanted to flex, I wanted to watch him fail, I wanted him to hurt.

Finally, we stopped at the weights. A man had just got up from a bench, leaving a puddle of sweat on the seat. I backed Liam onto it, and watched his shorts soak up the moisture. When he stood up in suspicion, I put a barbell in his hands. I'd had another idea.

'You're swaying quite a lot,' I said halfway through his first set of dead lifts. 'While you're lifting. Can you feel that?'

He stilled. 'Maybe. I'm not sure.'

'Makes me think your core stability needs extra train-ing.' *Stabili'y*, that was fun to say.

'Like some side dips or . . . ?'

'Get on your knees.'

'What?'

'Try the movement on your knees. It'll work your core harder.'

'Here?' He tapped the fake-wood tiles with the toe of one shoe.

'Yep.' I took the barbell while he lowered himself smoothly to the ground.

'Is there a mat?'

'You need the solidity of a hard surface.' *Solidi'y* was fun too.

He winced and shifted his knees as I stepped close, and his head dropped for a second. I nearly told him to pray. Instead, I tried to sound reasoned, reasonable.

'Tell me if you need to reduce the weight. You can always work back up as you feel more stable.'

Was this revenge? Could you call it that? It wasn't bloody, it wasn't done in the dark, it wasn't permanently damaging. I was just wasting his time, ordering him about, deceiving him. His knees would be sore tomor-row. I felt a little flat, though.

Liam continued his set, uncomplaining, and I watched two young women working out together on nearby mats, matching ponytails spooling against the padded vinyl. They smirked at each other as they made each successive bridge more suggestive, pushing up their pelvises and grunting until they giggled.

That's what I was missing. Someone to share this experience with. My old gang.

Brunch, back when I had friends. Four of us, like characters on a TV show, dressed up, made-up, on the up. Our parents would have been at a greasy spoon, tea and two sugars, white toast and marge; we were all macchiatos and courgette soda bread.

The table was already littered with muddied coffee cups – I was late arriving because Liam had pulled me back into bed after our post-run shower. I'd had to text Tanya my breakfast order while I was on the bus.

'Sorry, sorry,' I said, dumping my bag under my chair. 'What have I missed?'

'Daria's pregnant,' Lauren announced, suggesting a belly curve with one French-manicured hand. 'She phoned me yesterday.'

'Oh shit. What's she going to do?'

'Fuck knows.'

'Poor Daria,' Michelle said, using a straw to chase a lump of unblended pineapple in her smoothie.

'Yeah. Scary news.' Lauren sucked air in through her teeth.

'Can you all stop acting like having kids is the end of

the world?' Tanya said. 'Maybe she's happy to be pregnant. Jamie's employed. They have a nice flat. It's not like it's a fate worse than death.'

I exchanged looks with Lauren. Her geometrically perfect eyebrows arched.

'Sorry,' I said. 'How *is* beautiful Ashlie?'

'Yeah, what's she up to this morning?'

'Steve's taking her to Bounce and Rhyme. She's okay, thanks.'

'Aw, Steve's a good one.'

'The best.'

'And she is *so* cute,' Michelle said. 'Course she's not worse than death.'

Our food arrived. I was having sweetcorn fritters stacked with bacon and avocado, a spray of scarlet sriracha sauce. It was the kind of food made to be photographed. I got out my phone.

'Oh my God. No cameras,' Lauren said. 'Don't be basic.'

'Fuck you.'

'No, I'm serious, Cass. If you put that on Insta, I will *troll* you. *So* hard.'

I took my pic, took another, stood up to get a better angle. Snapped Lauren scowling at me. Some rugby lads at the table behind did macho-men poses, polo collars popped.

'Make sure you get my good side,' one called.

I was smiling, shaking my head, as I sat down.

Tanya was shaking her head too. 'It's not for social

media, anyway,' she said, drizzling maple syrup on her buckwheat pancakes. 'It's for Liam.'

'For Liam?'

'So?' I hit send and threw the phone into my open bag.

'He planning on coming here?' Michelle asked, her voice almost too soft in the noisy restaurant.

'Er, I don't know.'

'Gonna look up the recipe?'

'That's not why people take pictures of food, Shell.'

'What's he want it for, then?'

'He likes to see what she's eating,' Tanya said. 'Count the macros, or whatever.'

'Count the macros?' Lauren said.

I tensed. 'What's wrong with that?'

There was an exchange of looks. I caught the tail end. For a minute I didn't move. A chunk of fritter balanced, trembling, on my fork. I'd never not been part of an exchange; I'd never been the subject of one.

'She sends him photos of every meal,' Tanya said.

I ate the mouthful of fritter. 'Not every meal – that would be a bit excessive.'

'Every meal *out*.'

'Loads of people do that.'

'Does he do it too? Does he send you photos?'

'Of course.'

'How many a day?'

'I don't know. Jeez, Tanya. We like to stay in touch, to share what we're doing. You're making it out to be something creepy. He's just interested. In my day. In me.'

'Aw.' Michelle smiled at me. She hadn't been part of the exchanged looks either, but then she rarely was.

'She sends selfies too,' Tanya told the others.

Lauren looked up from her chorizo hash and winked. 'Long as your head's not in it, I say send away.'

'Not nudes. Photos of her at work in the morning and at home in the evening.'

'I'm tracking my progress – he's helping me track my progress.'

'You *are* looking incredible now,' Michelle said.

'Yes, fucking gorgeous.'

'Not that you weren't always gorgeous.'

'Yeah, yeah, obviously, you're just extra smoking hot now.'

'Thanks,' I said, cutting through the fat on a bacon slice.

Tanya was silent while she stabbed eight blueberries onto the tines of her fork. 'He's tracking your location, is what he's doing.'

I dropped my cutlery. The rugby boys perked up. 'Oi oi!'

'No, he's not. Why are you being weird about this?'

'What happens if you don't send a photo?'

She knew what happened. I got texts. I got phone calls. 'He gets worried sometimes.'

'Aw,' Michelle said again.

'So, the photos *he* sends *you*,' Lauren said, scooping the milk foam from the bottom of a coffee cup. 'Any of them shirtless?'

'Huh?'

'Just saying, you know, in case you ever feel like

sending them on, helping out your single friends.' She licked the spoon suggestively.

'You asking me to send you spank bank material? Of my boyfriend?'

A shrug. 'He's nice to look at.'

'I can send you some photos of Reece if you like,' Michelle said. Reece, who was listed as *Fuzzy Duck* in her contacts.

Lauren tucked the spoon into her saucer. 'Nah, you're all right, darling.'

There was laughter. But not from Tanya.

There was laughter by the hip adduction machines now. The pelvis thrusters working their inner thighs. I'd let Liam stand up again and he was finishing a set of very pretty bicep curls.

That prettiness was the reason I'd stopped going to brunch; I hadn't been able to see past it. I'd missed lunches, too, and drinks and dinners. It was too painful catching those exchanged looks and realising my friends were talking about me even when they weren't talking about me. Realising the group vocabulary had changed, that the word 'escalation' kept coming up, that everyone was suddenly an expert on 'narcissistic personality traits' and the definition of 'gaslighting'. That it was my fault. Liam's fault.

He passed me the dumbbells now and stretched one arm across his chest, released, flexed, sighed. 'Think you could help me?' he asked. And was there a hint of exasperation there?

'What d'you need?'

'I can't get the angle . . .'

He grimaced when I pressed on his elbow, but wanted more. He always wanted more.

'Will you hold my arms behind?' He turned and let me take his wrists.

'Feel like I should be reading you your rights,' I said, lifting them slightly, slowly. But it wasn't quite like arresting him. This was the way witches were tortured: hoisted by the wrists, strung up so their shoulders dislocated, bone sucked from socket, tendons tearing. It was their own body weight that did the damage. Just like a pull-up.

I'd been working on those since breaking up with Liam. I'd needed a new goal. It's frightening at first, to drop your weight onto your arms, the reversal of force like being upside down. And it's precarious, tenuous, impossible, until it's not. Then all the connections tighten, each muscle and ligament recognising its role, and the body becomes a rope, a chain, hung meat. The hands become hooks, the wrists gristle, the flesh below dry-curing in the breeze. It was strangely dehumanising. I was getting good at it.

'Mmm. That's what I've been missing,' Liam was saying, his voice close to a moan. 'Partner stretching is always more intense.'

'Depends on the partner.'

'Sure. I can be quite hard on mine.'

I kept my breath behind my teeth. 'How d'you mean?'

He shrugged and then groaned as the stretch deepened further. 'I used to train with my ex-girlfriend. I could be . . . demanding. I imagine that's what she'd say.'

'Oh yeah? And what do you think?' Hearing him talk about me produced a kind of vertigo, a feeling of falling, like a window had opened into another life.

'I don't think there's much point arguing. She wrote me off. I didn't tell her about my diagnosis. I'd like to *think* she'd be sympathetic, but I'm not sure. Maybe she wouldn't feel I deserve any pity.'

I kept my voice flat, even flatter than usual. 'Bad break-up, huh?'

'Well.' He thought for a second. 'I'm not good at being vulnerable, I'm not used to it. I wish I'd been better at letting her in, but I've always been the one who looks after people, not the other way round.'

I turned to let out a single heaving exhale. 'Is that right?'

'Yeah.'

Another stretch. Across his chest this time. I lifted his supporting arm to work the shoulder.

'I love spotting the potential in someone and then motivating them to achieve it,' he said. 'Not that it's always appreciated. Some people don't have the drive. Some people are happy getting stuck on the journey. Ah! That's too deep.'

'Sorry.' I let the pressure off and he switched arms, changing position. I followed without thinking, fitting my body to his, feeling the pulse in his wrist, watching the tick of an artery, the rise and fall of his chest. I could imagine all the ticking and pulsing inside him, the sparks firing, the levers lifting. The strength, the relentless strength, even after months of atrophying. He'd already lost that surprising softness, gained a few millimetres of muscle. He was good at being fit, a natural, no wonder he'd thought he could live for ever.

A shift, a resettling and he was suddenly angled towards me, his face above mine, his mouth curling into a smile as my stifled sigh fanned his chin. Again, I asked the question that was always on my mind: was he looking *at* me?

He pursed his lips and returned the breath, blowing gently, like he thought this was a game.

'Have you thought about leaving your body to medical science?' I asked.

He jerked in my hold, features frozen.

'I bet there are scalpel-wielding students out there who'd love a go.'

I watched his Adam's apple jump. 'I'd have to die first.'

'Yeah, obviously. Ideally.' I laughed, firmed my fingers. 'I was just thinking – you say you like looking after people.'

The slightest struggle against my grip. 'That's not really what I meant.'

I held on harder. 'We should all have a donor card, though. At least then you know your organs will be useful.'

'I find them quite useful myself, thanks.'

'Now, maybe.'

My hands were shaken off, shaken away. 'Yes, and I plan to be using them for some time.'

'How much time?'

'What?' He held his own wrist, pressing the joint against his chest, over his heart. He was near to panting.

'A year? Two years? Longer? Don't be selfish, Liam, mate. Someone else might need them.'

Week Four

'Close your eyes and open your mouth.' The laugh that followed these words couldn't have been more sinister.

'I don't think so, Ashlie.' I'd been caught before.

'Please, Auntie Cassie. Just close your eyes, then.' She stroked my hair.

'Why?'

A look that said I *knew* why. 'It's a surprise.'

I shut one eye only. I knew not to trust a six-year-old. Every sense counted, but especially sight. The little girl was leaning over my lap, knees digging into the sofa cushions, her face intent and malevolent, looming near mine.

Tanya's kitchen was like a banner that said *I've made it.* Bifold doors, American fridge, granite countertops, enough room for a sofa. It was the kind of kitchen posh girls like Susannah Parker and Jessica Ewing had had, the kind we'd pretended we weren't staring at when we were kids, invited for tea and expected to eat sausages or fish fingers *without ketchup*. At least Tanya was still dedicated to condiments, and nowadays I could openly stare.

Ashlie noticed. 'Close your eyes! Pleeeeeease,' she begged. 'I'm just going to *kiss* you.'

'Ugh. Fine.' I did it. Grimacing, wanting to put my hands up in front of me.

'Squeeze them shut. *Tight.*' I felt her lean further, hand heavy on my shoulder. Her hair had been braided, each plait tied off with beads, and they clicked together close to my ear, followed by the wet tick of her mouth opening.

'Eugh! Ashlie.' She'd licked me on the cheek and squealed with laughter as I wiped my face and made a show of horror.

'Okay,' she said when she'd calmed down. 'Close your eyes again.'

'Ashlie, I'm not an idiot.'

She was relentless. 'Close your eyes . . .'

'Ash,' Tanya said, coming back into the kitchen with a tray of sequins, a toddler holding her leg. 'Leave Cass alone now, yeah?'

'She's all right.' I ran my finger through the little girl's beads.

'She's got a cold. Green snot. Still don't mind if she licks you?'

'Ugh. Get away from me, disgusting child.'

'Here,' Tanya said. 'Sort these sequins out.'

Best job ever. We settled at the table and I helped Ashlie tweezer the tiny foil scraps into piles while Tanya sat little Noah on a ride-on ladybird and began to cut carrots into batons. The sun came in through the bifolds and sailed over us, making everything under our hands sparkle. I felt like I'd carb-loaded. Sleepy, content.

'That nutmeg?' I asked. 'That smell?'

'New diffuser. Don't worry, I know not to bake you anything.'

I'd been refusing even home-made treats for a long while. It was a sore point and I let it alone. The nutmeg was warm and strange in the sun, but Tanya had a thing for winter scents: pine, cinnamon, cloves, mulled wine, even in August.

'So,' I said, after a few minutes. 'Guess who came to the gym a couple of weeks ago?'

The slam of the knife into the chopping board stopped.

'Liam.' I said his name with a kind of flourish. It was exciting, and especially exciting to say it without bad news.

Of course Tanya assumed the worst. 'Oh God. I'm so sorry. And you thought maybe this time he'd given up for good. Oh, love.'

She must have properly focused on my face then, because she picked up the knife.

'Why are you grinning like that? What's going on? Oh no . . . You haven't . . . I can't even say it. You haven't done something stupid?' She was about to run over into condemnation, so I stopped her.

'It's fine. He's blind.' There was a bubble of laughter stuck in my stomach.

'What?'

'He's blind. And he thinks my name is Steph.'

'What the fuck?'

Her kids were in the room, but her language was my fault; I'd dropped the news without warning. I started again. Carefully explained in the least swear-inducing way what had happened with Liam, gave all the relevant circumstances and mitigating details. Tanya still had an outburst.

'Have you lost your mind?'

'You don't think it's, like, a beautiful irony?'

'No. I don't. I don't understand. How can you be near him? After everything he put you through.'

'Things are different this time.'

'You've thought that before.'

I shrugged. 'He wasn't blind before.'

Noah took a run at the dishwasher, the wheels of his ladybird crashing into the gleaming chrome front. Tanya gently turned him around, like a robo-vac. She had one of those as well.

'Cass, Liam is still a threat. This could just be a new way to manipulate you.'

'I don't think he knows it's me. I think *I'm* the threat now.'

I jumped as Noah backed up and slammed into the dishwasher again.

'You're playing with fire.'

'Blind fire.'

'Fire doesn't need to see to burn you.'

She dropped the knife in the sink and Ashlie looked up from her piles of red, purple and silver foil, the sequin trance broken. 'What's happened?'

'I have an enemy, Ash, and I think I should do something, should fight him somehow. But your mummy thinks I should walk away.'

Ashlie turned her head, keeping her eyes on mine. 'Are you going to punch him?'

'Er . . .'

'Because you shouldn't punch people. My teacher told me. Even if you are a real actual ninja and it's part of your culture and traditions. Also, when you bow in karate, you don't say *namaste*.'

'Okay. No punching, no saying *namaste*. So . . . What would you do?' I asked. 'If you had an enemy?'

She smiled at her growing pile of gold sequins. 'I'd trick him,' she said, her voice going throaty, rasping. 'I'd play a really mean trick on him.'

'Excellent advice.'

'No. Tricking is not good either, Ash.' A little plastic bowl of carrots landed on the table. 'Tricking is like punching.'

I winked at Ashlie. 'Depends on the trick.'

Tanya was only half-amused, and Ashlie and Noah were ushered into the living room to watch TV so I could be properly berated.

'You really think it's a coincidence he turned up at your gym?'

I stood and brushed a few sequins from my skin. I was sweating. 'Ours is the only one reaching out to people with disabilities.'

'Don't try to make it sound noble.'

Tanya was not a fan of our CEO. She'd have totally joined in the social-media pile-on if she'd had any time or energy left after posting pictures of her kids on Facebook.

I stepped out of her way as she put the uncut carrots in the fridge. 'I'm just saying it's not a coincidence, it's circumstance. He wouldn't fake having a tumour. I know that much. It's his worst nightmare.'

She smacked the fridge closed. 'You're sorry for him?'

'No. I don't know. Does it matter?'

She studied me then, my eyes, my mouth, my cheekbones. She was very calm, her lovely face placid. She wasn't thinking I had a lovely face.

'You know what?' she said, finally. 'I don't care. That's not the concern. The concern is this . . .'

She paused again, and I listened to the indignant hum of the fridge, the call of a bird outside, the TV through the living-room door: high-pitched American voices trying to out-cute each other.

'Yeah?' She'd paused for so long, I'd almost thought she'd forgotten.

'I don't know how to phrase it nicely, but basically I don't want you to pity-fuck him.'

'Oh. Oh! No. That's not going to happen.'

She took a step towards me, then another. 'You find him ugly now?'

'No, he looks pretty much the same.'

'So.'

'So what?'

'So, he's still hot, only now he's all vulnerable and needy and apparently non-threatening, and you're totally going to fuck him.'

Was I? It hadn't crossed my mind before that moment. Honestly. Did the idea tempt me? What would it be like with him unable to see? Would I give away my true identity? It would be a challenge to stay in character.

'You're imagining it!'

She knew me too well. 'Just thinking logistically.'

'How could you even contemplate letting him touch you again?'

'I wasn't. Not really.' I didn't mention the way he held my arm as we walked from cardio to weights, or the time he'd pinned me between his legs.

'Cass?'

She was too close and I backed up into the hall. 'Tanya. I hear you, but I *can't*, I can't give it up. I have to take this chance. Wouldn't you, if you were in my place? Wouldn't you want to *do* something? Wouldn't you want to at least enjoy the *possibility* of doing something? Getting your own back? Taking revenge?'

'No! Cass. Seriously. If you do this . . . whatever it is. If you get entangled again . . . then *I* can't. I can't be involved. I don't want to hear about it. I don't even know if I can see you.'

I'd been edged to the front door, the welcome mat

making its dry crunch under my trainers. I looked through bevelled-glass panels into the living room, at the cartoon kaleidoscope and the back of Ashlie's head. I willed the little girl to turn, to see, to help somehow. Relieve the tension, persuade her mother. But the cartoons held her rigid. I remembered that feeling – something happening and nobody noticing. Tanya was the only one who'd ever noticed, ever got involved.

'Cassie. I was there when you needed me. I will always be here, but not if you deliberately put yourself in this position. Again. Honestly, mate. I can't take it.'

'But . . . I thought you'd be into it. I thought you'd want to be part of it.'

'I don't. I want to be as far from anything to do with Liam as possible. He scares me. He used to scare you too.'

'Maybe if you could see him . . .'

'Cass, seriously. Call me when you've come to your senses.'

'And if I don't?'

'Don't call me.'

I didn't call her. Even when I spotted a bus-stop advert for a Siberian-fir scented candle, even when I found a sequin gilet for Ashlie at TK Maxx, not even when Jessica Ewing from primary school walked past with the streakiest fake tan I'd ever seen.

I stayed silent and went home. To my one-bed flat where the badly fitted laminate flooring stuck to the soles of my trainers and the downlights buzzed and the plastic kitchen countertops had deep burn scars from the previous tenants stubbing out their cigarettes. I stayed silent and heated some white-bean and kale stew on the two-ring hob, and I didn't think about Tanya's perfect kitchen.

My flat was above a pub that had been shut down for licensing issues and then shut down again for fraud. So at least it was quiet. Not like Tanya's place, which I wasn't thinking about, where the kids would be giggling in the bath, Ashlie trying to explain the rules to a complicated game based on whatever cartoon she'd just watched.

The most recent game had involved characters who'd been turned *evil*, the word evil always said with that same throaty voice she'd used to suggest tricking Liam. If Twilight Sparkle was *evil*, then Rainbow Dash had to perform a series of tasks to turn her good again. I liked the idea that the correct pattern of actions could turn a person good. As long as the apples were collected, the spell spoken and a delicious pie made, and as long as Twilight Sparkle could be tricked into eating it, then everything would be okay.

Did I want to turn Liam good? Was there a magic sequence for him? A combination I hadn't tried in the five years I'd known him?

I couldn't answer that question. I didn't want to. So I did what I usually do to stop thinking. I went out for a run.

It was nearly dark. Streaks of orange in the sky, streams

of cold in the warm air. I could hear the clink of glasses in the distance, in some beer garden somewhere, and the smell of pizza and Indian takeaway drifted past as Deliveroo cyclists weaved through the empty streets, but there was no one visibly enjoying themselves. I wasn't enjoying myself either. My breath was out of rhythm, my shoulders hunching, and I could feel the ghost of a stitch every time my heel hit the pavement. I was glad there weren't many people around to witness this mess.

The quickest way home was through a long street of garages. Lock-ups for the council flats by the railway. They were set out in a pattern: three together, then a break, three together, a break, three together, and so on. My dad had a lock-up like that when I was a kid, we kept holiday stuff in it: bodyboards, windbreaks, parasols, lilos. Every trip to our static caravan at Selsey began with a visit to the lock-up, with waiting for Mum to point at boxes and for Dad to climb over half-mended engines and pull out stacks of brittle, sun-bleached buckets and spades. Hot concrete under the backs of my thighs, the smell of motor oil and damp cardboard, a watery ice lolly in a long plastic tube.

Fine in the day, with your mum and dad, but not somewhere you should go at night, alone and female (not unless you're stashing a body), and not when you've been looking over your shoulder for years. Hard to resist, though, hard to turn down such a nice clear stretch of white concrete, such a perfect shortcut – I'd be through in a flash, and most importantly: Liam was blind.

I plunged into the dark, steps echoing, my stride lengthening, leaning left because the ground sloped slightly to a gutter. A perfect track, filmic. Motion-detector lights flashing on as I passed. I forgot how bad my form had been, the stitch stopped threatening. I wished I'd started a playlist.

Until I caught a movement. For a second I thought there was a window or mirror between two sets of garages and I turned, expecting to see my reflection, but it wasn't me.

Rusted garage doors blocked my view for fifteen steps, then another glimpse: someone in a hood and neon-orange trainers. Someone running parallel, keeping pace. Garage, garage, garage, orange trainers, garage, garage, garage, orange trainers. My heart itself began beating the words.

I held back behind the next set of lock-ups, internal organs sloshing about inside me, stitch stabbing me under the ribs, and walked. Walking after running is miserable, so slow, so heavy. It must be like that for birds when they land. How disappointing to be waddling along when you've been soaring, when you've been floating free, to suddenly find yourself chained to a body again, a lump that you have to drag along.

It took for ever till the next garage gap.

And there was no one there.

Upping the pace again – eight steps, ten – but that stitch was hooked to my insides, my calf muscles were bunched, and the line of lock-ups no longer looked friendly. The lights were switching off behind me, gaining ground. In a minute I'd be left in the dark. And then I heard a scuff of rubber on concrete, slightly out of time with mine.

I stopped again and waited, looking around, dragging in lungfuls of the dust that collects in ridged concrete, calming my breaths till I could hear beyond them: a distant siren, the thump of a car sound system getting closer and then further away, a metallic rustling like a fox in a bin. My sweat cooled, but I locked tight against shivering, standing like a statue till every light went out.

It was unnaturally dark, the blind wall around the estate just a void, the lock-ups blocking out light from the street beyond. I carried on staring, watching for neon trainers, ready for the flood of halogen, because surely someone else was standing, waiting, too, expecting me to spotlight my location.

Seconds ticked by, or maybe minutes. My ponytail making a disconcerting brush against my spine. Leaves stuttered over the concrete, like a sigh, like a whisper.

The light flashed on, six blocks up. Hood, broad shoulders, orange trainers.

I bolted. Doubled-back. That stitch trying to murder me from the inside. But I was fast. Too fast for the lights – they couldn't catch me, they couldn't keep up, and neither could the man. Was that because he couldn't see me? Or didn't want me to see him? Or was this just a reminder that Liam wasn't the only danger in the world?

*

I wanted to ask Tanya, talk to her, lay myself bare, let her dig through the major and minor pectorals and inspect my heart, check the valves and ventricles for venom. But she'd told me not to contact her, and I hadn't *come to my senses*. I felt angry, betrayed, hurt, and didn't know what to do with myself. I ached when I thought of her – she was a piece of me I couldn't soothe, and I kept poking at the phantom limb, replaying our conversation, the hollow pain better than nothing.

I leaned against the windowsill, half-hidden by a smoke-stained curtain, looking out at the street below. After a swift, skittish search of the flat, I'd turned off the lights and gone to stand sentinel. No suspects had appeared. No figures lurking under lamp-posts or crouching in doorways, no echoing footsteps in the empty street.

After fifteen minutes of watching, I got out my phone and tried my brother. *Congrats!* Gavin's voicemail told me. *Congrats!* Endlessly celebratory, even on the fourth, fifth, sixth time of trying. I gave up and scrolled through my contacts, searching for someone who wouldn't be too shocked to hear my voice. I hit a name, waited out the three or so rings. Cringed slightly at the wary 'Hello?'

'Hey, Jamal.' I was breezy, normal, like I'd done this a hundred times, like I hadn't relegated him to WhatsApp-only in the communication hierarchy. Liam had made me feel weird about him, but I'd thought after our assessment day that we could be friends, and a couple of times we'd swapped day passes from the gyms we worked at. He'd even helped me navigate a climbing wall.

'Cassie?'

I swiped the condensed breath from the window and turned, as if the street below might distract me. 'Hi. Sorry to bother you. I just . . .' What? Wanted to bother you?

'No, you're fine. No bother.'

I wondered if that was true, and realised I didn't know much about Jamal's personal circumstances. Did he have a girlfriend? Or boyfriend? Parents? Siblings? What did his life look like outside of the gym?

'Um,' I said.

'What did you think of the Colorado Health Club. Very white, huh?'

'It was . . . yeah, it was quite white, I guess.'

'But I wrote an essay on the place. Least they could do is give me a job. Ha ha ha.'

'Of course. I'd forgotten that was the gym you wrote about.'

'It's the only climbing-focused place around. I mean, you can find gyms with a bit of a bouldering wall, but it's not the same . . .' Jamal was running out of steam, seeing as I wasn't being very talkative. I could imagine his big wet eyes shining. He was so pure. 'You should maybe come and do another session with me sometime?'

'Yeah. Great. What are you up to now?' I asked.

'Now?'

'Never mind. I didn't see you out running earlier, did I?'

'What?'

'You didn't follow me?'

There was a pause on the line, a murmuring in the background; he could have been out, but it could also have been the TV.

'Look, Cassie, I really like you, and it's been great sharing workout tips and everything, but I'm, well, I'm married.'

'Oh.' I was hot, the mock-neck collar of my running top suddenly rough against my skin. 'Yeah. No, look . . .'

'I don't wear a ring because of the risk of degloving, which, by the way, I don't recommend looking up. Ha ha ha. Pretty gross. And, yeah, I know that sometimes a bare finger sends the wrong signal. But I'm not interested in, like, extracurricular activities. Ha ha ha.'

'Ha ha ha.' I laughed, sort of. 'No, Jamal, that's not . . . I'm not . . . either. I'm still getting over a really bad relationship, so, no, I wasn't . . . I didn't mean that.'

'Sure. Of course.'

'Sorry I called,' I said. 'I've just had a few weird things happen lately, or I've thought they were weird because I'm in a weird place. Like, mentally. Ha ha ha.' Oh God, I'd caught his tic. 'And I guess I was just looking for a simple explanation.'

'Right.' There was no amusement in his tone now.

'But I really am sorry to have bothered you. See you around. Take care. Bye.'

I squeezed the phone tight and knocked my forehead on the glass. I was still hot, and there was a brief steamy smudge when I lifted my head. Gone in a second. Gone faster than my embarrassment, which would never ever fade.

Tanya would have found it funny, would have absolved me. Lauren, too. Michelle would have misunderstood till I was too frustrated to be self-conscious. But I couldn't call them.

I'd tried to reconnect with the gang after I broke up with Liam, but it was obvious they'd all spent too long discussing me to feel comfortable with my actual real-life presence.

And then Liam was still getting in the way. Not only had I stopped going out, or answering my phone, or making plans, but whenever I had seen anyone, I'd ended up constantly talking about him. I hadn't been able to think of anything else to say; every subject ended at the monolith that was his name. It was like being in a new relationship when the merest hint of a lover in the conversation is a pleasure. Only it was a misery and it was tedious. And in order not to bore, or annoy, I sat in silence, listening and then half listening and then not listening to my friends.

So there wasn't anyone obvious I could just spring a phone chat on. Not now.

But I had Liam's number. And I knew how to block mine from appearing. He'd taught me that technique himself. And I felt like it was about time. Nuisance calls are, fundamentally, a classic of the genre. I wanted to hear his voice, I wanted to know if he was outside, if he was out of breath.

I switched the lights back on, put lentil soup in the microwave, perched on one of my ripped pleather bar stools, and dialled. Four rings before he picked up.

'Hello?' His voice, so normal and familiar, seductively familiar, was almost a comfort. Someone answering the phone to me, for me. I wanted to talk. I wanted to settle into him, into us, into how we used to be.

Shocked at my own reaction, I let my mouth hang open, absorbing the expanding store-cupboard scent of lentils and spices.

'Hello?' A little puzzled this time, but not angry. I let the flap of a pigeon's wing lead my gaze to a roof across the road and enjoyed knowing there was some-one on the other end of the line.

'Hello?' Ah, the very beginnings of irritation. The air got caught at the top of my lungs, some sense bleed-ing in.

He hung up. I stared at the phone. As an act of retribu-tive justice, nuisance calling was a little anticlimactic. I'm surprised it's so popular.

I dialled again.

'Hello.'

I hung up this time, sweaty fingers sliding on the screen. I'd been toying with the idea of heavy breathing, but at the last minute it had felt too comical. Oh fuck it. I dialled again.

'Cassie, is that you?'

I swear I hadn't done even half a heavy breath.

'Sweetheart?'

Sweetheart. The fucking cheek. The air left me in a genuine hiss.

'Cass?'

I cancelled the call, covered my phone with a towel, and squeezed too much lemon juice into my soup. I was rattled, which was annoying. He was the one meant to be rattled.

The next day was spent looking for orange trainers. Trainers the same colour as the construction workers' hi-vis jackets, the same colour as the kimchi pancakes in the Korean café, the same colour as the Berocca that Tommy had left fizzing on the desk in the office.

I watched the bubbles rise while my client tried to get himself together.

'Sorry, I'm so sorry.'

Clifford was in his fifties, close-cropped grey hair, poor muscle definition and a bit of a gut. He had very old gym gear on: an oversized, too-heavy cotton T-shirt and thin, nearly threadbare tracksuit shorts. His trainers (not orange) were cheap, stiff, like two halves of a baguette, and under them were black silk suit socks, worn as if he was announcing his refusal to commit to training, as if he'd already decided it was pointless.

And he was sobbing, nearly incoherent, darkened splotches on his shorts where tears had dropped.

'It's just . . . I've been in pain for so long . . . and now . . .' He sniffed and I pushed another wodge of tissues into his clammy hand. 'It's the hope . . . you know?'

He had chronic back pain and no one was certain what was causing it. He'd put on weight and that was definitely making it worse, but exercising was agony. I'd helped him use a roller, watching his gritted jaw relax and strain, then tried him with very light weights, sticking to fixed machines, controlling each movement, taking lots of rests and making time for long, slow stretches, flossing the nerves inside their myelin sheaths.

By the end of the session he could bend and straighten more easily, and the radiating pain in his legs had dulled. He wasn't cured, but it was something. And he'd burst into tears as he pulled on his beige cotton jacket.

I watched his loosened shoulders shake and didn't rush him. This wasn't unusual; exercise can make people emotional. *I* was emotional.

Clifford smelled a little of pine air freshener and I thought of Tanya and all the things I hadn't told her yesterday and all the things I couldn't tell her today.

She'd have an opinion about running in the dark, about choosing a route through a blind alley. There'd be a lecture for sure, but there'd be reassurance too. She'd take the fear on, absorb the sick, jittery feeling into herself, she'd be sensible and calm, and her disapproval would make me feel lighter, ready to be me again.

I pictured her face when I first met her in Reception, explaining that you had to draw around a shape before cutting it out. I'd just been hacking at the paper, approximating a triangle, shredding the edges till it was a tiny, unrecognisable fragment, and I'd felt silly until she held up her own precise hexagon. Then I'd realised it didn't matter how good mine was – it'd never be as good as hers. I was free.

I wanted to go and hold my carelessness up for inspection now, let her compare my chaotic life to hers, receive my blessing and my curse. But then I remembered how she'd looked yesterday, practically barring her front door.

I'd never been cut off from her company like this before. Not even when I was with Liam and he'd hidden my keys as I was leaving to meet her, or when he'd called me every thirty seconds while we were at the cinema, or that one time when he'd 'accidentally' locked me in our flat an hour before her birthday lunch. None of that had broken our connection.

'I know you don't like her,' I'd told Liam, turning a chicken thigh under the grill. 'But she's been my best friend since I was five.'

'I like her fine, I just think she's not the best influence.'

'She's a total mother hen.'

'A mother hen with a dirty mouth and a plate of cake to shove in it.'

'You mean she swears? And bakes?'

He'd put away the sweet date syrup I was going to add to the salad dressing and opened a bottle of apple cider vinegar. 'Look, I know you *think* of her as your best friend and this might be hard to hear, but she's deliberately sabotaging you. Or perhaps not deliberately, but certainly unconsciously. She's jealous. You have the discipline she lacks.'

'I don't know . . . I don't think she needs discipline.'

She'd gained weight from having kids and her face was round, her breasts bigger, her hips wider, but she was sexy, womanly. Soft and gorgeous. No hip dips for her, just one unbroken curve, waist to knee.

'Yeah, well, it's okay for her,' Liam said. 'She's still attractive when she's overweight. Not everyone is so lucky.'

'You mean me.'

He shrugged. 'People have different optimum weights. Don't let her get in the way of your progress.'

I *had* let her get in the way. *Bake Off*-inspired, she wouldn't stop with salted caramel bars and mini tea loaves and honey upside-down cake. Wouldn't stop offering and offering until I got tired of saying no and resigned myself to going home heavy and sluggish.

'Go on, Cass,' she'd say. 'It's not *cheating* – it's your life. It's enjoying your life.'

Dangerous words. And they made a little chink in my beautiful, hard-muscled armour.

Liam saw it. 'Unhealthy people are always surrounded by unhealthy people,' he said when I suggested enjoying life might also be a decent goal. 'You have to cut them out the way addicts do.'

I hadn't cut Tanya out; I'd just stopped picking up

anything she peddled. I was thinner and straighter, the bones in my face stark. It suited me, that was true, it revealed a spare sort of beauty more fashionable than Tanya's. And I couldn't be tricked into mediocrity again with magic apple pie. I was suspicious when she acted like I'd been turned evil. I was annoyed by that resentful nod as she stacked uneaten syrupy lemon squares back into their Tupperware.

'Are you . . . ? Are you crying?' Clifford was staring at me, his eyelashes still wet. 'I made you cry too?'

'No, well . . . I guess so. Sorry. I'm being really unprofessional.' I wiped my eyes with one of the tissues I was holding. I'd been angry when Tanya had tried to guilt me into eating, but now I thought, would it have killed me to make her happy? To have tried her cinnamon buttercream?

'Has something happened?'

'I kind of fell out with my best friend. But I don't normally cry. Sorry. Didn't mean to hijack your moment.'

There was a cursory knock, the swoosh of the office door. Tommy's clown trainers (not orange) scuffed the filing cabinet.

'Hey.' He picked up his lurid liquid vitamin mix. 'Oh. What's this? Some kind of therapy session?'

Clifford laughed, or made that raw sound that stands in for a laugh when your throat's full of tears.

I crumpled my tissue, dropped it in the bin. 'You'll probably be a bit sore tomorrow, Cliff. Just to warn you.'

'I can cope with that.' He started to fold his tissues, pocketing them.

'Same time next week?'

'Yeah.' He stood up and we both blinked at the smooth movement. 'I hope you work things out with your friend.'

With an hour till my next appointment, I hopped on the treadmill, determined to lay the ghost of that stitch. I wasn't sure when I'd be ready to run outside again. The image of a man, lit up and waiting, hung in front of my vision and I couldn't help pasting Liam's face into the space under the shadowed hood. Only the gym's dazzling lights dimmed those neon trainers in my mind. In the gym, I could relax, lose myself to the bounce, feel each stride turn from a tight step into a moon leap, breath rising until it seemed to hang about my shoulders in a mist, creating my own atmosphere.

Finally, I said to myself, finally. This is what I'd been needing all morning. There's a hunger to personal training, for movement, for momentum. During a session, you stand next to machines, watching your clients getting fit, and yet the most you do is hand over weights or demonstrate an action. Sometimes I demonstrate a few extra times, just to give my muscles the memory of exercise. I can see the client getting annoyed – yes, yes, they know how to do it – but I push my luck anyway, thirsting for the burn they get so easily.

I cycled through familiar songs, in the familiar order – I never shuffle – my body ready for each tempo, relaxing naturally in anticipation of a slower beat or tensing for the full-blast intro I knew was coming. When I got to 6K, I turned off my music, slowed down, set the incline high, leaned forward. What would it be like? To run without seeing? Was it even possible? I held the handles, shut my eyes. The throbbing rhythm was nearly unbearable without sight to steady me, and I remembered the swaying Liam had done, waiting for me in the foyer. When I opened my eyes, I found I'd got dangerously close to one edge. I straightened up and tried again.

One foot in front of the other. Kind of. Maybe. I couldn't tell. The gym's anonymous music was louder in this dark space, and a rapping percussion I'd barely registered now sliced its way into my head. I felt like I was listing, my body at an awkward angle. The belt was going too fast. I'd let go of the heart rate monitors.

'What are you doing!'

Tommy. Eyeing me as he smacked the red stop button. I blinked at the lights, bracing myself against the halt of the tread belt, a hand on Tommy's arm. I locked eyes with a man in lime-green shorts who was waiting out his rest time on a chest fly. The gym was busy, limbs everywhere, in every shape, like marks on paper – perspiring punctuation or the chiselled characters of an ancient language. No Rosetta stone needed for a translation. The message was obvious: run, snatch, clean, jerk, lose weight, get fit, keep going.

'You could seriously hurt yourself doing that,' Tommy said.

'My client is blind, I was just trying to imagine what it's like for him . . .' I panted, shifted my feet. The right one had been a millimetre from the frame.

Tommy threw off my hand in disgust. 'This is why it's a fucking stupid idea to have these people come here. Look how dangerous it is.'

'Well, I've done three sessions with him so far, and it's been okay.'

'Why did everyone have to go so mental over one dumb video?'

'I took him off your hands, didn't I?'

'Now I'm meant to work out how to get this kid with cerebral palsy to lift six kilograms without dropping the weight on his foot.'

'I can do some research on cerebral palsy if you like, if you'll help me now.'

'I'm done helping people.'

'Please, Tommy, I want to know what it's like. I'll keep my eyes shut and you train me.'

He leaned in close, breath sweet with synthetic banana. 'If you want me to train you, Cass, you'll need to pay me, like everyone else.'

'Not proper training. Just a couple of cardio machines. Some free weights. Please? It'll look good on your CV if you can say you've got some experience in guiding the blind.'

'You're not blind, though. If you want to practise, then it's me who should pretend to be blind.'

'But I want to *experience* it.'

'Well, now *I* want to.'

'What? No, you need to guide me.'

'No. You train me.' He closed his eyes, put his arms out like a zombie.

'Oh my God. How are we arguing about this?'

'What's going on?' Our manager, Steph. She side-stepped an ab-crunching machine and rested her clipboard on the treadmill's digital display.

Tommy recovered first. 'Cass is being weird.'

I let out a long sigh. 'I just wanted to experience the gym as my client might. For a few minutes. You know how it can help to put yourself in your client's shoes so you can tailor the sessions—'

'She was engaging in risky behaviour on the tread-mill.'

Steph frowned. 'How d'you mean?'

'She had her eyes shut.'

'Cassie?'

I cleared my throat. 'Many people use treadmills with-out seeing.'

'Yes. But they usually start with a trainer there to guide them. To tap them on the hip if they get too close to one side.'

So that was how it was supposed to work. Tapping.

To be fair to Tommy, it *was* annoying – our gym's CEO had offered our services but given us very little professional training to help anyone with particular needs. We had to depend on our imaginations.

Steph wrote something on her clipboard, added a full stop with a jab. 'Is there something you need, Cassie? Something I can help with?'

'No. Well. Yes. My client is supposed to be blind.'

'*Supposed* to be?'

Tommy stepped back to perform shock. 'You think he's faking it?'

The clipboard was hugged tight. 'Why on earth would anyone do that?'

'He—' I stopped. Was I going to admit I knew him? That he was my ex? That I thought maybe there was a possibility he was there to get close to me?

'Cassie, I don't like the idea that we're suspicious of our clients. After everything that happened, you know, we're having to work hard to inspire . . .' She looked at her clipboard. 'To inspire an atmosphere of trust and sincerity. It's really important that all our staff are on board.'

'Yeah,' Tommy said, 'we're in a new era of caring and inclusivity.'

Flashing him a glare, I turned to Steph. 'I get that. I do . . .'

'So . . . ? Is there something going on? Something you need to tell me?'

I hesitated. I could say it now and, whatever the truth, it would be over. Liam would get a different trainer; he might be asked to attend a different branch of the gym, or be banned altogether. I wouldn't have to see him again. Of course, I would have to admit to a lapse in judgement, I'd have to explain why I'd agreed to train him until now, why I'd let him call me the wrong name. I'd have to recount my history.

'Cassie? This would be a good time to say something if you have any issues, especially as you have a review coming up in a couple of weeks.'

I was looking at her, at the stretchy work trousers, at the way her fringe lay limply over her forehead, but I could also see my old manager holding out her hand while I slipped off the bank-branded silk scarf. Shame made my cheeks hot. Given the option, I wouldn't have admitted to transferring money. Given the option, I wouldn't have run straight to Liam and allowed him to take control. Given the option, I would never tell anyone how pathetic, how practically non-existent, my resistance had been.

'I just meant we don't do any checks, do we? We don't ask for a doctor's note or anything.'

'Of course not. We're not in the business of storing medical records.'

'It's a confidentiality issue,' Tommy told me, drawing a solemn mask over his grin.

'Yeah. It just makes it hard to know what level of visual impairment I need to prepare for.'

Steph gave me a little pat. 'I understand, but you have to let your client lead you.'

'Fancy a go on the treadmill?' I asked when Liam turned up for his fourth session. It was not a client-led suggestion.

His trainers were grey, clean, a cyan stripe across them. But that proved nothing. To avoid injury, it was important to alternate trainers. I had three pairs. Today's were royal blue. I was wearing a royal-blue tank top to match, and black workout leggings with a thigh phone pocket and mesh calf panels. I had on a crimson cross-strap sports bra and black blister-resistant socks. My underwear promised no visible panty line. I felt fresh, tight, inspired, photobank-prepped. I felt ready to train a blind man.

He was less ready. 'I'm not sure about running . . .' he was saying. 'It seems a bit advanced for me. Currently.'

'When was the last time you ran?'

'God. I don't know. Ages ago. Last winter?' He didn't look like he was lying, he looked pretty miserable.

'Miss it?'

A hand scrubbed over his face. 'Yeah.'

'Well, then, this is your chance. I can set the incline high, make it more comfortable. I've tried it myself. I tried it with my eyes closed. There's no reason you can't do it.'

I moved into his sight line and out again, monitoring every twitch of his eyelid, each minuscule blink, staring so hard at his face I'm surprised he didn't bruise.

When he agreed, I offered the use of my arm again but held my elbow just out of reach, and I watched him cast about for it, catching me only on the third attempt.

'You tried it yourself,' he said softly.

'I wanted to see what it was like . . .'

'You think closing your eyes is the same as being blind?'

'No, and no offence or whatever. I was only trying to help.' I took a step, but he resisted.

'Close your eyes now,' he said, reminding me of Ashlie. 'Go on. Close them.'

'Okay.' I stared up at him.

'You've still got them open, haven't you?'

I laughed, caught. 'Okay, okay, I'm doing it now. Really.'

'I'm trusting you.'

'They're closed.' They were. The noise in the gym intensified. I couldn't distinguish each sound, nor was I suddenly better at interpreting them, but they meant more, as a collection, as proof that things existed – the thin thread of a song in the speakers, the thump of feet on treadmills, the thud of a weight dropping to the mats, Liam, his breathing. Still real, even when I couldn't see him. Like he'd been after we'd broken up. A promise, a feeling, a creeping sense.

I was braced for touch, a hand on my hair, fingers on my face. I was sure it was coming, I thought I could feel the air move, hear the swish of a sleeve against torso. But there was just his breath.

'How d'you feel?'

'How should I feel?'

'It's not a test. Just be honest.'

'Twitchy,' I said. 'Vulnerable.'

'You don't like it.'

'Who does?'

'You're not often vulnerable?'

'Not any more.'

'Hmm.' His voice was deep, quiet, near my ear. 'I wish I was just closing my eyes. Sometimes I think if I concentrated, I could open them. I mean, I know they're open, I can feel they're open, but then I think, maybe there's an extra muscle I'm not using, and if I could flex it then it would all come back.'

'Your sight?' I let the light back into my head, let the lenses bounce it around, let my brain make sense of all the patterns and flashes. I was mostly trying to make sense of Liam, his planes and furrows, the reflective surface of his skin.

The space between us narrowed, his body brushing mine. 'Stupid, I know. But I can't seem to crush the hope.'

'I can understand that.' I didn't *want* to understand it, though. I didn't want to feel the clutch his words caused in my stomach. I stood and looked for something – anything – to focus on. A woman was pulling a tissue from the zip pocket of a sweatband on her wrist. She pulled and pulled; the tissue got longer and longer, like a magic trick. At the last moment, it ripped, leaving a ragged white strip caught in the teeth. She frowned as she blew her nose.

'It's such a *normal* thing, seeing,' Liam was saying. 'I can't really believe it's something I don't do any more.'

'I'm sorry.' The words were wooden; the woman was pulling something else from her wristband.

'Are you?'

Was I? 'One hundred per cent,' I said, a bit too chirpy, tugging him on again, towards the treadmills.

'If only there was an exercise for my eyes.'

'Right.'

'You'd help me?'

'No doubt.' I'd lost track of what I was agreeing to. I was watching a long white earphone wire emerge from the wristband pocket, and hoping the next item would be a long-eared white rabbit. I would not imagine how it felt to wish, despairingly, for your sight back. 'Left here.'

He let me hook us through the space between the weight racks and balance balls, and when I looked back he was sporting a sly smile.

'What's funny?' I asked, feeling duped, feeling stupid. He'd been playing for sympathy and I'd lost the game.

'You said left, but you took me right.'

I glanced at the balance balls as if they could give me a signal.

'It's okay. A lot of women can't do directions. If my ex was guiding, she'd probably walk me into a wall.'

'Your ex . . . ?' He was talking about me, the fucker. 'She'd walk you into a wall, huh? Sounds painful. You must have been a shit boyfriend.'

'I was the best boyfriend.'

I stopped, took my arm back, let him feel about with

his stick, let him find his way up onto the nearest treadmill.

'I thought you were demanding? You said, last week.'

'Yeah, but I was exactly what she needed, even if she didn't always know it.'

'Huh.' I was rough pressing his hand against the heart rate monitors, but if he noticed he didn't say. The belt rose.

'She couldn't stay the course, that's all. Had a problem with commitment. As well as directions.'

I increased the pace, and he stayed central as he found his rhythm. He didn't need any taps or nudges, but he also didn't let go of the handles.

I moved behind him and watched as he ran, glaring at the back of his head. I'd rarely seen him this way. When we'd run as a couple, I'd always been in front.

'You stay ahead of me, Cass,' he'd often said. 'Give me something worth chasing.'

'That's how you see it?'

'Go on. Set the pace.'

He said set the pace, but if I slowed he had a sharp jab in the rhomboid muscles ready for me. Muscles that were already sore from delt flyes and lat raises. I was relentlessly sore. And I needed prodding. I'd never have got out of bed otherwise, and think of what I'd have missed: the syncopated rhythm of our steps, loud in the dark morning, our breath streaming from us in matching white clouds. Once, the air was so frosty that Liam's eyelashes turned silver. We weren't allowed to skip a run, though, even when it was icy, and I slipped so often that my map of bruises joined together into a land mass, a continent.

Another benefit: when I was in front, he could check my technique, tell me when I lifted my elbows or dropped my hands, watch I didn't waste energy on too much vertical bounce.

'Breathe into your belly!' he called when he thought I was flagging.

'I'm trying.' I wasn't. I was barely breathing at all, and I couldn't work out where the air was supposed to go.

'Forearms parallel to the ground, Cass. You're doing really well, you can easily keep going.'

So I kept going. Past a row of squat houses with wide windows, where bare bushes bore tiny golden apples and a woman stared out at us from her yellow-lit sitting room. She and her armchair seemed to have formed into a single organism. I was utterly disgusted and achingly envious. I must have slowed – I got a poke in the shoulder blade.

'Don't lose momentum.'

I wondered what the woman would do if I mouthed 'Help me' as I ran past. The idea made me smile and I picked up my pace, tried to open up the top of my back to see if any oxygen could be squeezed in there.

'Turn left,' Liam said. 'Cass! *Your other left.*'

But he was right about me: I didn't know left from

right. My brain stopped functioning past the 8K mark. I was lost in a maze I had no hope of escaping. That must be why they make marathon routes so clear with all the barriers and everything. I leapt across a road.

'Watch out! There's a car coming.'

I turned my head blindly, mouth open. The car, with its staring headlights, was a concept I could only just grasp. But it was a long way off and moving slowly. Had he really needed to shout?

We followed the path to a street I recognised, big lime trees interrupting the pavement. I was a tiny Cassie, trotting along beneath the canopy, but Liam's presence didn't shrink; instead, his shadow loomed ahead, detached itself from the trees and darted after me. I'd nearly convinced myself I was being chased, when I was yanked back.

An arm against my throat, rigid and crushing. My hands were already scrabbling at his skin, my feet suspended mid-step. I toppled sideways, or was dragged, and a second later I was on my hands and knees, teeth gritted, a sour taste on my tongue. Liam was patting my hair and wiping saliva off his arm.

'That car was about to pull out,' he said. 'Didn't you see? You scared me, sweetheart. You nearly got run over.'

I hadn't noticed a car move, anywhere. I hadn't heard an engine. I'd missed it completely.

I kept running after we broke up, even though the breathlessness reminded me of Liam, made him present. And then one day he *was* present, a shadow splitting on the other side of the road, matching my steps, then slipping behind, following me, overtaking. The gust of air as his body came within a few inches of mine; the shine of street lamps on his reflective sports top. He didn't look back and I thought I must be imagining him, that I was finally going mad. I kept him in sight, though, the white soles of his trainers flashing at me.

Across the gleaming road, under those great dark trees. Halfway through a web of chicane bike barriers he stopped dead. A grin on his face as he looked round.

'Bit weird you following me like this, Cass.'

The heat of the run was catching up with me and I seemed to burst into sweat. I was sliding around inside my clothes.

'If you want to run together, you only have to say.'

I shook my head, turned, twanging a metatarsal in my haste, and had to limp ten steps before I recovered my pace.

'We can go this way if you like,' Liam called, turning too. 'Reversing a route is a good way to avoid injury.'

I didn't have the breath to tell him to go away, or the strength to outrun him. I could feel the vibrations of his steps as we pounded over a footbridge, and I could already feel the arm around my neck. But when I got to the main road and looked back, he was gone.

'I'll come out, next time you want a run,' my brother had told me. 'Be good. While I'm in town. Work on this gut

I'm getting.' He patted his belt, winked at Mum. 'So call me, yeah?'

'I run most days, Gav.'

'Okay.'

'So I'd be calling you tomorrow.'

'Okay. Yeah. Let's do it. Then if he gets close I can blap him one.' A little weave and punch, a little performance. I didn't buy it. Gavin had never stepped in before.

But the next morning I waited, shivering, in the shared house where I was place-holding a room for a friend who thought that maybe she might make a new life in Portugal. She'd given herself three months, at the end of which I'd be kicked out either way.

The room was all gauzy curtains and batik, the walls behind the hangings slick with damp. It was fine as long as I could get out early. But Gavin didn't arrive for our six o'clock appointment, and I sat huddled in the patchouli-scented mandala bedspread, watching the blanket of the night draw back, the shopfronts outside paling to grey, the points of tree branches sharpening against the lightening sky.

I could just go, I told myself, I could just put on my shoes and go. Instead, I turned away, and turned down the covers. I'd turned coward.

Unable to face the run, I didn't leave the house for a week. Survived on a pack of coconut and cashew protein bars. What did I need the protein for if I wasn't working my muscles?

When I called Gavin later, the next day, the next week, the next month, he was in Riga on a stag weekend, or on a business trip to Belfast, then at a country hotel with a mother-of-two he was shagging on the side. So he was no help at all. I suspected at least one of those trips had been made up. He didn't really want to face Liam, who was taller and broader and more muscle-bound than him.

He's a born salesman, Gavin. Gives good talk, but there's never any action, you can't count on him. Not like Liam: the day I finally tore myself from bed, he was there, ready, in his running shoes.

It was one way to raise my heart rate. And I thought per-haps I could do the same for him. Standing near the mats, I watched the two girls from last week run through a routine together. This time the blonde held her squat longer, the redhead cheering: 'Queen!'

They moved on to mountain climbers, stretching out and skimming their shins over the floor. The redhead finished her set while the blonde puffed and collapsed, but still had enough energy to clap for her friend. 'How's the view up there?' she called, as if they'd actually climbed a mountain, and I looked away before they caught my dumb smile.

Liam had slowed the treadmill to a walk, thirty

seconds of cooldown to go, a small white streak on the belt disappearing under his right shoe every sixth step.

'What about some lateral jump squats?' I asked, as he let me guide him onto unmoving vinyl.

'I don't know about that, Steph.'

'Yeah, you do. We've missed some key movements, and you don't want to lose any range of motion.' I was going against everything I believed in; I can't stand the leaping about that some PTs swear by. Give me a slow, controlled movement any day. But slow and controlled would get me nowhere with Liam.

He tensed and relaxed, tensed and relaxed, undecided. 'Is there enough space?'

'Plenty.'

He felt about with the stick before handing it to me. 'You'll tell me if I'm getting close to anything?'

'Of course.'

'Am I in a good position here?'

'Yep. Go for it.'

'Okay.' He was grimacing as he took a tentative side-step, as he let out a sigh. 'I can't.'

'You can.'

'I don't feel safe.'

'Of course you're safe. I'm here.' I smothered all the sarcasm in my voice. 'Trust me.'

He took a moment, lifting his hand, his fingers brushing against my forearm, my stomach, my hip. 'I really can't. I'm sorry.'

There was something blank about his stance, like an Action Man in its box, secured to the cardboard by loops of wire, waiting for a hand to give it life, to bump it over a playroom floor, to make it grip a tiny plastic gun.

'Fine.' I could do that, I could bump him along. 'Reverse lunges?' I said. 'How about that?'

'Sure.' He put his hands on his hips, took a big step back, dipped, pushed, switched legs. He was a little wobbly but getting steadier. 'This feels good,' he said.

'Great. Keep your heart rate up.' Mine was up, in anticipation.

I wanted more. The girls were stretching towards the pink-to-blue lights; a skinny boy was dipping his head in time with each bicep curl; a bunch-shouldered man on a lat pull-down looked as though he were worshipping a demanding god or begging for his life, or both. I watched him breathe out and rest, and wondered if his prayers had worked. Did they ever work? For any of us?

Everywhere I looked there was a call to a higher power. But I wanted the opposite, something base, something ugly. What could help me? Reebok step, medicine ball, foam roller . . . ragged printout that had continually failed to remind people to wipe down their machines after use. I pulled it off the wall.

'Six more,' I said, then slipped the piece of paper under Liam's back foot as he made contact with the floor.

A hiss of paper on vinyl. His leg slid into a scary-looking, hip-opening yoga pose, knee smashing into the ground. He caught himself on his hands, bit his lip, swore.

'Oh my God! What happened?' I asked, hoping the thrill in my voice sounded enough like shock.

'Skidded.' He panted below me. If he'd known what I was doing, he was frighteningly committed to appearing blind – so committed he'd let himself get hurt.

'Anything broken? Want to try again?'

'No, on both counts.' He rested his forehead on his wrist. 'Shit. This is the kind of thing I was worried about,' he said. 'Falling. Hurting myself. It's embarrassing.'

'No one saw.'

'You saw.'

'I'm no one.'

'Not to me.'

If things were different, we might have made eye contact then. If things were different, we might have been making another kind of connection. If we were different people. I wished we were different people. Steph and . . . Patrick? Meeting for the first time in this gym. No history, no animosity, no screwed-up narcissistic personalities.

'Falling is . . .' I was going to say it was nothing to be embarrassed about, but instead I said, 'When I was nine—' then stopped, not sure where I was going or how much I wanted to share. How much of me – the real me. My heart was pumping as if I'd done a hundred push-ups.

'When you were nine . . . ?' He wasn't looking, but he was focused, he was listening, breath shallow, mouth open as if to taste my words. Not demanding, not sitting there suffering my story, but waiting for me to go on. This was new: Liam as an audience.

'I fell a lot,' I said. 'Tripped. Tree root, raised kerb, bit of uneven pavement – you name it, if it was there, my foot would find it. I don't know why I'm telling you this.' What was I doing, treating him like a real person, treating this like a real conversation?

'Go on,' he said. Urgent. His expression so earnest. He wasn't quite facing me, but he was trying to. 'Tell me.'

'A childminder used to collect me from school, and on the way back to her place, I'd often just . . . I don't know. One minute I'd be walking, the next I was down, on the ground. And the look on Jackie's face was always like, *for fuck's sake*, you know? Not that she ever said that, but I irritated the hell out of her. She obviously thought there was something wrong with me – and, yeah, it *was* embarrassing.'

It hurt, too. My hands were always grazed, my knees permanently shredded. We went through plasters, through leggings. I was always picking at a scab. And I was sick of the feeling – those layers of skin scraped away, the grit in the graze. I was sick of being told off, for daydreaming, for not paying attention to where I was going. I was sick of feeling out of control. It was like some unknown force was coming for me, waiting for me.

'Do you trip often now?'

'No. It stopped soon after I turned ten. One day I realised I hadn't scraped my knees in months. Maybe I'd come to the end of a growth spurt? Got my balance back? Anyway.' I cleared my throat. 'Shall we do some stationary benchwork?'

'That would be great.' He stood and rotated his leg a couple of times, soothing his hip joint. 'I think I'm getting *my* balance back.'

At the free weights, I helped him onto a bench, got him to lie flat, Sleeping Beauty on her thorn-ringed bed.

'Thanks for telling me,' he said. 'About the tripping. It makes us even.'

'Even?'

'Yeah. It levels things out a bit.'

'Right. Good.' But it wasn't *good*. It wasn't what I'd wanted.

I felt conned, exposed, stupid for telling him something painful, something I'd never told him before. Why had I done it? I was raw and angry as I looked at him below me. I wasn't going to cut through the thorns and wake him with kisses. I held the barbell over his face. Perhaps I could drop it, to cheer myself up, to feel clean again. Perhaps I could break his nose or his teeth. Or – I moved it further down, hovered it over his throat – try and crush his windpipe. But I wasn't so jacked up that I didn't think of consequences. Prison, for instance. Losing my job, losing my clients, getting banned from the gym. Still, I didn't want to be *even* – I wanted to be *on top*, I wanted to *win*.

I gave him heavier weights than he'd asked for and studied him struggling.

'Finding it tougher today?' I asked, innocently.

'I can do it.' He was going red.

'Great. Let's try an extra set, then.'

I made the dumbbells mismatched and watched him try to keep himself centred.

'I seem to be favouring my left. Can you see?'

'You look balanced to me.'

'Are they definitely both eights?'

'Yep. Maybe you need to give your right arm a rest?'

While he was on a bike, I got his bag from the lockers, switched his peanut protein bar for a Snickers from the vending machine – good luck with the sugar crash later – and dumped his spare T-shirt in the lost-property box. Even? I'd show him even. I took his water bottle into the Ladies, filled it from a toilet bowl and waited for him to gulp at the bottle halfway through the session.

Finally, this felt like revenge. I was out of the labyrinth; it was all a memory, no map needed. I could enjoy the scenery. Enjoy looking. So I looked. The tautening skin, the stirring muscles, those green eyes, vibrant despite their sightlessness. I stared at him as if he were a picture. I stared at him the way women never get to stare at men: with no fear.

When he called his taxi, I was annoyed. A whole week till our next session. It was too long. I was impatient. There was so much more to do. More to get away with, or more he'd let me do. I didn't care either way, I was amped up and ready, my limbs vibrating. And the minute he left the gym, I couldn't keep an eye on him. Once we were back out there anything could happen. He didn't have to pretend. He could put on orange trainers and run alongside me; he could come to my flat and go through my bins.

If he wasn't really blind.

I was still holding the hoodie he'd brought to keep his muscles warm. The foyer lights swept his high cheekbones, pink, purple, blue, the colours reflected in his blank eyes.

'Catch,' I called, and threw the hoodie.

It hit him in the face, and he jerked back into a vending machine. There was a metallic thud.

'Oh. Christ. Sorry.'

The hoodie hooked for a moment on his man bun before it slid down, and he slapped his chest to stop it slipping further. 'Yeah. *Catching* is not my gift.'

'No. Obvs. Sorry. I don't know what I was thinking. I wasn't thinking.'

'It's okay. Just a hoodie. But no cans or keys or anything in future, yeah?'

'Shurikens only. Got it.'

He laughed and leaned his stick against the table, a table that was holding his dirty water bottle. 'At this point I wouldn't be surprised. It's been kind of a rough session. For me.'

'I'll take it easier on you next time.'

'No, that's okay.' He shrugged on his hoodie. 'I like it rough.'

I didn't answer and he let his smile fall, turning to feel for his water bottle.

I surrendered a groan. 'Don't drink any more of that.'
'What? Why?'
'It must be warm by now. I'll get you some from the cooler.'

I emptied the bottle in the bathroom and rinsed it out. He'd already drunk some. Would it make him ill? Would he guess what had happened? He'd always been so afraid of getting sick, of injury, of illness, of death, and so angry whenever I was sick, taking it as an insult.

Food poisoning was a weakness, catching the common cold proved I'd transgressed – had consumed alcohol or sugar behind his back, skipped a rest day, had too many rest days, forgotten to take a supplement, not finished my morning bowl of watercress.

He had a tendency towards germophobia, a fear of contamination, an almost superstitious need to keep active. When his anxiety was peaking, there was no escape. The shiver-inducing sound of him muttering the national anthem under his breath while he made me scrub every scrap of skin on my hands, the permanent chemical taste from constant gargling with antibacterial mouthwash, the exhaustion from the cancellation of rest days.

Because it was fat people who died of simple viruses, he said, couch potatoes. That wouldn't be us. We would be out every day, before dawn, startling the old people quietly walking their dogs. We wouldn't let anything get in the way. Not even my asthma.

'Who says you've got asthma?' he'd asked during a dew-drenched morning workout.

'What d'you mean?' I was gasping, trying to recover from a round of circuit training on slippery wet grass, the air chilled and damp enough to trigger a tight chest, shallow breaths. 'I've had it since I was, like, two years old.'

'According to who?' He seemed angry, and I was already learning to be wary of that.

'I don't know. A doctor?'

'Oh, a doctor.'

'Who else?' I jumped up, announcing I was ready to go again, wanting to change the subject, ignoring the squeeze of my lungs.

He didn't move. 'What happens if you don't take your inhaler?'

'I get wheezy ... Did we start with bear crawls or burpees?'

'Then what? What happens after you get wheezy? What's the next stage?'

I let my arms slap my sides. 'I don't know, I've always had an inhaler for that part.'

Which proved I'd never tried to quit my medication,

that I was addicted to Ventolin, budesonide, formoterol, that I was ruining my body with steroids.

A few days later, we went to the pharmacy, where I picked up my usual prescription and stocked up on our usual mouthwash, where I spent ten minutes deciding on a new flavour of lip balm, sniffing at the samples of orange brandy and peppermint, and where Liam made a fuss about hiding whatever it was he was buying.

'It's a gift,' he said. 'Don't peek.'

I had to wait till bedtime.

'So? What is it?' I asked that evening, propped against the headboard, rubbing vanilla-scented beeswax into the corners of my mouth.

'Tape.'

'Sounds fun, but I'm kind of tired for role play right now.'

He smiled, distracted, as he opened the small cardboard box. 'It's not for that. It's surgical. For you to wear while sleeping.'

'For my joints?'

'For your mouth.' The ripping noise of the tape coming off the roll was loud in our peaceful bedroom. He used the blade of his hand to wipe off my lip balm. 'You're overbreathing, and this will help.'

'But I don't want to be *under*-breathing, you know?' I said, ducking away from his hand. 'Like, I think maybe I'm quite happy with all the breathing I'm doing.'

'Cassie, don't be annoying for once.'

'For once?'

'Yes. Just for once, can you do what I ask? And not make everything into a joke? Can you just be a grown-up and make a sensible decision?' In the soft light, he was all the teachers I'd ever disappointed, all the bosses I'd let down, and every previous boyfriend who'd backed away.

'Sounds like sensible decisions are not my forte,' I said, a rasp to my voice.

'Then let me make them for you. Can you do that? Can you let me help you?'

'Fine,' I said. 'Fine, I guess I can try and do that.'

And I did try. I stayed still while he came close, hands warming my cheeks, fingers tracing my lips, lining them with tape, smoothing, stroking, studying.

'Okay?'

I tested the system, pulling in a couple of wafer-thin breaths, gave him a thumbs up, scooted under the soft green tartan covers and lay flat. I looked at the curtains, the pale chevrons on a charcoal background. Usually I thought of the pattern pointing to the sky, the stars, in-finite space, but now they seemed to be directed down, they seemed to be depressed, to point to disaster. That wasn't helping. I moved my gaze to the ceiling. The ceil-ing was calm. The ceiling was also white like the tape, it was straight-edged, like the tape, it had brushstrokes just visible in the paint, like the creases in the tape. I ripped off the tape.

'Need a sip of water,' I said, sucking at the sports bottle I kept on the bedside table. I admit it was anxiety thirst; I didn't like the idea that I wouldn't be able to drink anything during the night. 'Sorry. Right. Sorry. I'm ready.'

He was patient as he measured another length and smoothed it on, the side of his hand glistening with lip balm. I tried to smile, feeling the inflexible material crumple slightly, pulling at the delicate skin on my face.

'Great. Let's get some sleep.'

I nodded. Then: 'I forgot to use mouthwash.'

Yes, I'd peeled it off, leaving a papery layer of me, my epidermis, stuck to the glue. How many times could I do this? How many layers were there?

A scramble to the bathroom, not looking at Liam's expression, not wanting to see it. My face in the mirror was carefully blank. I rinsed my mouth, gargled, pressed my fingers to my lips and took a few deep breaths, feeling the cold air on my minty tongue. And I was slow returning to the bedroom, where it was half-dark, the square room rounded with lamplight.

Liam held the white roll on his thigh, a finger hooked through the middle. 'Last chance, Cassie. I don't want to lose my temper.'

'Is the tape expensive?'

'Jesus. No. That's not the point.'

'Yeah. Okay. It's just, I'm kind of scared.'

'You mean you don't trust me.'

'Of course I trust you.'

'Then prove it.' A hard *t*, a warning.

I sat down and presented my face. I didn't make any jokes, I didn't touch the tape. I gave him a double thumbs up this time and snuggled into bed against his chest. He stroked my hair, whispered how well I was doing, told me he loved me, but I could hardly hear him. My breath echoed inside my head.

Liam was pleased, though, excited, his heart beating fast under my ear, his dick hard.

'That's it, Cassie, let go now.' He lay very still, incredibly still, while I struggled to sleep, a jolt of alarm waking me every time I relaxed and expected to gulp oxygen in through my mouth.

In the morning, I was tired, foggy, and I wondered if all night-time nose-breathers had this drunk sensation on waking. I wasn't cured, I still needed my inhaler during the day, but that was okay, Liam said, it was a process, it was a promise.

The tape became a routine. I hated it. I knew it was supposed to help, but each night I felt like I was agreeing to be suffocated. My lips were chapped and sore, and I dreaded bedtime. Occasionally, I'd wait until Liam was asleep and then pull the tape off, crumpling it, letting it fall to the carpet, attracting dust, attracting disapproval. The mornings after were hard, silent, lonely. Those mornings were loveless.

Finally, one evening, the covers rucked up around my knees, I resorted to begging: 'Please, Liam. I can't. Don't make me. I can't do it.'

'I thought we'd got through this,' he said. 'This resistance. It's pathetic. It's idiotic. It's insane. But, fine, you don't want my help? That's absolutely fine.' He threw the tape across the room and turned over; didn't hold me as we went to sleep.

It was a punishment, a caution, an ultimatum, but there was no time for worry – I was out like a light, happily dribbling onto my pillow.

Hours later, I woke, panicking, fighting for breath, to find he'd put that tape over my mouth again anyway, had done it while I was asleep. Muddled, muffled, I scratched red lines into my upper lip, and then there was Liam above me, stopping me, holding my hands to the mattress.

'It's for your own good, Cass,' he was murmuring. 'It'll reduce your blood pressure and cure your asthma, if you let it, if you commit to it. I know it takes some getting used to, but you need it. Please? For me.'

The intense look on his face when I tried to speak, my nostrils flaring. He couldn't hear the words, but he must have known I was pleading behind the gag. He kissed me carefully on the shoulder, on my neck, on the strip covering my lips.

It wasn't long before I was putting the tape on myself.

Week Five

There is one basic admission that all kinds of fitness obsessives eventually make, from the runner that you see on the street, to the clean-eating, film-star-funded wellness guru, to the down-and-dirty boxing-gym instructor, to the slick, seductive YouTube model touting his 'secret weapon'.

The admission is this: we want it; we want to be aching; we want to be hungry; we want to be out of breath; we want our muscles to tear; we want our hearts to thud in our chests.

This is the premise, the first principle, of being truly fit.

We want this. We like it. We like to be sore and we like to be stiff and we like to be tired.

Everywhere in the Western world these feelings are being cultivated, and PTs and their clients are bruising and tearing and hungry and aching and high. So high. So happy, so pleased with ourselves and our low body fat and our extra cardio capacity and our long stare into a healthy future. We assume. We hope. We promise.

*

I was hungry and I was enjoying it. As if to try and tempt me, the fridge was humming, loudly, with a low rattle and a top note that was almost a voice. I had half a mind to join in – add my part – but I was self-conscious. My eyes were shut, a sleep mask over my closed lids, and it's curious how *not* seeing makes you imagine you're lit up, on a stage, as if you've taken down some defence, withdrawn your boundaries, become a target. I knew that in reality no one was looking in through my kitchen window, but try convincing my lizard brain.

So I stood still and silent, listening to my tongue unstick from the roof of my mouth with a tiny, tiny click. It made me think of Ashlie, and how I'd known a split second before feeling her tongue that she was about to lick me.

I'd already tried walking about my living room, grimacing, flinching at nothing, fighting a strong urge to raise my forearm in case something hit me in the face. Sightless, I moved as though I was injured, with dainty steps, giving my weight to the table, the kitchen counter, the back of the sofa. It reminded me of the days after I left Liam, when I paid close attention to my body, had to pay close attention, because there was no one else to do it for me.

What was Liam like at home, alone? Did he find the fridge noise insistent? Did he ever hum along? I wished I could watch him, follow him, peer in through his windows. But it wasn't my first wish. It wasn't a third or fourth or fifth. It was something from the past, like a hoped-for GCSE result.

I discarded the sleep mask, stretched, checked the time and gathered my rubbish: a black bag full of coffee grounds, protein-bar wrappers, yogurt lids and greasy brown paper; a cereal box stuffed with tiny grapefruit soda cans and ripped-up receipts. Since finding my bills strewn across the pavement two weeks ago, I'd been smuggling out my refuse and dumping it in the big public bins at the back of a supermarket car park. Just in case.

I'd got used to doing this back when Liam loved to look through my litter, and it wasn't like I was fly-tipping. This was the last time, though. I was, I'd decided, being more paranoid than sensible.

I made my stop, clanging the bin lids back into place with a satisfying finality, then stood at a zebra crossing and closed my eyes, feeling the hint of rain in the late-summer breeze, finding an echo of my fridge's song in the distant wail of an ambulance.

I knew I'd be imagining Liam's state for a while, speculating, gloating. I'd rubbed my belly like I was pregnant the whole time Tanya was carrying Ashlie, imagining falafel-induced wind was the flutter kick of a tiny human. Now I tried to interpret the red blur of my eyelids' blood vessels as I waited for an aural clue to cross the street, but sounds just endlessly swirled, and when I looked, a driver was waiting, impatiently edging her car over the black and white stripes. I flashed my palm in thanks, in apology.

I'm sorry. I'm really sorry. I was texting Tanya. *I miss you.* Her reply slid in: *I miss you too.*

I tried calling, three rings before it went to voicemail, enough time to notice the quiet, leafy side street, the pavement flanked by houses.

Me: *You rejected my call? WTH? I just want to talk.*

Tanya: *Have you passed Liam on to another PT?*

Me: *Not yet. Can I come round later?*

Tanya: *Have you told your manager who Liam is to you?*

Me: *No, but I chucked a hoodie at his face.*

Me: *Made him drink toilet water.*

Me: *Don't you think that's funny?*

Me: *I thought it was funny. I wish you'd join in, Tan.*

Me: *I thought you were my best friend.*

Me: *This is ridiculous.*

Me: *This is stupid.*

Me: *You're being unfair.*

Me: *Ashlie's my goddaughter FFS.*

Me: *You can't ignore me for ever.*

I was walking, swaying, as I texted. Feeling for the slight incline in the pavement while I navigated the screen. The growling of a nearby car roused me, and I pushed my phone into my jacket, quickened my step, realised I must look suspicious zigzagging slowly along, only just dodging the wheelie bins waiting on the pavement for collection.

A row of sunflowers faced me curiously, radiant against the darkening clouds. They bobbed as if excited, and I put a hand up to touch one before I saw it was seething with bees, all pushing their little black suckers into tiny yellow openings. I dropped my hand and listened to the buzzing for a few moments. The sound mixed with the loud wheezing of an engine fan.

The car was still there, idling. Looking for a house or following me? I had a creeping sensation as I walked on, but I didn't know if it was a premonition or just a reaction to the heavy pressure of the day, to the promise of a change in the weather.

Twenty seconds, thirty seconds. The car – a grey hatchback – crawled along, matching my speed.

I sidestepped a snail who'd found a stream of wet on the hot concrete. Above us someone had been watering a window box and there was a slowing drip, drip . . . drip . . . onto one of the wheelie bins.

I stood still a moment and the car huffed, impatient. I put out an experimental foot. Then, gradually, casually, I moved again. The car crawled. I stopped. It stopped.

I remembered leaving my old flat several months after breaking up with Liam, cheap cowboy boots tapping, long lilac skirt flapping. I remembered how his car had zoomed and idled as I'd made my way along the edge of an empty old industrial road. I'd known it was Liam then, even though I hadn't looked, hadn't wanted to look. But surely it couldn't be Liam now.

I took a deep breath, began a gradual turn, imagined my spine twisting: click, click . . . click. And found the orange indicator already ticking, the wheels scrunching, the car pulling away, too fast for me to see more than the driver's baseball cap and sunglasses. I glanced back at the snail, as if it might have seen more, but it was retracting its tentacles.

'Some snails can regrow their eyes,' Sophie told me when I got to work.

'Oh yeah? That's three. Keep your knees turned out.' We were giving her hip joints some attention, doing squats. Well, I was doing squats. Sophie was dipping a little and then watching me. But it was better than nothing.

'Like, if someone chops a snail's eye off its stalk.'

'Chops it off?' I got a wave of sickness, so sudden it felt Freudian.

'There was a kid at my old school did it. During garden time.'

'Really? That's horrific.'

'I know.' She shrugged. 'Garden time was really dumb.'

'I meant about the kid.'

'Oh. Yeah. He was kind of a psycho.'

'But the snail was okay?' I put a gentle hand on her back. 'Try again. You don't have to get very low. At all.'

She dropped a centimetre. 'No. It was fucked. Wrong kind of snail. My teacher put it out of its misery with a rock.'

'Christ.' I retracted my hand. 'What happened to the boy?'

'Nothing.' Another dip. 'Who cares about a snail?'

'I care.'

'Take it up with my old teacher.'

'I might.'

'Great.'

'Great.' I caught her smirk. 'Nice try, Soph. You've still got six more to go.'

'Ugh. Fine.' She performed two more squats, more like curtsies, and then raised her eyebrows. 'Happy?'

I wasn't, but there was a reward at the end of our session: a large, pale blue box on the table in front of the noticeboard.

Steph had abandoned her clipboard in favour of a paper plate.

'One of our members brought cake. Isn't that nice?'

She gestured at a guy in horribly shiny shorts. I knew his face. He wasn't the guy who used the cross-trainer with bare feet, or the guy who did hip thrusts at the mirror, or the guy that dropped dumbbells next to people's heads. But he seemed familiar; he seemed okay. I waved, then looked in the box. The icing read: *ank ing est!*

Sophie frowned. 'What did it say?'

'That we're the *greatest* or *best*, or something like that,' Steph said. 'And *thanks*. Or *thank you*? I cut it before I took in the message, to be honest.'

I laughed and tried for another – covert – look at the guy. 'He into you?'

'No.' Steph's fork hovered halfway to her mouth. 'I don't think so.' She glanced at him. 'Surely not.' Finally the cake made its target. 'Want some?' she asked, chewing.

'Yes,' Sophie said, taking a plate.

I shook my head. 'Nuh-uh. Not for me.'

'Really? It's good. There's lemon curd in the middle. From the Robin's Egg bakery.'

'I can't. I can't do cake. Thanks, though.'

I was still thinking about the snail. And I hadn't had breakfast yet, and I felt good about it. There are days when I wake up and all I want is to fill my belly. Then there are days when my body slips its tether to food and floats free. I was energised, blood running like water. I knew to hold off, to hold on to that feeling. Flexing my willpower, pushing for an extra lift, putting the tape back on my mouth. Liam wasn't there to monitor me, but these days I policed myself.

We'd been together about eight months when one of Liam's friends signed up to do a three-day cycle ride for charity. *Mike's bike hike.* For weeks Liam had been full of disapproval, saying Michael would wreck his joints, and the donkey sanctuary wouldn't thank him for it, but the morning of the ride he'd been keen to 'go and be a cheerleader for the idiot'.

The 'race' was starting in a fancy suburb on the other side of the city and it had been a rush to get ready in time. I had a turquoise clip in my hair that kept sliding down, and I was worried it looked ratty, childish, lop-sided. Liam's friends were fine, but they had a way of smiling at me, of talking to me, that made me aware of my careful accent and how I'd learned to rephrase my thoughts. Looking right mattered.

I was searching for my reflection in every shop window we passed, fiddling, fussing, when the smell of freshly baked doughnuts hit us. And suddenly I wanted carbs, wanted them with a tight-muscled intensity. Food I didn't even like called to me. Train-station pasties. Supermarket chocolate eclairs. Flaccid white bread.

I was disgusted by them too. Poison. Everything had to be lean in those days. Lean protein, lean muscle, lean meat. I was sick of the word lean. 'Like this?' I'd said the night before, tilting to one side, and Liam had told me I was cute.

'I'm going to have a cheat day,' I said, dipping my tur-quoise clip at the doughnuts in the bakery window.

'What?'

I thought his expression was indulgent, amused.

'I'm going to get a doughnut.'

'No.'

I laughed. 'Yeah, I totally am.'

'You'll undo all your work.'

I shrugged, got my wallet out, gave him a flirty smile. 'It's called dirty bulking.'

And then he was storming off, striding across a road, his neck stiff. I gave a half-second longing look at the doughnuts, but of course I ran after him.

'Liam!' I'd thought he was joking. No one could be that angry about baked goods. 'Liam?' I was breathless, cheerful, unbelieving. But he was spittingly furious. I grabbed at his arm and he shook me off. I was aware of strangers staring, that I still had a stupid smile on my face.

'If you're going to be disgusting, I don't want to have to see it.'

The sky here was too big and white, the trees too spindly, there was no shade, no cover. I limped along at his side, a just-kicked dog. I didn't want to be disgusting. 'Sorry,' I said, mortified at the sound of my own voice. 'It was just a joke. I'm not going to eat a doughnut. I'm not going to eat anything.'

'Looking after your health isn't funny.'

'I know.'

'I thought we were a team.'

We both crossed a road without waiting for the lights to change. Dust gusted around us as traffic passed close. A car honked.

'We are.'

'It hurts me, Cassie, when you don't take care of yourself. It hurts.'

Was he calming down? He was still walking. I was still jogging to keep up with him, tagging along, more like a child than ever.

'I know. I'm sorry. I'm very, very sorry.'

He began to slow his steps. I tried to think of something else to say, to make him happy, to make him kind.

'And I'm grateful. For your . . . guidance. To be on your team. I'll try and be better. I'm sorry.' My body felt loose and weak and I *was* grateful when he pulled me to him for a hug. That warm body, that soft fleece jacket, the strength of his squeeze. I'd done it, I'd persuaded him, won him round. I was safe.

'Don't scare me like that again,' he said, as if I'd hung out of a window or narrowly escaped a speeding car. 'Come on. I don't want to be late.'

As Michael's huddle of supporters came into view, I dragged the clip out of my hair.

Of course, I thought, waiting for Liam in the gym's foyer, I could eat a doughnut in his presence now and he wouldn't be forced to witness it. I could bring some into the gym and eat them right in front of him while he squeezed the chest press. I could do lots of things. But only if he turned up. The clock ticked past his start time, and no taxis pulled to a stop outside, there was no tap of a stick against the front step. I leaned on the BMI machine till a woman shyly shooed me off.

He wasn't coming. Had I pushed him too far?

That occasionally happened with other clients. They didn't like the regime, or they got tired of being told what to do, or they just wanted to use the gym to relax. Or to relax somewhere else entirely. I understood. I'm not very good at being trained myself. Enthusiastic at first, I soon resent being bossed around. It's why I thought Liam couldn't be controlling me. Because no one had ever controlled me.

I was aggressive, I was crass, I was ungainly, careless, loud.

'You need to learn how to behave, Cassie,' my mum said constantly when I was a kid. 'Control yourself. Calm it down. You're not being ladylike.'

She'd meant to make me ashamed. And it worked. I did feel shame, looking at other girls at school or my cousins on holiday, seeing how easily they sat still and talked quietly. I was never doing the right thing, even thirty seconds after I was reminded of the right thing. *Calm down, keep your voice down. Sit down, pipe down. Eyes down, arms down, put that down.*

I wasn't stupid. I learned to fake it, to copy the care, the quiet, the calm. But it never lasted long.

When I was twelve, my mum and I took the train down to the caravan at Selsey Bill. The rest of the family was driving – my grandparents, aunts, uncles, cousins, all bombing along the A3 in a convoy of old Fords and new Vauxhalls. But I'd provoked a last-minute Friday detention, so Mum had to wait for me to get out of school.

We caught a late train because my detention had been extended and I'd dawdled on the way home, knowing there'd be trouble, and then there *had* been trouble, which had made us even later.

So it was after eleven when the train drew into a deserted, hanging-basket-decorated station with an announcement to tell us we'd be waiting there a few extra minutes. Mum might have grumbled, but she'd fallen asleep on the seat opposite mine, and it was just

me in the empty carriage, conscious, alert, reading Sweet
Valley High and eating a packet of Skips, letting the salty
starch tighten on my tongue.

I'd nearly finished my crisps when I realised there was
someone standing on the opposite platform. Two some-
ones. Men, in jeans and belts, holding pints of beer in
real pint glasses as if they were in a pub.

It was slightly surreal, almost cosy. I felt like a kid in
one of those books my grandparents gave me, optimis-
tically, every Christmas: I was going home from boarding
school in the 1930s, wearing a boater and long socks,
and while I was on the train I'd be getting involved in a
magical adventure.

The men were friendly and raised their glasses. I copied,
raising my empty can of Lilt, and felt like something was
about to happen. A portal would open, maybe, or a wizard
would appear. I tried to go back to Sweet Valley, but I was
excited, and I couldn't help looking again.

When I did, I saw the pint glasses resting on the platform's yellow safety line. The men had put them down
to unbuckle their belts, to drop their trousers.

One was bent over, the other was playing with his
half-flaccid dick, a smirk on his face as he made eye contact with me. The shock ran from my neck to my
feet — bypassing my head. I'd been deceived, I'd been
defeated, there was no magic, no adventure. I slammed
my hand against the window.

Mum woke up.

'Get hit by a train, you fucking nonce!' I was mostly

shouting at the one looking. The other was just a weird pale camel in my peripheral vision. I spat at the glass.

Mum was horrified. But not by the men, not by a couple of blokes exposing themselves to a twelve-year-old – by me, by my reaction.

As the train began to pull away, she tightened her lightweight anorak round her shoulders and withdrew into the seat.

'You frighten me, Cassie, sometimes, you really do.'

Had I frightened Liam? Had I defeated him? I'd tricked him, just like Ashlie had suggested. I'd pushed him. I'd hurt him. And maybe he'd realised when he got home, or someone had seen what I'd done and told him. Maybe I'd gone too far with the toilet water and he was sick, had dysentery or cholera. Maybe he was dead.

My free hour was spent slouched in front of the office computer, researching blindness, trying to find my conscience, digitally sifting through the different kinds of white sticks. Long or short, telescopic or folding, rubber-tipped or with little rotating balls on the end. I watched videos that simulated going blind with fuzzy lenses and black-edged screens; videos that tried to give an approximation of greying out or tunnel vision.

I followed a link to a site about guide dogs. It was fifty pence to get one, apparently, but over fifty grand to breed and train one from birth to retirement. The difference was funded by donations, and members of the public could sponsor a puppy for a fiver a month. I signed up. There was a space to say why you were donating. I wondered about typing Liam's name and giving honest reasons, confessing to making him slip over and throwing a hoodie at his face, but in the end I baulked at writing the sentence: *I feel bad for being a twat to a blind person.*

And actually, my grandmother went blind, in her eighties. Macular degeneration. The centre of her sight a widening hole. Soon she couldn't drive, couldn't cook, couldn't read. She'd liked thrillers – ones where the main character was on the run. But her life became one room, one chair, one aspect: facing the garden, remembering the shrubs she'd planted. Sometimes she thought she could make out faces in the privet hedge, but it was just her brain filling in the gaps. If there really had been faces she wouldn't have been able to see them.

'People tell me how pretty you are, Cassie,' she'd said the last time I'd visited her. 'Wish I could see for myself.'

I thought she'd have been disappointed if she'd suddenly got her sight back. I wasn't that much to look at.

I stuck her name in the donation form, added *Thinking of you, Nanny*, and clicked confirm on the payment details. My good deed for the decade.

Michael's good deed was a little more significant. His bike ride raised over six grand. Not for donkeys either, for a research trust for motor neurone disease. There were twenty or more other riders, all with their own charities, their own lurid Lycra outfits, their own supporters. Everyone was in clumps of garish colours, so I noticed the woman, detached, alone, in a dark green jacket and slim black jeans. A blonde woman, wearing scuffed Chelsea boots instead of trainers, who was staring at me and Liam.

He'd been cuddling close, dropping kisses onto my hair, keeping me within touching distance as he talked to Michael and Ollie and some of the race organisers. After his furious reaction to my doughnut joke I was pathetically grateful for this sign of forgiveness. And he was so handsome, assessing the bikes, the route, the gear, laughing with his friends.

In their narrow shoes, elongated helmets, padded gloves and wraparound sunglasses, the racers seemed sleek and vibrant, like another species. I was glad I hadn't carb-loaded; I felt bulky enough in this company.

When Michael went to line up, Liam cupped my neck, gave me an ear-tickling whisper.

'My ex is here. Pippa. Thought I should warn you.'

I looked up then and locked eyes with the blonde woman. She wasn't a cyclist, but she was high-fiving Michael as he got on his bike. That was Pippa. I didn't have to be told.

'If she says anything to you, you know – it's just to try and get at *me*, to try and ruin what we have. She doesn't think I deserve to be happy.'

'But why?'

'I embarrassed her when I dropped out of uni. She doesn't think anyone without a degree deserves to be happy.'

'I don't have a degree either,' I said.

'And look at us now.'

I squeezed Liam's hand and watched Pippa reattach a water-bottle holder, jiggling it to make sure it was solid. She was tall, capable, healthy. She looked clever; she looked like she'd smell good. Michael patted her shoulder and she picked her way out of the crowd to stand at the edge, ready for the countdown.

Her figure was an irritation, a bit of dust in my eye; no matter how often I blinked, I could still see it. She lifted her hands high on the word 'Go!' and somehow I heard her joyful cheer over all the other noise. The cyclists shot off with a quiet, anticlimactic whir, leaving behind a whiff of WD-40, and their supporters snapped shut tubs of peanuts, crackers or watermelon chunks.

'Did you see Mikey slapping on Deep Heat?' Ollie asked.

'He'll be regretting that at the fifteen-mile mark,' Liam said.

'Before that, even. What an idiot.' Ollie looked at me. 'It draws blood *away* from your muscles.'

'Yeah, I know.'

'Oh, you know, do you?'

Stocky, fat-faced, no matter how low his body fat percentage, curly-haired and ruddy, Ollie had earned my instant dislike when Liam had introduced us six months before. But he had that posh-boy way of making you want his approval anyway.

'Yes,' I said, and took a breath, counting to five, reminding myself who I was, who I wasn't. 'Liam and I have discussed that in the past.'

'*Liam and I,*' Ollie mocked.

The breath turned heavy in my chest. It was Liam and *I*, wasn't it? Not Liam and *me*?

'We should ask about cross-promotion,' Liam said, gesturing at one of the park cycling trailers. 'I don't want to push merch, but they could be a perk for new recruits, or new franchisees.'

'You think?'

'It's probably the right demographic.'

'Sure, okay, worth a try.' Ollie let Liam get several metres away, then gave me a look. '*Demographic* means a particular section of the population.'

'Thank you,' I said. 'For explaining that.'

'You're very welcome.'

'Do you actually think I'm an idiot, or is this some kind of long-running joke?'

He smiled. 'I haven't decided yet.'

'How long will it take you to decide?'

The smile turned nasty. 'How long do you think you and Liam will last?'

I lost my breath at that. I thought of the doughnuts. I pictured Liam's back, taut with anger as he stalked away. It was easy to imagine him leaving for good, and it was easy to imagine Ollie's expression when he heard about our break-up. I toed a yellow leaf deeper into the mud, felt the break in the stalk.

'Hi.'

We both turned at the voice. It was the blonde in the green jacket.

'Pips,' Ollie said, arms open. 'Been a while.'

'Thought I should come and be friendly.' She wasn't smiling, though, and she wasn't looking at Ollie. 'Cassandra, is it?'

I nodded, even though no one called me that. My pale grey Air Max trainers were muddy and I wished they weren't.

'I'm Pippa.'

'Hi.'

She looked at the deserted starting line. 'Hope Michael will be all right. He's got a knee injury . . .'

'That's what he's using Deep Heat for?'

'Yes. Couldn't be talked out of it.'

'Idiot,' Ollie said again.

Pippa ignored him. 'I don't know if you know, but Liam and I used to be a *thing*.'

And I thought *I* was direct. I opened my mouth, but my lips froze when I tried to reply. I could feel Ollie's attention, his amusement.

'How long have you been together now?'

'Er. Eight months. Ish.'

'Living together?'

'Uh-huh.'

Her gaze darted between my eyes. 'And how *are* things?'

'Yeah,' I said. A rush of sound. 'Yeah. Great. Things are great.' I couldn't help the frown, the disbelief in my voice that she'd ask, that I'd have to answer.

'Great.' She pushed back her heavy blonde hair. Shifted her weight on those long legs. She did smell good; her perfume made me picture big pink petals, as if the smell alone could create a projector-screen image. 'I remember what it was like at eight months. When you think you're *made* for each other.'

I couldn't tell if she was being sarcastic. The last of the crowd, wives and dads, were gathering up empty granola-bar wrappers and stuffing puffer jackets into bags. Someone with a megaphone was giving out times and locations, where to meet your loved ones after the race. The noise mixed with Pippa's voice, muddling the tone.

I might not have been able to decipher her meaning, anyway. She was *so* posh. The kind of woman I avoided, even as a client, even though that type usually had money. I felt small and mean next to her, some lumpy little peasant, low-browed and stunted. She and Liam must have looked good together. Shiny and fit. Like a couple of racehorses.

She hummed a little, watching the crowd. 'You're a fitness fanatic too, I hear.'

'Liam's whipped her into shape,' Ollie said, and Pippa's gaze snapped to mine, fierce, forceful.

But her voice stayed distant. 'Right.'

'So, how've you been? How's Singapore? What tidings from the world of international business?' Ollie turned to me. 'Pippa's an analyst. Extremely brilliant. Got a first from Oxford.'

'Wow,' I said. 'I bet she knows what demographic means and everything.'

A faint line between her fashionably unplucked eyebrows. 'Demographic?'

'Private joke,' Ollie said.

She swallowed hard, and even her swallowing was posh. 'You want to be wary of those.'

'How's Tattie? How's Figgy? How's Pookie? How's Bumps?' Ollie began asking, each name sounding more made-up than the last. Pippa didn't really answer, just gave a location for each: Bergen, Avignon, Doha, San Francisco. Her accent was so round and sure. My hard-won middle-class tones were cheap in comparison.

'God, mass dispersal,' Ollie said.

Pippa pushed her hands deeper into the pockets of her green country jacket. 'Well.'

We both turned then, as if from the same instinct. Liam was stepping off the trailer.

'Better be off.'

Ollie followed our gaze. 'Not going to stay and say hi to Liam?'

'I don't know. He can be . . . a force of nature.' She

gave a trilling little laugh at her own phrase, then looked down at me. 'Like a tsunami or something.'

Ollie leaned in close. 'A tsunami is a tidal wave.'

I dug again at the yellow leaf.

Liam didn't even look at Pippa as he got close, it was as if she didn't exist, despite her obvious awareness of him – her whole body stiffened at his nearness – and he was grinning as he reached me.

'I got us something,' he said, and I had a sudden irrational hope that it was doughnuts. 'They're selling these great shirts.' He held a dark green moisture-wicking tee to his collarbone, then shook out a smaller version and pressed it against my chest.

'Matching?' I said, looking down at the logo on the left breast.

He smoothed the shiny fabric over my shoulders. 'Of course. Like you said, we're a team.'

'What about *this* team member?' Ollie broke in. 'Don't I get a gift?'

'Different team,' Liam told him, looking up. 'Hey, Pip,' he said, casual, dismissive.

She raised a hand, gave a gracious little smile, side-stepped till she had a clear path to turn, and walked away.

'Lovely to see you too,' Ollie called after her, gently sarcastic.

Then Liam was kissing me and I stopped paying attention, only vaguely aware of Ollie's sigh of disgust as he edged away.

I wonder what Pippa would have done if Liam had walked into her place of work and interrupted her research into Japan's cat-café phenomenon, or whatever it is that business analysts do. Called security, I imagine, then disappeared into the crowd the way she had after the cycle race.

But I wasn't built like that, like a racehorse, jumping a fence to get away from the whip. I was a donkey on the beach, plodding back to my master, hoping for a carrot, hoping I could get away with a quick kick in revenge.

He still hadn't appeared; he wasn't coming to the session. I sifted through the sands of Liam's internet presence, letting his Instagram posts bounce over and over, hoping for an update. There was nothing after February: a final picture of tyre tracks through dewy grass. His company website still listed him as a director, the *About Us* page still showed a picture of his face. He'd never displayed his abs, or poked his tongue out at the camera like our CEO, but this photo of Liam was especially solemn, with a studio background, all mottled blue.

To sign up with our gym, he'd had to give us his phone number and current address, so I knew he was still living in the flat we'd once shared near Kennington Park, an area I'd mentally cordoned off, marked as enemy territory. I hadn't crossed the line since our break-up, not even digitally, but I googled the postcode now and swished around on Street View, studying the blurry-faced people who disappeared between frames, and zooming past elongated buses forever pulling away from the pavement.

'Bloody buses,' my next client said, when he arrived an hour later. 'I was stuck two hours on one the other day. I could have got off, mind you, and walked. But the rain, you know.'

Richard was slight, compact, shorter than me, his lean muscle hidden under thick tracksuits. 'I'm very modest,' he'd told me during our first session. 'I save the skin for the sauna, you know?'

He was in reasonable shape, was confident about cardio, but he liked me with him for the free weights. 'You can keep all those Neanderthals away,' he said, averting his gaze as we slipped past two men switching places on a barbell bench. 'Protect me from the grunting and sweating. I can't abide a masculine atmosphere, you know?'

'Maybe you should try the Pilates studio on the high street.'

'What, with the frosted windows? Where all the skinny mums go? No chance. Have you ever seen any of them come out again? God only knows what goes on in there.' He played with his helix piercing for a moment. 'You trying to get rid of me?'

'Of course not. I'm just worried about your delicate sensibilities.'

'Don't joke. I need you, Cassie. And I need this place.'

'No joke. You're my precious flower, Richard. My desert rose.'

'Stop.' He was smiling. His smile was very pointy, pinched, almost a pout. 'Go on, then, give me the twenty-twos.' He was fucking strong under his modest attire.

'How was the Japanese place?'

'Eh? Oh.' A rest. I took the dumbbells. 'Mixed, if I'm honest. I wanted to swim in the ramen, it was that good. But the sushi was terrible. I still ate a lot of it, though. Coconut rice rolls. Sweet ones. I walked out like I'd stolen the silver.' He clutched his belly and blew out his cheeks. 'Impossible to resist, though, aren't they? Bad things. The minute something's bad, I just can't help it, you know?' He squinted at me as I handed back his weights. 'Do you know? Are you ever tempted by anything, Cass? Anything at all?'

I was tempted by one thing. And it dragged me towards the shadow world of pixelating frames and spiralling fish-eyed focus. But Google wasn't enough. After my shift, I walked north, the real world jarring in comparison. Having a body in this space was completely different: feeling the light rain misting my skin, enjoying the smell of damp soil, looking up at the way the treetops cut through the lowering clouds and reached into slices of sunlight.

It seemed momentous to deliberately march into Liam's territory, to cross that invisible line and feel my thread weaving through the maze behind me.

Our old flat – Liam's flat – was in a block: a square building, solid, white and grey. A sixties build with big slabs of windows. It looked like something from a smoky old spy film. I'd loved it once, and I'd missed it. There *had* been good times: coming home with food from the market, getting back after a long, cheerful run, being carried up the steps when I'd sprained the extensor at the front of my ankle, Liam's arms tight around me.

Impossible not to remember stumbling out that last time, though, weak and brittle. So I stepped warily on the mossy tarmac, holding the railing next to the pelican crossing as if my weight might set off a trap. I felt like an animal sniffing at a perimeter, only this time maybe I was the predator. Or, at least, not the prey.

Liam's car was in the car park. A Golf R. Turbo-charged engine, three hundred horsepower. Nought to sixty in four seconds. 'Sporty little number', my dad called it – not quite praise. The windscreen and bonnet were leaf-covered, the lapis paint dulled with dust, and soil had built up around the tyres: Liam hadn't driven it in a while. If I'd needed proof of his condition this would have been it. He loved driving that car. Loved parking outside my place, my places, wherever I was. Loved staring out through the windscreen, or leaning against the side, or leaving it empty, as a reminder that he'd be back.

There was a spattering of raindrops, advance notice of weather to come. I used the moisture to wipe the passenger window, rubbing it with my sleeve, but there was nothing to see – nothing on the seats, or in the centre console – so I kicked the tyres, just for something to do, and then turned to the row of large wheelie bins backed against the building as if they were hoping to be forgotten. The recycling bins were locked, but the general waste wasn't. I lifted a lid, the smell coming at me as I moved. I gagged. But it felt right, it felt obvious, looking through his rubbish. After all, he'd done it to me.

I pulled my top lip flat over my teeth, tried not to breathe, reached in and tore open a bag. Polystyrene, cling film, sachets of cat food. Not Liam's. I tried another: tissues, wine corks, plastic packaging from a PAW Patrol toy. Not his. I ripped open the next: empty protein-shake bags, the wrapping from a shoulder support, plastic clothes hangers with sports labels on them. This was Liam. I spread the bag wider. At the bottom were a lot of ready-meal trays, smeary with the dregs of creamy, tomatoey sauces. Proof of his microwaved diet. How the mighty had fallen. I reached into my pocket for my phone, planning to take a photo. And then I stopped.

What the hell was I doing? Arms elbow-deep in rubbish, hands covered in sludgy, stinking filth, I was scrabbling about in my ex-boyfriend's waste. And for what? What was I hoping to achieve? I couldn't tell him I'd found out he was subsisting on Tesco Finest lasagne for two. I couldn't torment him with the eye-watering macro count in an Iceland chicken korma.

I drew back my arms, mindful not to touch my face.

'Hey there.'

A woman was coming out of the security door. I knew that clinking latch, the squeaking hinges. I didn't know the woman, though, her flat face or her yellow peasant blouse, her appliquéd jeans or her thick-sandalled feet.

'Can I help you with anything?' She paused a second as the breeze caught her, caught the long gauzy scarf that she'd tied in her hair. 'What are you doing?'

'I'm a cleaner for flat twenty,' I said. 'My client thinks I threw something away. I'm looking for it . . .' Was that believable? My mum had been a cleaner for big Chelsea houses when I was a kid, but she'd always talked about the clients rather than the work, about the affairs and the deaths, and the problem kids failing their degrees. About that gift she got from a woman who never looked her in the eye: a pillar-box-red Karl Lagerfeld blazer that was apparently too much trouble to return.

'What is it you're looking for?'

'A watch?'

'You think you threw away a watch?'

'Well . . . no. I mean, I think I'd have noticed. But I promised I'd check, so here we are.' I shrugged. I felt small and stupid. I suddenly wished for shoulder pads.

'Don't you have any gloves?'

'Ah. Gloves. Yes. I forgot them. This is actually my day off.'

'You came to look through the rubbish on your day off?'

'Er . . .'

A taxi drew up, turning slowly into the car park, sun reflecting wildly over the building, first-floor windows flashing as if in recognition. If it was Liam, I didn't want to wait around.

'What does the watch look like?'

'Gold?'

'You threw away a gold watch?' She sounded horrified; she sounded like she'd hoard all her unused blazers.

'No. I don't think so, but I promised I'd look. Anyway. It's not here. I'd be able to see it, you know, glinting and everything.'

The taxi's passenger door opened and a trainered foot hit the pavement. The woman peered into the bin, her pretty scarf perilously close to the muck sliding over the side. I wanted to lift it clear, but I didn't. I shut the lid.

'Oh,' the woman said, trying to pull back, realising she'd been trapped. 'Oh dear. I'm caught somehow. Can you . . . ? Where are you going?'

I ran. There were voices, there was a shout, but I didn't look back. The bin lid wasn't heavy – the scarf would slither out. The woman would be free in a second if she'd just stop to think, if she'd calm down.

I calmed down in the park, where the squat, red-brick toilet block was open, its barred doors swung wide in welcome. There, I rinsed off the worst of the bin grime, adding another layer to the building's bouquet of stale water, bleach and urine.

We used to run in this park, Liam and I. Circuits. Measuring the kilometres by the number of times we passed the building site for a Northern Line ventilation shaft. The work was finished now. A neat, boxy, windowless structure sitting in its cordoned-off corner, breathing for the Tube, letting out the stale air, silently panting. Like me.

I'd missed it here – the woody smell of the rotting leaves, the thud of conkers hitting the grass – and I jogged a little, for old times' sake. Circling, sniffing the damp air, greeting raindrops on railings with the tips of my fingers. The drizzle became a shower, the rain beginning in earnest, and my jog became a walk. One lap, two, trainers pressed to the pavement, my quick-drying clothes tested to their limits.

Then another test: Liam, tapping out his path, hood up, a curl of hair untucking from the drawstring rim. I might not have clocked him without his white stick, but that distinctive accessory alerted me, suggested I peer beneath the waterproof shell.

My skin was numb, and for a moment I thought perhaps I was watching him on a screen, swooshing along, clicking arrows, dropping a little yellow man into circles on a map. And Liam's slow movements were disorientating, unnatural, almost performative. Carrying himself like a too-full cup of coffee, careful about where he let each trainer land. It didn't seem real, it didn't seem possible.

He was managing, though, making progress, keeping

to the edge where tarmac met grass, and reaching for the iron gate at the entrance to the park.

It was raining hard as he got to the street, even the heaviest footsteps covered by the wash of car tyres on the water-rushed roads. I jerked forwards, catching up, and followed him, matching his sedate pace, watching the ball of his white stick plop into puddles. He traced a route along the road, gripping railings, brushing brick, bouncing off a row of bollards. He was sluggish, painstaking, stiff. Pulled into himself.

I had an urge to take his arm, get him home quick – pure impatience. I had an urge to leave him to it and get myself home. Caught between, I stayed. My hair was draggingly wet, the stream of water making me squint. I'd begun to shiver. The weather was hostile, but to me or to him?

Up on the corner there was some scaffolding – a church in the process of being made into flats – and rain was pouring off the various levels, deafening as it pounded down.

Liam stopped there, at the kerb, and cocked his head.

A car went by, then another. The sweat under my shirt mixed with the rain, and I wondered how long Liam would wait before he dared to cross. I wondered if I could shove him into traffic.

But then he put out a foot, weight shifting forward. And there *was* traffic. Nearly silent under the sheet of rain: a car coming, too fast. I didn't think – there wasn't time – I lunged. Yanked him back, my hand catching at anything it could, fingernail bending backwards against the shiny material of his waterproof jacket. Already unbalanced, he fell, and I saw, rather than heard, his gasp, his curse, his stick clattering down next to him.

A man across the street, face green-tinged under a child's frog-head umbrella, gave me a thumbs up and shouted after the car. I waved back and didn't need to fake my shock. I'd saved Liam's life. Had I meant to? If I'd had longer to weigh the pros and cons, would I have made a different decision?

I watched him slowly pick himself up from the pavement. Alive. He groaned and peeled his sodden trousers from the backs of his thighs. Alive. Felt around for his stick. Alive. Living.

I probably wouldn't have killed him, probably couldn't have pushed him in front of that car, but pulling him back seemed perverse. How to explain it to anyone who'd heard me howl about his behaviour? How to explain it to my mum or dad? Or Tanya?

Liam was on his knees now and I focused on him, held out a hand, moved my mouth to make it look like I was talking to him, so the frog man across the road didn't think I was just creepily watching this blind guy flounder. But I offered no real help and stood back when Liam rose to his feet.

'Is someone there?' he asked, voice a little slurred. His face was wet and for a moment I thought he was crying. 'Hello?'

I flicked a glance at the frog man, but he'd moved on,

pulling his umbrella close. I took another step away, itchy in my wet clothes.

'Ugh. God.' Liam shook his long hair, scattering droplets, and brushed his fingers over his neck.

I thought of him wrenching me back while I was running. At least this time there'd really been a car.

He stood at the corner again and waited, he waited a long while, the rain scouring his scalp and sleeking his hair. Waited until a woman walked by, stopped and touched him on the shoulder.

'Excuse me? Are you okay?' She was middle-aged, with a hipsterish fringe of grey hair and a leopard-print beret. Her slender voice cut through the muddle of rain.

Liam replied, forced to move out of that rigid, concentrating stance. But I couldn't hear his response.

'You're facing the road. Park behind you. Church on your left. I know it's easy to get mixed up if you stop.' She made a sympathetic face that Liam couldn't see. 'My father-in-law was sight-impaired.'

Liam angled his head, said something, asked something.

'No,' she said, as I ducked behind a parked van. 'I can't see anyone.'

Week Six

The palms of my hands were thick across the inner knuckles, yellow with callouses, rough where I'd dug my nails into the unfeeling skin. Between rowing and pull-ups, I'd worked my hands hard.

The morning after I saved Liam, I fitted the bars of weights into those raw creases and rubbed the flesh to redness. In the mirror, my regime looked like a slow-motion tantrum: kicking my legs out, gritting my teeth, pushing things out of the way, stretching them, lifting them up over my head. I would have seemed furious if I'd done it fast, if I'd yelled, but the movements were tempered and silent, and no one in the gym paid me any attention.

By the end, my chest and back hurt, my legs were jelly, and staying quiet had become too much. I let out a snort, a gasp, a spluttering laugh. Suddenly it was all so funny. I'd saved Liam's life. Despite everything, I'd saved him. It was hilarious. It was brilliant. Life was good. I'd be fine. And, okay, Tanya had told me she didn't want to see me, but I needed to talk to my best friend.

I went to shower away the sweat I'd worked for – fighting water with water – and dressed fast in clean clothes, clumsily French-braiding my damp hair as I left the gym. Tanya was still ignoring my calls, my voicemails, my texts, so I went and did step training on the kerb by St Saviour's Primary School and waited while other, more punctual mothers lined up along the iron railings. Some had little babies curled into carriers or splayed in prams. The women all seemed to be hunched over, as if the kids had stolen their internal structures, made them collapse into heaps of human flesh. That would never be me.

Liam had been dead against having kids, and a few months into living together, he'd started to take an interest in my contraceptive arrangements.

'You shouldn't be on the pill,' he'd said. 'It's bad for you. Causes blood clots. Strokes. It can make it harder to lose fat.'

There was also a risk of heart attacks and liver cancer. He made me stop the prescription, said we'd use condoms instead. I'd never known a guy so ready to renounce bareback. I was touched.

Of course, he immediately began forgetting to suit up: 'Sorry, Cass. It's not my fault. You're so hot, you make me lose my common sense. You're probably fine, though, right? Your period was over two weeks ago.'

Tanya had asked if he was secretly trying to get me pregnant. I didn't think so. In fact, I suspected he'd lose it if I told him I was having a baby. Which meant month after month of living in dread. The accusing look when my period was late. His disapproval a weight in my belly. The only thing in there, I hoped. A foetus would ruin everything.

How lucky, then, that he was tracking my cycles. Especially as the morning-after pill was also banned. It had a lot of nasty side effects, apparently. But then so did pregnancy.

'Tanya's going to persuade you to try for a baby,' Liam said one day, after I got home from seeing her and Ashlie.

I was crouching in the hallway, cleaning my trainers, rubbing a bobbly disposable cloth over the rubber soles till they gleamed white again. 'Hardly. She's told me *not* to get pregnant.'

'What?'

Liam's quietly furious tone took me by surprise. I put down the shoe. 'She just . . . I mean . . . I just mean she's not pushing kids on anyone. Ashlie's birth was kind of—'

'She told you not to have my baby?'

I put down the cloth. 'Not yours specifically.'

'She warned you off?'

'No, she—'

'This is exactly what I've been talking about. What I've been saying. What the fuck has it got to do with her if we have a baby? Huh? What business is it of hers?'

'But you don't want—'

'I'll tell you why she's invested. Because that's *her* role. That's who *she* is, right? In your group? She's Mama Bear. And God forbid she'd have to share that title with anyone else, with someone who'd make a better mother, even. Talk about selfish. Talk about controlling.'

'So you mean . . . *Do* you want kids?'

'That's not the point. That's not the fucking point. Listen to me, can you? Fucking listen to me.'

But I thought I had been listening. I thought I'd understood. We were going to beat death, stay healthy till they found a cure, and children didn't feature in the plan – what was the point of kids when you were going to live for ever? There was no need for a legacy if you didn't die. I'd half assumed he liked all those fit old women in the pictures because they were past child-bearing age. I envied them a lot more than I envied Tanya.

At sixteen minutes past three, Tanya arrived, yawning into a disposable coffee cup, Noah drowsing in his push-chair. I watched their progress across the road, then joined her at the school gates and pulled her in for a hug. Her response was stiff, but it didn't matter.

'You look amazing,' I said.

She was pleased, though she didn't want to be. Her

hair was curled into layers of flat, wide ribbons. She tamed her hair the way I tamed my body – without mercy.

'You're making me crave pappardelle, though, and you know I can't have carbs. Ha ha!'

'Everything's about food for you.'

'Food is good.'

'*That's* a new one.'

Ashlie appeared, trailing after her teacher in a line of other grey-dressed children. I waved, accidentally elbowed someone next to me, and stumbled off the kerb.

'Cassie, you're high.'

'I'm not. You know I'm not.'

'Not on drugs. You're *high*. Like when you've worked out.'

'I just did a workout!'

'Yeah, I can see that.'

A woman in densely packed daisy-print dungarees got out of an SUV, its hazard lights flashing, tyres on the double yellow lines. She waved to another woman who was wearing a strappy satiny dress, showing off her ham-like arms.

'Watch out, here comes Big Fat Mum Club,' I said. Not loud. I wasn't loud.

'Cassie.' Tanya raised her palm. 'Can you just not?'

Dungaree Mum and Ham-Arms pushed to the front and retrieved surprisingly sweet-faced kids. A dad, waiting at the edge of the group, lifted his chin and rubbed a hand down his neck, his Adam's apple bobbing. I thought for a second he looked familiar, but it was just the way he was dressed, ready for the gym.

'Auntie Cassie?' Ashlie said, waving a flapping concoction of paper plates and masking tape.

'Ash! What's that you've got?'

'Space station,' she said, holding out her cardboard creation until Tanya took it.

The action reminded me of Liam, and it was like a drop in temperature. A dulling of my bounce.

Then the space station was launched into the pushchair's basket and we were moving, ready to explore the outer limits of South London.

'So I'm assuming, as you're here, you've given up?' Tanya said.

'Given up?'

'Training Liam.'

'Oh. That. No. I'm very much still doing that. No giving up for me, not yet, no siree.' I suppose I was a little hysterical.

'Really, Cassie? You know, this thing with Liam – it's like whatever they're called. Endorphins. But you're going to crash, and then what happens?'

'You don't crash after an endorphin high,' I said. 'It's a gentle comedown. And it's probably not endorphins that make you feel that way, anyway, it's actually like these endocannabinoid things that bodies make naturally?'

It made sense – I always went home and grinned into the shower spray after a run, and I'd definitely done that after a joint too, in my late teens, when *drugs* were my drugs. Tanya was less keen to discuss the body's ability to produce mood-enhancing molecules. She turned sharply into a road by the estate and helped Ashlie climb onto a low wall around a communal garden.

I waited for a moment and then jumped up too, balancing, concentrating, trusting myself.

'Auntie Cass?' Noah shouted. 'Super super.'

'Super?'

'I told him you have an enemy,' Ashlie said, trotting along, watching her own feet on the narrow brick. 'He thinks that means you're, like, Spider-Man or Spider-Girl, or someone.'

'Oh.' I leapt down to the pavement and back again, but I'd done several sets of squats already today and my legs were wobbly. 'I'm not a superhero,' I told her, 'but I did save someone's life yesterday.'

'Whose life?'

'Liam's.'

Noah squeaked as the buggy was yanked backwards, Tanya's fists tight on the handles. '*What?*'

I shot her a smug smile. 'He nearly got hit by a car. I swooped in, pulled him back.'

'Swooped, like flying?' Ashlie asked. She'd turned, assessing me, searching for wings or magic or web-shooters.

'Um, more like running, or lunging, if I'm honest.'

'Oh.' A hop. 'So you can't fly.' I couldn't tell if she was disappointed or relieved.

'You're with him, then?' Tanya said. 'You're going out with him again?'

'No, no. I was just following him . . .'

'Following?'

I was grinning and my cheeks hurt, but I couldn't stop. 'Yeah. I get how that sounds, now I say it out loud.'

'You're starting to be as obsessed with Liam as he was with you.'

'Obsessions are fun,' I said, my tone still up and rising, even as I could feel my mood sinking.

'Mum? I'm hungry.' Ashlie abruptly sat down on the wall, and I only just avoided falling on her.

'We'll have tea when we get home.'

'But I'm hungry *now*. *Muuum*. I want something now. You always give us a snack on the way home.'

There was an awkward pause. Tanya was looking at me; she was looking at me and she was embarrassed. Something was going on, but I couldn't understand what.

Noah was squirming against the buggy's straps, wanting to go, to be off, to get somewhere, getting ready for a tantrum. 'Snack!' he yelled. 'Snack! Snack!'

'Fine.' Tanya pulled her eyes from me and pulled a pack of prawn cocktail Quavers from her bag. They were for Ashlie. There was a Freddo for Noah. 'I know crisps and chocolate are bad,' she said quietly, not looking at me now. 'So you don't need to tell me, okay?'

The wall was rough under my hands except for

cushiony little patches of moss. I caught a glance from under her pappardelle hair.

'I wasn't going to say anything,' I said. It was time to rest, to let my muscles cool, to give into the post-heat hurt, to admit I was human.

'Good.'

Ashlie's munching, the crinkle of the crisp packet, Noah kicking his feet in joy as Tanya unwrapped the chocolate. A cosy scene, comfortable. It made me think of Tanya's kitchen, of PG-rated jokes and mild gossip, of raising our voices over the crunch of carrot sticks, the rumbling boil of the kettle, the clipped narration of a property show on the TV. If I went back with them now, that's what I'd get. I wanted it. But I had to win Tanya round first.

'I made him fall over,' I said as she sat down next to me. 'If it makes you feel any better.'

She looked away, but there was an edge of amusement. 'I'm glad you're having fun.'

'He nearly did the splits.'

'Yeah. And then you saved his life.'

'That was a blip.'

'Hmm. Sounds like you've got it all under control.'

She was being sarcastic, but she was serious too. I could feel my energy leaving me, and my knees were sore. Noah leaned out of the buggy, done with his chocolate, and pushed his little cuddly elephant into my hand. The curled trunk fit my palm, cool against the blisters I'd sprouted since the morning. I squeezed, feeling the pressure build under my skin's surface.

'Control,' I said. 'That's what it's all about, I guess. I never had any before.'

'That's not true.'

'Isn't it? Who got drunker than me? Who was louder? Who ate the most, swore the most, got in the most fights? Me. It was always me. Before Liam, anyway.'

'You don't owe him anything, Cass. You know? Not even revenge.'

'But I do, Tanya. I have something I need to give him, give him back . . . I can't explain it, I can't help it – I can't *control* it.' I looked at her. 'I wish I could convince you, make you understand.'

A soft hum. 'Yeah.' She stood up and brushed the back of her jeans. 'Nothing's changed, though, Cass. I love you, and I think I get it, sort of. But I can't watch.'

'I'm sorry.'

Ashlie finished her crisps and offered the empty packet to her mother. Tanya stuffed it into the side of the pram bag. 'Don't be sorry, Cass. Just be careful.'

She pushed the buggy on, and Ashlie turned to wave. I didn't move. I sat on the wall until my bum numbed. I wished I could numb my brain the same way. I had the fluttering feeling I get sometimes during a cardio session, my mind looking for somewhere to land. But there was nowhere safe, nowhere that didn't make me feel worse. My mother, Tanya, the gym, the street, my clients. I kept picturing Sophie's snail with its eyes cut off, imagining it trying to push up its little stalk stumps.

I had to meet another client in half an hour, but my legs

were weak from over-exercise. I usually revelled in post-workout exhaustion, that ring of lactic acid like a wreath of laurels, but I felt vulnerable, out in the world, out of control, trembling. I didn't want anyone to see me. I wasn't up to a race with orange trainers. I pulled my foot up to stretch my quads, and found I still had Noah's elephant.

'That better not be for me!' Amara called, leaning over the handle of her trolley. 'I don't respond to insults, even if they come in cute, cuddly form.' She tilted further, toes just touching the dappled supermarket floor, to scrutinise the elephant. 'It is cute, though.' She dropped onto her heels. 'Okay, I'll take it.'

Amara was a bride-to-be. Bubbly, cheeky, irresistibly likeable and frustratingly self-indulgent. Ten weeks till her big day and she was still a big girl. I doubted her fiancé cared about her size, but she cared, she insisted she cared. Really. And there was a dress – by a designer I was supposed to have heard of – hanging in the back room of a local bridal shop, waiting for its final fitting. It wasn't exercise she needed help with – I'd never met someone with stronger glutes – it was eating. I'd offered to go food shopping with her, to keep her on track. She said she was full of good intentions when she left the gym, and full of food the minute she was in a supermarket.

I tucked the elephant into the corner of the trolley, steadied myself. 'It's not for you. It's my friend's – her son's.'

'Oh. And here I was thinking you'd brought me a gift.'

'An insulting gift?'

'I was prepared to overlook that.'

'Remember, you're not paying me for this,' I said.

We'd made a pre-wedding meal plan, full of kale, full of beetroot, full of beans, and I was there to keep her honest, guiding the trolley along the aisles and putting items back on the shelves. No more packs of coconut mochi, or sandwiches made with a whole wedge of Ossau-Iraty. No more sugary mocktails or bottles of Riesling or boxes of fennel-seed tarallini. She didn't need to eat *everything* the *Sunday Times* mentioned in their glossy supplement.

Especially as she had a hen weekend at some fancy spa to get through. There was no chance she'd come away from that with a calorie deficit.

I knew about the excesses of hen dos. Michelle's had been at a chocolate workshop where we'd downed tubs of melted cocoa like they were shots, then spent the rest of the day groaning at the mere idea of sugar. Tanya's was in Crete, which meant nights adding spoonfuls of honey to our raki and screaming '*Yamas!*' in each other's sweaty faces, and days roaming baking-hot ruins, trying to focus our aching, hungover brains on murals and mosaics.

My friend Lucy got engaged while I was living with Liam. I missed the announcement and the planning, and assumed I'd missed the hen do until a WhatsApp group popped up on my phone. I was touched, grateful to be included. It had seemed like a second chance – a final chance. And they'd had T-shirts printed: *Bride on the Luce.*

But Liam didn't want me to go and he didn't talk to me as I got ready, as I dug through my stained make-up bag and tried to remember how to attach eyelashes, as I smoothed a dress down over the points of my hips, the muscles of my thighs. Instead, he made dinner – cod and chorizo casserole, luxurious by our standards – sprinkling the plates with parsley and setting the table for two, even though I wasn't going to be there to eat. Then he gently, reproachfully, reminded me to take my curcumin tablet.

I went out, but I felt guilty. I went out, but I spent half the night wondering, aloud, if he was okay. I went out, but I may as well not have been there for all the fun I brought. At 3 a.m., I was alone, leaning over a sink in the disabled toilet, staring at my own eyes in the mirror and trying to calm my breathing. I didn't want to rejoin my friends with this weight around my neck. I didn't want to show them the heavy-lidded and grey-skinned version of me. I didn't want them to see the panic. I wanted to spend my time, my money, my goodwill. Even though I knew there'd be a debt to pay.

I woke up at midday, bleary with daylight sleep, to

find Liam stewing in the living room, sitting very still, hands clenched together.

'You okay?' I knew he wasn't, but I was used to starting conversations with false assumptions, with lies, with deliberate, defensive disingenuousness.

'I'm sorry, Cassie.'

My stomach flipped. I had a feeling he was sorry for something he was about to do.

'I've been pushing you too hard.'

The breath left me in a long sigh of relief. 'No, it's okay, you haven't.'

A sad little smile. 'I obviously have. If I hadn't been pushing you, then you wouldn't have fallen off the wagon so completely.'

'I didn't. I didn't fall off. I danced, I tracked the active calories, I kept hydrated, I engaged my core . . .'

Quietly: 'Is that part of our programme?'

It wasn't.

'It's okay. I'll make it up to you, Cass. I will. I'll make it up to you now. In fact, I've bought us a treat.'

He held up a plastic bag. He'd been shopping while I was asleep. He'd been to buy a bottle of Jack Daniel's and a Colin the Caterpillar cake.

I started shaking. Alcohol and sugar were banned substances, and it was frightening to see them in our flat.

'What are they for?'

I couldn't read his expression as he got up, but he sounded like he was happy. 'For us. For you and me. We can do it together, be bad together.'

I took a step back. 'I don't want to be bad, Liam. I wasn't bad last night, I was good. I was sensible. I don't want to ruin it.'

'You were *good*?'

'Well, I was . . . I didn't drink or anything.'

'You mean you had less fun than usual.'

'Not necessarily.'

'You had less fun because you didn't want to let me down.'

'Well, I guess. Yeah. I never want to let you down, Liam. Ever. I know I didn't make our run, and I'm sorry, but—'

'No, Cassie, that's what I'm saying. *I'm* sorry. I'm sorry all I do is ruin your fun. Keep you from partying, from indulging, from letting go. You must hate me sometimes.'

'Of course not.'

'So let's have some fun now. Together. Let me prove I can do it.'

I tripped on the coffee table as I tried to back away, but he caught me, cradled me. And I let him sit me between his thighs as he cracked open the bottle and unfolded the cake box.

'We deserve it, don't you think?' he said and his *t*'s were so sharp. He'd never had a glottal stop. 'We'll jus*t* have *t*o *t*rain *t*wice as hard *t*omorrow.'

Then his fingers were digging into my jaw, my teeth slicing into the soft inner flesh of my cheeks as he forced my mouth open. And the chocolate was so much, so rich, so spongy and suffocating, I could hardly swallow it. Liam helped by tipping up the whiskey, letting it pour over my chin, letting it burn into my lungs. I choked, chocolate buttercream up my nose.

I was struggling, pulling against his hold, dragging ragged breaths through crumbs, tears in my eyes, but when he said 'More?' I nodded and watched him scoop up more cake with his big, blunt fingers.

To be fair, he gave himself the same treatment, shovelling chocolate into his mouth and gulping at the bottle. We were united in the brutal sugar crash, the stunning hangover, huddled on the sofa in front of *Fitzcarraldo*, shivering so hard we couldn't read the subtitles. I hate the humourless little guy in all those dumb films. I hate the witless plans to find legendary gold or move a ship across a continent, and the misery it causes for other people. What a fucking waste of everyone's time. But Liam was happy, and he held me tight, tucking a blanket round us, nuzzling lovingly into my hair.

And the next day we were out in our running gear at 5.55 a.m. I'd wrecked my form and added forty seconds to my time, and that hurt worse than anything.

I still can't look at Colin's smug, slobby, sticky-out-tongued face.

Luckily, the cake section of the supermarket was generally off limits. For me and, I hoped, for my clients. Amara had gone to choose between bistro- and Italian-style salad bags and I was alone, focused on counting the carbs in lentil pasta, when Ollie came round the corner of the aisle.

'Cassie? I thought that was you. Great to see you.' He came in for a cheek kiss and I went stock-still. His hair was sticking out above his ears, and he was trying to grow a little beard on the point of his chin. He looked like those pictures of satyrs I'd seen in Crete.

'No horns?' I said, because seeing him had given me a shock and I'd lost control of my mouth.

He stiffened. 'Horns? Oh. You mean I'm the devil, or something?'

'I was thinking more like a goat.' I let out a bleat.

'Jesus, why did I think I could have a normal conversation with you?'

I wanted to be normal, I did, but I'd warmed up now, I was too far gone. 'Whoooo's going trip-trap over *my* bridge?'

'Cassie. Stop it. I know last time was . . . I'm sorry about that.' He gave a little eye roll, as if the last time we'd seen each other he'd done something harmlessly embarrassing, heckled a wedding singer or pissed on a wheelie bin. 'But be serious, will you?'

I shook my head slowly, remembering a brilliant autumn day, the scent of bonfires in the air.

Three months post-break-up, and Liam was still following me on runs, calling from new or withheld phone
numbers, waiting for me outside coffee shops. I was
working at a gym in a converted police station that
offered high-heel aerobics and face yoga. That's where
Ollie found me.

I was leaving; he was looking at the class timetable in
the porch with a faintly disgusted expression. I could
imagine him repeating the class titles to someone later, a
sneer on his too-red lips: '*Fifty Shades of Slay.*'

I pushed up my sunglasses to greet him, but I was
wary. His car had been outside my flat several times in the
last couple of weeks – Liam sending someone to act as
sentinel when bootcamp sessions were keeping him busy.

We did an exchange of small talk, asking after each
other in broad categories. But I knew what was coming.

'Liam's in a bad way.'

'Okay.'

'Okay? That's all you've got? This break-up is really
hurting him.'

'Thanks for letting me know?' I slid my sunglasses
down, covering my eyes again, and stepped into the
street. It was a quiet street, full of Victorian houses with
white tier-shuttered windows. Every single resident had
complained about the nineties rave workout sessions the
gym offered and I tended to keep my head down on the
way in and out, hiding the logo on my T-shirt.

Ollie didn't mind being conspicuous, didn't mind raising his voice. 'Cassie, why are you being like this?'

I didn't answer. I was backing off, putting pavement between us.

'I don't get it. What's he got to do to make you happy?'

'I don't want him to do anything.'

'Are you seeing someone else? Cassie . . . can you stop walking away? I'm talking to you.'

'I don't want to talk here.' A woman was looking out of a nearby window, pretending to dust the slats of a blind while she watched two of our regulars – wearing headbands and leg warmers – pour their half-drunk coffees into the pot of an olive tree. One of them lifted a neon-gloved hand to wave. I crossed the road.

'Okay. I've got my car,' Ollie said. 'Let's talk in there.'

'I don't think so.' I kept walking. The hedges along the path were all green and gold, and a seagull called and spun through the air, and I thought I was free, but then Ollie rushed ahead to cut me off.

He smelled like an old betting shop: tobacco and damp wool coats. He didn't smoke, he wasn't wearing wool; he had this aftershave that was meant to be manly. He was a joke, but not a very funny one.

We were next to a dark BMW, shiny and confident. He opened the door.

'Get in, Cassie. Come on. We need to talk. I'll only take up five minutes of your time.'

He crowded me till I had to make a scene or fold down onto the leather seat. I folded. And I scuffed my head on the frame and knocked my sunglasses into my lap, but he didn't notice or didn't care. He just shut the door and ran to the driver's side. It was so clean in there it felt like a fancy taxi, and it smelled new: carpet and cleaning products. The creak of leather as he settled in beside me. We were close, and when he turned I shrank back against my door.

'Go on, then, get it over with,' I said, feeling like a sullen teenager.

'Where's this attitude coming from?' He may as well have added 'young lady'. That was the tone. I was a stubborn student, someone who needed telling off.

I made myself sit up. 'Ollie. Listen. Liam made me sick.'

'It sounds like you were already sick.'

'No, seriously. He put something in my food . . .'

'Oh, God. You really are mad. He told me what happened. It's not his fault you ate your weight in sugar and then had a bad reaction. You're what? Thirty, nearly? You need to take responsibility for your actions.'

'Okay. Thanks for that.' I reached for the door handle, but he gripped my arm.

'Wait. Wait. Look. I get it. Liam can be intense, laser-focused. Bit of a stickler. That doesn't suit everyone. You should have seen him at uni . . . He was . . .' Ollie shook his head. 'But you were so good together. *Are* good together. And he's miserable without you.'

A traffic warden appeared on the corner.

'Ah, shit. I'd better move the car. Buckle up.'

I sighed, but strapped myself in and leaned back into the seat as we pulled into traffic. The engine was quiet, the ride comfortable. Ollie knuckled the seat warmer on and I thought, if he could just not talk for a bit, I'd be quite happy here, watching the bare branches of trees against the sun, feeling the heat relax the muscles in my back. No such luck.

'Liam's at my place.'

I went stiff. There was intent in that statement.

'Why don't we just go back there and I can give you a few moments alone?'

'No. Ollie. No. I don't want to. Stop the car. Let me out.'

He kept his eyes on the road, his hands tight on the wheel. A children's playground flashed by in a blur of blue and red. 'I'll let you out at my place.'

'Why are you doing this? It's nothing to do with you.'

'It's got a lot to do with me. Who d'you think has to pick up the slack at work? Liam's missing sessions because he's so worried about you, feels he has to check up on you.'

'Harass me, you mean?'

'No, actually, I don't mean that. Cassie— D'you know what, that doesn't even matter. This is my business because Liam's my friend. And the least you owe him is an explanation after your psychotic behaviour.'

'*My* behaviour?'

'Honestly, Cass, at this point I don't really see the attraction. He's put up with your manipulation long enough. But it's Liam's choice—'

'No, it's *my* choice. And I don't choose him.'

'So there *is* someone else?'

'Ugh. No. I choose no one. I'd rather be alone for the rest of my life than with Liam.'

'No need to be a bitch, Cassie.'

'I'm just trying to make you understand. It's over. Me and Liam. We're done. This isn't cute, Ollie. You're not doing a good deed. You're not Cupid. Right now, you're kidnapping me.'

'Fucking hell, you're dramatic.'

I shrieked my frustration at the ceiling, which probably didn't do much to convince him of my sanity. The sun flashed in at us as we passed some tall railings, making our movements jerky and frightening. At the end of the railings there was a church with a sign: *Try Praying*.

'Calm the fuck down,' Ollie said. 'I told him I'd pick you up, but I didn't agree to put up with a tantrum.'

'You said— You mean Liam put you up to this? All that "Just talk to me, Cassie" stuff, that was a lie? I cannot believe this.'

'Shut up, we're nearly there.'

In his temper, he hadn't noticed the lights change and had to slam on the brakes to avoid hitting another car. My sunglasses fell into the footwell, but I didn't have time to retrieve them. I opened the door.

Ollie flung out a hand. 'Cassie, don't be a cretin!'

The light turned green. He tried to pull away, but I was half out, stumbling. I fell onto the pavement and he reversed across my path, bumping over the kerb. But I was free, forcing myself up, legging it, limping along

an alley between two houses, Ollie shouting my name
as I ran.

'Doing some food shopping?' he asked now, as if he'd
never tried to kidnap me.

'No, Little Billy Goat, I'm here with a client. She needs
some encouragement with her diet.' The supermarket
was too bright, the hundreds of food packets lurid,
mocking. My face was stiff, my breath shallow.

He ignored the first part of my sentence; he was good
at ignoring bad behaviour. 'You're still working as a PT?'

'Yep.'

'Good for you.'

Yeah. Good for me. I could see Amara squeezing a
loaf of olive and basil sourdough. I needed to get to her,
make her stick to the list. Maybe I'd make her carry a
pumpkin home.

'Still at that pole-dancing place, are you? The rave
place? Where weightlifting means wearing a heavy layer
of make-up?'

'Nope. Sorry to disappoint you.'

'I'm not disappointed. I'm relieved. Liam thought you
were too good for that gym.'

'Did he?'

'Yeah. He's changed, Cass,' Ollie said, picking up a
pack of quinoa and tossing it from hand to hand.

'I'm sorry?'

'Liam. He's had a tough year. A tough few years. We all have. People choosing gyms over parks. CrossFit over bootcamp. We lost a few franchisees and had to dip into our reserves. Then you left, and then . . .'

'Then what?'

He sighed. 'I know he went a bit mad. I've never seen him like that. But he really loved you. Loves you. Even now.'

'Lucky me.'

'Don't be like that.' God, the disapproval. How did he do it? And so fast.

I put down my pasta. 'What do you want, Ollie?'

'Liam decided not to contact you. He sort of gave up for a bit. On everything . . . But I told him you'd want to know. I think you will want to know.'

'Know what? Get to the fucking point.'

'Always so aggressive.'

'No. Not always. Only when my ex-boyfriend's pompous mate is winding me up. What should I know?'

'About Liam's brain tumour.'

It wasn't hard to act shocked, it was shocking news. But I was a step ahead for once. I was prepared. And Amara had stopped groping the bread. Progress.

'Yeah,' he said, his tone so, so serious, gravelly, like he'd been practising. 'It took us all by surprise.'

'How long have you known?'

'A few months. It's not cancer. It's not like that. But it's bad. He tried to keep it from everyone. I don't think he wanted to admit it to himself, but I knew something was up. He got a blinding headache during a sponsorship meeting, very nearly cost us the deal. That was a while ago. I'm over it now.'

'You're so magnanimous.'

'What?'

'That means forgiving.'

'This isn't really the time for jokes, Cassie. This is real life here.' A long indrawn breath; dealing with me required patience. 'Anyway, the point is, I've been wondering if some of the more . . . extreme parts of his behaviour were due to this . . . thing in his head.'

'Maybe.' So he was admitting Liam had acted badly, madly. Once that would have helped, would have stopped me feeling like I was mad myself, but it didn't matter any more. I'd lost track of Amara, and the next aisle was full of fancy foreign snacks – true temptation. I really needed to go and supervise. I'd *promised* I would supervise.

'A tumour can do strange things to you. Physically,' Ollie was saying. 'It can give you fits. I mean . . . Cassie,' he dropped his voice, 'he's fucking blind. At the moment, anyway.'

That got my attention.

'What d'you mean, at the moment?'

'Well, it's not certain, but he'll probably get the tumour removed in a few months – I mean, he's on a waiting list – and then there's a possibility they can perform some kind of procedure that takes the pressure off the optic nerve, or rather, they reinflate the tube that the nerve runs through. Something like that. I've looked it up. It's worked in other patients, apparently.'

I couldn't react, not for a moment.

'Optic means related to sight,' he said, because he couldn't resist either.

'So he'll see again?'

Something surged into my throat – up up up – and kept coming. Or was I falling? It was all the same. I'd thought I was free, but I was still stuck in the labyrinth.

'The consultant is hopeful. And I found a woman online who had this decompression thing done. She'd been blind longer than Liam, and her vision came back within a couple of days. Ish. So, yeah. Probably. Hopefully. But it's been really hard on him, Cassie. It's changed him.'

He kept talking, but I'd stopped listening. Liam was going to see again. I was running out of time.

I watched Liam closely when he came for his training that week. He was different again. Not actually different, not physically, but I had yet another lens to study him through. This Liam was temporary. This Liam, the one I could look at, get close to, would soon be gone. His tumour would soon be gone, and his sight might be back.

My blood had pounded in Ollie's wake. I'd nearly dropped the pink Prosecco Amara had been trying to load into her trolley, and although I'd kept my hands in my pockets after that, she'd noticed. Wondered why I was shaking.

But there's always an excuse for trembling muscles. Fatigue, for instance, when you've reached your limit and been made to keep going. Or low glucose levels, when you haven't had enough food and the fridge is locked. Or cold, especially a swift drop in temperature, like a warmed-up body suddenly submerged in an ice bath.

'Wasn't sure you were coming,' I said, taking Liam's bag, clenching my fist against a tremor. 'After you didn't turn up last week.'

'Yeah. Sorry.' He gave a roll of the shoulders. I'd last seen them in that rain-slicked coat, hunched against weather and traffic and attack. They were still hunched, I realised. And he was stiffer than usual. 'I messed up the times. It's hard keeping track,' he said. 'I haven't got the hang of the calendar yet. It skips sometimes, or the voice goes too fast.'

'You always have the best excuses.'

'Does that mean I'm still in trouble?'

'You asking to be punished?'

'Depends on the punishment.'

I didn't need that kind of temptation. I settled him on the cross-trainer for a short warm-up, and then went to stow his stuff, to fill his water bottle, and to wonder at the realness of him. At his legs forcing the pedals to move, at his hands gripping the handles, at his breath disturbing a few strands of bun-escaped hair. It was amazing that he could be here. Amazing that anyone could be. Everyone in this gym. How fragile it was, life. All of that. All that chance.

'You're leaning a bit,' I said, touching his hip, causing a yelp. His hold spasmed on the pistoning handles. 'That was dramatic,' I said. 'You injured?' I was already pulling up his T-shirt, the shiny fabric slipping over my fingers. Underneath was an atmospheric nightscape – mottled purple sky interrupted by a large yellow moon. 'Oh, you *are* injured.'

'How's it look?' He'd stopped moving, the cross-trainer's whir suddenly silent.

'Sore.' I grimaced at my face in the mirror. At *Steph's* face. Not my manager's face, not mine. I stared at this half person I'd invented, that I was pretending to be. She looked sly. She looked unreal. She looked like she shouldn't be here either, like she should have died last week. And I guess I'd have been saying goodbye to her, too, if Liam hadn't come back.

But he was here and he'd taken the hem of his T-shirt in his own hands to show, yes, an ugly bruise on his back, but also a very neatly cut set of abs, the muscles shifting slightly and constantly as he held steady for my inspection. He'd lost the roll of flesh from week one, and a woman walking the treadmill in an oversized Cookie Monster vest top was openly staring. I didn't blame her.

'Looks like you've already had some punishment.'

He shivered, cooled by my breath. 'It's healing, though?'

'I'm not a doctor.' I wasn't medical, I didn't know about bruises, or tumours, or the *decompression of the optic nerve.*

'Well. It doesn't feel so bad now.'

I ran a fingertip over the skin, felt his flex. 'How'd it happen?' I asked, but I was hardly listening. I'd forgotten what he was like, what this part of him was like, the way the muscles hummed, the dips at the back of the waist, the line of strength each side of the spine.

'Tried to walk round the park alone. I got disorientated, lost my balance.'

'Alone?'

The self-deprecating smile slipped. 'A route-learning officer took me out last week, helped me memorise the directions, the grooves in the pavement, where the railings and the pelican crossings are. I'm meant to be able to do it alone.'

'After just one session?'

'It should have been easy.'

'But why are you in such a rush? Don't you have the rest of your life to learn routes or whatever?'

'I guess.'

'It's not like you're ever going to see again. *Is it?*'

He didn't answer. He seemed to be staring at the wall, but of course he wasn't.

'Well, are you?'

'No.' He cleared his throat. 'No.' And there were tears, actual tears, two, then three, then four, filtering through his beard. 'No. I'm never going to see again,' he said.

He inhaled jerkily, filling his lungs in two, three, four heaves. His shoulders shook. He didn't cover his face and it seemed so naked, so raw, his eyes neither searching for nor avoiding mine. I had to turn away instead.

The woman on the treadmill was glaring; the Cookie Monster seemed stunned too. This probably didn't look great.

'I'm sorry,' I said. 'I'm really sorry, Liam. I didn't mean . . . Let me get you some tissues.'

I ran to the office and found Tommy relacing Steph's trainers while she sat and self-consciously curled her socked feet under the chair.

He pointed at Liam as I tried to get by. 'What is it with you and making your clients cry?' Tommy asked. 'Didn't take you for a tough-love type.'

I ignored him. 'Mind passing me the tissues?'

Steph reached for the box and leaned to look at Liam, who was resting his forehead against the cross-trainer, the picture of despair. 'What happened?' she asked.

'He's had some bad news,' I lied. 'About his condition.'

'Maybe you should wrap up your session.'

'Yeah. Yeah. Good idea,' I said as I jogged back across the gym. 'Very good idea.'

Cookie Monster woman was slowing her walk, eyes on Liam, she was stopping the workout on her watch, she was gathering her bottle and towel. She was setting her face for sympathy. But I got to him first.

'Here.' I pushed some tissues into his hand. 'I don't think it's a good idea to carry on with the session. I don't want to risk further injury.'

He pressed the tissue against his face, then blew his nose. 'I can cope with injury.'

'Can you?'

'I've got a fucking brain tumour – how much worse can it get?'

'I don't think you're in a good state for a workout.'

He swallowed with a thick, wet sound, nodded. 'Fine. My taxi won't be here for a while, though,' he said. 'Is there somewhere I could wait?'

'There's . . . there's a café across the road.'

The café across the road was a bowl place. You know – everything's a bowl: breakfast bowl, salad bowl, rice bowl, broth bowl. I pushed through the door and breathed in the steamy smell of spring onions and noodles. I felt exposed and nervous; I'd stepped out of the gym and into the real world and I didn't know how to navigate here. Liam seemed taller, bigger, stronger. He seemed more familiar. Was it the same for him? Would he, could he, know me without the camouflage of coloured lights and the fizz of a high-frequency soundtrack? Even my thoughts seemed louder, clearer.

I tried not to think too hard, tried not to look back. He held my elbow lightly, half a pace behind, his stick held in the other hand, the end running over the pavement, the step, the vinyl tiles. He was hesitant but trusting, the connection between us gentle but insistent.

In the café I read out the menu and Liam ordered pork broth with extra mushrooms, a mineral water, some edamame beans. 'Want anything?' he asked me. 'I'm buying.'

'I wasn't going to stay.'

'This hour's mine, isn't it?'

'For training.'

'What's the difference? Order something.'

I knew what he was doing – buying his way out of vulnerability, asserting his financial dominance.

'Jasmine tea?' I said.

'That's free. Pick something I have to pay for.'

'Thanks, but I don't want anything. I'm on a fast day.'

That shut him up. The king of calorie control. We found a table, and I put his hand on the stool so he knew where it was, slid onto the seat opposite and sat up straight to try and get our eyes at the same height. He turned, as if to show me his profile.

It was worth showing. The line of his forehead and nose so clear, as if he was in better focus than everyone else, his face given just a few more pixels. And to think I used to kiss those pixels.

My tea came in a tiny handleless ceramic mug, and I warmed my palms on the bumpy glaze, rubbed the rough line of clay at the base.

'I'm really sorry,' I said again. 'I was insensitive.'

'That's okay. You're making it up to me.'

'Is that what I'm doing?'

'I hope so.'

'And . . . the tumour . . . ?'

A raised eyebrow. '*My* tumour, you mean?' He was indulging me; his tears had certainly dried up quick.

'Yeah. Er. What happens about it?'

He pulled some bamboo chopsticks apart and rolled them. 'I should get an operation, eventually.'

'And that means . . . ?'

A slash of chopsticks across his head. 'They cut the fucker out.'

'But your sight?'

He made a show of swallowing, shaking his head, letting the corners of his mouth turn down. He made a show, but here, in the café, it wasn't such a convincing performance. Here, sitting face to face, I could see how his jaw muscles twitched.

He was lying. Trying to get sympathy from me, from any woman, from innocent little Steph, the personal trainer who'd been so very nice to him. Apart from the odd hoodie to the face, I amended; apart from a few sips of toilet water.

'So, when's the operation?'

He shrugged. 'I have a scan next week. Before our session. I'll find out after that.'

'But, like, days, weeks, months?'

'Weeks. I think. But it seems pointless. They may as well leave it. What do I care about having a stroke, about death?' He spat the last syllable, but even that seemed calculated, as if saying the word was a price he was prepared to say to keep up the act.

'One pork, extra mushrooms.' A jangle of napkin-cushioned cutlery as the waitress put Liam's food down in front of him. He thanked her, felt for the edge of his bowl, poked the chopsticks in and gently mixed everything together.

I picked up the soy sauce pot. He used to avoid soy

sauce, the high salt content, the oestrogen triggers. What good had that done him? He needed to loosen up a little. I waited till he moved his hand to take a bite, then tipped the spout over his bowl and added a long stream. He didn't notice. I set the pot back in the wooden holder and picked up a bottle of hand sanitiser instead. One pump, two. He swirled the liquid in, taking his punishment, unknowing.

Week Seven

A week later, I was standing in an alley. It was eight o'clock in the morning and my shoulder was skinned from a brush against brick, my feet freezing from puddle-riddled tarmac, my mind wrapped round and round with hazy intention. Wrapped like my keys, all the bite, all the malice, muffled and softened. They poked their sharp brass and silver points through wool as I squeezed, a nasty surprise inside soft, balled socks, but no surprise to me.

Last week I'd poisoned Liam's soup. Why had I done it? If the waitress had seen, if she'd come over and asked me, what would I have said? That I was angry because he'd lied to me, and because I'd been unable to confront him, and because a confrontation was the last thing I wanted, but also the only way I'd get the answers I needed.

Luckily she hadn't come over, and hopefully she hadn't seen what I'd done. And luckily there *was* another way to get answers. Because surely there would be some in his flat? I still had the keys for that flat.

When we'd been living together, Liam had kept a tight grip on his keys but had often found reasons to lend mine out – a friend asking to store something; a heating engineer wanting to check the boiler; a colleague needing to pick up some equipment. And then my sawtoothed little set, the closest thing I had to a weapon, would take a long time to come back to me, notched in the pocket of the borrower, or lying neglected in a drawer. Or, as it turned out, neatly stashed in Liam's car, where he'd hidden them while he acted as my gaoler – letting me in and out of the flat, locking up at night so I had to ask to leave in the morning.

'Want to frisk me too?' I'd asked once.

'What?'

'Well, you probably should, I might be smuggling in contraband.'

He gave me that grim smile. 'Cute, Cassie. Very cute.'

I was always cute, hadn't he worked that out yet? I was also careful, and cooperative, and I had actually let him frisk me. It had been pretty fun. But I was weary of the prisoner role play. I wanted to come and go freely; I wanted the means of escape.

So the next time I regained the keys, I knew I needed copies. It wasn't that I didn't trust Liam, exactly, it was just for convenience, it was just so I didn't have to bother him, so I wouldn't have to annoy him and hear the nasal sigh he made when I was being demanding, unreasonable, too much.

And I did it during my lunch break, when Liam wouldn't be around, not because he wouldn't approve, or because I'd be in trouble, or because it would cause an argument, but because I wanted to take the burden of this decision off his shoulders.

The locksmith's was just a kiosk in the mall, and when I arrived the shutter was down. A note on it: *Back in 5*.

I only had half an hour for lunch, but it was cool, I was fine, I was breathing, I could wait. I had to wait, because who knew when I'd next have the keys.

I found a pound shop and made myself browse in a quiet aisle. I was hyper. Wild. Seeing everything. Every jagged, glaring colour, orange and leopard print and turquoise. Every brain-warping shape: curly mermaid tails and thrusting sunburst mirrors, fake orchids with their little snapping beaks. I shut my eyes and felt along a shelf until my hand caught something soft. A pair of fuzzy socks. I squeezed them tight as I went to the checkout and bought some suspiciously brittle chocolate.

When I got back to the locksmith's my heart was steady and the shutter was open. I inhaled the shoe-polish scent and grinned at the aproned man behind the till. He took the keys for copying and I tapped on the counter while the machine scraped away at the metal.

'How long will it take?'

'I'm nearly done with the first one. You in a hurry?'

'Yeah.'

'Well, you should have left more time for this, then, shouldn't you?' He was probably younger than me, but that apron made him think he was someone's patriarch.

I couldn't tell if he was teasing. 'I was here ten minutes ago. Not my fault you shut up shop halfway through trading.' That's what my dad would call it – 'trading'.

'Gotta take a piss now and then. I'm on my own here.'

'You tell all your customers about your toilet habits?'

'Only if they ask as nicely as you.'

I gave a laugh then. He'd earned it.

'There's one.' He handed over the first copied key and I flipped it several times on my palm. It was still warm. I dropped it into one of the fuzzy socks.

'And that's the other two. Want a ring?'

'You ain't even proposed yet,' I said, but the locksmith just rolled his eyes. My heart hadn't been in it. I'd forgotten how to deliver that kind of line.

I paid and added the other keys to the sock, balled up the pair and stuffed them in the pocket of my body warmer.

Back at work, I unwrapped the white-streaked chocolate. I didn't eat it. I looked at it, I sniffed it, I *remembered* it. Then I chucked it in the bin. And I didn't use the keys. I stashed them in my sock drawer, but I felt better knowing they were there.

I felt better now, peeling them from the socks, holding them in my hand. I'd had all week to think, stew, ruminate. I'd had all week to work myself up. But probably, really, I wasn't going to do anything. I'd cancelled all my morning clients, but I wasn't going to do anything. I'd dug out the keys, and was standing in the alley opposite his flat. But I wasn't going to do anything.

The alley was a mossy stretch of cracked tarmac and cigarette butts where someone could easily lounge and not be too conspicuous. I'd stared along it when I'd lived with Liam, wondering idly about the smokers who hunched their shoulders into the (surprisingly rough) brick wall.

Strange to be the one in the alley now, staring in the other direction.

He'd told me he was going for a scan this morning, but not the time of the appointment, so I'd arrived early. The morning was warm but dull, sun not yet burning through last night's rain clouds.

In the flat, I could see Liam moving through the three rooms that faced the street. Big windows showed him in the bedroom, pulling his hair into that habitual bun; in the kitchen, where he turned on the tap, flicking water onto the pane of glass; in the living room, feeling for something on the windowsill. He was slow, a hand on the wall or door frame. I had to stand well back to see a few feet into the rooms, and there were long moments when he was out of sight. Still. I knew where he was. I knew what he was up to. I knew he wasn't causing any trouble. I liked that.

A group of kohled-up students walked past, smoking, eyeing my cosy little alley. I looked at my phone as if I was waiting for someone. Smoking would have been a better cover, obviously, but there were limits to how uncomfortable I'd make myself in this pursuit. I plucked at a bit of moss while I thought about that. Pursuit as in a hobby? Or pursuit like I was in pursuit?

I had to wait nearly an hour before anything happened, before a taxi drew up outside the building, the engine idling, the driver checking his phone, just like me. It was nine fifteen when Liam disappeared from his second-floor stage, and a couple of minutes later when he appeared on the street. The taxi driver guided him into the back seat, slammed the door and drove off.

Time for me to heft my bucket, Marigolds, bleach – I'd come with props for my cover story, in case I met the scarf woman again – and amble, inconspicuously, to the security door. Not so secure: my key slid smoothly into the lock.

Inside, a smell of cooking, cleaning fluid and bike oil. The stairway was dark at the bottom of each flight of steps and light at every turn, where a window filled the wall. It was all so familiar. Up I went, my trainered feet silent on the rubber treads, up until I found the door. It had a peephole in it, which seemed amusing to me.

I fished out the final key, felt a click of submission, then the beautiful give in the hinges as I pushed open the door. Memories held me at the threshold for a moment before I stepped inside, breathing the breath he'd left behind, wading through his scent, his skin cells, his dissipating energy.

On went my Marigolds as the door – a fire door – clunked shut behind me. I remembered that clunk, how the action of the closing arm was not quite smooth.

The corridor was T-shaped, living room on the left, bedroom on the right, kitchen in the middle. There was a tiny spare room, a bathroom and some cupboards on the internal wall. It was a nice flat. I'd been impressed when Liam first brought me here. The wide, sectioned windows let in a lot of light: in the living room the view was all tree; in the bedroom, pure sky.

I needed a wee after all that waiting, and I listened to the rattle of the extractor fan as I sat on the loo. Such a familiar noise, the ticking and whirring like the sound-track to a movie I hadn't seen in years. I shivered, wiped, flushed and washed. Shifted my feet over the pebble tiles that I'd persuaded Liam to have laid, dried my hands, and thought, well, why not? And squeezed the bottle of expensive no-parabens shampoo into the bath.

In the living room, things were neat, spartan. It looked as though a pathway had been cleared in the proud expanse of carpet. A folder by the TV told me when a carer had been in to help Liam, squiggles after the names and times. I stared at the remote for a while, then picked it up, took out the batteries and put them back the wrong way. It was petty and it made my heart race, and I liked it.

I went through the drawers in the Ikea unit, hoping for something medical/official, but everything was categorised and everything was practical. There'd been some effort made to help Liam find the categories by adding tactile stickers to the drawer fronts. I picked them off.

Then I muddled the categories: hats in with joint braces, hand sanitiser in with stationery, headphones in with sunglasses. Sunglasses. Here were the sunglasses I'd abandoned in Ollie's car. Peachy-brown, two-hundred-and-fifty-quid Chanels. For a second I didn't want to touch them, even with gloves on. It was like greeting myself, somehow, a shadow self. A Cassie who was brighter, more sure; a Cassie who planned to sit in the sun. I wanted to be that woman again. I put them on. They felt right on my face. Heavy, grounding. The world became a little mellower, smoky, subdued.

It was through those glasses that I spotted the letter pinned to the wall. A letter about today's scan, then, underneath it, another inviting him for an *endoscopic trans-nasal transsphenoidal decompression* of his optic nerve. It was close enough to Ollie's description to be true.

There were more sheets behind this letter, a dozen, perhaps, dating back to the spring.

We see from our records that you failed to attend the practice for your ophthalmology appointment.

He'd missed several, the letters getting increasingly stern.

There is no charge for wasted surgery time, but you may be placed on probation . . .

We are very concerned that you have not managed to attend any appointments . . .

This letter is a final warning.

So he'd been putting off treatment, or maybe diagnosis. Not a surprise, knowing Liam, and it told me something about the angst he'd felt over losing his sight, over the realisation that he was ill.

I got out my phone, took a note of the date for his operation – six weeks away – and went to the kitchen, to the fridge, where I pinched turkey ham out of its packet, chewing as I surveyed the rows of prepped meals, zoodles and salad dressings. He'd ditched the ready-made lasagnes I'd seen evidence of in his bin. I wondered if someone else had been coerced into sorting this food for him. It all looked delicious.

I took a scoop of Greek yogurt, then a second. I crunched on a carrot and a sugar snap pea pod, then wolfed down a raw chocolate protein bar. I tipped a punnet of blueberries directly into my mouth. Smiling around them. Imagining him coming home. *Who's been eating* my *fruit?* This wasn't a labyrinth, it was the Three Bears' cottage. I wondered which chair I should break. I was quite likely to break one; my family couldn't be trusted with chairs. That had been the consensus, anyway, when my great-uncle's birthday party was being planned.

'You should see the ones the village hall is offering,' Auntie Sal said. 'Look like they're made of sugar or something. We're not using them. If you want to sit down, you can bring your own chair.'

She was organising the event and I didn't want to argue, but I didn't know how I was going to carry furniture on the train. Gavin said he'd hire some for the weekend, that a conference company owed him a favour, but I knew better than to rely on my brother. I'd been complaining to Liam, but I hadn't expected him to come with me, to offer to drive me.

'It's an eightieth birthday party. With all my family. I don't think you'd enjoy it. There won't be any caviar.'

'Someone's got to keep an eye on you.' He'd already carried two folding chairs down four flights of stairs, and was wedging them into the car.

'I can't get up to much mischief with that lot.'

'Your mum said they're getting a toffee crumble cake.'

'You want some?'

'No. But you do. Don't you?'

That's what this was about, I realised, holding the car door and working my heels between stones. He was worried I'd eat birthday cake.

He closed the boot. 'Not just birthday cake, Cassie. There will be a hundred kinds of carbs on offer. Mini quiches and cheese sticks and pizza bites, knowing your family.'

'What's that supposed to mean?'

'Only that it'll be Iceland's favourites.'

'And what would your family have? M&S? Waitrose?'

'I don't know. Probably not. I doubt any of my repre-hensible relatives would self-cater.'

It took forty-five minutes to get to the village hall, a low garage-type building in a scrubby wood, the lichen on the trees lurid in the party lights. The hall had been hung with plasticky decorations: cut-outs of flamingos and hula girls, little Union Jacks and dinosaur balloons, all mixed together.

'What's the theme?' I asked my auntie Julie.

'Oh, whatever we had left over from the kids' parties. The flags were already here – it was VE Day last week.'

They'd splashed out on coloured lights but not both-ered to turn off the overhead fluorescents. And there was a bubble machine that was mostly being ignored, even by the children. I put my gift on a table and went to greet Stan. He was sitting on a sturdy wooden dining chair in the middle of the dance floor, begging to be moved because he was sick of the women dancing around him.

'I'm not a pole,' he was saying, bubbles popping unnoticed on his bald head. 'Even if my name *is* Stanislav.'

'I didn't know your full name was Stanislav,' Liam said.

'It's not,' I told him. 'That's his idea of a joke. Hello, Uncle Stan. Happy birthday.'

'Oh, Cass, love. Get me a beer, will you? There's a good girl.'

The bar was shut; the family had bought their own alcohol at wholesale prices. As I made my way to the drinks table, all I could see were my aunties' flabby arms and my cousins' double chins. I felt disloyal noticing those insignificant features. Especially when everyone seemed so happy to see me.

'Cassie. Gorgeous one. Glad you're here.'

'Oh, Cass. Give us a hug, girl.'

'Cassandra! Look at you. So slim. And who's this?'

Liam was pinched and kissed, and won immediate favour by offering to run to the shops to buy extra ham for the kiddies' sandwiches.

'Lidl, is it?' he asked.

'That's right, love.'

He started to leave, then came back for a kiss, pulling me close in front of everyone. They thought that was romantic; they didn't hear him whispering in my ear, 'Nil by mouth, Cass, till I get back.'

He'd been right about the mini quiches. They came out while he was still at the shops. Also oven pizzas, cocktail sausages and bowls of Bombay mix.

'Old Stan loves a bit of Bombay mix.'

'Only with a gin,' he shouted, his voice creaky with the effort. I gave him his beer and was handed a baby.

My cousin Jenny was fidgeting. 'Just for a sec, Cass. Everyone else has already done a hold and I need a wee.'

She disappeared and I moved to the edge of the dance floor, then to the doorway of a room stacked with those chairs Sal thought were too fancy for the likes of us.

Royal blue with gold trim and delicate carved legs. I
could see why they'd made her nervous.

I tried to bounce the baby, who was not happy to find
her mother gone, and I was getting a decent warm-up
from the swaying movement, the semi-squat, by the time
Liam got back.

'Doesn't suit you,' he said.

'What?'

He nodded at the baby, who was now settled nicely
against my collarbone. 'Don't go getting any ideas.'

'I wasn't.'

'Women gain between twenty-five and thirty-five
pounds during pregnancy. It would be a waste of all your
hard work.'

I handed the baby back to her mother. It's not like I'd
been wanting one. But I felt a bit restless as I held my
palm over the cooling wet patch of dribble on my chest.

I watched the dancing, wanting to join in but knowing
I wouldn't without a glass of wine. Liam wasn't so shy.
He gave me a plate of drying carrot sticks to hold and
told me to stay where I was, then asked Uncle Stan's wife
to dance. She was thrilled, smoothing her lacy blue dress
and clinging to Liam as she box-stepped delicately over
the floor. He couldn't have made a better move.

'What a good boy,' people said. 'Well done, Cass.
Don't you want some pizza, love?'

I was proud. Pleased. It was me had brought the nice
lad to the party, the handsome boy. A gentleman who
would dance with the older ladies. I lapped up the praise,

but it wasn't enough. I was hollow, ravenous, humming with hunger. I wanted that pizza.

As Liam twirled my great-aunt, I turned and let Sal push a slice into my mouth.

She chuckled. 'Leave me my fingers, love, will you?'

I rested my forehead against the wall while I chewed, feeling the warmth come back into my limbs. I didn't need much, just this, just this, and maybe one more bite.

Then a different kind of warmth: Liam at my back.

'What d'you think you're doing?' He drew a fingertip through the tomato sauce on my cheek.

'It's a party,' I told the wall. 'It was one bite. It was Sal.'

'You thought I wouldn't notice.' His voice was low, excited. 'But I knew you didn't have any self-control.'

He refused to look at me for the rest of the evening. I sat on one of our own folding chairs and drank water to wash away the salt from the cheese, and laughed when someone teased me for not joining in, for not drinking, for not eating, laughed as I resisted holding the baby again. I laughed and said I was fine, that I wanted nothing, but I was made of want. I was a gigantic, shapeless monster, stretching, gurgling, lumbering, and I was a sliver of bone, brittle, whittled, lonely, afraid.

I tried saying something to my mum after Stan had been driven home, explaining quietly as we unhooked balloons from the car park gate. Trying out the phrases for the first time. 'It's just that . . . sometimes . . . he won't let me eat.'

'What is it?' she asked with a sigh. 'Don't we give you

enough attention as it is? You have to go and make stuff up?'

'No. I'm not . . . I don't . . .' I jerked my face away as a clutch of balloons hit me on the chin.

'Everyone wants to be thin, Cassie, and in good shape. You hear women every day wishing they could find some system, some secret to sticking to a diet. Well, you've found it. Be grateful.'

And, yeah, diet and exercise are all about having a system, a way to survive the pain. Hunger pangs and getting a stitch and feeling your lungs burn. They're hurdles at first, but then, as you get fitter, they start to diminish, to seem small and easy to clear. Going hungry because of someone else is not the same. Just as pain inflicted by someone else is not the same. I loved my next-day muscle ache, even the very worst kinds. But I didn't want to be hurt. I liked fasting because it was an achievement and I could feel proud of the results. But I didn't want to be starved.

A few days after the party, I came home from work to find a lock on the fridge.

I was resting my fingertips on the steel wire when Liam came in. 'Thought we should give your willpower a rest,' he said. 'This way you can relax. The decision of what to eat, or whether to eat, is out of your hands.'

'But——' I said.

'And it means I'll be doing all the cooking. So you can sit back. Let me look after you.'

'Okay. So . . . can I eat now?'

'No.'

'Liam . . . ?'

'Wait till dinner.'

It was three o'clock. I hadn't had lunch and I needed to prep for evening clients. 'I just want a yogurt.'

'Wait till dinner.'

'Or some chicken. Liam . . .'

He walked away. Left me holding the fridge as if I could appeal to the appliance for help. It hummed, un-cooperative, almost defiant, flaunting itself and its status as the home's hub. And I thought about turning it off the way my uncle had switched off my nan's fridge after she died, and I remembered the shocking silence in the seconds following the unplugging, and how it was the first time I'd really believed she was gone.

But Liam wasn't gone. He was in the living room, waiting to see what I'd do. I found a packet of pumpkin seeds in the cupboard, made a black coffee, filled my mouth, filled my stomach. I could be uncooperative and defiant too.

The next day the cupboards were bare.

I finished chewing the blueberries and shut the fridge door. Opened it again, battling its resistance. Closed it. Opened it. Look at me, I thought, just opening Liam's fridge whenever I want. And I could have left then, after that triumph, but there was still the bedroom to explore.

It was neat. The chevron curtains pulled back and tied, those arrows pointing up or down, depending on your outlook.

The right bedside table held a lamp with daylight and night-time settings to comply with circadian rhythms, as well as the dangling ends of phone, watch and earphone chargers. On the other table was a pink-shaded lamp. Fluffy, fluttery, filmy. I knew without switching it on the warm glow it gave a room.

He'd kept our dark green checked sheets, soft, worn, washed and tumble-dried. The bed was made and it looked cosy. A sick fatigue smoothed my tense muscles and I sank onto the mattress.

I was so tired. I'd eaten . . . well, the yogurt alone was probably two hundred calories. And now I was having a crash. And tomorrow it would all begin again. Waking up early to get in a workout, pushing myself, upping my reps, prepping my food, weighing my food, logging my food, planning for every molecule that went in my mouth. It never ended. If I skipped calorie-counting now, I'd have to fast later, and hunger pangs felt dangerous these days.

I lay back and rested my phone on my ribs. The weather had brightened and light bounced off the screen, forming a watery square on the wall. I breathed deeply, making the square shimmer wildly over the plaster. Then

I tightened my muscles and breathed without letting the square move an inch.

It was so warm there, the sun heating the end of the bed, dust dancing in the rays. I shut my eyes and bundled into the duvet, arranged my head on Liam's pillow.

Once during the months he was following me around, appearing out of nowhere, trying to get in touch, I found he'd parked his car on my street. It must have been the twentieth time and I was so tired of fighting that I went and leaned on it, pressed my cheek against the roof, muttered, 'Come and get me.' Luckily the alarm went off, which shocked me out of it. I ran back to my flat and locked the door.

There was no alarm in Liam's bed. I could easily fall asleep. I wanted to fall asleep. I was so tired I could cry; I was so tired I *was* crying. For all the hours and days and years ahead of me. For the rest I could never let myself have. My tears soaked Liam's pillow, and I sobbed until I began to drift off, my body humming and happy, warm and aligned.

Someone shouted in the street below. I gave myself a pinch. Oh God, I really was Goldilocks. And Daddy Bear was going to come back and find me in his bed. I looked at the window, wondering if I could jump out of it if I had to. Two storeys up. Thirty feet down. Best to resist the attempt.

I lifted my head from the tear-wet pillow. Would it still be damp when Liam went to bed tonight?

Probably not; that square of sun would creep right over it, dry it out. I shivered as I left the warmth of the covers and knelt in front of the wardrobe. I wasn't a cliché, I didn't touch his clothes or cut out the crotches of his trousers, I just patted the pockets of his winter coat and, when I found his car keys, slipped them into my own pocket. That VW was just sitting there, asking to be driven.

Liam's old gym bag was at the back of the wardrobe, the black canvas a little dusty, smelling of shoes and stale air. I was surprised he hadn't chucked it – once something was no longer in use he usually jettisoned it from his life. I'd taken that as a warning in the first few months of our relationship, not realising that being dumped was the opposite of my future problems.

Inside were a bunch of mementos. Couply photos of us that had sat on the bookcase in better times; medals we got from a 10K run we did together, the ribbons plaited; an old Fitbit that I'd had engraved for his birthday; a hat he'd bought me during a daytrip to a zoo.

I smiled, but it was no time for smiling. There were other things in the bag.

A roll of duct tape, a bunch of cable ties, a Stanley knife, some bleach spray, a wad of microfibre cloths and a pair of rubber gloves. I held the gloves in my own gloved hands.

What had he been planning to do with these? For a moment I pretended I didn't know, that it was a mystery, that a simple, innocent explanation would suggest itself if I kept my mind blank a little longer. But I knew. This was a kidnap kit, a murder kit, a kill-Cassie-and-get-away-with-it kit. I felt a dragging, phantom pain, suddenly frightened in a way I hadn't been for weeks.

In the front zip pocket I found keys.

They were attached to an alpaca key ring Tanya had brought me from Peru – her last holiday before kids. The little corn kernels were missing from the alpaca's saddle bags and the bead eyes had come unstuck, but I'd thought the snazzy colours would stop my mum losing this set. Because, yes, I'd given these to my mother. The spare set to my old flat, to the place where I was living six months ago.

So Liam and I were both key hoarders, key thieves; both storing the means to each other's spaces, waiting to let ourselves in, to take something or leave something. Keys really were power.

But my power had been confined to a pair of balled socks and his jostled against a more sinister collection. Had he been planning something worse than terrorising me from afar?

Had he been planning to tie my limbs? To shut my mouth with a new kind of tape? To cut me with that knife? To cause enough mess that he had to clean it up? It was hard to focus on these questions because, as I left the flat, I imagined him soaking blood off the laminate floor of my old hallway, his face splattered, red running under the rubber gloves and seeping into his cuffs.

*

I could have called the police, but what would I have said? That now my ex-boyfriend was blind, I'd thought it was time to break into his flat? To search the place, mess with his stuff, eat his food. I wasn't sure that'd end well.

I could have called my mum, but that would have given her a chance and I wanted to see her eyes, wave the evidence in her face. So I knocked, without warning, on my parents' draught-proof front door and waited, staring at the fuzzy alpaca key ring, furious enough to subdue the fear.

Mum had on a pale pink jumper, *Kindness Always Wins* written in sequins across the front. I didn't bother with hello.

'You gave Liam the keys to my last flat.'

'No.' She wasn't exactly shocked by my question. Point against her.

'You're lying to my face, Mum.'

'I'm not. Would you come in? You're giving the neighbours a show.'

I followed her into the house. It was too hot. It was always too hot.

'What have you got yourself worked up about?'

I dangled the keys between us. 'This is what I'm worked up about.'

'Well, I can't remember ever giving Liam *any* keys.'

'He had this set – the set I gave you – in a bag in his bedroom.'

'You've been in his bedroom? Are you . . . Have you made it up, then?'

'No, I've – it doesn't matter. That's not the point. The point is your betrayal of my trust.'

'Oh, *betrayal*, is it?' The word was too dramatic for her, for real life, for taking seriously.

'Yes. Betrayal. Why, Mum? Why did you give my abusive ex-boyfriend the keys to my flat?'

'*Abusive.*' She was this close to rolling her eyes.

'Mum.'

'Well, I've already said I didn't give him any keys . . .' She was working out her defence in front of me as she put the kettle on, as she reached for mugs. 'And that's true. But,' she put the mugs down, 'I have to admit, I did wonder if he'd taken them. He visited us. Before Christmas.'

'And you didn't tell me?' I was screeching, competing with the hiss of the kettle as it reached boiling point.

'And I did notice they were missing a few weeks later. But then you moved anyway, so I didn't see it mattered. And he didn't do anything with them, did he?'

'What's going on?' Dad came in to look in the fridge – a family trait.

'Liam had my keys.'

'He got in your flat?'

'No, the keys to my old place.'

'Oh. Well.' He turned, Petits Filous in hand, and left again.

Mum raised her eyebrows at me. *There we are*, her eyebrows said, *that's the reaction you can expect from anyone reasonable.*

'What else have you given him?'

'Nothing.'

'What did he want when he came here before Christmas?'

'What he always wants. To talk about you. To ask about you. To make sure you're well and safe.'

'You mean you told him my movements.'

'Look, I know what I'm supposed to do. Okay? I told him I couldn't give him your address or your number or tell him where you worked or any of that. But I don't see why I shouldn't have a civilised conversation. He never did anything to me.'

'He terrorised your daughter.' Oh, *terrorised*, is it? my brain said, because part of me didn't believe it either. The past had stopped seeming real. In my mind, Liam had always been blind – how could he have terrorised me? How could it have mattered that he was standing outside the café where I was ordering brunch? I must have been making it up. I must have wanted attention. I must have *wanted* him to see me, when he couldn't.

'You don't half exaggerate, Cass.'

But, no, I wasn't exaggerating. I had evidence. 'There's a bag in his wardrobe with . . . it was . . .' How to describe it so she'd understand? 'Mum, what would you do with duct tape, rubber gloves, a knife, cleaning products and somebody's keys?'

She thought for a second. 'What kind of knife?'

'Not a butter knife, if that's what you're hoping.'

'What do *you* think he was going to do?'

'I asked you first.'

She poured boiling water into the mugs, jabbed at the teabags with a spoon. 'He said he wanted to surprise you.'

'Fucking hell.'

'Language.'

'Mum!'

'All right, all right. Yes. Fucking hell. Fucking hell!' She threw the spoon in the sink. 'He said he was going to do something romantic and you'd understand . . . Fucking hell, fucking hell, fucking hell.' She threw the mugs in the sink too, hot water splashed her jumper, dripping down the sequins, but she didn't flinch. 'He said everything would work out and everyone would be happy. That he'd make you . . . that there was no way you'd turn him down again.'

'Yeah, well. Can't turn someone down if you're dead.'

Now she'd tell me I was being dramatic. But nope. She took the mugs from the sink, fished out the handle that had broken off one of them. 'I'm sorry, Cassie,' she said, pressing the rough edges of china together, trying to make them fit. 'And Gavin's in fucking Malaga like he always is when he's needed. Fucking hell.'

'Okay, Mum, that's probably enough now. And Gav wouldn't be much use, you know that.'

'I heard smashing,' Dad said, returning with his empty fromage frais pot. 'You holding a Greek wedding in here or something?'

'Or something,' Mum answered.

*

I was full of tea, toast and biscuits by the time I left my parents, carb-loaded for a marathon and only a bus ride to get through. It was nice to be weighed down by something wholesome, though, something real, in my belly not my brain.

I looked at the sky as the bus drove along; the thick cloud seemed to mirror my own muffled state. I'd been afraid and I'd gone to hide my face in my mother's lap, and for once she'd patted my hair and told me I was a good girl. And because she'd been on my side I'd let her fill me with white bread and full-fat milk, sugar and palm oil. I still felt dirty when I thought about the bag, the ties, the knife, about what might be in Liam's mind. I still felt like I was the one covered in it, stained by it, soiled. But I was okay. I'd be okay. When I got another look at Liam's face, at his eyes, I'd get a reminder, would feel his vulnerability in contrast to my power.

I got up as the bus pulled into my stop, lurching and panting like an exhausted animal, its hot breath ruffling the long skirt of a woman waiting to get on. Above the skirt she wore a T-shirt that read: *My personal trainer has four legs and a tail.*

Woof.

Her personal trainer was with her, dragging her arm back, sniffing under the long plastic seat in the shelter. It was one of those curly types that everyone gets in the city, furrowing its curly brow as it explored the other passengers. It gave a bark as I stepped off the bus, a real bark, and the crowd of queuers scattered and regrouped.

I'd have liked a dog, one day, maybe. A creature bouncier than me. Someone to growl so I didn't have to. I was thinking I might ask my landlord about pets when something caught my eye. No, not something. And not caught. Because, as the bus pulled away, I *saw*, I straightforwardly *saw*, orange trainers.

They were at the far end of the road, the legs above them bare, tanned, male. A dark jacket, hood up, no hair visible, and from this distance the face was nothing, a pink blur, a promise of human features. But I was sure he was looking at me, I was sure he was coming towards me.

I felt a swoop of fear, but I couldn't run. I couldn't. I was stuffed and sick and sluggish, half a loaf like a brick in my stomach. I was living one of those dreams where you're running and not getting anywhere, except I was awake and I wasn't even running, instead I was stooped, resting my hands on my knees, trying to find the energy to move. How stupid to eat, to give in, to choke all the gaps that made it possible to move. I may as well have poured concrete down my neck. I'd never get away from him, whoever he was, whatever he was planning.

It *was* disgusting to eat doughnuts. I *had* undone my training. And now I could only hide. I could only hope to be invisible. But the bus had left with most of the other pedestrians, and I was exposed.

I pushed upright – it was an effort with my thudding heart so heavy – and turned a corner, heaving my weight, dragging my feet. My shoulders had hunched up to my ears and they relaxed painfully as I stepped into the first shop I saw.

A fancy plant shop. The floor dirty plywood, the pots glazed into galaxies. It was warm and sweet inside, some white flower winding its scent through the air, through my trembling trachea. I pretended to study a *Monstera something-something* while I really scanned the street.

People passed, people in brogues, in boots, in flip-flops, people in conservatively coloured trainers. Several curly dogs came by. Then that flash of orange, the legs, the shorts, the hood pulled up, directing the face hole at the shop windows on the other side of the road.

I moved back into the steamy dark of the shop. Air like a clump of dough in my throat.

'Looking for anything in particular?' The girl at the counter was plump and pretty, verdant with green shimmery make-up and a septum ring.

'Um,' I said, sure I could feel the glow of orange somewhere behind me.

'Are you a new plant parent or expectant?' She raised her silver-lined eyebrows. She was only half joking; she knew how people were about their *photosynthesising phriends* – there was a poster on the wall displaying those exact words.

I stuck out my belly, rounded for once, puffed up with processed grains. 'Few weeks to go,' I said, rubbing at the ache. 'Hope it's not a monstera I'll be pushing out my vag.'

The girl's guffaw made me smile, made me brave. I

straightened and looked through the window again. Orange-trainer man had stopped by the Robin's Egg bakery, and as I watched, he stepped inside.

'Fancy a creeping fig?' the girl asked.

'No, I'm just keeping an eye on him.'

'What?'

When I turned, she was holding a tiny pot with a tiny plant nestled in the soil.

'It's free.'

'Why?'

She shrugged. 'I screwed up the cutting. It might not survive.'

As I reached for the plant, my phone vibrated. *No Caller ID*. I hit cancel, but my hand shook and I dropped the pot, soil powdering the floor. 'Shit. Sorry. That wasn't a very good start, was it?'

'It's okay.' The girl crouched and scooped the roots and compost back into the pot. 'Like I say, you're its only chance.'

And this was my chance: Orange Trainers was still in the bakery; the street was clear. I thanked the girl and dropped into the cold, breezy high street. The air out here was not sweet, not humid, it was sharp and tasted of car fumes. My heart rate was too high. I could feel the shifting blood in my chest, in my neck, in my carotid arteries, all that undigested food forcing my organs, my veins, my oxygen into narrow channels. I'd gummed myself up, couldn't even turn to check if anyone was following me, so I just plodded forward – hoping, trusting – the tiny fig plant shivering, giving away the tremor in my hands.

'You look like shit,' Tommy said as I walked into the office. Big, tall Tommy. He was physically solid, if nothing else. I wanted to hide behind him. 'You look like you've seen . . . Oh. *Have* you seen it?'

'Seen what?' For a second I wondered if there was a ghost, if the gym was haunted. Were the orange trainers a vision? The soul of an angry would-be weightlifter?

'The mouse,' Tommy said. 'Did it give you a scare, hey, Cass? Would have thought you'd be brave about it.'

'Mouse?' I said, setting the fig on the desk. 'What mouse?'

Apparently, a tiny pelty body had been spotted scurrying past the water cooler – an early-morning exerciser had flushed it from the stack of steps – and now Tommy was stalking about with a cricket bat while Steph went to call an exterminator, outside, where no one could overhear. Whoever it was that kept gifting us cake was also attracting vermin.

I watered the fig, then went to give the mats a thorough clean, searching for any holes in the skirting boards, ready with wire wool and Polyfilla. This was also the ideal level for watching and analysing trainers. I ticked off red, yellow, green, blue, indigo and violet. No orange.

I tried to be subtle about the colour-matching and the mouse-hunting – I didn't want to put off the members – but it was difficult not to wince at every crumb of protein bar dropped from a packet, or to start whenever the reflection of an orange Sainsbury's bag flashed on the newly polished floor. It was hard not to flinch and peer and follow some deep hunting impulse.

Although these days, my hunting impulse left something to be desired. My killer instinct was non-existent. I pressed the pad of my thumb against the one short nail on my right hand, the nail that had broken against Liam's jacket. I'd saved his life. I'd dragged him back from the brink. Snatched him from the jaws of the underworld. (Well, okay, I'd stopped him stepping off a kerb.) I felt cheated. I hadn't had all the information. It wasn't fair.

For over an hour nothing orange entered the building, unless you counted a half-drunk bottle of Fanta, and the cleaning had calmed me down, the repetitive action a balm. The mats shone, the air smelled of bleach. It was like the aftermath Liam had been prepping for with his microfibre cloths. I wadded the damp blue paper roll and chucked it in the bin, put the cleaning spray back in the office, gave my tiny fig another tiny drink of water. The leaves shuddered when Tommy came to get me.

'Your client's here.' He gestured with his head, watching Liam sweep the floor with the end of the cane. 'Poor guy.'

I got up and let the swivel chair roll into the filing cabinet. 'Sympathy now, is it? You said he shouldn't be allowed to train here.'

Tommy shrugged. 'He's in better shape than most of

my clients. Wonder how he keeps it up. He only does one session a week.'

'He's got a regimen at home.' I assumed. He always used to – one for both of us. Precise minutes of warm-up and weight training, focusing on muscles in isolation, narrowing in on inches, millimetres of tissue. Then cardio. Then foam rolling to get the blood flowing, rolling, rolling till the skin on the backs of my thighs bruised. Then, finally, body-weight exercises: planks, crunches, bridges. Push-ups.

'Down. Eight more.'

Grit under my palms. The smell of the almond wood polish he'd used to clean the hallway floorboards. My arms shaking. 'Liam, I can't.'

His voice cold. 'Eight more. Or you don't get dinner.'

I laughed the first time he dropped that threat. I wasn't laughing when I had to watch him eat sweet potato and feta frittata, my mouth watering at the smell of fresh parsley and chives, at the way the crumbly cheese was just melting into the deep orange of the potato.

'You're angry with me,' Liam had said, digging his fork in.

I'd swallowed and lied. 'No.'

He'd swallowed his bite of frittata. 'You think I'm being cruel.'

'No.' That wasn't a lie, but I could feel the tension in my body. He'd never been cruel. Not deliberately. It just *felt* cruel.

'But you want dinner?'

I shrugged.

Fork raised, a chunk of egg and feta, a glassy sliver of onion. 'D'you think you've earned this?'

I *was* being honest when I said, 'No.'

It was the correct answer. He finished his last couple of mouthfuls and then got up, got behind me, got his hands on my shoulders. I leaned back and could hear the slight gurgling of his digestion.

'Thank you,' he said, circling his thumbs over the knobs of my spine, warming the back of my neck. His breath, all feta and chives, made my stomach rumble. 'Thank you for finding the strength to resist. I can't do this alone, Cass. I can't always do this alone.'

I was hungry, but it wasn't so bad, because Liam was kind, he was loving, and his thumbs had found the aching sinew just under the line of my shoulder blades. He wanted me to achieve my goals. That was all. And I needed to help him, to step up.

Last week, I'd watched him eat again. I'd sat in that café while he ferried mushrooms from soup to mouth, noodles trembling in the chopsticks' grip. Last week,

I'd pumped some sort of isopropyl alcohol into his food. But only a couple of squirts. This week the knowledge of the evil he'd been considering, packing for, spread through me like a poison, like DNA-damaging free radicals.

My heart was tense, my heart was diseased, my heart had been broken and it couldn't be trusted. I was sweating with the effort to keep it beating. I'd been sweating more than usual recently, and the tops I'd worn when training Liam smelled strange. I'd thought it was the residue of fear, until I remembered the Armani Code I'd been liberally spraying to throw him off my scent.

'Hey,' he said as I took his bag. A bag so like the one in his flat that I shivered at the sight of it. 'Sorry I'm late. A new carer's been added to my rota and she seems to have moved all my stuff around. I can't find anything.'

Yesterday that would have cheered me up, but I had no space for it. 'No worries, mate,' I said.

'Also, I've been walked all over the hospital getting different scans, so I feel like I'm well warmed up. Think we can skip straight to weights?'

'Sure. Whatever. Come to the mats.' My gleaming mats – what a pity he couldn't see them, couldn't admire my work.

And to think there was a mouse, somewhere. Hiding, cowering, waiting for its chance. I looked into the corners of the room, narrowing my eyes at crevices, at shadows, at a raisin from a granola bar.

'How am I looking?' Liam asked, pulling my gaze

back to him. 'I feel like I have more muscle. Am I imagining it?'

He wasn't. He was gaining muscle fast, his body remembering its shape, colouring inside those lines.

'I've been doing a lot at home. Callisthenics. The basics. And I've set up my weights again. It feels good, and it helps to pass the time. Like prison, or something. Or maybe not that. But what d'you think? Am I making progress?'

'Yeah,' I said. 'You're getting there.'

He seemed disappointed by my miserly assessment, but I couldn't give him more. I couldn't praise him. I'd had to perform admiration all the time when we were together, when we were working out.

'You need to check your left elbow,' he'd say. 'You're locking it.'

'Thanks,' I'd answer. 'Your form is perfect. Beautifully smooth motion.'

I was always ready with my superlatives: beautiful, amazing, wonderful, awesome. There was a danger that I'd do that with clients, that I'd cover up every awkwardness – when they weren't doing a movement properly or could manage fewer reps than last time – with compliments, with sweet talk, with ungrammatical acclaim: *You're doing brilliant.* It's lying, but perhaps it's the good kind – fitness success is ninety per cent psychological, after all. What's the odd insincere 'Impressive' or even 'Inspirational!' if it encourages someone to keep practising?

EMMA HEALEY

But I didn't want to fall back into that with Liam. I was going to be objective, I was going to keep to the facts. I would never use a superlative again.

And having seen what he was keeping in the wardrobe, I was cautious. I was reserved. I didn't want to push him or make any mischief. I'd opened that bag out of mischief, and look where it'd got me.

'You're quiet,' he said, unfolding to standing, and holding out his dumbbells after a set of skull crushers.

'Am I? Sorry.'

'Something happened?' He turned his face to me. The picture of sympathy.

'Man troubles,' I said. It was basically true.

'Right. Of course.'

'Why of course?'

'Well. You're the type to have trouble with men. Beautiful girl like you.'

I spun to look at him, one weight on the rack, the other dangling from my left hand. 'But you don't know what I look like.'

'What, because I can't see, you mean?' He shrugged. 'I can still tell.'

I felt a tiny twitch of relief at him confirming his blindness. 'How?'

'You have an attractive energy. A sexy aura. You're in good shape, too?'

'Oh, you mean you're assuming I'm hot because I'm a PT.'

'Well, are you in good shape?'

'Depends on your definition.'

'Let's see,' he said.

And then his hands were on my waist. I made a tiny noise, a breathy little retch – he probably didn't hear it over the music – but I didn't stop him, didn't move. Couldn't. When was the last time he'd had his hands on me like this? Two years, just about.

'Good obliques,' he said, gripping. His hands were warm, big, heavy. 'You're really solid, you must have good core strength.'

He was jerking my waist now, sharp, shallow movements, back and forth, to test me. I tensed automatically, and he pressed his thumbs in at the front. I turned my head. A twenty-minute spin class was finishing, three rows of people stretching their arms into the air as their legs wound down and down. The light in the foyer changed and the scene became watery.

'Nice abs,' Liam said. 'Now let's check if you skip leg day.' Already bending to find the front of my thigh, he patted it. 'Nope. You're definitely putting in the work here, too. Big quads. I bet you're a squat queen.' He squatted as he said it, always in competition, and ran his hands down over my calves. I felt my legs move involuntarily, like a nervous racehorse before the starting bell. 'Great gastrocs.'

Below me, his brown hair was shiny, the man bun he'd pulled it into neat. I was still holding one dumbbell. I could hit him. I could swing my arm high and let the fifteen kilos of metal do the rest. My own kind of skull crusher.

But he was up again, closer now, running those searching fingers along my arms, squeezing my shoulders, assessing biceps, triceps, deltoids. He stroked my trapezius and I watched his face, close to mine. I could feel his breath, smell the hint of cumin – I remembered how he used to like chickpea curry for lunch.

Those blank eyes seemed to look inwards, and I wondered if he could recognise me from the feel. I thought of my mum asking if my blind client ran his fingers over my face. He'd known my physique intimately, once; he'd practically sculpted it himself. But I had a bit more padding now, was a bit curvier. I focused less on cardio and more on weights, on strength, on those pleasingly effortful pull-ups, perfecting that smooth upward thrust.

Last time he'd touched me, I was lean, hard, my body fat so low that my periods had stopped. These days I had bigger biceps, but also breasts, more flesh on my hips, a squidgier inner thigh. My periods had come back. Those parts of me were like the weeds that grow through abandoned buildings, proof that nature always wins.

Could I have picked *him* out with my eyes closed? I used to think I could, had thought he was familiar on the outside, at least. It had been the inside that was alien: a terrifying stranger wearing the face of the man I loved.

'Your pulse is a bit fast,' he said, feeling for my subclavian artery. 'It's like a little butterfly in there.'

I thought my pulse might stop at that. But obviously not. Obviously my body just went on and on. I was a machine. A set of muscles to train. Of course he thought

I was attractive. He didn't need to see me. What more could he want than a body that he could define, dissect, make into an anatomy lesson?

'You're in great working order.'

His hands rested on my shoulders, palms over my collarbones, and he wasn't pushing, wasn't even giving me his full weight, but I was trapped. In the middle of the gym, surrounded by colleagues, I had nowhere to go.

I swallowed and he felt it, and there was a look of triumph on his face. He'd got something he wanted: my compliance again, my obedience, my fear.

Week Eight

I called Tanya, left a message, left another. Braced for her saying 'I told you so.' I'd take it: the censure, the derision. I'd accept it. I was dumb and disgusting, careless, stupid. I was everything she'd thought I was, and I should have listened.

She never got back to me.

I knew because I checked my phone every few minutes. I didn't watch TV, I barely slept. I was too warm all the time. I needed to pee. I needed to move. I walked into shops and then straight out again, unable to concentrate long enough to buy anything.

Finally, I went to the gym and rowed. Fifteen minutes, twenty, twenty-five. My shoulders burned, my sit bones ached, I struggled to match my breathing to the movement, but after another few minutes the change came, that moment when it becomes beautiful, easy, what you're made for.

In my mind, the movement turned from a row into a climb – not up a rock face, or one of Jamal's walls of bolt-on holds, but up a tree. Up, up into a massive tree, a pine or fir, which stood with ladder-like branches, letting out its winter-spice sighs. And I was forcing through wet needles, rainwater dripping down my spine, and it was just inhales and exhales, and suddenly stopping wasn't necessary, or even possible. The tree might grow, might stretch up for a hundred miles, it wouldn't matter. I could keep going.

There are stories of people climbing trees in North American forests and never coming back down again, disappearing for ever. I wonder if they were like me, if their bodies felt like mine, and they just couldn't stop climbing.

After forty minutes, I was high enough, sore and smiling as I tucked the handle against the machine. I gave my back a cursory stretch as I uncurled from the seat and Tommy raised his bat, thinking I was signalling, then lowered it in disappointment. He'd been trying to get the job as assistant manager and seemed to think personally dispatching the mouse would make him the obvious choice.

'Enough of the guard duty,' I said, dragging a jacket up my sweaty arms. 'You'll never catch it with a bat anyway.'

'You know that only makes me want to prove you wrong?' he said, with rare self-awareness.

I hadn't applied for promotion. I could still feel Liam's hands on my waist, and I suddenly, desperately needed to be out of reach, needed to be gone, hidden, before he regained his sight. I liked this gym, but there were others. Cheaper places where no one ever wiped the equipment or replaced the worn rubber on the machine handles; fancier ones with pools and cafés and spas; yoga studios and CrossFit gyms. I could work somewhere else. I needed to work somewhere else.

But if I had to move, I wanted a *job*, not just the opportunity to advertise on a crappy pinboard while I worked twelve hours a week as an unpaid cleaner. I'd had enough of that. So I got my CV together, my certificates, my best professional outfits. I got interest, I got replies, and a few days later, I got an invitation for an interview at an upmarket 'leisure club'. It was a relief.

The sight of Liam's car, still in its space, was another kind of relief. The leisure club was in the middle of nowhere, past the suburbs, out of the range of public transport. I'd asked Gavin if I could borrow his car, but he'd driven up to Kilmarnock and said he wouldn't be back till November. My interview was in a week. Not much time, but enough for a temporary loan, a test run. Liam would never know, and I'd already pocketed the keys.

I hummed, for courage – half a half-forgotten tune – and crossed the milk-lit car park. It wasn't yet six in the morning and a weak mist lingered. To look round would have tempted fate, invited Liam's attention, so I kept my neck stiff as I brushed the dry leaves off the bonnet and cleaned the windscreen with some cucumber-infused face wipes. They came away black, gritted with debris, and my fingers didn't escape the dirt, but it was satisfying work, exposing the inner recesses of the cabin, uncovering a little nest I could be safe in.

The locks clunked, the sound loud in the hushed car park, and I was sure when I looked up at Liam's windows that he'd have been alerted, that he'd be looking down at me from thirty feet up, watching a crushable little Cassie scurry about thinking she was clever. But there was no one there.

I slid into the driver's seat. It was set right back and I took a few moments adjusting everything, mirrors, seatbelt, steering-wheel height, before firing up the engine. I'd been worried it wouldn't start, but it was fine, purring happily on a quarter of a tank of petrol. No atrophying here, no weight gain, no brittle muscles.

Aches and twinges usually comfort me, prove I've worked hard, but I had a nasty splintering feeling in my left lower back, and this pain was an old enemy, a tight muscle I could never quite work out, a fist next to my spine. I switched on the seat warmer to soothe it, put the car in gear, and pulled out of the parking space.

I'd done it. I was driving away. I wished we called it grand theft auto in Britain. *Taking a vehicle without the owner's consent* didn't have the same ring. I wished I had a drop-top, maybe even a cliff to drive off. But doing it alone seemed too tragic, and Tanya still hadn't called me back.

Also, I didn't really want to die. I was beginning to enjoy myself, to appreciate every mundane detail – flicking the indicator, slotting my phone into a cupholder, turning on the air conditioning. Mundane and glorious. Here I was. King of the road. Master of my domain. It was weird. To be in charge, to be on this side of the car. Liam had been the driver in our relationship, with all the driver's entitlements. He'd been the driver when we'd travelled to meet his mum.

'This is going to be good,' he'd said, tapping the steering wheel as we crawled across the bridge. 'This visit. Because you're here. It'll be different with you at my back.'

I didn't want to think about backs. Sweat was trickling down mine. It was a cold day outside, but a fucking stifling day in the passenger seat. Liam had whacked the blowers on full and the temperature to twenty-three. I was swelling inside my skin, but the driver had control of the air con, that was the rule.

'You make it sound like your mum might stab you.'

'Not physically,' he said, finally finding space in the traffic to actually move ahead. 'But there is a kind of . . . puncturing that she specialises in.' A swerve up through a wide street, just us and a few taxis. 'You're my armour, my insulation.'

'Don't say insulation,' I whined.

He changed gear. 'Another layer, then.'

'Don't say layer.'

'My safety blanket?'

'Ugh.'

'What's wrong with you?'

'Maybe I could take the wheel for a bit?' I said.

'We've barely started. I'm not tired. And you need to conserve your strength.'

'Surely it's you that needs to do that?'

'I'm used to her, Cassie. I can handle it. With you there, anyway. You make me feel like I can do anything. Like I can face anything.'

'Oh God. This is stifling.'

'What?'

'You're suffocating me.'

He stared at me long enough that I was worried he wouldn't stop at the next queue of traffic. But he did, his attention sliding in and out of the car as he slowed diligently, perfectly, angrily.

'Can I please turn down the heat? Please? I know it's driver's preference, but I can barely breathe.'

He gave a tight nod and I leapt for the dial, showered myself in a freezing breeze, watched the city recede in a blissful chill. I spread my arms and legs and we didn't speak for several miles.

Liam's mum's house was chilly in a less blissful way, all plastery, white and chalky, little shapes above the doors and windows – triangles, ovals, berries and leaves. There was a balding gravel driveway and huge, noisy trees, wheezing in the wind.

'Darling!' Madeleine said, coming to the door, her hands up in reverence, as if she were tracing the contours of Liam's face, despite not touching him. She was very thin, with a chunky cardigan nearly down to her ankles and a polo neck underneath.

'Hiya,' he said, his voice flat, the word ending in a hard *a*, almost a glottal stop to rival the ones I used to trade in as a kid. He sidestepped into a tiled hallway filled with mud-crusted boots, avoiding her touch, pushing me forward.

She took the cue. 'And this must be Cassie.'

'Lovely to meet you.' The phrase seemed to make her wince slightly.

'Come in, come in. I've got lunch ready. I've got . . .' She shook her head. 'It's in the kitchen. I'll bring it through.'

We went into a dining room with long dark gold curtains and a big but fragile-looking table. Lunch was a small packet of Co-op bean salad in vinaigrette, some unpeeled, undercooked boiled potatoes with a lot of chives sticking to the skins, a baguette lying beached in a too-small pasta bowl, a porcelain plate of sliced tomatoes, and a huge wheel of Gouda, which sat waxy and unbreached throughout the meal. The cutlery was delicate and silver but tarnished, and nestled into horseshoe-shaped metal rings were proper napkins, the fabric stiff and starched, and stained.

'Well, *bon appétit.*'

'You sound like a waiter,' Liam told his mother.

'Do I? Is that what waiters say? These days?'

I picked up my napkin ring and studied it so I didn't have to answer. It was heavy, with little eye-shaped stamps along the curve and a blocky sun on each end, and it reminded me of the copper bangles people wear, the ones they swear soothe swollen joints.

'You're admiring my manillas,' Madeleine said.

'I . . . was wondering what they're made of.'

'These ones are bronze. Rather discoloured now. My grandfather brought this lot back from Nigeria.'

'Did he?'

'I've always thought they looked a little like teething rings. Not that I'd give one to a baby.' She sighed. 'Still, I had hoped one day to pass them on to my grandchildren.'

'Mum.' Liam's voice was a tired warning.

'Oh, fine, fine. I'll shut up. I know it's a touchy subject. I know young women today think they have better things to do than rear children.'

I looked at Liam. I hadn't had a period in a couple of months, but it wasn't because I was pregnant. We were still playing Russian roulette with unprotected sex and I'd been relieved when I stopped bleeding altogether. The intense workouts two or three times a day, and the strict fasting several times a week, had forced my body fat so low that my hormones had given up, my breasts had deflated, my hair was lank. I'd lost all my curves, my body harder, straighter.

Stopping my periods made me feel I'd won somehow; beaten messy, corporeal Cassie into submission. I didn't think of myself as a woman, or even an animal. The need to defecate was horrific. My poos came out in tiny, hard-won rabbit droppings. I was disgusted by the parts of myself that reminded me I wasn't just a machine around a brain, a set of muscles I could train and then train harder.

Eating seemed shameful. Fuel was acceptable, and I could manage if I thought of it as pouring oil into an engine. But to enjoy it? Revolting.

Luckily there was no chance of that with Liam's mum. After fifteen minutes of savouring the vinegary beans, forking them one at time into our mouths, sharing out the tomato and pushing the inedible potatoes around, Madeleine suddenly stood up.

'God!' she shouted.

I coughed into my water glass, and thought for a moment we'd missed saying grace. But no.

'I made soup!' She ran out of the room, something tinkling as the floor joists bounced, then ducked back in. 'I suppose it's a bit late, is it? At the wrong end, I mean.'

'No, no,' I said. 'Sounds lovely. I'm up for soup.'

She seemed relieved and brought me a shallow bowl, barely filled with something thin and lentilly.

'Up for soup,' she said as she set the dish down, chuckling as if I'd made a pun.

She served Liam and herself and we scooped up the few spoonfuls and then sat looking at each other.

'I do so enjoy that tree,' she said, gesturing at the

world beyond the window. 'I can tell the weather by it. If the wind is high, or what a lot of sun it's shading from the ground.'

'It's a lovely tree,' I said. 'Big one, too.'

'Yes.' She relaxed again for a moment and then jumped, pricked by a thought: 'Coffee?'

'Lovely.' Apparently I couldn't stop saying 'lovely'.

The coffee was instant, but Madeleine insisted it tasted better if you vigorously mixed the granules with milk before you added the hot water. I didn't have the heart to tell her I took it black.

We sat in the sitting room to drink it, on sofas that were hard yet sagged forward, so you were in constant danger of sliding to the floor.

'I'm very attached to that tree,' she said again. 'I sit here . . . or in the dining room . . . and I work out what sort of day it is . . .'

I nodded, and wondered if she had the beginnings of dementia. But, no, it was the awkwardness. I tried to think of something to say, to help, but it was hard to concentrate. I couldn't stop shivering. The house was beautiful, with high ceilings and tall windows onto a green-yellow lawn, but it was also uncomfortably cold and damp.

Everything was elegant, the little side tables and the pearly lamps and the inlaid chests full of tiny drawers, and yet it was also dirty. Dust and grime in the corners, upholstery that seemed wet to the touch, like the cushions in our caravan in the winter. The spindly dining table had been sticky with rubbed-away varnish, old food lingering in the wood grain. There was a drains smell everywhere, faint but sure.

My noticing was a judgement on me, though, somehow. I wasn't lofty enough to be unaffected by hygiene. There was no loo paper in the bathroom and I felt it was my fault I had to fish a packet of tissues from my handbag.

Liam didn't seem to notice, all his attention on the windows, on the garden. Perhaps he also enjoyed the weather-telling tree.

'You know him, darling,' Madeleine was saying when I came back from the loo.

I wondered about telling her she was out of paper, but I didn't have the courage.

'He was your doctor when you were small. D'you remember? Maybe not. You were very tiny.'

'I don't think so,' Liam said, his eyes finding then leaving me.

I began to sit down, slowly, demurely, not drawing attention to myself, but as I got close, his arm came around my neck and I was pulled, pressed against his body, cheek to ribcage, half lying on him. 'Liam?' I whispered.

'Well, congratulations,' he said to his mother, insincerely.

'Thank you, darling.'

I shifted a foot forward, trying to take the pressure off my obliques, breathed against his chest, making his shirt damp.

'Does Dad know?'

'Liam,' I said again, pressing a hand to his stomach and wriggling. He tightened his hold. At least he was warm. At least he smelled good.

'Mmm. He's sent me a lovely card ... somewhere,' Madeleine said. I thought she was probably looking about for it. 'And I've got an invitation for you too . . .'

I was starting to hurt, the sideways position making my waist burn, my spine ache. My neck and shoulders were held in unnatural positions, fighting against the periodic bunching of his bicep. 'Liam,' I said again. 'Let go.'

He looked at me then, almost in surprise, as if he'd forgotten I was there. His muscles slackened, and I slipped from his hold.

'I'm gaining another son, that's what Matty keeps saying. Rather sweet.'

I rolled my shoulders, gave Madeleine an embarrassed glance. I had no idea what was going on and was surprised again when Liam reached for me, settling back, snuggling, struggling on the sofa.

'How absolutely delightful,' he said, hand sifting through my hair.

'That was sarcastic, darling.'

'No. Genuinely.' Red was creeping up from his collar, gathering behind his ear, blotchy. 'I'm thrilled for you.'

Madeleine sighed. She did a lot of that. 'Let me just go and find this invitation. I want you to take it with you. I must have left it on the piano, or maybe in the hall?'

I shifted, but only a little, suppressing my desperation for spinal alignment. The movement attracted Liam's gaze.

'My mother is marrying again,' he said.

'Oh. That's what you were talking about . . . I didn't know she was seeing anyone.' I pulled away slightly to look at his face.

'And she's acquiring a stepson. So that's nice for her.' His hands moved, one over the other, up my rope of an arm.

'You're not pleased?'

'Oh, I'm delighted. Matteo has a gold medal, you know? Alpine skiing.'

'Wow. That's . . . not a very useful skill day-to-day.'

He laughed and leaned into my neck, squeezing the flesh above my elbow. 'You can't ever leave me, Cass. Promise?'

I tensed, looking at the door Madeleine had passed through.

'Cassie? I know I'm replaceable. Evidently. Eminently. I'm just asking you *not* to replace me. Please.'

'Of course,' I told his hair, and the smooth strip of skin around his ear where the red was fading. 'Of course I won't.'

He let go, knocking a moth-eaten blanket off the sofa arm. 'You said I was suffocating you. In the car.'

'That was the heat. That's all. I'm sorry.' I got up to replace the blanket, looked down at him with a smile. 'I was just hot.'

'You understand, though, don't you? Now, being here? You understand I just want one person in my life to put me first, just one . . .'

He slumped forward, pressing his face against my stomach, arms around my hips, the rest of his words muffled, and I sensed I was seeing – holding – the little boy he'd once been. Lonely, hungry for love. I wanted to make up for all the neglect, the pain, and silently promised that I would.

The door rattled. Madeleine at the threshold, invitation in hand. 'Goodness,' she said, very softly.

I felt caught, compromised, but also defiant. I stroked Liam's hair as I held her gaze. I was better than her. I loved him better, and I'd prove it.

I didn't once touch the car thermostat on the way home.

I touched it constantly on my illicit test drive, though. Adjusting and finessing it so that I was climate comfortable every mile, every minute. It was nearly ten o'clock by the time I parked near my parents' empty caravan at Selsey.

This stony outcrop of the Sussex coast with its beach and caravan park was the promised land when I was a kid. The place our grandparents always wanted to be. *Down the caravan, down Selsey Bill. Gonna see you down Selsey Bill, yeah?*

It was where we all met, uncles and aunties and cousins. Where we were allowed to run free and stay up late, where even *my* voice, my attitude – usually too loud and untamed – couldn't compete with the crash of the waves.

The tide was high now, and a few silhouetted figures were wading through the light coming off the water. I sat on a concrete sea defence and watched an old couple split a bacon sandwich. I wanted to do that one day: eat with someone. Share food with someone, without guilt or doubt. I walked to the shore, slapping the water with the soles of my trainers. It was calmish, and I was restless.

It was hard to believe I had clients this afternoon, even harder to believe Liam would be booking his taxi in a few hours, setting out, groping his way towards me. Groping, literally. His hands hadn't left marks where he'd touched me last week, but my skin prickled at those points. I'd checked several times, expecting a burn, a bruise, a brand, only to find there was nothing visible. No one would be able to tell what had happened. I could strip down to the cheap bikini I'd bought at a supermarket and still keep my secrets.

My family always say September is the best time to swim, after the sea's been warmed all summer. That's obvious bollocks; it was fucking freezing. But I forced my body forward, the waves licking up my calves, thighs, lower back. That tight muscle got a shock, got a taste of its own medicine.

Finally it was worse to be half in, and I plunged,

shivering and laughing, pushing off the sand. I got hori-
zontal. Drifted, stiffened, relaxed, swam. I swam for a
long while, up and down the shallows, checking now and
then for my pile of clothes.

A frisbee game started and moved on, a group of
little kids came to gather stones and were ushered back
up the beach for a snack, a pale-furred dog wandered
lazily into the waves, stranding its owner on the shore.
The sun was high, all the shadows hiding.

My eyes were stinging and my mouth was salt-
puckered by the time I emerged, but my back was
numbed, supple again, and I glowed inside as I wrapped
myself in a plaid shirt. I checked my phone, wincing at
the reflected glare, and realised I had to leave soon if I
wanted to be back in time for Liam's next session.

The pale dog – medium-sized, droopy-looking, hair
in its eyes – dragged itself from the surf nearby and
used one paw to dig half-heartedly through a bundle of
seaweed. The owner smiled at me as he waited, ten feet
away. He was in his thirties, with strong, tanned legs in
baggy shorts, broad shoulders under a big woolly jumper.
Not lean. A walker more than a runner. A feeder more
than a starver. The kind of guy you could split a bacon
sandwich with.

I wrung out my hair and smiled back.

'Not many people out there today.' He gestured at
the waves. 'You're a strong swimmer. Couldn't help
noticing.'

'Thanks.'

'I was impressed. You a pro?'

I laughed and flashed him, indicating my hideous bikini. 'Yeah, sponsored by Tesco.'

He looked, but he was careful not to look too long. 'Tesco'd be lucky to get you.'

A tired whine from the dog. I reached to pat its flank, the fur still running wet. 'What kind? I only know the big brands, Labradors and that, sorry.'

'That's all right. She's a bearded collie. Name's Brenda.'

I said hello to Brenda, slipped on my leggings and picked up my shoes. The breeze flattened my shirt against my body. The man looked again, but shyly.

'You staying nearby?'

I shook my head. 'Here for the day.'

'Ah.' He gave me a playfully disappointed pout.

I answered it. I liked him. I could imagine another scenario, a walk along the shore, a stop in a pub, the tang of beer washing away the salt on my lips, the night cooling while we talked, the warmth as I shrugged on his big, cosy jumper. I sighed. There was nothing beyond that.

But the fact that I could imagine it at all was progress. Liking a man, wanting a man.

Trusting, though. That would be harder. Trusting myself, trusting my instincts. I'd ignored my instincts the last time I'd been on this beach, when Tanya and her kids had borrowed my parents' caravan.

I had wanted to stay in the caravan too, of course, but Liam had lost his temper when I suggested it. A shock to us both. Life had been peaceful for a while: I acted as though I had nowhere else to go and no other people to see, and our routines had reached the level of sacred rituals. We'd made up fast, as if to erase the fight, and I told Tanya we couldn't get away from work. She'd said I sounded just like Steve.

But then, one morning, Liam surprised me: he'd re-arranged his clients, got someone else to take his classes, made a picnic, and was ready to drive me down for the day. I was too astounded to be happy, couldn't believe it until we were parking by the sea wall.

Late July, hot and dry. Pebbles clinked against each other on the shoreline, seagulls let out their distant, falling calls, and the air tasted of salt. The light was white, the sea hard to look at. I winced when I took off my sunglasses to pull my dress over my head, but it felt like a privilege to be at the beach.

Tanya had a bright-striped Peruvian throw spread over the shingle and we lay on it for a moment, pleased with ourselves. Noah, not long born, was curled into a peach towel like a soft grub in a leaf, and Ashlie hung over him, adoring her little brother, kissing him on his chubby leg. Her hair was in two tight, waxy plaits, frizzing above her forehead.

Eventually, Liam caught us up, carrying drinks from the shop and the rest of the stuff from the car. He pierced the sand with an umbrella, plunging us into relieving shade, and got out the factor 50 sun cream. He began to squirt it on me, rubbing it into my skin even when I complained he was dragging the flesh off my bones.

'Can you be less rough?'

Why did I bother asking? He pressed harder. 'Got to make sure it's all over. You can do me after.'

Ashlie had factor 50 on too, but Tanya hadn't rubbed hers in so thoroughly – the little girl was smeary, streaks of white on her brown skin.

'Look, Auntie Cass, I'm a ghost! *Whooooooooo.*'

She jumped at me and I rolled her about, threatening to bury her up to her head. She picked up sand like a lint roller.

'Yes! Yes! Bury me!'

Liam plunged into the sea, not afraid of the freezing water, and came back periodically, droplets spattering the stones around us. 'Come on, Cass. It's lovely. Come on.'

'Come on, Auntie Cass, dig! Come on!'

'All right, you two, give me a chance.'

'Didn't realise we'd brought *two* toddlers with us,' Tanya said.

I laughed, but it came out nervous. Liam wasn't a fan of Tanya, and comments like that didn't help.

When the sand proved too dry for digging and our hole was overwhelmed by a second shingle avalanche, we decided to break for lunch. Tanya pulled out shop-bought sandwiches, a KitKat and a bag of Pom-Bears. Liam unpacked a lemon-dressed cucumber salad, a separate Tupperware of cold roast salmon, and a tiny packet of crushed pumpkin seeds. A meal in three parts.

'What's that?' Ashlie asked, very suspicious.

'Salad,' Liam told her, arranging the salmon over the cucumber and sprinkling the seeds on top. 'Want some?'

'Nuh-uh.' She eyed the salad as if it would jump at her.

'You sure?' He handed me my half on a little melamine plate with a thick paper napkin and a wooden fork. Tanya pulled a face at the fancy set-up.

'I hate cucumber,' Ashlie said.

'The dressing makes it taste nice. Try it.'

'Nuh-uh. Yuck.' She stuck out her tongue, fake retched.

Liam didn't find that as charming as the rest of us, and studied her as he ate his own pretty plate of food. 'But this is good for you. Unlike those crisps you've been stuffing your face with.'

'Liam,' I said sharply. 'She's *eating*. Not stuffing her face.'

He ignored me and set aside a slice of cucumber. 'Try a piece.'

'No.' She turned her face away.

'Why not?'

'Don't like it.' She turned her face the other way.

'You haven't tasted it.'

'Don't need to.' She turned right round so her back was to him.

'Yes, you do.' He finished his last few bites.

'Can't make me.'

He stood up all of a sudden, making Ashlie scramble away in surprise.

'Yes, I can,' he said, picking up the single slice of cucumber.

Ashlie shrieked as she ran, and Liam danced after her, flapping the bit of cucumber in threat.

Tanya was laughing now. Grains of sand had stuck to the glue on the sandwich packet and must have been working their way into her food, but she didn't seem to mind. 'He's good with kids, huh? I'm surprised. Doesn't mind joking around.'

But I wasn't sure. I wasn't sure if he was joking. I watched them get further away, their figures whittled by the light. They were nearing a chunky groyne that cut the beach into sections and I didn't want them to get out of sight.

I pushed my feet into flip-flops. 'I'll just check . . .' I left the thought unfinished and hoped I didn't sound worried. Jogged awkwardly over the beach, half falling into dips in the shingle. It's meant to be good for you, running on sand – helps endurance because it's bloody knackering, and takes the pressure off injuries. I was thinking about that when I rounded the groyne.

Liam was in front of Ashlie, bending towards her, his hand on her face. She was still shrieking. I called Liam's name.

'Cass? Hello! I found an alien.'

'Lead me to your . . .' Ashlie began in a squeaky monotone. 'What was it, Uncle Liam?'

'Take me to your leader.'

'Oh, yeah. *Take me to your leader.*' The cucumber slice had been stuck to her forehead and she pretended to use it to look closely at me.

'Hullo, human,' she said, the alien voice deepening; she was trying to make me laugh.

I did laugh, but it was mostly relief, and I refused to think about why, about what I'd expected to find, or what I would have done.

'Hello,' I said to alien Ashlie. 'What planet are you from?'

'Planet biscusging cucumber.' She was giggling, holding the cucumber so it wouldn't fall off, thrusting her forehead down, then up. 'I'm looking at the sand. I'm looking at the sky.'

Liam headed back towards camp and Ashlie followed, 'looking' at everything. When we got back, she wanted to be caught again.

'I'm an alien!' she shouted. 'Chase me!'

Liam did, racing along the shingle, but Tanya soon took pity on him. 'Okay, alien. I think it's time you did some research on this planet.'

Ashlie slumped forward and the cucumber fell into the sand. Tanya picked it up and stuck it back on her forehead with a grimace of disgust.

'Run to the shore. Pick up a pebble and bring it back to study with your alien eye.'

Ashlie ran off, her chubby little arms waving.

'That's a good trick,' Liam said, leaning on his knees.

Running with Ashlie had exhausted him like nothing else I'd ever seen.

'Yeah,' Tanya said. 'You learn to sound really enthusiastic about pebbles when you've got small children.'

Ashlie came back with a shiny white stone, smooth and pure. She balanced it on her palm and we all looked.

'Hmm. What does this tell us about Earth?'

'Erm. It's rocky.'

'Excellent. What fantastic scientific knowledge your planet must have.'

'Think you can find a bigger one?' Liam asked.

'Yeah!' The pebble dropped like a meteor into the sand as she ran back to the shore.

'Now you've got the hang of it,' Tanya told Liam.

This time, Ashlie cradled a fist-sized rock.

'Ah, an interesting specimen,' Liam said. 'What about a bigger one?'

'Careful not to drop any on your feet,' Tanya called as the girl ran off again. She turned to me. 'Noah needs a change. I'm going to take him back to the caravan. I'll only be ten minutes. Do you mind? You'll keep an eye on Ash?'

'Course.'

She heaved Noah up and set off across the blistering sand. I felt exhausted just looking at her and thought I'd lie down, as Liam and Ashlie seemed to be getting on so well.

But a minute later, Ashlie's shadow passed over my eyelids. The cucumber was gone, leaving an oily smear on her head. 'Where's Mummy?'

'She went to change Noah.'

'Get back to it,' Liam ordered, hands on hips, the distance of two long shadows between us.

Ashlie took a step, but wasn't entirely convinced by my answer. She needed more, her toes scrunching into the sand beneath the stones. 'Mummy's coming back?'

'Of course, love. You having fun with Uncle Liam? Or d'you want to have a sit-down?'

'We haven't finished,' Liam said.

'I'm hot.'

'It's cooler by the shore.' He prodded her, just there, where a little crease had formed under her shoulder blades. 'Bit more running for you. Burn off those Pom-Bears.'

'Liam, come on. Kids don't need to worry about that,' I said.

'You think?'

'Yeah. Don't say stuff like that to her.'

'Someone's got to.' He was heading back towards the water, stiff and angry.

Ashlie curled under the umbrella, her resemblance to Noah suddenly stark. I could feel her eyes on me as I lay in the sun. 'It's okay,' she said. 'I don't mind.'

'But it's not nice to comment on the way people look.'

She thought about that for a moment. 'Mummy's fat, isn't she?'

I sat up, not knowing what to say. I felt like I'd been hit. 'Your mummy's curvy.'

'Liam says she's fat.'

I glared at Liam's back, at the swell of water as he sank beneath the waves. 'He shouldn't have said that. And anyway, it's not . . . it's not important.'

'*You're* not fat.'

'I just have a different kind of figure.'

'Because you eat vegetables and exercise.'

'And because people come in all shapes and sizes. Your mum's had two children . . .'

'Liam says you work hard to look like you.'

I tried to stop it, but a warm little glow formed at the praise.

'He says I need to work hard too.'

'You're four, Ash. You don't need to work at all yet.'

She gazed at Liam, his gleaming movements as he purified himself in the surf. 'Yeah. He said you'd say that.'

When Tanya came back, Ashlie was doing drills, Liam barking at her as if he were leading one of his park boot-camp sessions. The little girl was running and running and wouldn't stop when Tanya asked her to, when sausage rolls and pink-iced cupcakes were offered, when her forehead turned dark red. She wouldn't stop till Liam let her.

I knew what that kind of motivation felt like. How Liam could foster it inside you, the need to keep going, to pump, pull, pant until each memory of each prohibited prawn cocktail crisp and every wangled wine gum was purged, sweated out, shucked off. Until you were pure again.

When would I be pure again? What would it take? How long would it take?

For ever. That's what I felt. That Liam had tainted me, stained me, and unless I could reverse our roles I would always be marked as someone who'd been tricked, manipulated, deceived. I'd always be the victim. I wanted to mark him instead, to wipe my shame onto his skin.

I sat until the man in the woolly jumper was a dark speck against the bleached strand, his pale dog – the exhausted Brenda – invisible. And then I ran up the beach, stones dashing my ankles, scratching my calves.

I glanced at myself in the rear-view mirror: hair wet and sculpted by the wind, cheeks scraped clean. I looked mad. I liked it. Grains of sand detached from my skin and fell into the immaculate upholstery. I grinned, keen-eyed for the clock, heavy with the accelerator, and as I whipped past a sign for CENTRAL LONDON, I thought I caught the flash of a speed camera.

I got back a few minutes late for the session, ran to the Ladies and changed into the spare kit in my locker. As I unfolded the T-shirt I saw it was the one Liam had bought for me at Michael's bike race. Dark green, expensive. A shame to wear it while I was salty and unshowered, but there was no time to get clean.

When I got onto the main floor, Liam was there, being led towards a recumbent bike, talking to Tommy.

An aborted breath slammed through me. I was too late.

He'd caught the thread and Tommy's words were leading him out of the maze, leading him towards the light. Because surely Tommy had greeted him, chatted to him, questioned and answered him, forgotten my request and called me Cassie? It was over, it was all over.

'Finally.' Tommy, hailing me across the floor. 'Where you been?'

'Er. Nowhere. I mean, I'm here. I'm right here.' I couldn't see Liam's face in the mirror, the bike's screen was in the way, but his shoulders were relaxed, and he hadn't begun to accuse, or yell.

A mocking bow from Tommy, a gesture at the whirring machine and the man powering it. 'I started Liam on his warm-up. You're welcome. *Steph.*' He winked as he said the name, the emphasis obvious, revealing.

'Thanks,' I said, my jaw hurting where I'd clenched it. 'Well, you can, you know, piss off now.'

'Okay,' Tommy said. 'Wouldn't want to get in the way. Have a good one, *Steph.*'

'Everything all right?' Liam asked as I guided him to the next machine, slotting his limbs between metal and padding, adjusting the heights, the weights, the angles, and swearing when the pins didn't immediately lock into place.

'Yeah, fine.'

'You seem a bit . . . flustered or something.' A flirty little flash of concern before he pushed down, working his triceps. 'And you were late.' Another rep. 'And you were a bit rude to poor Tommy.' Another push. 'And you smell like the sea.'

I glanced at the office. I hadn't had time to spray on my armour; the Armani Code was undisturbed in the lost-property box.

'So what's going on?' He was resting before the next set. Letting his muscles think they were done, giving them a moment to relax before he hit them again. 'Is it a new perfume?'

I moved my face into his. I wanted to headbutt him. 'Would you rather I get Tommy back?'

'What? No.'

'You were having a cosy little chat.'

He took a moment to process that, then pressed down on the machine, forcing me back, and gave an uneven sigh, very like a laugh. 'Are you . . . jealous?'

I laughed too, drily, unconvincingly, the hem of my T-shirt bunched in my fist. 'I'm going to refill your water.'

I needed to be away, to be somewhere he couldn't hear the waves of my breath, and where I couldn't easily reach out and smack his smug face. I needed to calm down, to remember where I was. I looked at the people working out, focused and frowning, and maybe it was just my mood, but it seemed as though we were all here to punish something. The machines, the equipment.

Pounding the treadmill under our feet, dropping the weights as if they'd offended us, unsettling the battle ropes and squashing the balance balls. Squeezing and stretching and pulling elastic wires as if they were the strings of sinew exposed during a flaying.

Liam was more tender in his movements, self-restrained, coaxing the weight up up and down down, letting the iron come to rest quietly on the pad. If he was trying to punish anything, you wouldn't know it.

I fitted the refreshed bottle into the machine's holder, aware of contrasts, of the water sloshing in the bottle, of my mouth, paper-dry, of Liam's smile and my scowl.

'I saw my ex-girlfriend this morning,' he said.

I imagined myself creeping through the car park under his window, the sun glinting off the car's freshly wiped windscreen, and suddenly everything seemed to be on the other side of a pane of glass. I had the smothered feeling of wearing earphones when there's no music playing.

'*Saw* is maybe not the right word,' he said, 'but you know what I mean. She came to my place.' He let the weight stack smoothly, gravity a biddable force in his hands. 'It was a bit of a surprise.'

'Surprise?' I tried to step back, but gravity wasn't obedient to *me*; my feet were leaden, magnetised to the floor.

'Yeah. She bumped into a friend of mine last week, and he told her about me, about everything.'

I thought of Ollie in the supermarket. *He's fucking*

blind. Of course he'd told Liam he'd seen me, of course he had. And Liam would have been expecting me, waiting for my conscience to kick in, my sympathy to rush his way.

'It obviously got to her. We didn't have the best break-up, but she's been kind.'

'*Has she?*'

He tilted his head, puzzled by my tone. 'Yeah. She was concerned, and she sorted out some stuff for me, re-organised my drawers, cleared old food from the fridge.'

I could see all the stuff mixed up in the baskets, the headphones and joint supports; I could taste the blue-berries I'd chewed through. I remembered the Goldilocks feeling of lying in his bed, and then the moment I'd opened the bag in the wardrobe. He was dangerous and he was playing with me. And worse, he knew I'd been trying to play with him. I scrubbed a sweaty palm down my thigh.

'It was especially nice of her, because she had to delay her flight to help me out.'

'Her flight?' I thought of the ride down to Selsey, the race to freedom.

'Back to Singapore.' He shifted in the seat, stretched. There was a deep, satisfying click near his collarbone. 'She flew out this afternoon.'

Pippa. He was talking about Pippa. The relief raised and repelled me. I could move, I could breathe, I could take a few steps towards the door. I could see past myself and imagine Pippa swooping in, flipping her thick hair out of the way while she rummaged through Liam's out-of-date food and explained where she'd stowed his batteries or supplement bottles, blonde strands falling lightly on the sheets while she straightened his bedding. I wondered if she'd looked in the wardrobe.

'It was weird being near her again after so long,' Liam was saying. 'Without being able to see her, I mean. Her voice wasn't quite how I remembered it. More melodious, more beautiful, even. Maybe I didn't appreciate it when I could see?'

'Makes sense,' I said, muted and unmelodious. I'd slipped free of his notice, but it made me angrier somehow, more aware of the residual fear. I could barely stop myself from kicking him. By the time we were through with the power-lifting machines I was feeling vindictive. I didn't trust myself to speak.

'Free weights next, I think,' he said, sure, demanding, amused somehow, as he waited for my arm, for my steps, for my gentle guidance. 'Need to work more on my chest.' He lay down on a bench and held his hands up, expectantly. I went to find a barbell. 'I'll do three sets, maybe four. Keep track for me?'

'Mm-hmm.' My hands were fists, my teeth gritted. I'd been cheated of my confrontation, thinking it was coming, wishing for it, seeing it rise up in front of me only to disappear again, a shadow retreating in the high sun. And what was I supposed to do now, with all this hard resistance, with this aggression, with the defences I'd built and the weapons I'd primed?

Something. I had to do something.

For the first two sets I was honest. I stood by the top of his head, counted reps and collected the barbell. During the final rest, though, I took a twelve-kilo plate off the right side and added it to the left, spinning the screw with a violent flourish.

No one was in our little corner, but I kept an eye on the mirrors anyway. It was hard to lift straight and I had to brace a foot on the wall to get the weight to him in the correct position. Lowering the bar horizontally, the line of it corresponding to the bench, to the racks, to the salt-hazed horizon in my mind.

He took it. I let go. And the bar hit him in the cheek, the whole thing capsizing, toppling left and pounding onto the mat below. Gravity wasn't always his to command.

'Whoa!' I said, putting the full amount of disapproval into my voice, as if he'd been reckless. 'Steady there. Are you okay?'

I lifted and racked the weight, and he curled off the bench onto the floor, cradling his face.

'You should have told me if you were getting too tired.'

He groaned. I wanted to savour the moment, but now people were watching. A perky yoga type who'd propped up her phone to film a sequence of tangled-limb balance poses turned the lens towards us.

I patted Liam's man bun. 'Wait there.'

Our first-aid kit was in the office. I pulled an instant

ice pack from it and raced back, squeezing it to freezing. Liam was still on the mats, still on his knees; the yoga type had stopped filming, but was hanging about, adjusting her halterneck top, smoothing her seamless shorts. She hadn't realised he couldn't see her tensed glutes, her arched back, her thrust-out tits. I got down next to him.

'Here. Ice pack.' I touched it to his cheek and he flinched.

'Take it,' I said. But he wouldn't. So I knelt there, holding it to his face.

We were so close I could see the pores in his skin, tiny and clear, the tempting dip in his top lip, the straight line of his nose. He was perfect. On the outside. Had Pippa got this close to him while she was reorganising his fridge? Had she had the same thought?

Slowly, he brought his hand up to cover mine. He didn't close his eyes, he didn't need to close his eyes, but I felt he was relishing this, that he was delighted, concentrating. When I shifted, he tightened his grip, kept me there.

'Does it still hurt?' I asked.

'Yeah.' Croaky, performative.

'Want to go and sit by reception?'

'No. Just wait. Please.'

But I couldn't wait. The longer we stayed like that, squatting on the ground, the more panic I felt. His eyes seemed to be on mine and it was a struggle not to pull back, to throw the pack at him and tell him to leave me alone, get out of my head, my gym, my life. I pressed harder against his skin.

He swore, and that made me feel better. More in control. But my fingers were going numb. I watched the skin turning whiter, the nails a pink ombre. Cold is great for muscles. People always want to put hot-water bottles on their sore bits, but apart from period pains, that's nearly always wrong. It might be comforting to curl up with a heat pack, but it does nothing to reduce swelling.

Cold showers and ice baths became an obsession in the last few months of our relationship. Liam recommended them over and over. I was reluctant; I like to be warm. But I'd been having problems with my shoulder muscles – they weren't recovering as fast as they had – and I was pulling my neck more frequently. I knew an ice bath was better than rotator cuff surgery, but I wasn't keen.

'I'll try a cold shower in the morning,' I told him one evening. 'I'll let you know how that goes first.'

He seemed to accept that and sent me out for a walk. A good warm-up walk to make my muscles relax.

'We'll skip anything more intense for today.'

I was relieved and pleased. He'd been so determined

about everything recently, it was nice to see I could occasionally change his mind.

But when I got back, he'd run a bath, filled it with ice cubes. The bathroom was dark, and he'd lit a candle as if this was going to be romantic.

'Ice baths are good for your muscles,' he repeated automatically when I again started to refuse. 'They've been proven to reduce swelling.'

I knew all that, he'd told me that, but I didn't want to get in one. I undressed slowly, arguing but complying, playing for time. And I pulled away when he reached for me, trying to get my balance on the pebble-effect tiles that I'd thought were so stylish. Now they were bumpy and hideous under my bare soles.

'Come on.' He stepped into the water, the ice cubes hollow-clinking against the cream enamel.

You wouldn't have known the bath was cold; he didn't react, except for the hair on his legs lifting as if in a breeze. He splashed a handful up, across his knees. The candle flame hissed in the wax and threatened to go out.

'Stop building it up in your head,' he said. 'It's not as bad as you think.'

I thought maybe it would be like swimming in the sea, a bit chilly but bearable, invigorating. My mistake was clear the second my toes touched the ice.

I swallowed a lot of water in my panic to get out, gashed my head on the tiles. The shower curtain was dragged off its rings and never hung straight again.

'I had to hold you down,' he said later, stroking my damp hair. 'You didn't have enough willpower.'

And my muscles *were* better. He was right about that.

Liam worked through his last round of cardio without complaining. His cheek had swollen a little, and he'd probably have a bruise, but the impact hadn't broken the skin. He'd be fine. He was fine. I called a taxi for him, helped him to it – cautious, solicitous. I could be kind, even if my voice wasn't beautiful.

When I got back to reception, Tommy was waiting.

'You trying to get us sued?'

'Huh?'

'You dropped a fucking barbell on his face.'

I was ticklish with glee and it was hard to hide, the fear and anger still echoing. 'I did not. He just lost control of it.'

'You weighted it wrong.'

I ignored him, aimed the spent ice pack at the bin, threw a perfect arc and watched it land. Swish!

'*He* might be blind, but *I'm* not. If a barbell moves a millimetre out of alignment, you step in. You know this. We all know this. What's going on? You let him get hurt.'

The yoga woman chose a step trainer nearby, obviously listening. I dropped my voice to a hiss. 'Don't be dim, Tommy. Why would I want to do that?'

'I don't know. If you hate training him so much, I can take over.'

'I don't hate training him.'

'What is it, then? He turn you down?'

Yoga woman smirked at herself in the mirror, and I felt my face getting hot. 'No. I'm not interested in him like that.'

I retreated to the office, rearranged the first-aid kit and packed everything away. How much had Tommy really seen? I hadn't expected him to be paying attention. He followed me, leaning against the door frame.

'What's your deal with him? Something's going on. He said something to you, Cass? Tell me. Because I really don't get it. He seems like a cool guy.'

'You think?'

'Yeah. He set up that park bootcamp business. Made it a proper brand. It's everywhere right now. That's kind of cool, don't you think? And you know, you can buy a franchise? Use their programmes and equipment? He said he could do me a deal, actually. Pretty sweet. I really would be okay to take him off your hands if you don't want him.'

'Oh, you just *loooooved* him so much?'

'He's interesting. Knows a lot about the industry, has a lot of contacts.'

'You think he's going to get you free merch?'

'No. It's you that's into designer gear. We've got other stuff in common.'

'What stuff?'

'He also has a mental ex.'

'Does he now?' I wondered if it was meant to be me or Pippa.

'You think women can't be mental?'

'No, no. I can very well imagine you making a woman completely insane. Go on, then,' I nudged him. 'What did he say? About his mental ex?'

'She made him do all the cooking.'

I waited for a moment. 'Oh my God. Is that it?'

'No . . . I can't remember everything right away.'

'Okay . . . Should I wait, or will it take a very long time for the thoughts to form?'

'Well, he said she got herself fired from her job so he'd have to support her.'

'Right.' It was me, then. Pippa wasn't the kind of person who got fired.

'And she let her friends disrespect him all the time, and was always sneaking out to see them and flirting with other guys, and she pretended to be into fitness, but actually she was a slob. Basically, the second she got into a relationship she let herself go.'

That hurt. It shouldn't have. I knew it was lies, but my self-worth was totally tied up with my fitness, my self-control, my dress size and calorie intake, my constant workouts. The idea that I'd let any of that slip, even in Liam's fantasy version, made me wince.

'At the same time, she was constantly on at him to be fitter, to build his muscles and everything. Like, she only cared about him if he was looking tight.

Apparently she trawls gyms looking for her next sucker boyfriend. But I'm wise now. I will definitely make sure I avoid her.'

'What was her name?'

'Huh?'

'Did he tell you her name?'

He thought for a moment. 'Nah, I don't think so.'

'How you going to avoid her, then?'

He looked around the gym, thinking, but also perhaps studying the women on cross-trainers and leg presses who might be out to catch him, who might be sirens, ready to date him, then get fired and fat and force him to work out. He stared at the yoga woman on the step trainer, lust and terror combined. He seemed genuinely panicked. I considered offering to tie him to the free-weights stack to keep him out of trouble.

'I'm sure you're too smart to get caught, anyway.'

'Yeah. Well. I know what to look out for. *My* ex was a bitch too. Always cancelling on me to see her kids.'

'Wow. Okay.'

'Anyway, this isn't about me.'

'If you say so.'

'This is about you sabotaging a client.'

'Oh, *sabotage*, is it?' I thanked my mother for that condescending reaction.

'Well . . . carelessness, then,' he said, lowering the stakes.

I let out a shocked laugh. The tactic had actually worked. No wonder Mum used it so often. 'He was fine.'

'He was hurt.'

'He walked away fine. He'll have a bruise at most.'
More's the pity.

'Sure. Just know . . . I'm watching you.'

Well, I was used to that.

Week Nine

I'd dismissed Tommy's threats, but I was nervous about how his surveillance might affect my job, my plans, my power over Liam. I'd half expected him to be outside my place when I went to the shops, but that was just my conditioning, an echo, an old piece of my personality. Over the last few weeks, I'd thought someone was going through my bins, following me in a car, and searching for me on the high street. It was as if I had to be watched these days to feel alive.

I'd stood in the mossy alley again last night, looking up at Liam's windows, watching him – a shape pitching about in the half-lit interior. It felt good to be the audience instead, to know where he was, to find him contained and mundane.

To look is an act of faith: trusting you won't see something too traumatising when rubbernecking at an accident, daring to look into a seaside peep show, or uncovering your eyes during a horror movie. It's also an offence, an intrusion (imagine a stranger seeing you naked). *I can't look* and *Don't look at me* transmit the same sense of distress. Which one was I? I wasn't sure any more.

The day of my interview dawned dull, a hard pattering on the roof as I *borrowed* Liam's car again and took it up the quadruple carriageway, out of the city. I was fleeing. Or perhaps I was being expelled, a toxin in the bloodstream.

All the photos on the club's website had focused on the blue expanse of pool, so I was surprised by the new-age building with its glassy dome. Inside, it was white and bright. The café was serving salmon and you could smell it from the foyer. Women in fluffy bathrobes poked at their pink fish and spun champagne flutes by the stem. They looked happy, they looked mischievous, they looked how I would have liked Tanya and Lauren and Michelle to look in thirty or forty years.

The reception had a marble top and behind it was a circular window into the pool area, where you could see people lying on loungers. A delicate scent of chlorine mixed with the smell of the lilies arranged in a big display in front of the till, as if to hide the fact that things still needed to be paid for here.

Several older men pushed into the queue while I was giving my name – they were sorry, but they were in a hurry; they were sorry, but they had an appointment; they were sorry, but they were much, much more important than me. Apparently, no one ever bothered to remember their membership card, so I waited while half a dozen people were located on the system and verified.

Just being there made breathing easier, and it wasn't the leafiness of the surrounding area. It was the knowledge that Liam would never accidentally turn up. I could find a cheap flat in the closest commuter town, buy a second-hand car and hide myself away until I was ready for a bacon-sandwich-eating man in a big woolly jumper. I could be quiet and middle class and unremarkable. I could watch detective shows to discuss with clients, I could keep an eye out for the new spring/summer collection at Marks & Spencer, I could read the *Daily Mail* and learn the names of all the minor royals. If I was sensible with my wages, I could get a dog.

By the time the manager came to collect me for a tour, I was invested in this new life, I was passionate. This was it, the answer. Why hadn't I thought of it before?

'Thanks again for coming all this way for an interview,' Lisa said as we climbed carpeted stairs. She was very smart, hair piled up high, wearing a wrap dress and heels and carrying an iPad. No yoga trousers for her, no clipboard. 'I know people like to do them remotely now, but I wanted you to get a feel for the place and for the place to get a feel for you.'

I peered enthusiastically through the narrow glazing in the door to the cardio room, through a long window into the studio, through a tiny, steamy square into the sauna. Each time, middle-aged or elderly people turned with indignation borne of shame and I began to feel I was spying. I was too intense in my study, too used to seeing them as goals, as photos on the fridge.

Lisa, by contrast, was fine. Lisa didn't notice, didn't care; she saw only the sprung floors and the curved treadmills and the kaleidoscopic switchboard in her office.

More lilies in here, and when Lisa popped out to photocopy my passport, I pressed my face as close as I dared, breathing in that churchy smell.

'So you've been fully qualified for over four years,' she said, sliding my passport across the huge live-edge desk. 'Your insurance is valid . . . And you have an up-to-date first-aid certificate, which is great. Have you ever had to use it?'

'First aid?' I thought about holding an ice pack to Liam's face. 'Only the most basic parts.'

'Good to know. We've never had a bad accident here either. Touch wood!' There was lots to choose from, and her fingers found a long, resin-filled crack in the desktop. 'What are your strengths as a PT, do you think?'

I'd been expecting this. I had an answer ready. 'I'm adaptable. And I'm good at pushing my clients out of their comfort zones.'

It was the wrong answer. I got a sharp look over the iPad.

'Are you?'

'Er. Well, I mean I only push when it's wanted. I do think it's best to let the client lead whenever you can. Obviously.'

'Obviously.' She kept a smile, but it got tighter, cooler.

'What would you say the most important part of training is?'

'Building trust.'

'Ah. And how do you do that?'

I thought of Liam. I couldn't help it. I thought of sliding a sheet of paper under his foot, of filling his bottle with toilet water, of throwing a hoodie at his face. I thought of the barbell. 'Um,' I said, looking at the window behind Lisa, looking at the curved glass panes and the wavy wooden art on the walls. 'Um.'

'It says here you're interested in rehab, and working with disabled clients.'

'Yes.'

'That must require trust?'

She was trying to help me, but I couldn't respond. I kept thinking about the moment the bar crashed into his face. About Tommy telling me he'd seen. My mind flinched from one image, only to recoil at the next. I put a hand to my own cheek, feeling for a bruise I knew wasn't there.

'Are you feeling unwell?' Lisa asked. 'Would you like some water?' She got up with a quick smooth of her dress and filled a paper cup from a cooler.

'Thank you,' I said, gulping. 'Sorry. Sorry, I'm okay now.'

'Excellent. I was asking about rehab because, the thing is, we have a lot of older clients. As you might expect. Retirees. And we get quite a few wanting help due to mismanaged golf swings.'

'Right. Yep.' I set the paper cup on the edge of the desk.
'How would you go about helping with that?'

'It's about flexibility, so I'd focus on stretches. Gentle ones.' I wouldn't think of forcing Liam's arm too far, making him wince, making him cry out. I wouldn't.

'Great.' She seemed relieved that I'd managed a full sentence. 'But your usual clients are more of the *inner-city* persuasion?'

'I'm sorry?'

'The kinds of people you regularly train. I'm just wondering what they expect from you, usually, in terms of *conversation*, or expression.'

'Conver—? Oh.' I wasn't posh enough. That's what she was saying. And I realised then that I'd been using my *Steph* voice. That I'd let grown-up Cassie's veneer slip. I'd said 'deligh'ed to be here', I'd said 'flexabili'y'. It had never happened before. Not since the last year of secondary school. I felt like I'd come to the interview naked.

'I guess, erm, I guess I tend to keep things business-like and listen more than I talk.' I tried to patch the crack in my glossy exterior, to touch my tongue to my teeth on every *t*. But my accent sounded false, self-conscious. I sounded like I was taking the piss.

I stumbled through the rest of Lisa's questions, red-faced, disorientated, and was relieved when she let me go.

The smell of lilies followed me, the rain trapping it inside the car, and at a red light I checked the rear-view mirror and saw that the bridge of my nose was stained orange with pollen.

I said goodbye to the green hills, the neat fields, the high hedges; goodbye to the safe, anonymous flat in a commuter town, and the little white Jack Russell I'd been planning to rehome.

Ollie had talked about getting a dog the whole time I was with Liam. He'd wanted a white one too. A Sealyham terrier. A pure breed. Rare. But his landlord didn't allow pets and it took him a while to commit to buying a flat. In the context of their affectionate but competitive relationship, it had seemed strange that he'd let Liam get ahead on that front. Liam thought so too.

'Finally,' he said to me, a few days after we heard Ollie's purchase had completed. 'I don't get how it's taken this long.'

We were wandering around a designer homeware store, looking for a house-warming gift.

'Feels farcical getting a present, congratulating him, when he's dragged his feet for so long.'

'Can't turn up to the party empty-handed, though. You said.'

'That's true,' Liam admitted, sniffing at – and then passing me – a pine-scented diffuser. 'Nice to know you listen to me.'

I got a smile, one of his original smiles, warm and wide. I liked it, and I liked this shop in an old warehouse with huge rounded windows. Spare and sparkling, the place was staffed by an elegant pencil-skirted Italian and an older woman who wore plain black clothes and dramatic red-and-purple glasses.

Arranged over three floors were large pieces of furniture, sofas and dining tables, but also rugs and lamps, cushions and vases, candles and cards. And you were allowed to admire everything because it was *all* tasteful, it was all middle-class-approved, even if that was sometimes surprising.

I looked greedily at the display of china, as patterned and gaudy as the old sets my nan had kept in her corner cabinet, but permitted here because the designer of these plates was from Sweden, not Staffordshire.

'Gorgeous,' I said of a collection of crockery covered with daintily painted fairy-tale animals.

'Not really Ollie's style,' Liam said. 'His girlfriend might appreciate them, though. Just like the stuff she eats off at nursery, I imagine.'

Ollie's girlfriend was twenty. Ollie's girlfriends were always twenty – each successive one arriving with an expiry date.

'It's not even a nice flat,' Liam said. 'It's dark and it's right by the main road. The pollution's terrible. The windows are permanently grimy.'

'Plant pot, then?' I suggested, pointing at the shelf ahead. 'You could give him an aloe.' Liam had been worrying over air quality recently, researching the best plants for oxygenating a flat, compiling a list of the ones that helped filter out contaminants, trying to save us from formaldehyde, xylene, benzene.

'There's more upstairs,' the Italian woman reminded us, calling from the till, waving order papers at the ceiling. 'Feel free.'

I thanked her and started up the floating staircase, eyes darting. 'Oh. Here we go, that's Ollie to a T.' On a shelf above us was a fluttery hundred-leaf lampshade in various shades of pink. It looked like a huge head of cherry blossom and made the light in the stairwell romantic, cosy, glamorous.

'I think I'm just going to go with whisky,' Liam said. 'He doesn't stint himself. Never worries about muscle retardation. Might as well indulge him.'

'Oh, sure. Okay.' I was disappointed, had relished the idea of buying something from the shop, even if it wasn't for me. I lingered under the lamp.

'I kind of love it, though,' I said.

'Get it, then.'

'You don't want that in your flat.'

'Our flat.' His tone was sharp. 'If you like it, get it.'

'I can't.' I went up the rest of the steps, just so I could stop looking at the lamp. Up into the bright jumble of clean, clean lines.

'You can.'

'I can't. Really. I need, maybe, six more clients before I can get out of my overdraft.'

There were no other customers on the first floor, where the items for sale were larger and significantly more expensive. This corner of the shop was set up like a stylish apartment, the warehouse windows softened with gauzy fabric, a fluffy rug laid under the coffee table, a bowl with ceramic fruit. In here even ceramic fruit was stylish! All the furniture (table, sofa, desk, floor lamp) had legs that stuck out, stark, splayed, like they were newborn giraffes trying to find their balance. The pine-needle smell was still in my nose, and gave me the impression that the pale wood furniture was still alive and growing.

Liam stopped and turned, a hand on the back of the sofa. 'You're in debt?'

I shrugged. 'Well, there's debt and there's debt.'

'How, though? I mean, why didn't you ever say anything?'

'I don't know. I just don't really talk about money, usually.'

'What about your savings?'

'I used them when I lost my job, when I was getting qualified as a PT and everything. It's okay. I have a plan, I know how to budget.' The sofa cushions were sharply rectangular, but velvet, irresistible.

'But it's idiotic to be in your overdraft if you don't have to be.'

'Exactly.' I sat down. 'That's why I'm not buying a lamp.' There was a thick woven throw draped across the seat and I tucked a corner around my thighs.

Liam came and stood over me, shins against my knees. 'Let me pay it off.'

'No. Thanks, but no.'

'You shouldn't have paid me rent when you moved in. I told you not to.'

I sank further into the sofa cushions; they were softer than they looked. My head lolled. 'I remember. Liam, it's fine. It's not your fault. I can handle it.'

He went and prodded a space-age rocking chair, testing it, wobbling it back and forth. 'You don't trust me to look after you, is that it? You think I can't afford it or something?'

'What? No, of course not.'

'Or that I'll let you down somehow?'

'I know you won't let me down. But it's good to be financially independent. I don't want you to think I'm taking advantage.'

'Why would I think that? Why wouldn't I want you to be able to depend on me?' He paced between the windows. 'Why won't you let me help?'

'I would, I do. Liam . . .'

He picked up a ceramic fig, weighing it. For a second I thought he was going to throw it, then I thought he was going to take a bite. His face was white. 'What do you need independence for, unless you don't trust me?'

'It's not about trust . . .'

'Then let me give you the money. Let me fucking support you. Stop being a stubborn cunt.'

'Can I help with anything?' It was the woman with red-and-purple glasses, studying us keenly through them.

I felt a flash of outrage, as if this woman had walked

into our living room, our real living room. I'd forgotten where we were, forgotten we were in public. We'd been acting like we were at home. My fingers had found their way deep between the sofa cushions and I slipped them out slowly, hoping I hadn't damaged the nap with my sweaty palms.

'No, sorry. We were, er . . .'

'My girlfriend would like that pink lamp,' Liam said, recovering faster.

To recover from the disastrous job interview, I needed a strict boundary, a self-imposed rule, a five-hundred-calorie day. By the evening, I'd eaten – and tracked – quinoa salad with spiralised broccoli stalks for lunch and a boiled egg on an Irish potato farl for dinner, I'd snacked on grapes and carrots, I'd drunk black tea, I'd weighed and counted and totalled, and felt like I was back in control, but somehow I'd recorded five hundred and eleven calories. I was just rechecking the maths for the fourth or fifth time, jabbing at the calculator, when the phone hit back, pulsing against the rowing callouses on my left palm. *No Caller ID*. I tapped decline, locked the screen, but before the picture could darken there was a knock on the door.

I had a strong feeling it was Liam, Liam from the past, come to tell me off for the sixteen grams of grapes I'd forgotten to log until it was too late. Not that I needed telling off. I was kicking myself hard enough as it was. The red of my tracking app punishing me every time I looked at my phone.

But when I got to the bottom of the stairs and peeked through the peephole, I saw Tanya, hood up, lips pursed, and I slipped on the laminate in my hurry to open the door.

'You said you've got Ghostie.'

'What?' I was staring at her. She wore the parka with a broken zip I knew so well. I could feel the fake fur on the hood without putting my hand anywhere near it.

'Noah's elephant.'

'Oh, yeah. Come in.'

She glared at me, but went ahead up the stairs and sat on the sofa, struggling with the zip on her coat. There was a smell like mulled wine, like cloves and oranges and alcohol on a cold day. It made me hungry, and the hunger made me ashamed.

I went to get Ghostie from my wardrobe, breathing in the dusty, unappetising air, filling my lungs instead of my stomach. My mind kept bouncing through numbers, through portion sizes and grams and millilitres, trying to find a mistake in my calculations. How could I have gone over my limit? I was so careful. I even carried a spoon to measure the milk that went in my tea. I counted each drop of oil, vinegar, ketchup, chilli sauce, even if I didn't eat most of it. I weighed everything and my kitchen scales were sensitive to the last gram. I usually overestimated in the morning, and then shaved off calories as I measured exactly what I was about to eat. I always came in under the estimate.

It wasn't like I never took a break, but if I was going to have a cheat day, I planned for it. This was *un*planned. This was disorientating.

Tanya accepted the elephant from my limp hand. 'I thought you'd be pleased to see me. What's going on?'

'Nothing.' I tried to shake it off. Comforted myself with the idea I could go for a run, but this was supposed to be a rest day – probably part of the reason I was so jittery. I hated rest days, not having something to tick off, not seeing a number tick up, not watching time tick down. I hated knowing I'd wake up tomorrow without sore muscles.

'Cassie?'

I checked through my app again, sure I'd logged something twice. Tanya got up and grabbed the screen.

'You're freaking out about overeating.'

'Not freaking out.'

'You're sweating.'

'I'm not.' I was usually cold on a fast day. I took my phone back, shoved it in the pocket of my tracksuit bottoms, tried to change the subject. 'Why exactly is the elephant called Ghostie?'

'Elephant, phant, phantom, ghost, ghostie.' She spread her hands.

'Noah's a weird kid.'

'Ash named it.'

'Ah, I should have guessed.'

'She loves you.'

My phone was a weight against my hip, I traced its shape with a finger. I must have made a mistake. I usually capped out at four hundred and seventy calories, maybe four ninety. How had I made it into the five hundreds? 'Aw. That's nice. I love her too.'

Tanya waited.

'I do. I love her very much.' My words were flat, we could both hear it.

'Cass? It's eleven calories. Can you get it together?'

'I'm fine. It's fine. It's nothing. I'm fine.'

'This is Liam's doing. This is what he made you do. This is what you used to be like. Remember?'

She was right and wrong. Liam had been strict, but I was stricter. That's why the locked fridge had been such an insult. I was already in a prison of my own making. I didn't need Liam to add any bars.

'She still pinches her belly, you know, when she looks in the mirror.'

'What? Who?'

'Ashlie. He called her fat, Cass. That day at the beach. He dressed it up all fancy, but even a little kid can get that kind of subtext.'

I stopped my hand in its journey to my own abdomen, forced the fingers away from the reassurance I was after – that the skin there would be taut, lying flat against the muscle, unrippled under the bunched waist of my tracksuit. 'That's awful. I'm sorry. She's gorgeous.'

Tanya gave a nasty little laugh. 'And me?'

'What about you?'

'What am I?'

'You're gorgeous too. Seriously, Tanya, you're fishing for compliments now?' It was fine, I told myself. I could absorb eleven calories into tomorrow's plan. I could do that.

'No,' Tanya said, 'I'm just wondering what you really think.'

'I think you're fit as fuck. You know that.' But I also thought: maybe I should eat more, in that case. Absorb *fifty* calories tomorrow.

'I don't believe you. Because . . . d'you know what? It's not just Liam. It's you. You make me feel like I'm huge and repulsive.'

'How do I?' *No*, a voice in my head was saying, fifty calories would lead to a hundred. And there was no knowing where it would stop. *This is why you have daily goals.*

'Your little digs – oh, not directly aimed at me, but at other people. "Big Fat Mum Club", for example.'

I smirked at the name, till I saw Tanya's face. 'I was trying to back you up,' I said. 'You hate those mums!' Driving fancy four-by-fours, always going on about their spa weekends. They loved to half invite Tanya to events and then never follow through, and one of them hadn't bothered to show up for a play date. Ashlie had cried for hours, collapsed with disappointment. I could happily throttle those women; the least I could do was insult them.

'By calling them *fat*? I'm the same size as them, Cass. How d'you think that makes me feel?'

'Are you? Okay. Well, that was dumb, then. I was dumb. But I don't . . . I mean . . . who cares what size someone is?'

'You do. I can feel the judgement. Every time I eat something, whenever I sit down or say I'm tired or admit to having missed a spin class.'

'I'm not judging you!' I wasn't. I was jealous. Just eating when she felt like it, baking and sitting down, and letting her mind wander. How did she do that? How did she manage without all the systems and structures, the barriers that kept you straight? I couldn't remember.

'They say that scrolling through Instagram is bad for your mental health. Have you heard that?'

'What's that got to do with—'

'You're like if Instagram was a person, Cass. Being with you is bad for my mental health.'

'Best stay away from me, then,' I said, and Tanya gave me a half-frightened look.

No wonder. It sounded like a warning.

Perhaps there were other people I should warn. I had to protect Amara from my judgement. I had to protect Clifford and Sophie from my wrath. Perhaps I should warn Tommy, too, to get out of the firing line.

He hadn't been joking about watching me – when the time came for Liam's appointment, he hung about the foyer, flicking a cloth half-heartedly over the handlebars of a step trainer and sending me glares. He was like a teenage girl waiting for a member of a boy band.

'Jesus,' I said, when a minicab drew up. 'Don't get jealous. I'm not going to get in the way of you giving him a blow job in the back of the tour bus later.'

'You're really crass, you know that, Cass?'

'Disapproval in rhyme, that's a new one.'

'You're a freak.'

'And I shouldn't speak?'

'Huh?'

'Never mind. Want me to fluff him for you?'

'Piss off, Cassie.'

The taxi stopped, but it wasn't Liam's taxi: an older man got out, carrying a bunch of files towards the bank next door. I waited. Tommy waited. The gym lights cycled through the rainbow. And again Liam didn't come. There was no apology, no call to the gym, no email, and when I tried to ring him I got his answerphone. Had he decided to quit? Was he ghosting me? Just because of a little knock from a barbell?

I couldn't believe it. I felt outraged. I felt off-track, too, untethered, unable to get in touch with him, to find out where he was. The walls of the labyrinth were closing in on me; his thread had broken, and I was left holding the frayed end.

I'd taken the piss out of Tommy, but I felt a similar sense of expectation, and I busied myself straightening the noticeboard by the office rather than finishing the admin I'd been assigned, hoping for the familiar minicab.

I repinned the signs for mindfulness and nutrition
workshops, weeded out old business cards, and wondered whether to bin the call for extras (*female only, 18 to
25*) for a YouTube video. I'd just decided it seemed like a
dodgy project when a man approached from behind.

'Hi.' He was smiling as if he expected a warm
welcome.

'Hi?' The drawing pins had dug under my nails, but I
was used to that level of pain, inconvenient, insignificant. I turned back to the board.

'It's Greg,' the guy said, coming to lean against the
wellness sign I'd just uncreased. His shoulders were
slightly sweaty, a few wiry hairs poking out from under a
multicoloured tie-dye vest.

'Oh. Okay. Hi, Greg.'

'You never eat my cake.'

The sentence made me think of Tanya, of the moment
she prised a lid from a Tupperware, the warm, sugary
smell, the promise of friendship, the *price* of friendship.

'So, then.' A nudge on my arm. 'Let's talk dates,
shall we?'

'Dates?' I thought of the fruit. Of a date loaf Tanya
had made when she was pregnant. Of the word Med-
jool; of fine-grained skin and treacly innards. I was
fasting, making up for my calorie slip. I was hungry.

'You and me,' Greg was saying. 'Dinner. You can skip
dessert as you're such a freak about sugar. No sneaking
a bite of my tiramisu, though.' He was wagging a finger

314

and I watched the tip, confused. Did we know each other? He was acting like we did.

'Weekday evenings are better for me.' He had his phone out, scrolling. 'And I don't think you have too many evening clients. I haven't seen you with many.'

'Seen me?'

A movement made me look down – a mouse, scrabbling over the discarded battle ropes, running across the mats. My clean mats. Yesterday I'd scrubbed too hard and removed a layer of latex, but I barely spared them a glance. Something else had caught my eye: orange trainers. This man, Greg, was wearing orange trainers. Neon orange.

'Were you . . .' I started, but I couldn't think how to phrase the question. It was going to come out hostile and angry, provocative. I was still holding a spare drawing pin and I drew the point over my palm.

'You need someone in your life,' he was saying. 'Don't think I haven't noticed, and you can't tell me you're taken. The only bloke I ever catch you with is blind.'

That made me look up. At *Greg*. Greg with his florid tie-dye vest and his close-cropped hair and his carefully shaved face, at the angry laughter lines around his mouth.

I squeezed the pin. 'Losing your sight doesn't mean you can't have a relationship.'

'Oh, pull the other one. Girl like you? You want to be admired. He can hardly do that.' His shoulder shifted, dragging the paper sign from the pins, making tiny, ragged holes.

'I don't want to be . . . I don't want that . . .'

'Let's stop doing this dance, shall we? Tuesday. Seven. There's a Portuguese place you're going to love. And there's an *espetada* on the menu that I'm going to love watching you eat.'

'I'm not really into red meat.'

'Live a little.' Greg lifted his chin and rubbed a hand along his throat. I recognised the action.

'Did you . . . ? Do you have a child? At St Saviour's?'

'What? No. I don't have kids.'

And yet he'd been there, waiting in the knot of parents. Waiting for a child he didn't want to admit to? Or waiting for me?

'Look, I'm flattered.' I wasn't, but what else were you supposed to say? 'Thing is . . . I don't really like being asked out at work.' Pathetic. That was practically an invitation to be accosted in my free time.

'Well, you never pick up your phone.'

'Yes, I do.'

He smirked. 'Liar.'

My hand went to my pocket. The buzz of an ID-less caller had punctuated the last couple of weeks. I'd always hit decline. 'You've been calling me?'

'See?' A shrug, a smug little shrug. 'I tried the usual channels.'

'How did you get my number?' I thought of the rip in the recycling bag, the old bills fluttering. 'Have you . . . been through my bins?'

He gave me a pitying look. 'Your number is advertised.

PT services. Come on. It's just dinner. I know you don't live with anyone.'

'How do you—'

I was cut off by a bang. Tommy and his cricket bat.

'Fuck,' he said from the lockers. 'Nearly got it that time, I swear.' He let the bat hang from his grasp. 'What's going on?'

Greg hooked his thumb at me. 'I'm trying to get *her* to be reasonable.'

'What you got your knickers in a twist about now, Cass?'

'She's playing hard to get.'

'Oh yeah? You two a thing, then?'

'Yeah.'

'No,' I said, pressing the spare pin into the board. Tommy was all I needed. 'He asked me . . . but I'm not looking for . . .'

'I've been after her for weeks. Spent a fortune on that Robin's bakery place. It's time for my reward.'

'I didn't ask you to buy anything.'

Tommy was in my periphery, hovering, vibrating. I didn't want to look, to see the mirth, the amusement. I thought he must be loving this.

'That's okay. I wanted to. My treat.'

'But why? I don't know you.'

'Be real, babe.' Greg put a hand on my hip. 'The amount of eye contact you give me? There's chemistry here. Can't you feel it?'

Tommy stepped closer, knocking the offending hand away. '*I* can't feel it.' His grin was gone.

'Well, it's between me and her. You're not involved.'

'Oh yeah?' He turned the bat, weighing it. 'You know, in point of fact, in the matter of organisational relations . . . Well, as I'm her supervisor and she's at work, I think I *am* involved.'

I ignored his weird quasi-legal phrasing, his claim to workplace seniority, and took the opportunity to answer Greg while I had a concrete pillar of a man as a buffer. 'I don't want to go out with you. No offence – I'm just not interested in anyone, at the moment.'

'You heard her,' Tommy said. 'Better luck next time. Back to the hundred-pounders, mate.'

'I lift one forty, actually. And I run a six-minute mile.'

That was a lie. He wasn't a runner, anyone could see it. Stocky muscles bunched and stiff, a little bit of extra flesh all over. He'd be slow. If he was behind you, he'd be easy to lose. I glanced at the trainers again. 'Did you follow me? A few weeks ago? Did you follow me off Trinity Road into the estate?'

He stared hard at me for a moment, then shrugged. 'I saw you out running.'

'You waited in the dark.'

'I waited to check you were all right. I was being chivalrous.'

'Then why didn't you say anything?'

He shrugged again. 'What should I have said? Women like you, crying assault at a conversation.'

'Okay,' Tommy said. 'That's it, mate, no more one-forty lifts for you. It's time to go.'

'Go where?'

'Away. We don't allow workplace harassment here. Get your stuff. Find a new gym. I'll organise a cancellation. You won't be charged for this month.'

'You can't do that.'

'I can.' Tommy spun the bat.

Greg looked at it. 'Are you threatening me?'

'I don't know, mate. Are you threatening Cassie?'

'No.'

'Then no.' He gave a bland smile, but up there it did seem a little threatening.

Greg hesitated, looked at me, looked at the bat, looked at me again. 'Unbelievable,' he muttered, turning, the psychedelic swirls on his vest spiralling with the movement. His voice got louder as he got further from us. 'This is fucking ridiculous.' Then, head in his locker: 'What a bitch.' And passing reception: 'Cunt!'

I watched him leave, pulling his bag over his head and adjusting it with sharp, angry jerks. Then I switched my stare to Tommy. He'd put down the bat and was stretching, his long arms reaching for the nest of pipes on the ceiling.

'What?' he asked, dropping hands onto hips.

'Thanks.' I sounded stunned, even to me.

'You really think I'm a prick, don't you?'

'Yeah.'

He shook his head. 'I told you. Relationships are fucking risky. Lot of psychos out there. Gotta watch out for each other.'

'Right, you're right. Actually . . . I've got a psycho ex too.'

'I knew it. You've got that energy.'

'Have I?'

'Yeah, nothing to be ashamed of. We all get burned, man.' He was rotating his hip now, flashing his pale inner thighs as he moved, showing that vulnerable skin beneath his shorts. 'You're too worried about saving face, Cass. You know that? Pretending you're all posh and that, but I've noticed you can't sustain that accent.'

'What are you talking about?'

'And you don't have to keep doing the act either. The tough-girl act.'

'So if he ever came in . . . my ex . . .'

'You just point him out to me.' He reached for the bat, raised it, then lowered it again and grinned. 'I probably wouldn't actually beat him up, though. Don't want to go to prison.'

'But you'd block his membership? You'd tell him to leave? You'd take my side?'

'Of course. What the hell, Cass? We're mates.'

Mates. I was stunned. It wasn't like I'd never had an ally. There'd been times Tanya had offered – threatened – to call Liam for me, to tell him I'd be late, tell him I was going to share Ashlie's birthday cake, tell him to leave me alone and give me a rest, but I'd never let her. I'd thought it would only make things worse. I didn't think people went away when you told them to.

And I'd half expected Greg to be waiting for me when I left the gym. But my new *mate* Tommy had come out to make sure the street was clear, carrying his bat and trying to keep a straight face.

'You okay getting home?'

'I don't need a bodyguard.'

'Yeah, I know. I've seen your clean and jerk. Wouldn't want to come across you in a dark alley.'

That had made me feel brave. Still, I jumped when someone stumbled onto the street, letting the door to their building slam, and, out of breath, I stopped for several minutes under a railway bridge, protected by the dark. I liked the way the passing trains were so loud they made your head rattle, inspired a primitive fear, a clean, blameless fear. I touched the vibrating brick. There was bright graffiti sprayed across it. Once, I'd known the boys who tagged spaces like these, but they were all DJs and hotel managers and estate agents now, and younger kids had sprayed over their marks. The territory was lost.

My territory was shrinking. And what was I going to do? Fight for resources? Pee on the boundary? Apply for a restraining order?

I didn't even know who to fear any more. It hadn't been Liam in the orange trainers in the dark, and it hadn't been Ollie either, doing his friend's bidding. That bag in the back of the wardrobe was probably still dusty and neglected. It should have made me feel better, except I couldn't help wondering if I was marked. Was there something about me, something I did, that attracted the craziest men? Had that woolly-jumpered guy on the beach been a secret serial killer?

I was looking behind me, scanning the faces of fellow pedestrians as I neared my flat, and I didn't see my parents before they shouted.

'Cass, love!'

I felt the jolt of panic shoot through my toes, hamstrings, shoulders. And I knew then that I wasn't brave, because the steadying sight of my mum and dad, their cosy, normal appearance, their straightforward expressions, made my throat feel full.

'You're jumpy,' Mum said, studying me.

'Sorry.'

'What's happened?'

'There was this guy at work, asked me out . . . It doesn't matter.'

'Ooh. Go on, what guy?' She was excited, pulling at the boat neck of her swing top, hoping for gossip.

'Not like that. He went a bit weird. My colleague had to ban him for harassing me.'

She glanced at Dad. 'Harassing you, eh?'

'Yeah.'

'Talking to you, d'you mean?'

'No, I don't mean *talking to me*.'

'Okay, okay. Just. You know. Try to keep things in perspective, eh, love?'

I opened my mouth and then shut it. It was still nice to see a familiar face, it was good to have some company – better to be safe than happy. 'What are you doing here, anyway?'

Dad had both hands on a clear plastic box, bundles of grey dust preserved in the bottom.

'Your CDs,' he said, with a heft that made the cases clack together. 'I'll carry them up.'

'Thanks?'

'We thought it was about time you had them back,' Mum told me as I unlocked the door. 'They're just taking up space in the loft.'

'And you want that space for something, do you?'

'We're not just a dumping ground for you and your brother, you know.' Behind me, her feet stumped up the lino stair treads. 'We're not just where hi-res audio goes to die.'

I laughed, and the sound bounced through my kitchen. 'Hi-res audio . . . ? Where d'you get that phrase?'

'It's *my* phrase.' There was a frown, though, which told me it wasn't. It sounded like one of the Radio 4 comedians she listened to when Dad was out.

'I'll put them here, shall I?' he said, shifting the box against a wall, masking a portion of the floor where the laminate planks didn't meet the skirting board, and where my own dust had formed into balls.

'Great. Yeah. Great. I'll put the kettle on.' A favour for a favour.

Mum sat at the counter and dabbed a finger onto one of the burn marks. 'Smells funny in here.'

'You're welcome to my hospitality.'

'It's just the truth, Cass. What is it?' She made a show of sniffing.

I shrugged. 'Pipes, probably. I don't know.' There was a sourish smell, stale water and old takeaways, the ghost of spilt beer. I didn't rent the place for its glamour.

'Aftershave, more like.' Another sniff. 'It's you, it's coming off you. How close did you let that bloke at work get?'

'Oh that.' *That* scent, the scent I'd needlessly armed myself with in anticipation of Liam. 'Someone left some perfume in a locker. Thought I'd try it.'

'Nice perk of the job. Talking of – Gavin said you had an interview?'

'Did he?'

'Said you wanted his car?'

'I only asked. It was just in case.'

'Well?'

I got out mugs. 'It's not important, Mum. I didn't get the job anyway.'

'But you would have needed a car, would you?' She was really digging her fingernail into the burn now.

'It was a gym. In Surrey.'

'Bit of a commute.'

'I would have moved, probably.'

A dramatic pause. 'And you're only telling us now?'

I pulled teabags from the shelf, milk from the fridge. 'Well, actually I'm not telling you, Gavin told you. I wouldn't have bothered because, like I said, I didn't get the job.'

'Use your loo?' Dad said, eyes on the hallway.

'Course.'

'But you're looking to move away, are you?' Mum kept on.

'Maybe. I mean . . .' The kettle let out a long, controlled breath, and I poured boiling water into the mugs. 'I'm not safe here. I don't feel safe.'

'Safe?'

'Liam—'

'Oh, I knew that'd be it. Liam, again. Liam, Liam, Liam.'

'Yes, Liam. You agreed, you said it yourself – he's dangerous.'

'*Dangerous.*'

'Don't do that, don't do that voice. I told you about the bag, Mum, remember? The stuff inside. My keys . . .'

'You obviously still had *his* keys. Does that make *you* dangerous?'

'That's not the same thing!'

'Yeah, well,' she said, adjusting a strand of her honey-highlighted, ceramic-straightened fringe. 'I been thinking about everything you told us, you know. And to be honest, Cassie, I don't think anything's all that clear-cut.'

'What?'

'Exactly. *What* can we really know about that bag? *What* was it really for? *What* made you jump to conclusions?'

My mouth was open – I could feel the air drying my

tongue – and the teaspoon seemed to bend in my hot hand. Things were swimming, things were shadowy and fragile. Things like my sanity.

'I mean, did you take the bag, so you could show us? Did you get a picture, even? No. We've only got your word for it. First, Liam's *abusive* when he looks after you, then he's a *stalker* because of a few texts, now he's a killer? And this new fella *harassing* you.' She reached for her mug. 'I hate to say it, love, but you've got a bit of an addiction to exaggeration, you know. A bit of a taste for the dramatic. Ugh. Speaking of taste – got any sugar?'

'No.'

'No sugar?'

I rolled my lips over my teeth, bit down, let go. 'It causes joint inflammation.'

'Does it now?'

'Yes.' We'd gone through this before – she had sore finger joints, but wouldn't listen to advice on dietary remedies.

'Save the lectures, Cass, love,' Dad said, as he came out of the loo. 'It's me'll have to hear about it later.'

Mum took a tiny sip of tea. It was followed by a wince, then a hostile look. 'Don't s'pose you've got a biscuit anywhere either, eh?'

'Nope.'

She sighed. 'Glad I don't live *your* life, Cassie. *What* is there to look forward to?'

Week Ten

What *was* there to look forward to? A job in a strange town, if I could find one, a new set of clients and all the work it would take to attract those clients, to build trust, to build relationships, to make friends. A life without fear? Greg and his neon trainers had proved there was no guarantee of that. So what was I hoping for?

I'd had the answer to that question when I was living with Liam. Hoping he'd come home happy, hoping he'd come home kind, hoping he'd come home as the man I loved and recognised. And when he'd come home incensed and insulting, there'd still been a goal, something to work towards: calm and conciliation.

There was constant momentum around him, there was purpose. Liam, always moving with motive: cutting fennel bulbs for a salad, trimming insoles for my running shoes, ushering me into the passenger seat of the car just as dawn was breaking.

I'd woken that morning to find my clothes already chosen and laid out on the bed, breakfast packed.

'We're going somewhere,' he'd said when I questioned him.

'Where?'

'We're going to do something that not everyone gets to do.'

I'd ignored the plunging fear in my stomach as he hurried me into my clothes, down the stairs, into the car. It was damp and chilly, the light milky with the promise of a pale sun behind clouds. Birds turned glossy eyes on us and hopped about on a nearby fence. They shrieked when the engine started, annoyed to be interrupted during their dawn routine. The clock on the dashboard read 05:46. I huddled into my seat, asked again.

'Where are we going?'

Liam backed out of the parking space, shooting me a grin. 'It's a surprise. My client called me last night. It's . . . something he said he'd arrange if he could.'

'It's not flying or anything, is it?' I could totally imagine him trying to make me pilot a plane, or jump out of one.

'No, you'll be keeping your feet firmly on the ground.'

I sucked in a breath and held it till I couldn't. 'Liam, just tell me.'

'Don't ruin it, Cass. Come on.'

He didn't need to tell me twice. Good Liam was back. The one I loved. Happy and focused, affectionate. His hand on my knee at every traffic light.

We drove for nearly four hours, the sooty suburbs

turning to scrubland and then green fields. Finally, we slowed through a little flint-flecked town and took the road indicated by a brown sign with a generic elephant symbol on it.

'A zoo? Liam? A zoo?'

It was a small zoo with a big, low building at the entrance, a kiosk window winding up as we arrived. There were tickets ready under Liam's name and he bought me a boxy tourist's hat with the zoo's logo on it and made me wear it as we walked round. 'The sun's getting stronger,' he said. 'I don't want your lovely skin to burn.'

There was a big lake in the middle of the grounds, exotic with large-leafed plants, fat and furry-stemmed. The water gave off a sulphurous smell, mixing with the booze-sweaty stink of the marmosets in the closest cages. It was so strange to be there, I couldn't believe I'd woken up that morning in my own bed.

We wandered along wooden walkways, spotting tiny creatures in the backs of tanks, and I stood close to thick glass and chicken wire, hoping the bigger animals would wake up.

Liam stopped to check his phone in the tropical house, where the steamy air was filled with jasmine and alligators were submerged to their eyeballs in the artificial river. A bead of moisture tapped my head: the banana leaves above were dripping.

Liam wiped the drop away. 'Okay, the real reason we're here . . .'

Oh God, we were going to have to eat one of the

animals. That was my first thought. Some new research had shown that fresh – I looked wildly around – flamingo was the best protein for muscle-building.

'. . . while it's asleep.'

'What?' I'd missed his words while worrying about finding pink feathers in my food.

'A puma, Cass. They have to sedate it – her – to remove the ingrown claw, and while she's out you can give her a stroke.'

'Are you serious? A puma?'

We'd walked past the puma enclosure earlier and had been ignored by a sandy, compact creature. Fierce and muscular, and not hiding her muscles behind fluffy fur but showing them off under a sleek pelt. The strong shape of her jaw was almost human, the wide nose noble. I'd watched, wishing to find some affinity – for her to acknowledge an affinity – between us. As if that would make me into an untameable creature, someone to be afraid of. But she'd merely given a deep chuff, a clearing of her throat, and refused to look at me.

'How come? How are we allowed?'

'My client owns this place,' Liam told me. 'And when he said there was going to be a procedure on a puma, I asked if we could be there. I thought you'd like it.'

'I would like it. I'd love it.'

But first a scruffy, irritable little man in a logoed polo shirt had to meet us at a breeze-block building.

'You're Mr Moulton-Hatt's visitors, then,' he said, as he got us to wash our hands and display our short nails and lack of jewellery. 'He seems to think the animals are here as entertainment.'

'It *is* a zoo,' Liam said.

'A *conservation park*,' the man corrected, leading us in through a wire gate. 'Stand here. Don't move.'

He indicated a spot opposite an open cage. Inside, a pale teenage girl with a name tag (SCARLETT, TRAINEE) and a sinewy man in khaki shorts (GEOFF, SENIOR VET) were positioning the sleeping puma on her side, on a pile of straw. They looked like the cast of a strange nativity scene, wise men attending a feline Mary.

'Is she having a baby?' I asked, before I could stop myself.

Geoff looked up with a grin. 'Nothing so exciting. This is just a straightforward procedure. And very quick. That's why we've gone for a sedative rather than an anaesthetic.'

A strong, damp, mossy smell mixed with the faint odour of cat pee. Cables criss-crossed the ground, connected to blazing white lights that gave the vet a clear view. Scarlett held a tray of scissors and pliers, all methodically spaced and labelled. The scruffy man laid his hands gently on the puma's neck and kept track of her breathing while the vet knelt in the straw and pressed on her pads.

'Here's where the claw is digging in,' he said, holding up the paw. 'You can see this digit doesn't move as well as the others. The infection's blocking the action.'

He gripped the bloody ingrown claw with chunky metal clippers, cutting through it.

'Poor thing,' Scarlett said, watching him disinfect and sew the wound. 'She's been a bit hostile to the male recently and no wonder.'

The scruffy man snarled a laugh. 'Sounds familiar. I'll have to check my wife's toenails when I get home.'

Scarlett rolled her eyes but said nothing, concentrating on handing Geoff the set of heavy-duty pliers. The vet thanked her and moved round, clipping the other claws and grunting with the effort.

'They're rather horny,' he told us, with a chuckle. 'Bit like Eric here.'

Eric didn't like that, but the vet was grinning as he checked the puma's eyes, ears and teeth.

'Her canines are pretty worn. She's already lived longer than she would in the wild. That's the thing about captivity, you end up well preserved.'

I thought of Liam's nonagenarian cheerleaders, legs in the air, hair silky and dark, smiles on their eerily youthful faces. That could be me; that was the promise, Liam's promise.

'No mites,' Geoff said, 'and her fur looks good. We'll just give her a quick trim.' He shaved a small patch under the puma's jaw and took some blood for testing. Scarlett labelled the samples and collected the claw trimmings, then left with the vet, both waving cheerio.

As soon as they'd gone, Eric stood up.

'Right, well, I suppose you'll want to give her a stroke now. You've probably got a few minutes.'

We both moved forwards.

'One at a time!' He said it like we'd rushed at the sleeping animal, though we'd only shuffled a little in her direction.

I stepped back, but Liam nudged me.

'Go on, Cass.' He kissed me on the forehead where the tropical house's banana leaf had baptised me.

The puma's fur was much stiffer than I expected, like a Labrador's, like a guide dog's. You could feel the hot muscle humming under the skin. I knelt and brought my face close to hers, wishing again for that connection I was sure would change me. Her breath came in fast puffs and she stayed stubbornly sleeping.

So I rubbed the three undamaged paws, feeling the leathery pads, put my hands under her cheeks and along her sides, felt her soft tummy. I was gentle, but I wanted to touch it all. I knew her scent was rubbing off on me and it made me feel powerful. I was shaping her haunches when she twitched.

'That's it. Time's up,' Eric said. 'She's going to come round and get her own back for all that molesting in a couple of minutes.'

'I wasn't – it wasn't like that.' How to – *whether* to – defend myself or explain that there was nothing sexual in my touch? Shocked, shamed, my temper rose. 'Do you get a lot of people coming in here wanting to fuck the animals?'

He looked almost pleased at my words.

'We get all sorts,' he said after a moment. 'The boss'll let anyone in.' He looked at the puma, protective, possessive. 'Better go.'

She was really waking now, moving her paws, flicking her tail. I wished we could stay, even if it was dangerous. And then suddenly I didn't. Her eyes opened. It's what I had wanted all day, for her to notice me. But I'd been very stupid. This was a creature it was better to hide from. She hissed and I backed into Liam's arms, letting him guide me quickly along the corridor and through the gate, my heart banging.

At the sinks, Liam stopped to give me a hug. 'That was close,' he said.

'I got carried away. Sorry. You didn't get a chance to . . .'

'That's okay. Did you enjoy it?'

'Yeah. She's amazing. I never thought I'd get that close.'

'I'm glad.' He pressed on the soap dispenser and I washed my hands thoroughly again. When I was done he dried my skin with a long strip of blue paper towel and gently unrolled my sleeves before we went back to the public part of the zoo. To macaws squawking and children shrieking. I slipped on the mossy steps and Liam caught me, skimming his nose along my hairline.

'You smell like her,' he said. 'Like a puma.'

'Do I?'

His voice dropped low. 'You smell . . . feral.'

'Hmm. What d'you want to see now?'

'I like this top,' he said, his hands pushing under the hem of my T-shirt.

'You chose it.'

'I'm full of good ideas.' He looked away for a moment, scanning the grounds, then began to tug me towards a huge rhododendron behind the nocturnal creatures' house. The tree was blazing with dark red flowers and dense with glossy leaves that made a floor-sweeping canopy. Liam reached in and eased two branches apart. 'I've got another good idea.'

We were sniggering as we edged through into a secret, sandy cave of crossing limbs and shivering green light. Outside there were sounds of feet on gravel, of people asking each other for sun cream or ice lollies, the mixed-up calls of exotic birds, small children, monkeys. Inside, we kissed quietly, the maybe imaginary musky smell of the puma blooming under the vegetation.

I thought about the puma a lot afterwards. Kept an eye on the zoo's social media for updates. Someone occasionally wrote posts as if they were by her: *Enjoying my venison blood popsicle in the sun!* The photo a frozen puddle of gore melting against her sandy jaws. All the posts seemed slightly provocative (or was that just my interpretation?) and I wondered if it was the crabby, scruffy little man who was writing them.

Then, one day, a picture of her tilting her head coquettishly, peering through the netting of her enclosure, which shaded her eyes like a veil: *Devastated! My beautiful sister, Delilah, was killed by her mate last week. Here I am performing puma funeral rites.* The killing had happened at a zoo in Canada, where the puma had been placed only a few months before.

I read the linked news story and clicked on the next suggested article. That made me go on a scrolling marathon. And I found it wasn't that unusual for male animals to kill females when they'd been enclosed together for mating.

At the Krasnoyarsk zoo in Siberia, a female polar bear rejected her mate and he killed her; a year later, another female polar bear was killed during a 'breeding attempt' in Detroit. In London, a female tiger was killed by her 'perfect mate', and another was killed during a 'breeding mishap' in Sacramento, and another during an 'introduction' at Tacoma, and another in San Diego. At Neuwied Zoo in Germany, the female tiger who'd been supposed to 'keep the male company' was killed by him, and the same thing happened in Copenhagen. At Nihondaira Zoo in Japan, a lioness was 'choked to death' by her lion, and another lioness was killed in Dallas. Most recently, a male leopard killed the female during an attempt to breed them at Erie Zoo in Pennsylvania.

It was dangerous to be locked up with your mate.

My own period of captivity was drawing to an end. Only three weeks left of Liam's half-priced training programme. He'd sent a message of apology the day after his missed session, and arrived for this one clean-shaven and shiny, wearing a beanie pulled snug over his scalp. The man bun had gone, and he looked so much like the Liam I'd met in the park, the Liam I'd lived with and run beside and loved, that I was disconcerted, my body suddenly fragile and papery, like a cocoon.

What was inside me? Something beautiful, something properly equipped? Or a spineless little grub?

'You cut your hair?' I said at last, taking his bag.

'Thought it was time to remind the barber of my existence.'

'What about it giving you strength, or whatever?'

'That's what the gym's for. You should know that. That's what you're for.'

'Am I? Right. Want to give me your hat too?'

He put a hand up, spreading his fingers over the woollen scalp. 'No, thanks. I'd rather keep it on. Not used to the feel of a short back and sides.'

'Bit cold, huh?' I wondered about snatching the hat, but that would have been petty in the extreme. And I was on best behaviour, considering the barbell incident had been noted. I could always grab the hat later. 'Where d'you want to start? Cross-trainer? Or are you happy with the treadmill?'

'Very happy.'

His gaze seemed to rest on me in the mirror, and I stared back at his handsome face, then stuck my tongue out, just because I could. A muscle in his lip twitched, his body responding to mine without his even knowing.

But his movements were less coordinated in general, his muscles looser than normal, that careful control over his limbs gone. Maybe the hair *had* been weighing him down, grounding him somehow. His sight, his self-awareness, seemed worse. There was more fumbling for handles and stumbling over obstacles. When he got off the treadmill he was unbalanced, almost clumsy; several times his body collided with mine.

'Sorry . . . sorry.'

'No worries. You feeling okay?'

'Bit of a sinus headache, that's all. Seems to be messing with my balance.' He was breathing through his mouth and his voice was slightly nasal.

'Let's have a rest, then. We can check your progress.'

I'd been hiding in the office a lot since Greg, and all my clients had had extra assessments that week, bare feet on the monitors, biceps Velcro-wrapped, while I peered out at reception. I knew in theory that Greg couldn't just walk in, that his access had been deactivated, but I also knew from experience that there were no guarantees. That if a person wanted to get close, they could.

Liam sat on the office chair again to remove his shoes and socks, and I stayed back, remembering the way his legs had caught me before. I was always being caught. By something, by somebody. I was always running and looking over my shoulder, flinching. I was sick of it. I wanted to make someone else flinch.

As the blood pressure machine sighed out its time, I snatched Liam's hat.

'Hey!'

'Nice cut,' I said, my voice a little trebly with adrenaline. Liam's hair was flattened where the wool had pulled tight, but it looked soft and neat, showing the shape of his skull, and I knew how it would feel, the brush of it across my palm. Weird to think of a tumour nestled in there, growing, pushing everything else out of the way.

'You satisfied now?'

'I don't like secrets,' I said.

'Some secret. I got a number three fade, in case you want all the details.'

His laugh turned to a cough, and he held the back of his hand to his top lip, recovering. 'I'm sorry. Would you mind getting something out of my bag? I have a spray. In the side pocket. I don't know if it's a cold or hay fever or what, but this blocked nose is driving me crazy.'

Hay fever, like a human, I thought as I went to the lockers. And my hand rested on the metal door for a moment while I examined that thought. *Like a human.* Because part of me had seen Liam as a supernatural force, and the idea of him succumbing to grass pollen or tree spores was absurd. Even the brain tumour had made him seem special, with the dramatic nature of the problem, the spectacle of sudden blindness.

But he was just a man. He'd gained muscle, and the scales had shown fat loss, but it was within a normal range. He could do more push-ups in a minute and his heart rate was lower during cardio, but the changes weren't startling. He could hold a plank and a wall squat longer, but only by a couple of minutes. I'd have been pleased had he been anyone else, but he was meant to be a monster – monstrous in his abilities.

I fetched the spray, felt him curl his fingers around it, and waited while he squirted it into each nostril, performed some effortful sniffing.

'Thanks,' he said, tipping his head back. 'Can't afford to lose another sense.'

'Hah.'

'Okay.' Another sniff. 'I'm ready. Sorry. I'm back. I'm focused.'

'Let's do some fixed weights, then. Keep it simple.' Because he was just a man.

I thought it over and over while he pulled on bars and pressed on armrests, forced up footplates and squeezed thigh pads. I thought it when I secretly upped the weight, moving the pin from one seventy to two twenty, and watched him fail to lift the stack more than twice. I thought it at the end of the session, when he couldn't find the sleeve of his jacket and I had to guide his hand into the armhole. I thought it when he began rummaging in his gym bag. *Just a man.*

'I've got something for you, actually. Steph.'

'Oh?'

'Yeah. Tommy said people sometimes bring in cake and share it round? He said you have a particularly sweet tooth.'

'Did he?'

'Yeah – he said, "Steph's always after the goodies on the snack table."'

'Ohhh. I see. Yep, that's me. Munching away twenty-four seven.'

'Great. Well. It's somewhere in here . . . D'you mind?'

'Sure.' I slid the zip further open, and saw it immediately: a box of Quality Street. My hands were shaking as I stared at it and remembered one just like it, sitting in our flat, on our kitchen counter, sucking up all the light. A pleasure I wasn't allowed, a treat that was there to taunt me, test me. A delicacy that had destroyed everything.

I couldn't move my gaze, I couldn't bear to find out that this had all been a game, I didn't want to see the look on his face when he told me he'd won.

'These . . . are for me?' My voice was wobbly. I bit my lip hard.

'And everyone else. I mean, if you *want* to share.' He had the same tame expression as always, his eyes trained on the lockers rather than on me. 'Sorry it's not something more personal. I can't do my own shopping at the moment.'

'You're giving me this box of *Quality Street*?'

He frowned then. Just for a second. 'Ah, is that what they are? I asked for Lindt at the very least.' He shrugged, chuckled. 'I have a care worker who goes to the shops for me. She's . . . keen on a bargain.'

I felt like I did when I forgot to breathe sometimes

mid-lift. My neck was stiff, working hard to keep my head up. My brain was too heavy, then too light.

'Steph? Everything okay? Have I done the wrong thing? You can eat them, can't you?'

'Sorry, yes,' I said. 'Thank you, yes, of course.' Because I could. I could take the box and open it, offer the contents and watch people peel the colourful wrappers, and I could do it all while remaining calm and professional, because it didn't mean anything. Because he was just a man. And because he'd only ever once bought Quality Street deliberately.

We'd been in the middle of a total sugar cull – no fruit, no milk, no balsamic vinegar – so when I saw the chocolates on the kitchen counter, gaudy and alien, I knew they were a trap. I knew it and yet my mouth watered at the hollow rattle of the cardboard box. A virgin box from the shop, untouched. I stroked the smooth top, imagined the strawberry creams nestled inside.

That morning, Liam had made a bacon sandwich and covered it in HP Sauce, asked me if I wanted to take a bite. I hadn't even known there was HP Sauce in the fridge. Something was wrong, and I was worried.

In the evening, Ollie came for a crisis meeting. Four separate parks had suddenly revoked the bootcamp's usage licences, their liability insurance had gone up, and they were losing instructors, members and money. Liam had been feeling helpless, despairing, unable to control the situation.

Usually he would have had some sort of low-sugar, high-protein snack ready for Ollie, something he was interested in trying or making or showing off, so when he brought home the chocolates it felt like an upping of the stakes.

My parents had always had a tub of these, shiny and cheap, on the coffee table. Slowly the multicoloured insides would dwindle until it was just a sea of yellow – hard caramels that no one was really tempted to eat. Then, a few days later, a new tin would appear, as if they grew organically in the gloom of the living room, like mushrooms.

But there was nothing natural about the box being in our flat.

Liam opened it while he boiled the kettle, and the idea of the contents made me feel drunk. I kept squeezing my hands into fists. I'd rejected the bacon sandwich, but I was weak from wanting something good and tasty. When Ollie popped a Caramel Swirl in his mouth, I knew my expression was too intense – creepy, even; that it was obvious I was wishing I could *be* Ollie for a few minutes.

They had their meeting in the living room, and I went to bed hearing the drone of their voices as they strategised, as they insulted council workers and disloyal bootcamp members.

The next day, Liam left for work before I woke. He'd taken on two extra early-morning classes to make up for the shortfall, and it meant he had to skip our run.

But I wasn't supposed to let the routine drop, and he had ways of making sure – tracking my phone, or checking the soles of my trainers to see if berries from the big evergreen tree outside the building had been crushed into the rubber treads. And, yes, usually I had been for a run, but occasionally, when I was tired or out of time, I'd just gone downstairs and stamped on the berries, shuffling about, staining the pavement.

That day, though, after showering and dressing and putting on my berry-crushing, alibi-creating shoes, I found my keys weren't on the hook, and that Liam had locked the deadbolt.

It wasn't the first time. I didn't waste energy tugging on the handle, and I didn't bother to call him. There was no way out. Or, there was a way out, but it would mean using the secret keys I'd balled in that pair of socks and stashed under the collection of half-used make-up I kept in the bottom of the vanity unit. All powdery and grimy-looking. If Liam came home while I was out, I'd be caught. I'd have to explain why I thought I needed secret keys, I'd have to work to prove I trusted him, I'd have to apologise for piling emotional weight on him during this most stressful time.

So I took off my trainers and sat down. I had nowhere to go, but I also had nothing to do, and there was that nearly full box of chocolates sitting on the kitchen counter.

Liam hadn't chucked them after the meeting. In fact, the used coffee cups were still in the living room, a couple of discarded gold wrappers down the side of the armchair Ollie had sat in. I tidied up to take my mind off the box of temptation. Washed up, swept up. But I kept thinking about it throughout my second workout, my weight session, my online appointment with a client.

I thought, what if I opened the box? What horrors might emerge?

None. When I lifted the lid, there was no screaming, the lights stayed on, no one knocked on the door or rang my phone. It was just a collection of cocoa and milk solids, a bit of praline, a bit of fruit flavouring. I picked up a chocolate, sniffed it, swallowed the sea of saliva I suddenly seemed to be producing, and made a decision. I would just eat the Strawberry Delights – there were only three. And God I wanted them. The almost bitter shell, the sweet, tangy centre. It wasn't a question of willpower, so much as free will.

I set the scene: pulled the curtains right back to expose the flat to a rosy sunset, put on music, brought my fluttery pink side lamp into the living room and turned it on for ambience. I drank a large glass of water, prepared a big bowl of leafy salad, found furry slippers and made a black coffee. Snuggling into the sofa, I took a deep breath. This was perfect. Nothing would mar my experience.

The first chocolate lasted fifteen seconds. An amazing, wonderful fifteen seconds. Almost too good. My face contorting against the sharp sweetness, the expanding floral scent. I noticed the crack of the shell, the liquid stick of the filling, every moment savoured. The next survived eight seconds. Still good, still great. The last one I barely remembered eating. It was a bit of a waste. But that was it. I wouldn't have any more. I was done.

I ate the whole bowl of salad – the oil and pepper in the dressing nearly tasteless after the beautiful sugar – drank more water, and felt disappointed in myself. But how nice to enjoy life for a couple of minutes, or, indeed, for twenty-three seconds.

I screwed the wrappers into tiny red balls and pushed them to the bottom of the bin liner, put the salad plate in the dishwasher as evidence of my healthy eating and turned off the pink lamp. That was when the cramps started. And the nausea. And the sweating.

Then I began throwing up.

When Liam got home, I was lying on the bathroom floor, damp and miserable, wishing like hell I hadn't caved. Who'd have thought my reaction to sugar would be so strong?

'You ate the strawberry chocolates,' Liam said, standing in the doorway, looking at me with no sympathy.

'Yeah.' I smelled of sick; my breath was rank.

'I knew you would.'

I was too weak to react, to do more than groan and press my face to the cold tiles. But a horrible suspicion added to the pain in my gut. 'Maybe I'm allergic to sugar?' My voice was so hopeful, pathetic.

'Maybe.' He could have agreed with me, he could have left it there, life would have carried on as normal. But he was triumphant. He wanted me to know. 'Maybe *not*.'

I groaned again. 'You put something in them.'

He crouched and stroked my hair. 'It wouldn't have mattered if you'd controlled yourself.'

'What was it?' I pushed myself away from him, dragging a towel off the rail and curling up against the bath.

'An emetic. They use it on zoo animals. It'll wear off. How many did you eat?'

'Three.'

'Three? Really?' He moved, knelt closer so he could study me. 'Then you've ingested approximately sixty millilitres. Don't worry, that's not dangerous. My client gave me very detailed instructions.'

'Everything hurts.'

'You won't eat chocolate again.'

He was so hard. I squinted up at him. 'You hate me.'

'I love you.'

I started shivering then. It was the effects of the drug, the vomiting, the sweat and the cold tiles. But it was also what he'd said. His love was more terrifying than anything. He walked away and brought back the box of chocolates, resting it on the tips of his fingers, as if he were a waiter.

'Liam?'

He gave a polite smile, looking down. 'Thought you might want another.'

'No.' I dragged myself round, past the basin.

'No?' Pretending to be surprised, stepping closer. 'But you love these. Don't you? You'll do anything for them – ruin your diet, make yourself ill, betray my trust.'

'I just wanted a chocolate, Liam—'

'*Three* chocolates.'

'You bought them.' I was nearly at the bathroom door, but so weak I didn't think I could get up. Every now and then my stomach gave another convulsion and I gagged and had to put my head down. I was a little worm chopped in half, flailing about in agony, trying to move my bisected body out of the way.

'Here we go.' He squeezed the sides and the lid popped up. 'D'you have a preference? Or shall I choose for you?' A swirl of his finger, the sweets rustling in the box.

My head was in the hall, hands slapping the floor, body sliding along after them. I hardly felt human. I couldn't work out what I was.

'Orange Creme, Cass? I know you like the fruity ones.'

He was holding the unwrapped chocolate in his fingers. The rest were dropped on the floor next to me, crushed underfoot as he followed me towards the front door. 'Come on, Cassie. Open your mouth. Don't you want another?'

'Keep away from me.'

'You think you've learned your lesson?'

'Yes.'

'Good. You'll thank me, sweetheart, you know you

will.' He left me collapsed against the door, fetched some water and watched me drink. 'Let's get you into bed, shall we?'

The hard ends of his fingers digging into my ribs as I was carried, bundled under the covers and left alone to curl up and shiver, wishing – irrationally – for him to stay. I wanted comfort from him, I wanted to be held by him, despite everything. I think if he'd got into bed with me then, I'd have forgiven him. Ashamed as I might be to admit it.

But he went to clean the bathroom. The smell of bleach drifting into the bedroom, the sounds of a tap running and, yes, a podcast playing, the host talking about the health benefits of olive oil.

And wasn't he kind? Wasn't he thoughtful? I'd made the mess, but he was happy to clean it up. Nothing about me disgusted him, except for my lack of control.

I slid out of bed and crawled to my phone. My head was just a weight I had to drag around and it pinged off the door frame as I reached the hall, found my jacket, forced my feet into trainers.

Liam had shut the bathroom door to clean behind it and didn't hear when I opened the front door. I slithered down the stairwell, triggering the automatic lights, the floor lurching up through me, bile rising on the tide. But I kept my mouth shut, the taste of those churned chocolates in my throat, till I was through the security door and into the sweet-smelling streets.

It was all about sugar. This life. Any life. The different types and the effects on the body. Glucose, fructose, lactose, sucrose. The energising and inflaming, the eroding and inflating, the bloating and erupting and depressing consequences.

Sugar. Who pushes it and who polices it. Who is tempting you and why. Who is sneaking it into your diet. Because someone is always sneaking it in, so that *low-fat yogurt* becomes code for a pot of creamy corn syrup, and someone is always giving advice and someone is always wrong, and someone is always fighting over the disputed territory of a banana, a bowl of strawberries or a slice of bread.

Sugar. The high of it, the easy animation. The crashing, blackening, limping withdrawal. The longing and lapsing and shame. The endless miserable trawling for substitutes, for erythritol and xylitol and steviol glycosides. The enunciated need to *cut it out*. The promises and pleas. And the final realisation that the thrill is cheap, but that every time we bite into a cola bottle or a brownie or, yes, a Strawberry Delight, we are risking something, we are making a bargain.

I left Liam at reception and took his gift to the snack table.

'Ooh, chocolates!' Steph said as I opened the box.

'Thank God. I've been craving something sweet all day, and our cake donor seems to have gone AWOL. In fact, I think he's cancelled his membership.' She was already eating and her words came out sticky. 'Typical. Just when we've finally got rid of the mouse.'

'Have we?'

'Mmm. Exterminator found a nest behind one of the lockers. I asked for it to be removed humanely, but I'll be honest, I didn't stay to check.'

'Tommy will be sad not to have done it himself.'

'Will he?'

'He's been a man on a mission.'

She picked up another chocolate, pulling the twisted ends with a professional flourish. 'He's been asking about being assistant manager.' She looked at me. 'Think he should get it?'

'Yeah,' I said. 'I do.'

'Your client's taxi's here.'

I threw Steph's sweet wrappers in the bin on the walk back over, dusted my hands, though there wasn't really anything on them, and watched a dance class holding a half-squat. They'd been holding it several seconds already: sweat was breaking out on brows, stomachs were sucked up under ribs, one of the women had even pulled in her cheeks.

'Now draw up, through the centre,' Dani called, squatting too and grinning through the burn. 'Hold it tighter, tighter. I want you to imagine you're squeezing the air out, squeeze, squeeze. Hold it! Okay. Let go.'

A chorus of groans, a tangle of limbs flopping about, puppets with cut strings.

How weird we all are, I thought, tightening our bodies, sucking them in, vacuum-packing them until there's no room left for a soul. Who needs a soul, anyway? That old bloated thing. Not us. Wring it out, leave it to slither down the drain, discard it. And – bonus – that gets rid of a few pounds, lightens the scales, takes an inch off the waist.

What else might escape, though? What might I have accidentally expelled? Empathy? Guilt? A conscience?

'That's enough,' I said as I got near Liam. 'No more loitering.'

'What?'

I patted his back, a bit too hard. 'Your ride's here.'

'Oh. Thanks.' He swiped the cane in front of him, pushed the beanie into a pocket, shifted his shoulders, took my arm. 'How am I looking?'

'How d'you mean?'

'Well, do I look . . . ?' He sighed. 'I don't know. I'm meant to be going for drinks. That's where I'm off to. It's why I had my hair cut and everything.' A sheepish smile, head tucked to the side; he let go of me for a moment to feel his shaved face. 'What d'you think?'

'Er,' I said, urging him towards the car. 'I think you look . . .' Was I going to say it? Could I give him this? 'I think you look very handsome.' If I'd said anything else it would have been a lie.

'That's a relief.' But he sounded more smug than relieved as he lowered himself into the car. 'My friend thinks going out for drinks will be good for me, but it's been a while.'

'Has it? Me too.' I couldn't remember the last time I'd tasted alcohol or sat at a table, relaxing to the buzz of other people's chat.

'Oh really? Wanna come?'

'Where are you going?'

'Some tequila place, on a roof.'

'Sounds lethal.'

'Hope not. I've just got back to lifting one seventy.'

'Hah. Right. Good one, mate. Unfortunately, I've got a client coming in an hour. No rest for the wicked, eh? Maybe another time. See you next week.' I slammed the door. On Liam, on temptation, on the performance of Gavin's persona and the repetition of his phrases, on the recklessness that was rising in me. I could feel it, the need to do something big, mad, effervescent. I was the fizzy water you're not supposed to drink because it makes you fat. I'd been shaken up and was about to blow my top. A giggle escaped.

Imagine walking into the bar on his arm, imagine the looks on his friends' faces.

I stared at the taxi, idling at the lights, Liam's silhouette in the back window. He was off out, off to spend his afternoon on a suntrapped rooftop, arresting his muscle development with mescal. Imagine if I was going with him.

Imagine having somewhere to go that wasn't home or the gym. The bubbles popped, my water went flat.

Greg had said he knew where I lived, and for the last few days I'd taken tortuous routes everywhere, painstakingly surveying the street, expecting a heavy hand on my shoulder as I struggled with the locks on my front door, predicting a shout at least, a threat, a curse. I'd peeked out of my kitchen window the same way I did the office, waiting for trouble, not trusting absence. I kept the curtains closed and the creeping fig I'd been given was dying from lack of sun. I knew how it felt. I'd been doing all my runs on a treadmill.

It was uncomfortable to be on the street now, outside the gym, its security, its surveillance, and I was just turning to go in when my phone dinged. I jumped more than the sound warranted. But it was only a text from my mum.

Hope no one harasses you at work today. Lol.

I blushed, but it wasn't embarrassment. My stomach flipped, but it wasn't nerves. Heat ate up my skin, flooded my muscles. I was shaking, but it wasn't fear.

You weren't there, I wanted to tell her. *You weren't the one being chased, hounded, called names. You weren't the one who was starved and monitored. You weren't the one whose keys were kept with the tools for a murder. You didn't see the bag. You haven't been in his place. You can't understand.*

But maybe she could understand. Maybe I could make her see. Maybe I could make everyone see. That bag, that knife, that collection of cable ties and cleaning products, I could take a photo and send it on. To my parents, to Tanya, to Tommy, to Ollie, to Jamal, to the police. I could shove it in their faces. *Look what I've had to put up with, look what Liam really is – how could you expect me to act normally after that?*

And all I had to do was walk up four flights of concrete stairs to his door.

The smell of a windowsill basil plant hit me as I unlocked the door. That combination of cannabis and cat piss, worth it for the extra flavour the herb lends food, especially if you can't rely on salt or fat.

The scent was strong – the leaves baking in the afternoon sun – a kind of alarm pheromone, a warning, a boundary marker. I wanted to heed it. I wanted to turn back. It was harder this time, knowing what I would find; harder to make myself go in and rifle through his belongings, his preparation, the evidence of his rage.

But I was here now. I'd taken the risk already. And this was the only argument I had left. I crossed the bedroom, acknowledged the pink lamp, got down on the carpet and slid open the wardrobe door. The bag was there, less dusty since I'd had my hands on it, but just as sinister.

My mother's voice was in my ear as I grabbed the handle. *Maybe the cable ties are for actual cables, Cass, and the knife is just to cut the ties.* And I could already hear Tanya's *Told you so.* I paused a moment, imagining Jamal interpreting any picture I sent him as a come-on.

But there was still Ollie, Tommy, the police. And there was me. I needed to see the proof again.

So I dragged the bag towards me, feeling it skitter

over the floor, light, too eager. And before I even pulled the zip I knew – it was empty. No keys, no ties, no knife, no bleach. Nothing. The open bag seemed to grin at me, enjoying my confusion, my distress. I plunged my hand back in and felt about roughly, scratching at the inner piping, the plastic liner. There wasn't a secret compartment, or a forgotten scrap of evidence. He'd cleaned up, like he always cleaned up.

I felt how I often did during a long swim in the sea. I was sinking, caught in cross-currents, adrift, the only option a slow descent to the sandy floor.

When the key scraped in the lock, I really felt like I'd been underwater, and when Liam walked in, reality barely lapped at my skin. The shock was a moment behind, a wave crashing over me. I thought I might turn to water myself, right there, become a puddle he could paddle through.

I stood and flattened myself against the bedroom wall as the front door did its clunking close, as Liam took off his beanie and dropped his bag on the welcome mat. I held my breath, saliva pooling in my throat. It was too quiet in the flat; he'd hear if I swallowed.

His shadow slipped across my body, and I flinched. Because he could see light and dark, and he could tell when I waved a hand in front of his face, and surely he would catch me now, with the sun defining every movement?

But he passed on, sliding his hand along the smooth plaster of the hallway to the kitchen.

I waded closer, through memories, desires, fear. Watched him as he put away a teaspoon, a wooden spoon, a measuring cup, a couple of sharp knives. He was deliberate as he slotted them into drawers, running his fingers along the handles, knowing the space well enough to seem sighted.

He felt his way to the window, which had been left open on a security lock, and he shut it tight, cutting out the noise of traffic, sirens, a barking dog. I wondered what else he might do, what he might reveal, and if I should stay to watch.

Wasn't that what I wanted? Wasn't that what I was there for, really? To be sneaky and sinister. To be a hunter, bold and clever, a breaker-and-enterer, an evil genius.

But I didn't feel bold as he walked back to the front door and double-locked it: deadbolt, latch. And I didn't feel clever listening to the slide of the security chain. I was timid and uncertain, stiff and wide-eyed in the bedroom mirror. That's when I noticed something that made me wonder (it was only wonder at first, curiosity): a book, lying on the bedside table. Splayed, spine up, pages spread, as if it had been put down in the middle of reading. But who could have been reading it?

I spent the week after leaving Liam reading. Sitting in Tanya's garden with a blanket over my knees, like an invalid. I read whatever book had been left in the living room: a pictureless cookbook from the 1950s, a biography of a snooker player, a children's chapter book about a cat superhero. I didn't take much in. I barely moved. I could feel my muscles retreating, like disappointed brawlers, fists raised but no longer expecting the thrill of a fight.

Tanya had come to find me on my flight from Liam's. Freezing and fragile, I was a mile from the flat, too scared to stop walking in case Liam caught up, sure he'd come looking for me eventually. When she asked where I was going, I realised I'd been heading for the cemetery.

She'd scooped me up and taken me home, tucked her life around mine, its ordinariness a balm for my wounds. I slept in the neat spare room, where an electric drier heated the furthest corner, and Tanya fed me water and crackers, mashed banana and apple sauce, steamed carrots and liquorice tea. Finally, a few days later, there was a plain beefburger on a bed of plain white rice.

'I know it's not your usual perfect combo of macros or whatever, but you've got to try and eat *some*thing.'

She was right. But I couldn't face processed meat, or force down any more refined carbs. I'd left him and that was transgression enough. The T-shirt I'd borrowed from Tanya and her pair of drawstring lounge pants were looser by the day, but I couldn't make a decision about what to put in my mouth. I could only sit on the patio, where it was warm, where I could reach for a fallen sweetcorn cob, the kernels brown inside their papery husk, and hold it in my hand, soothe it like a bird. The garden was lush with overripe produce, with the hum of bees and flies, feeding.

The veg patch was Steve's and he was away, and Tanya had made it very clear when he'd brought in the raised beds and the two tons of soil that she would not be participating in the maintenance. So beans were splitting on the vines, jewel-red raspberries had scattered among the tall grass, and some of the artichokes were beginning to open – the two heads in the brightest sun had purple stamens springing from their centres. It was decadent, letting all that food go to waste.

'I could just pick some stuff,' I said for the third or fourth time.

'He has to learn,' Tanya said, her face hard. 'If he wants a garden, if he wants a *family*, he has to actually come home sometimes.'

Ashlie was on the trampoline, doing star jumps, doing bum jumps, doing a new jump that she really needed someone to see.

'Mum? Mummy? Watch! Watch me.'

'I'm watching.'

The metallic springs squeaking; the flash of Ashlie's shadow behind the safety mesh.

'I was thinking,' I said, 'maybe I'd have a satsuma, in a sec?'

'Help yourself.'

'Think that's okay?'

'You had fish fingers last night. If you can handle that, you can manage fruit, I'd say.'

'Yeah. And it wouldn't be bad to have one now, would it?'

'I've just said, haven't I? Oh.' She patted my leg. 'I see what's going on here. Gonna have to decide this one for yourself, mate.'

The jumping had stopped, the springs silent. 'See, Mum? Mummy? Were you watching?'

'Yeah. Excellent, sweetie! Keep going. Can you go from standing to knees and back again?'

The springs whined, there was a thwap of canvas, a long sigh as Ashlie noticed her mother's gaze waver.

'I could . . . weigh it. Maybe. The satsuma.'

'Yep.'

'Or not.'

There was some ironic nodding. 'Or, in fact, not.'

I smiled but it was creaky. 'I had quite a lot for breakfast.'

'You had one bowl of Weetabix.'

'Three biscuit things, though. Lots of milk. And what am I using the energy for?' I waved a hand over my inert body.

'You're healing.'

'My stomach's fine.'

'Psychologically, Cass. You're healing in here.' She touched her head. 'That takes energy too.'

'Mum! Watch!'

'I'm watching, baby. I've literally not taken my eyes off you.' Then, in an undertone, 'For fuck's sake.'

My smile was easier. 'Is there anyone who doesn't piss you off, Tan?'

'Noah's doing all right, just now.' He was asleep.

I let my head drop on the back of the bench, pierced by the glow of the sky, the dry smell of the wood. 'It's all so tiring. Deciding. I keep mentally writing texts to ask Liam what I should eat.'

'Are you serious?'

'He's good at that stuff . . . it's second nature to him.'

'*I'll* tell you what to eat.'

'It's not the same.'

'Why?' She waited, then tutted. 'You don't trust me.'

'You'll tell me to eat cake.'

'*Bien sûr, merci beaucoup.*'

I lifted my head from the bench, blinked into the sun. 'Am I having a stroke?'

'I was being Marie Antoinette?'

'I *am* having a stroke.'

Tanya's laugh merged with Noah's wail as he woke up. Another handful of raspberries fell into the grass. Ashlie called again: 'Watch me!'

'I'm bloody watching!' Tanya shouted, then, dropping her voice, 'I'm telling you, if Steve doesn't come home soon I'm filing for divorce.'

'I should move out.'

'What?'

'You've got enough on your plate.' I glanced at the flowering artichokes. 'I mean, not actually on your plate, obviously.'

'Oh, piss off. I don't even know how to cook a sodding artichoke. It looks like a pine cone.'

'Says here you can boil them and eat the petals.' I flashed the open cookbook. 'They're nice with lemon butter.'

She'd stood to go inside, but turned back to face me. 'So you'd eat that? If I made it?'

'They're loaded with nutrients.' I sounded like Liam. 'Yeah.'

'Fine.' She pulled the book off my lap. 'Artichokes it is.'

I took a step, reached out and touched the book. *The Power of Positive Thinking.* There were notes inside, but not in Liam's handwriting. The copy was second-hand. The copy was someone else's.

'Hi, Cassie.'

What is it like? To finally meet the Minotaur? To wake the puma? To come face to face with Daddy Bear? It's cold despite the warm day. A block of ice on your chest. Heavy. Wet. Suffocating.

When I looked up, I saw him in the mirror, his body behind mine, and I froze. Focused only on his reflection. But that was the wrong myth; that wouldn't keep me safe. He waited, smiling, standing between me and the front door. The door he'd just thoroughly locked.

'It's great to see you.'

'*See* me?'

He said nothing, but I knew.

'I thought you were going out?'

'Changed my mind. I'm allowed, aren't I?'

'But . . . You can see?'

'The operation was only two weeks ago, so you're a bit blurry, but yeah. Yeah, I can see who you are.'

'Operation?' I looked at his head, at the short hair and the undamaged scalp.

'They moved the surgery forward, which was a lucky break. What are you looking for? There aren't any scars. They go in through the nose. Sorry again about missing last week's session. I was still recovering.'

'Oh.' My voice was nothing. I was alone with Liam. The real Liam. The Liam of my nightmares. And the windows were shut tight, and the weapons were stowed away. I thought about the way his mouth had twitched when I stuck out my tongue, how he'd walked into the equipment, fumbled. I'd thought his sight was worse. But he'd been acting, playing the role of a blind person, overplaying it.

'I didn't want to miss today, though.'

He was looking right at me. Right. At me.

'You set the weight to two twenty when I asked for one seventy.' A pout. He struggled to hold it through his obvious glee.

'I must have misheard.'

'Hmm. Maybe you should get your ears checked. It's best not to ignore that kind of warning. I should know.' He unzipped his jacket with a vicious tug.

I didn't answer. Of course I didn't. I sidestepped into the kitchen; it was the wrong direction, but then I was famously bad with those. 'I should go.'

He ignored that as he shrugged off the jacket, contemplated me, his eyes roving over my figure. 'I wasn't sure how I'd react.'

'To the surgery?'

'To seeing you today. I've been surprised before. I had a feeling you worked at that gym – Ollie thought he saw you there months ago – but when you were introduced as Steph, I wasn't sure. I wasn't sure for weeks. Your voice was different, and it's disorientating, being out in the world. I've learned that nothing is ever as familiar as you think it'll be. But I thought I'd be able to smell you, if nothing else.'

'I smell?'

'Don't worry. It's a sweet smell, fresh. Mountain heather or washing powder? I don't know. I always liked it. But I couldn't catch it. I couldn't exactly shove my face into your neck. And anyway, you covered up with some God-awful perfume.'

'Armani Code.'

'That's what it was.' He chuckled, then flicked a glance around the flat. 'How'd you get in?'

'I have a key.'

'Do you? Interesting.'

'So you worked out it was me. When, exactly?'

'I don't know, *exactly*. But every week I got another clue. It was like a game.'

'A game? It's not a game, Liam. Ruining my life, my sanity, isn't a game.'

'Me ruining *your* life? How can you say that? *You're* the one that's been in charge. Aren't you? This whole time? You're the one who's been playing with *me*, with *my* life. You made the rules, Cassie. You broke them too. You came here.'

'Not for fun.'

He sighed, stepped closer. He was so calm. No, not calm – controlled. I wondered what would happen when he lost it. 'What for, then? What are you doing here, Cass?'

'I don't know,' I said. Because I really didn't know. It seemed crazy to be standing there with him.

'You've been training me for weeks. You've had your hands on me. You let me put my hands all over you. What does it mean, Cassie?'

'It doesn't mean anything.'

'That's not true. That doesn't make any sense. Let me tell you what I think: I think you wanted to be near me. I think you couldn't keep away. I think you wanted—'

'I wanted to hurt you. That's what it means.'

That stopped him. 'You didn't, though.'

I said nothing. I wasn't going to confess. I could see he was thinking back over the weeks, interpreting. Hoping.

'The barbell?' A startled laugh, forced up by his dia-
phragm. 'You did that deliberately? But why leave it
there, why not—' He'd remembered something else.
'When I slipped . . . When you threw my hoodie . . .
What else? What else? What am I forgetting? How many
times? Did it make you feel good, Cass? Did you enjoy
it? Did it turn you on?'

'Don't be disgusting.'

'Oh, I'm disgusting now? Yeah. Yeah, maybe. You
know what my first thought was, when I went blind? I
thought, if I never see again, at least I have Cassie to
remember; at least her image, in here, will keep me company, console me.'

'I don't only exist for your benefit.'

'No, you exist to fucking torture me, apparently.'

'That's your thing, Liam. It's you who likes torturing
people.'

'What are you talking about?'

'I saw it. In the wardrobe. That bag you had. All that
stuff. The knife, the ties . . .'

'That wasn't meant for you.'

'It had my keys in it!'

'I know that. I mean . . . You weren't supposed to see
it. I wasn't going to do anything, for fuck's sake. This is
what comes of snooping. It didn't mean what you think
it means. It didn't mean anything. It was just a kind of
stress reliever, a comfort blanket.'

'What kind of psycho has a kill kit for a comfort
blanket?'

He thumped the side of his hand into the wall, steadying, threatening. 'Be careful, Cassie. You don't want to say something you'll regret.'

'The only thing I regret is pulling you back when that car nearly hit you. *That* was a mistake.'

'A mistake?'

'An instinct I should have ignored.'

'That was you? You were there?'

'I wish I hadn't been there.'

'But you were. You followed me? You were watching. And your instinct was to save me.' A hard stare. An actual, real stare. We were looking into each other's eyes. He could see my every move, every expression. I couldn't hide any more. He raised a hand to my cheek. 'Here we are,' he said. A kind of awe in his voice.

I flinched away. 'Liam, no.'

'I love you, Cassie. And you love me.'

'I don't.'

'You were jealous. When I said Pippa had been here. I could tell. And, yes, I'll admit, it's the real reason I mentioned her. I wanted to gauge your reaction. You behaved just how I'd hoped. It revealed how you felt. Come on. Don't lie. You know you want to get back together.'

'I don't.'

'WHY ARE YOU HERE, THEN?' His sudden roar shocked me against the fridge, my head hitting the chrome.

'Because . . .' I could hear the despair in my voice. Why was I there? Why had I come? Why had I done any

367

of it? Why would you help a man you wanted to hurt, who wanted to hurt you? Why would you spend time with him? What was wrong with me?

'Because you know I'm right.' His voice was level again, as if he'd never shouted. 'You're being stubborn, as usual, but you know it's true. Let me prove it to you, Cassie. Let me show you.'

His face in mine, lips light over my jaw, my cheekbones, harder against my mouth. Each touch made me feel violent, towards him, towards my own skin. I wanted to scrape it off. I swiped at us both, not caring which of us I scratched.

'Cassie,' he said, an endearment, an admonishment, his hands coming up to hold my wrists.

I tried to shove him away and he took a step back but held on and I lost my footing, toppled sideways, a whistle of fear as I fell. But the landing was soft, interrupted by his grip. The grip he'd improved under my direction.

'Let go,' I said – begged – but he ignored that and got over me, heavy with intent. 'You can't do this. You can't.' My hair was caught in my clothes, then in his fist, and he wrenched me flat, my arms trapped beneath his shins. I pulled anyway, scalp smarting.

'You need to calm down, Cass. Are you calm?'

I thrashed pointlessly. 'Get off me.'

'Not until you get it together.'

I writhed against him, finding a little more purpose, trying to unbalance him, or at least get an arm free. 'I'll calm down when you let go. You have to let go. Please. Please, Liam, be sensible. Be normal.'

A jerk of my hair, hitting my head on the tiles. 'I *am* normal. I'm the normal one.'

I lay motionless then, watching him as he knelt over me, feeling all the places where I was pinned. My wrists were under his ankles, his thighs squeezing my elbows to my waist. He wasn't resting his full weight on my ribs, but the threat was there. I had nowhere to go, and nothing to do except wait it out. He had to release me eventually.

'Neither of us are fucking normal,' I said.

'It doesn't matter. This is it. This is love.'

'It isn't. Love? I don't even *like* you.'

He reached a hand towards the edge of the counter above us, breathing hard. 'No, Cass,' he said, opening a cupboard and speaking quietly into it. 'You do love me. You do. Weeks and weeks of contact. You didn't try to get away. You confided in me. Told me stuff you'd never told me before. We reconnected. This was working for us.'

'I was playing you. I was trying to get my own back.'

'No. It was working. Doesn't matter what you thought you were doing, it was working, *we* were working – why are you trying to ruin it? Why are you always trying to ruin it?'

He pulled a bottle of bleach from the cupboard and started to unscrew the cap.

'What are you doing?' Was that the same bleach he'd been planning to use when he murdered me? Did he have the knife handy too? Could I get away if he reached for it?

'I'm saving us.'

I wriggled again, forced a smile. 'By cleaning?'

'By switching places, Cassie. We're made for each other, but we have to stop competing. That's the problem. One of us has to be vulnerable. One of us has to make a sacrifice. I was blind for a while. Let's see how you like it.'

It took me a moment to catch his meaning, to believe it. I bit at my still-smiling lips. He was serious, he was insane, and he was pinning me to the floor.

'Don't worry,' he was saying. 'I'll take good care of you. I will never let you out of my sight.'

The sound of the liquid sloshing stopped my breath. But he'd shifted his weight when he reached into the cupboard. I bucked onto my side, wrenched my arms up, covered my face. He tried to get me in a better position for the bleach, but was hampered by the bottle in his right hand. One knee was behind my back, the other coming down near my wrists, trying to trap me. His left hand gripped my chin. 'Keep your fucking head still. Keep your head still.'

Liquid hit my temple. Panicked, I shot an elbow into his groin, felt the bone connect, felt the strength in my tricep. That calmed me. Because I'd been training too. I'd been training for a long time.

'Shit.' He fell forward and I squirmed out from under him as bleach sprayed over the floor.

A stream of it caught my hair, the shoulder of my top, and the smell made my nose sting, my eyes water. I swiped at my face, retreating, scrambling up the cupboard, onto the counter, grabbing the window handle and twisting the key, but Liam already had me by the collar, jerking me back, his left hand sliding around my neck. I remembered all those runs, him 'saving' me from phantom cars.

I clawed at him, his arms, his face, caught the edge of an eyelid with my nails and heard him shriek. The window was right there – I leaned on the worktop, slapped at the glass, frantically rattled the handle. It finally swung open with a sucking sound, swinging up, right up, over the street, and I crawled across the counter to lean out. The pot of basil fell from the sill and smashed a couple of seconds later, sending soil up like smoke. The ground was thirty feet below, part tarmac, part pavement, totally unforgiving. I felt the ghost of an impact in my stomach, a dizzy rush of understanding.

Some teenagers were smoking in the alley. They saw me, dropped their cigarettes and went for their phones. I screamed for help. Liam was standing again, bent over but determined, a hulking, blundering animal. His hands on my ankles, hips, waist, pulling me towards him. But there was so much bleach on the floor, he was sliding around in it. I kicked back, making him skid and lose his footing. His chin smacked the counter as he went down.

I swivelled. Thrust my legs out of the window fast, before I could change my mind, and backed out, shins skinned by the frame. I let myself scrape against the building, hands hooking, joints jerking, cheek to brick. I breathed, swallowed, eased from a dead hang to an active one; I knew all the moves, how to tighten each individual muscle, how to support every vertebra. I'd been practising for months. I could hold on.

Liam leaned out after me, kneeling on the kitchen counter, and for a second he just looked, just stared. 'What the fuck are you doing?'

'Fuck you,' I said. Eloquent to the last.

That pissed him off. 'Get back in here, you stupid cunt. D'you want to fucking die?' He grabbed my left wrist, leaning further, his knee half off the windowsill. The breath was stuck high in my chest, my shoulders burned, and I forced my toes into the line of recessed mortar, trying to take a fraction of my weight off my arms.

Liam let go of the window frame to grab me, but I clamped my right hand tight, and yanked with the other. Down. Hard. Twisting my wrist out of his grip.

He toppled forward, head first, his body briefly blanketing mine. His desperate fist clenched the hem of my T-shirt for a split second, but the force of the fall pulled his fingers straight off me. And he was gone. There was a sickening thud.

I clung for a moment longer, not trusting myself to move. I couldn't look down, hardly dared to breathe. Aware of the empty air below me, the precarious return path to safety, the stinging line where the bleach had caught my face and shoulder. A dog was barking. A sharp sound, *ha ha ha!* At least someone found the situation amusing.

Voices floated up, someone calling an ambulance, people asking each other what was going on. There were footsteps, shouts. My fingers were cold, stiff, aching, the frame cutting into the joints. I ignored them, kept my eyes fixed on the brick in front of my face and visualised the movement I needed. One good pull-up, that's all it was. I felt nausea rise at the idea, but I could do it. Smooth action, tight form. I could do that, I could do that, no problem.

I sucked in a breath and then shoved myself up, shoulders, back, biceps. For a second I knew I couldn't manage it, but then, feet braced, I felt the strength in my arms, found I was still going, slowly, slowly, holding on till I could see the kitchen counter, then up again. Tricep push-down. Easy-peasy. I'd been working on those.

I leaned forward, hooked my ribs on the window frame, grabbed at the edge of the counter, and I was in. I slid through the mess of bleach and threw up into it.

Week One Hundred and Thirty-One

Not brunch. Not dressed up, not made-up, not on the up. But there *are* four of us, and it *is* like a TV show, just not the kind I'd choose.

The table is littered with paper cups, juice cartons, cereal-bar wrappers. I wasn't late arriving, because the officers keep us on schedule. 'Hurry up, ladies, let's go,' they shout before the banging of a door, the turn of a key, the jingle of a chain.

'Thanks so much again for coming,' I say.

'As if we wouldn't come,' Lauren says. 'Our most notorious friend.'

I stick my tongue out at her, because, actually, my story barely made the BBC website. It wasn't that interesting, even though the victim and perpetrator were filmed dangling from a second-floor window. Those teenagers with their phones.

I saw the video while I was on remand. My lawyer showed it to me, said it was why I didn't get bail. I was just too much, as usual, frightening, a potential danger to the public. But I was impressed, remembering the way my muscles had burned as I pulled myself up. On film I made it look easy.

My friends, I found out later, spent a long time searching out reposted clips, monitoring the comments and defending me, trying to put my side of the story. But it was hard to sway public opinion, and what more could they do? None of them were in a position to offer half-priced personal training.

In the video, you can see people in the street, a cluster of curious faces – the smoking teenagers, a shrub-lopper, a kid with a dog, a woman wearing a gauzy scarf. Then Liam's drop, then, later, the paramedic leading me out.

I'd been trembling as I walked through the security door, gripping the paramedic's arm, talking and talking, because I needed to hear my own voice, because I couldn't believe it: that I was alive. I kept wanting to know if Liam was dead. 'And what about now?' You can hear me clearly, asking and asking. 'Is he dead now? And now? And now?' It had seemed fair to ask; he'd tried to blind me after all, and he'd have settled for killing me.

My friends told all those strangers on the internet that it was shock, but no one was buying it. Because Liam *was* dead.

I thought I'd lost Tanya, and Lauren and Michelle, but no. They couldn't reach me while I was with Liam, while I was dealing with Liam, but they've made an effort to reach me here.

'Want me to transfer you some money . . . ?' Tanya asks.

'No, don't worry, I'm fine. I don't need anything. And my parents have topped up my canteen fund anyway.'

'How were your parents, last visit?'

'Mum's stopped trying to find new evidence, at least. Though this has given her a taste for it. My dad's annoyed, said she's always got headphones on now, listening to true-crime podcasts.'

Mum has changed her tune. Again. Last time she visited she was talking about setting up a charity for women who've been driven to kill in self-defence, naming it after me. She's been pestering Gav to run a marathon to raise money. Which has its own pleasingly paradoxical logic. She's already mentally preparing for her MBE investiture – I can imagine her picture in the local paper, outside Buckingham Palace, in a mauve skirt suit with matching fascinator: *I am truly humbled to be recognised.*

She isn't the only mother full of surprises.

At the trial, Liam's mum said her son was a completely different person when I was around. She thought I'd forced him to perform affection, made him touch me all the time. That I'd wanted 'nothing less than worship'. The stress of this, the embarrassment perhaps, had occasionally made him rather curt with his mother. Very cold, unloving.

She thought I must have demanded that, as a show of loyalty. He'd intimated to her that I'd insisted on his *choosing teams*. And he'd been keen to make things work. He'd wanted the relationship to be successful. She didn't blame him for that, he'd seen his parents go through a

messy divorce and obviously wanted to do things differently. Even when he'd got ill he'd asked her to stay away,
to give me a chance to take care of him. He hadn't told
her we'd broken up.

So maybe it had all been a show, his hatred of his
mother, his angst, his neediness when she was around.
Maybe he'd been performing for both of us, and I'd
missed it entirely.

'So,' I say, shifting on the sweaty plastic chair. 'What have
I missed?'

'Daria's wedding. Which was . . .' Tanya searches for
the right word. 'Strained? Is that too mean?'

'Not mean enough,' Lauren says. 'Looked like she had
fish hooks in the corners of her mouth. Wasn't going to
let that smile drop for a second. Just in case we didn't
think she was happy.'

'Yeah, it was painful to watch.'

'Oof, yeah.'

'Her dress was beautiful, though,' Michelle says.

Tanya and Lauren give her blank looks, sighing.

Then Lauren perks up. 'Jamie mentioned you, actually. Gave a little "absent friends" toast.' She mimes the
raising of a glass, shimmies a bit in her seat.

'I was surprised I got an invite.'

'Guess he knew he was safe – you weren't going to
turn up unexpectedly, were you?'

'Laur,' Tanya says. 'Don't keep rubbing it in.'

'That's okay,' I tell Lauren as her face falls. 'Really.

Don't hold back. Bet Daria's delightful new husband enjoyed telling everyone exactly where I was.'

A grin. 'He didn't look *un*happy.'

Ollie didn't look unhappy either, when he stood up in front of the jury and told his story. He admitted animosity towards the defendant; said I made out I was a victim, but that I'd had an 'unbelievable hold' over Liam, that I'd got myself fired and then lived off him.

They made a lot of my getting sacked from the bank. Said it displayed a lack of impulse control, a propensity for rule-breaking, for thinking myself above the law. They suggested it was at my prompting that Liam had taken a load of money out of his company to pay my debts. He'd taken so much that the business was in danger of being prosecuted by the Inland Revenue; the withdrawals were unauthorised and there was a massive tax bill. Ollie had had to take a personal loan to cover the discrepancy. It was why he'd had to wait to qualify for a mortgage and had been stuck renting for so long.

No one believed I didn't know. No one believed me about anything. It didn't help that Ollie's triumphant smirk cracked at the end of his testimony. He burst into tears on the stand, his big round face ruddier than ever. Wishing, while wailing, that he had insisted Liam stay for drinks on the afternoon of his death, that he hadn't let him get a taxi home.

*

'Christ,' Lauren says, leaning forward. 'Who did that to her?'

I follow her gaze to Guinevere, who has half a dozen livid scratches down her cheeks. One cuts across her top lip and is the reason she's smiling at her visitor with only the right side of her mouth.

'She did it to herself,' I say. 'You should see her arms.'

'But—' Lauren stares till I nudge her. 'Why?'

I shrug. 'Her dad abused her as a kid.' I feel sorry for Guin, she's had a rough life, and I even understand her desire to mark herself. Without the scars she looks like the legendary queen she's named for, with her long hair and fine-boned face. But my first cellmate was a cutter and it meant constant searches, the prison officers looking for sharps she'd 'banked' to hurt herself with in the middle of the night. It was disruptive and annoying and it really tried my patience.

'She seems in a good mood now,' Tanya says.

'That's the speed she just took, probably.'

I'd got used to there being drugs everywhere during the months I was on remand. The women were open about taking them, about swapping tobacco for Valium or even smack. But I wasn't an addict on the outside and I wasn't going to start messing around with chemical highs. And anyway, I hadn't expected to be inside very long.

The trial took two weeks – it felt like an eternity, but it also felt like a rush, like a landslide, like a plummet from a window. I wore some work-style yoga pants to court (the real Steph would have been proud), where I pleaded not guilty and was sure I could tell my story well enough to persuade everyone inside the court that I was the victim. I hadn't counted on the litany of witnesses for the prosecution; I hadn't counted on the number of people who'd noticed my ten-week descent into madness.

Greg was a good witness for the prosecution. Amiable, attentive, sporting a smart suit and silk tie. They were trying to establish premeditation and, of course, he'd been watching me. He'd seen me hanging around the flat, the 'murder site', he called it. He'd seen me several times standing in an alley opposite and looking up at the windows, watching and waiting. He hadn't known Liam lived there until afterwards; he hadn't realised I was nursing an obsession. If he'd known, he wouldn't have asked me out. He admitted he'd been angry at my rejection, but understood now that he'd dodged a bullet, 'a fucking big bullet'. He got a warning from the judge over his language.

Liam's scarf-wearing neighbour told everyone I'd been engaging in suspicious activities (how people love a legal-sounding phrase), that I'd posed as his cleaner, trespassed in a *private* car park, thrown away a gold watch and then trapped her in a bin while I made a run for it. She'd been very distressed, apparently.

So they knew I'd gone through his bins, I'd entered his home illegally, and I'd stolen his car too. The prosecution produced a speed-camera shot of the Golf R hurtling down the motorway, the same Golf R that had been parked outside my flat, the keys in my kitchen. No way out of that one.

There's a scuffle on the other side of the room, a squeak of trainers on the lino, a visitor in a floral jumpsuit being separated from an inmate in shiny jogging bottoms. Suze. Her mouth wet from the prolonged kiss. I know her from the prison gym. She keeps her thin hair in a high, floppy bun, and is missing an earlobe from getting a gold hoop ripped out during a fight. She's in for robbery. Well, she's really in for growing up in a care home and having an addiction, but they got her for robbery.

'All right, all right,' Suze says, her head bowed to the officer. 'All right, miss. Sorry, miss.' She chances a glance up and catches my eye. 'Cass!' she calls. 'This is the ball and chain.'

I wave at the woman in the chintzy jumpsuit. She's young and pretty, in a tired way.

'Cass is helping me lose weight,' Suze tells her partner, and also the room. 'I've been getting to be a fat shit in here, in't I?'

'Nah, you haven't.' Her girlfriend's voice is low, shy.

'Yeah, I have, though. I was skinny when I come in. I was svelte.' She smooths her hands over her body, suggestive, mocking. 'One thing crack'll do for you, eh?'

'Suze. Don't joke.'

'Never seen a fat crack addict, have you? Nah. One pipe and . . .' She sucks in her cheeks, then cackles. 'I'm staying clean, though. When I get out. Gonna get addicted to endorphins, like Cass.'

'She means endocannabinoids,' Tanya says to me.

'So you do listen when I talk.'

At least there's a gym here. I was only locked up a few weeks before they gave me a job helping other women get through their PT qualifications. Circle of life and all that. Suze is a great client, an instinct for the movements, and she has some amazing relationship horror stories. Tommy would love her.

Tommy spent the first few minutes in the witness stand exclaiming over having only worked together a few months; apparently it had felt like longer (he didn't say if it was in a good or a bad way). He told the court my clients rated me highly, the ones I didn't kill, anyway. He said there'd been complaints about me not coming back, which was nice to hear.

He'd observed me with the victim, of course; he'd also observed I attracted psychos, which was unlucky, and he felt for me, having had similar problems. He was compelled to mention the fact that I'd hit Liam with a barbell, but he'd shot me an apologetic look and turned to the judge to stress that I'd only done it the once.

'Nice to see you're making new friends, anyway,' Lauren tells me.

'I'm keeping busy. There are some genuinely nice people here. I know that might sound mad.'

'Have you got a girlfriend in here, then?' Michelle asks.

'*Shell!*' Lauren blushes as if it's her love life under scrutiny.

'What? Lots of prisoners do – it's called "gay for the stay". Reece told me.'

'Reece needs to get over his obsession with women's prisons.'

'It's not an obsession, he just likes to know about things.'

'Well,' I say, 'you can tell him I haven't got a girlfriend, Michelle. In here or outside. I think I'm better single.'

I still find it hard to imagine being safe in a relationship. I think about the female zoo animals a lot, about being trapped with your adversary. I think about the Minotaur in his maze.

When it became obvious my case was going badly, I changed my plea. Admitted to manslaughter. I got four years. I can't help wondering what Liam would have got if *I* had slipped? The same? Four-years-out-in-two?

Ollie, Tommy, my stalker, the neighbour, all my prosecution witnesses would have defended him, so maybe he wouldn't have gone to prison at all. In an alternative reality I'm dead and he's just walking around like nothing happened. Sometimes I'm convinced he's doing that anyway.

*

'So. Open prison next?'

'Yeah.' At the moment I'm a closed-category prisoner. There's only open and closed for women, dangerous or not dangerous. At the moment I'm in high security, with gates on gates on gates, with fingerprint sensors and trauma therapy. It's crowded and there's no privacy since they moved a load of prisoners over from another facility. The single cells all have bunk beds squeezed into them and there's no screen for the toilet. I've been lucky with my current cellmate, but I'm looking forward to a change. 'I'll get to go to the supermarket and cook my own meals.'

'Sweet.'

'How are you feeling about it?' Tanya asks, more serious.

I nod. 'Good. Good.' A shrug escapes. 'Nervous. I haven't had to choose my own meals for a long time.' Tanya holds my gaze and I wonder if we're both thinking of the days in her garden after Liam's poisoned chocolates, when I couldn't decide what to eat.

'You should make noodle soup,' Lauren says, winking. 'With a nice little side of alcohol rub.'

'Lauren!'

'What? Too soon? It's been, like, two years.'

The trip to the café with Liam had come up at my trial. The waitress another witness. I didn't recognise her at first, in a sand-coloured blazer, her hair dyed red, and of course her name meant nothing to me.

She'd come forward after seeing the video of the 'tragedy' online, and she'd recognised me, marked my coming and going from the gym. Told the court Liam and I had seemed friendly. Told the court she'd seen me pour hand sanitiser into his noodle soup. She made it sound like I'd tipped a whole bottle into the broth, and then she cried when the lawyer asked her if she'd confronted me. The regret kept her up at night, supposedly; she felt her intervention might have saved Liam's life.

'People drink that hand sanitiser stuff for fun. That's why it's all foam in hospitals now, instead of gel,' Michelle says. Definitely another Reece fact.

Lauren makes an intrigued face. 'Maybe we should get some for your welcome-home party, Cass. I've been trying to find a theme.'

I let out a laugh, which, with a little encouragement from my friends, becomes a howl.

One of the officers shouts over my noise. 'Settle down, Cassie.'

'Sorry, miss.' I hunch into the protection of the group, smiling. I'll never be that scrappy little terrier again, but there's still a quiet growl inside me, and I recognise it as a kind of joy.

'Time's up anyway, ladies.'

Tanya hugs me across the table. She smells of cinnamon and cedarwood.

'See you soon,' she says. 'And, oh, Ashlie's been looking after your creeping fig, she wanted you to know. It's grown a lot – nearly touching the floor now. And she's been making you a book about what happens when you sow the sleep from your eyes instead of seeds. Spoiler: you grow a catnap plant that makes you doze off on the toilet so that it can eat you.'

'Wow. What a mind,' I say. 'Looking forward to that.'

'Ha, yeah. The pictures are . . . well. You'll see. But I'll wait till you're settled in the new place to send it.'

I thank her, hug the others and sit down while all the visitors are guided out. Suze whistles at her girlfriend to make her turn and wave. I wonder about doing the same, shouting, barking, forcing my friends to look back. But I don't. It won't be long till I can walk outside with them; it won't be that long till we can meet again for brunch, lunch, dinner and drinks. I'm going to start banking calories now.

Acknowledgements

Many people helped bring this novel into existence, including those at Creative Artists Agency and Hutchinson Heinemann and Cornerstone, especially Ailah Ahmed, Venetia Butterfield, Caroline Johnson, and of course my wonderful agent Karolina Sutton.

Early advisers, inspirers, readers and supporters include Cassie and Simon Cox, Andrew Cowan, Emmy Donnelly-Gallagher, Charlotte Gray, Hannah Harper, Kathryn Healey, Jack McDavid, Cora McKechnie, Kerry Snelling, Louisa Theobald, Rowan Whiteside and Lucy Yates.

I'm very grateful for help with research from Dr Alex Baker and Mrs Rupal Shenoy; from Sam Gibbons (Movement Mechanic) and Ross Lenton (Dynamic Fitness); and also from Nora Atkinson, Edward Bates, Bobs Beer, Jenny Fisher, David Foulds, Dan Harris, Mark Honan, Helen King, Judy Manning, Mark Smith, Diane Stewart, Charles Townsend, Maggie Wilkinson, and everyone at Vision Norfolk.

Finally, without my husband, Andrew McKechnie, this book would have been abandoned like so many others over the past seven years. I will be eternally grateful for his attention, belief, chivvying, dedication, encouragement, fortitude, grit, humour and insight. He says that's enough alphabetising, and so I'd like to end by praising his judgement.

ELIZABETH IS MISSING
EMMA HEALEY

'Elizabeth is missing', reads the note in Maud's pocket in her own handwriting.

Lately, Maud's been getting forgetful. She keeps buying peach slices when she has a cupboard full of them, forgets to drink the cups of tea she's made and writes notes to remind herself of things. But Maud is determined to discover what has happened to her friend, Elizabeth, and what it has to do with the unsolved disappearance of her sister Sukey, years back, just after the war.

A fast-paced mystery with a wonderful leading character: Maud will make you laugh and cry, but she certainly won't be forgotten.

'Both a gripping detective yarn and a haunting depiction of mental illness'

Observer

'*Elizabeth Is Missing* will stir and shake you: a seventy-year-old crime, the most likeably unreliable of narrators . . . real mystery at its compassionate core'

Emma Donoghue

'One of those mythical beasts, the book you cannot put down'

Jonathan Coe

WHISTLE IN THE DARK
EMMA HEALEY

Jen's fifteen-year-old daughter goes missing for four agonising days. When Lana is found, unharmed, in the middle of the desolate countryside, everyone thinks the worst is over. But Lana refuses to tell anyone what happened, and the police draw a blank. The once-happy, loving family return to London, where things start to fall apart. Lana begins acting strangely, refusing to go to school, and sleeping with the light on.

As Lana stays stubbornly silent, Jen desperately tries to reach out to a daughter who has become a stranger.

> **'Healey writes with such an ease and naturalness that it carries you effortlessly forward'**
>
> *Sunday Independent*

> **'A compelling modern family drama with witty and wonderful characters. Utter bliss'**
>
> Nina Stibbe

> **'Healey is a natural storyteller'**
>
> Claire Fuller